THE BEST PEOPLE

'Stay loose,' she advised. 'Remember it's not the real world; it's only advertising.'

'Thanks, Mom. I'll try to hold that thought.'

Tony and Paul were in the 'conversation corner' of the office, a casual grouping of sofa, chairs and coffee table set apart from the big desk. Serious conferences always took place here. As though the informality of the setting made the deadly possibility of disaster less real. Tony and Paul were struggling to maintain a posture of calm. Jackets off, ties loosened, Gucci-loafered feet on the table, they looked like two suburbanites relaxing at the country club after a round of golf. You had to be one of them to know that every nerve-end was quivering with fear. You couldn't blame them. The agency's commission on an eight-million-dollar account would be nearly a million and a half dollars a year.

Jim slumped into a chair, 'Either of you know what the hell is happening?' he asked.

Also by the same author, and available from New English Library:

THE HEART LISTENS
THE RICH AND THE RIGHTEOUS
THE MIXED BLESSING
ALWAYS IS NOT FOREVER

The Best People

Helen Van Slyke

NEW ENGLISH LIBRARY
Hodder and Stoughton

**For Lenore Lyon,
with love**

Previously published under the
title: *All Visitors Must Be
Announced.*

First published in Great Britain
by Cassell & Co. in 1973

© 1972 by Helen Van Slyke

First NEL Paperback edition
1976
New edition 1977
New edition 1979
New edition 1981
New edition 1986
11th impression 1988

*The characters and situations in this
book are entirely imaginary and bear
no relation to any real person or
actual happening.*

This book is sold subject to the
condition that it shall not, by way
of trade or otherwise, be lent,
re-sold, hired out or otherwise
circulated without the publisher's
prior consent in any form of
binding or cover other than that in
which it is published and without a
similar condition including this
condition being imposed on the
subsequent purchaser.

No part of this publication may be
reproduced or transmitted in any
form or by any means,
electronically or mechanically,
including photocopying, recording
or any information storage or
retrieval system, without either the
prior permission in writing from
the publisher or a licence,
permitting restricted copying. In
the United Kingdom such licences
are issued by the Copyright
Licensing Agency, 33–34 Alfred
Place, London WC1E 7DP.

Printed and bound in Great
Britain for Hodder and Stoughton
Paperbacks, a division of Hodder
and Stoughton Ltd., Mill Road,
Dunton Green, Sevenoaks, Kent
TN13 2YA (Editorial Office: 47
Bedford Square, London WC1B
3DP) by Richard Clay Ltd.,
Bungay, Suffolk.

ISBN 0-450-03351-1

Chapter I

For the third time, Casey Cromwell silently reread the formally worded letter written on heavily embossed Tiffany notepaper. 'The Board of Directors of 617 Park Avenue cordially welcomes Mr and Mrs James Flagg Cromwell as owners of apartment 14B and looks forward to their early occupancy. Sincerely, André Dubois Livingstone, President, 617 Park Avenue Corporation.'

She sighed with satisfaction, poured herself another cup of coffee, reached for the cream and sugar and remembered, just in time, that she had decided to go on a diet. Not that she needed to lose weight. It was just that if you were twenty-five years old and happily, almost complacently, married to a good-looking young advertising executive, you had to be careful if you wanted to keep on being a size eight. Especially with those sexy nineteen-year-old secretaries who worked at Jim's agency.

Across the breakfast table, the good-looking young advertising executive was riveted by an item in the New York *Times*. His mind was not on the sexy secretaries nor on the co-operative apartment that he and his wife had inherited from his grandmother. Mentally, Jim Cromwell was already in the office. Just as Casey reread her precious letter, he kept going back over the terse paragraph in the paper's daily advertising column. It said that the Weinberg Shoe Company had decided to look at campaign presentations from several top agencies before selecting the one to handle their eight-million-dollar account. Under Al Shriber's by-line, the story continued: 'Although all of Madison Avenue had expected Stewart, Sutton & Atherton to be awarded this new business, officials at Weinberg confirmed today that they would receive solicitations from other agencies before making a final decision. An announcement is expected within 60 to 90 days.'

The deceptively innocent-sounding item threw Jim into shock. His agency, Stewart, Sutton & Atherton – or SS&A as it was

5

better known – had been pitching the Weinberg account with everything they had. They had spent thousands of dollars in creative and executive time, and hundreds of hours putting together suggested advertising campaigns. They had invested heavily in research about the shoe business in general and Weinberg Shoes in particular. Admittedly, it was a gamble, doing all this work and spending time and money on 'speculation'. Some agencies refused to make such an investment 'on spec'. But Jim and Tony Stewart and Paul Gordon, the agency's creative director, had felt confident of the outcome. They had had what they thought was an informal acceptance from Lester Weinberg, the company's chairman and sole owner. Only last Friday there had been rejoicing at the agency when Jim and Paul had come back from making their final presentation to Lester and his executives. Now there was this hint that the celebration was premature.

Jim devoutly hoped that the *Times* was wrong. It had been known to happen. Though rarely. The *Times* ad columnist was good. He was one of the few who knew the difference between smoke and fire. But he knew when they went together as well. Al Shriber must smell trouble. So did Jim.

The Weinberg business was more than important to SS&A. It was crucial. By any standards, it was a big account. But for SS&A, it would be the biggest one ever to come into the agency. And with times as tight as they were this year, it would literally mean the difference between profit and loss. Jim tried to think of anything that might have gone wrong. He meticulously reviewed the meetings, the work they'd shown, even his personal rapport with Lester Weinberg. He could think of nothing that would suddenly cause the shoe company to have second thoughts about SS&A.

The gently insistent voice of his wife brought him back to the domestic scene. Her voice had a slight note of irritation, as though she'd been trying to get his attention for a few moments. He lowered the paper. Casey was waving a letter at him.

'Hey, aren't you even going to read our official acceptance?' she asked. 'I know you're used to such things, but it isn't every day that *I* get to own half of a seven-room apartment! It wouldn't hurt you to show a little enthusiasm.'

Smiling, he took the letter from her. 'Sorry,' he said, 'but my mind was on other things.' He read the brief note. 'Very nice, but it's hardly a surprise. We've known for months that we had the apartment. It was only a formality, this acceptance thing.

6

You didn't think the board would overturn Grandmother's will, did you?'

'I've heard of it happening,' Casey said defensively. 'Somebody told me just the other day about a guy who inherited a co-op apartment and the board refused to okay him. He had to sell it to someone who was acceptable to the building. How about that? I mean, nothing's really in the bag until it's signed, sealed and delivered, right?'

Thinking of the item in the *Times* ad column, Jim nodded in agreement. 'Right. So now that you know it's really true, you can start making plans to move. The apartment's in pretty good condition, but I'm sure you'll have plenty to do.'

'I still almost can't believe it,' Casey said. 'From a three-and-a-half room walk-up in the Fifties to practically a palace on Park Avenue.'

'From Swank to Schlumberger in one generation.'

'Now come on, Jim. You have to admit that it's kind of terrific. I mean, who do we know in New York who has a dining room and a maid's room and bath? When I think of those big, high-ceilinged rooms and honest-to-God fireplaces and all that lovely wasted space in the entrance hall and the butler's pantry . . . '

'Hold it,' he said. 'Remember me? I don't need the *House & Garden* tour. I lived there, on and off, between the ages of ten and twenty-one after my folks died. When I wasn't away at school, that was my home, if you recall.'

'I know. But it didn't really *belong* to you, like it does now.'

'True. And I also didn't have to handle the upkeep like I do now. Just because you own shares in the corporation, kiddo, doesn't mean that you literally own the rooms you live in. Or that you live free. The monthly maintenance on that place is a hell of a lot more than the rent we pay now. And even though as shareholders in the building, we get a yearly tax deduction, you have to remember that there's no kindly landlord to repaint every three years or give us a new stove when the old one conks out. All the repairs and upkeep are strictly out of our own pocket.'

For a moment, Casey looked worried. 'We can afford it, can't we?'

'Of course we can afford it. We're the sole heirs of the estate, which includes some nice, income-bearing, blue-chip stocks, along with the modest family jewels and the highly authentic

7

family portraits. Add that to my decent salary and we're practically rolling.'

'Being rich is very soothing. I think I'm going to adjust to the idea in about a minute and a half.'

Jim grinned. 'Don't let it go to your head. As some wise and learned philosopher once said, "The capacity for luxury is easily acquired".'

'Who said that?'

'I forget. Me, probably. Anyway, I agree that a fat bank account is almost as attractive as a thin wife.'

'You're pleased about the apartment, aren't you?'

Jim considered this. 'Yes, I'm pleased. Tom Wolfe to the contrary, maybe you can go home again. It's an outmoded way of life, but nobody can deny that it's comfortable.'

'Outmoded how?'

'Well, it's probably one of the last remaining "protected buildings". Very select. Very snobby. I don't think there's a Democrat in residence. Maybe not even a Liberal Republican. Most of the people who live there are the original settlers, or second generation like me. It's quite a small building, you know. Only thirty apartments on fifteen floors – two to a floor. It was one of the first co-ops ever built in New York. Must be forty-five years old. It's – oh, I don't know – very personal. Not like the forty-seven-story monsters they're putting up these days. Not that the new ones don't have their advantages, too. The plumbing's a damned sight better and, in spite of more tenants, you have more privacy. In 617 everybody knows a lot about everybody else. Too much, probably.'

He was suddenly aware that Casey had tuned him out in the middle of his somewhat introspective rambling about the building and its tight little clublike atmosphere. Knowing she wasn't listening, he said, at the same level, 'So I thought we'd turn the third bedroom into a harem and do it all with water pipes for the opium. Okay with you?'

'Fine,' Casey said absently. Then she suddenly came to. 'What?'

Jim laughed. 'The honeymoon is over,' he said. 'You no longer listen raptly as your lord and master expounds on serious subjects. Next thing you won't laugh at my old jokes any more. That's the beginning of the end. If you don't believe me, write to Ann Landers.'

'I'm sorry,' Casey said. 'I was just thinking of all the things I have to do before we really can get in. I thought I'd hop over there this morning and start measuring. We have to figure out how much of our stuff works and what we want to keep of your grandmother's things. I love the blend of contemporary and antiques, don't you? Some of her beautiful pieces are treasures, but I'm not sure whether they scream "Us". Anyway, we'll see. Then I have to find a good painter and floor scraper and make a date with the moving people and call the phone company. Lord knows when we'll get a phone installed! Everybody says it takes months unless you're an invalid . . . '

'Which is what you'll be if you don't slow the hell down,' Jim said. 'Take it easy. We can't move tomorrow. There are still a lot of final legal formalities, even if we've passed the social-acceptance test. For one thing, we'll have to get out of our lease here. It's bound to be two or three months before we can actually get in. This is October. I wouldn't count on it before the first of the year.'

'Nope,' Casey said firmly. 'We're going to have our Christmas Eve party there. That's a commitment. Even if I have to kill *everybody* to get the place ready.'

'Okay. Just don't kill yourself in the process. The apartment is too big for a lone widower. Besides, you do have help, you know.'

'What help? You're in that damned office every night until eight o'clock. Fine help you'll be.'

'I didn't mean me, dummy. I meant Euralia. She'll be terrific. And that's what she's there for.'

A look of pure surprise and something like dismay crossed Casey's face.

'Good Lord,' she said. 'Euralia. Of course. She's still living there. I completely forgot. What are we going to do about her?'

'Well, I kind of thought you'd want to keep her on. She was Grandmother's housekeeper for thirty years, but she's still only about sixty and strong as an ox. We have the space, so what's wrong with a live-in drudge? I admit she's not Josephine Jolly, but she's not a bad sort and God knows she's efficient. That's a big place, remember, and you'll need full-time help. Which, I gather, is not so easy to come by. Besides, even though Grand-mother left her a little money, I doubt that it's enough for her to live on. So I'd feel obligated to give her something extra at least until she's old enough to collect Social Security. I think it makes sense for her to stay, but it's up to you.'

'It's going to be quite a change for her,' Casey said slowly.

9

'Taking care of one quiet, elderly lady isn't like coping with us and our odd-ball friends.'

'I have an idea she'll adjust,' Jim said.

Casey hesitated. 'There's something else.'

'Yeah?'

'I don't think she likes me.'

'Oh, come on, honey. She barely knows you. She's only seen you a dozen times. That's kind of stupid.'

'Well, if you want to know the truth, she scares me to death. She makes me feel absolutely gauche, she's so bloody correct. I don't know how to handle servants, unless you count a part-time cleaning woman or the bartenders we hire for parties.'

Jim shrugged. 'Okay, if you feel that way we'll let her go.'

Abruptly Casey did an about-face. 'No. You're right. I am being stupid. I'm sure she's a jewel, and it's dumb of me to get the fall-aparts about dealing with her. I keep forgetting that this is a new world, and if Euralia comes with the territory I'd better get used to the idea. Probably it'll work out okay. And if it doesn't, we can always change.'

'You're a good, sensible kid,' Jim said, 'and I may keep you around for a while. Okay, I'm off to see whether SS&A has blown the Weinberg Shoe account like the *Times* says or whether, please God, we're still in the running.'

'You're kidding! I thought that was locked up!'

'So did I,' Jim said. 'And believe me, it had better be or we'll be trying to support that apartment strictly on inheritance money. Anyway, that's my problem. Yours is the new household. So have fun. Incidentally, if there's anything you need, check with Mike O'Shea. He's the super.'

She nodded. 'I'll try to charm him. At the moment, he's the second most important man in my life. Is he co-operative?'

'Bound to be. You're probably the best-looking thing he's seen in that building in forty years. He's eighty-five if he's a day, and stone deaf. But just yell for what you need and you'll get it sooner or later. Probably later.'

'I'll try, darling. But if I overdo the charm and he makes a pass at me, may I call you?'

'No,' Jim said. 'Call the A.M.A. It'll be medical history.'

*　　*　　*

As soon as Jim was on his way, Casey called the apartment.

'Mrs Cromwell's residence,' the voice answered.

Well, at least that's one habit she won't have to change, Casey thought. 'Good morning, Euralia,' she said cheerfully. 'This is Mrs Cromwell.'

There was a pause. Then the voice said, politely, 'I beg your pardon. Who is this, please?'

Bitch. 'It's Mrs Cromwell. Mrs *James* Cromwell, Euralia.'

'Oh, of course. Good morning, madam.'

'How are you, Euralia?'

'Very well, thank you, madam.'

Casey could imagine the impassive face at the other end of the wire. After thirty years of peaceful, genteel service with the senior Cromwells, their deaths, within a year of each other, were taken by Euralia as a personal affront, a sorrowful but annoying upheaval of her well-ordered life. Even now she probably resisted the fact that another Mrs Cromwell would occupy the apartment, give the orders, step into the shoes of the handsome old lady who had been her employer and, in a suitable way, her friend.

The 'new' Mrs Cromwell said she was glad to hear that Euralia was well. 'I'm sure it must be lonely for you,' she added.

No, Euralia thought, it isn't particularly lonely. I'm used to solitude, staying in my part of the house while the Judge and Mrs Cromwell lived in the rest of the rooms. It wasn't loneliness that made her sound so reserved and distant; it was fear. She was sixty years old and she didn't even know whether or not she had a job. Or, for that matter, whether she wanted this one. She waited, saying nothing.

'I'd like to come over in about an hour,' Casey said. She hoped her voice conveyed just the right amount of cheerfulness and authority. 'Mr Cromwell and I are looking forward to moving into the apartment as soon as we can, and of course we're hoping you'll stay on with us.'

There was another seemingly endless pause. Christ, Casey thought, at this rate it will take us half a day to plan a shopping list. The housekeeper's taciturn manner began to get under her skin.

'Euralia? Are you still there?'

'I'll be here, madam, when you come. Perhaps we should discuss our arrangements then if it is agreeable to you.'

Perhaps I should tell you to start packing now, Casey thought. You and I will never make it. Instead she said, 'Fine. I'll see you shortly.'

This time the answer was nothing more than a soft click as

11

the receiver was replaced. It was not what you might call an auspicious beginning.

* * *

Walking into 14B an hour later and knowing it now belonged to her gave Casey a kind of creepy feeling. She hadn't been in the apartment since Mrs Cromwell's death, and the very sameness of it was eerie, as though the old lady would appear from her bedroom to greet her grandson's wife come to pay a call. As one might have expected, Euralia had not changed so much as the position of an ash tray in the traditionally furnished, immaculately kept living room. Even the flowers on the Hepplewhite desk were as Mrs Cromwell had always had them – a graceful arrangement of white tulips that arrived twice a week on standing order from Wadley & Smythe. Obviously, nobody had remembered to cancel the order. Correction: Neither Casey nor Jim had remembered. Euralia would not have felt it her place to do so, any more than she would have taken it upon herself to disturb the arrangement of furniture which had remained, each piece in its accustomed place, for more than forty years.

Casey wandered slowly around the elegant room, admiring it with the dispassionate appreciation one gives to a museum display. It was lovely. But it was yesterday. She and Jim would want a warmer atmosphere, a more personal room where good things blended with sentimental touches. This room looked as though ghosts lived in it. And perhaps they did.

Euralia, impeccable in her white daytime uniform, watched her as she made her thoughtful tour. Finally Casey seated herself on one of the Louis XIV love seats flanking the big fireplace. She motioned toward its facing twin.

'Sit down, please, Euralia,' she said.

Slowly, almost reluctantly, the housekeeper took a rigid position on the other stiff little sofa. Hands folded, spine straight, eyes direct, she was the very epitome of the perfect old-fashioned servant facing an interview with a new employer. Her composure suddenly made Casey feel like an awkward schoolgirl. Nothing in her background had prepared her for this role. As she'd told Jim that morning, she wasn't used to dealing with full-time help. She groped for the way to begin. Nervously, she took a package of cigarettes out of her bag.

'Have one?' she asked, offering the pack to Euralia.

The trace of an almost condescending smile crossed Euralia's face.

'No thank you, madam.'

Ass, Casey scolded herself. First wrong move. You don't offer cigarettes to domestics. You're supposed to be firm and polite and slightly aloof. Which is the way they like it. They want to be employees, not friends. In a way they're like children; happy and secure only when there is discipline and authority. Well, now Euralia knows how little I know about handling 'staff'. To hell with it. She can take it or leave it. Annoyance with herself hardened her voice.

'Euralia,' she said, 'as you know, Mr Cromwell and I have decided to live in the apartment, and we'd like you to stay on unless you have other plans.'

'I've made no plans, Mrs Cromwell.'

'Then you'd like to stay?'

The housekeeper seemed to be searching for the right words. 'I've lived here for thirty years,' she said. 'It's the only home I know.'

'But you have reservations?'

As though she might offend, Euralia seemed to weigh her words.

'May I speak frankly, madam?'

Oh for God's sake, Casey thought, we're acting out some kind of nineteenth-century drama. People just don't talk this way any more. Euralia and I are doing a conversational minuet. It's insane. Then she softened. People who live in this kind of house do observe rigid protocol, she realized. Anything else would be foreign and frightening to the polite, respectful woman who faced her. Her voice was softer when she answered.

'Of course, Euralia. Please be frank. We must both be if we're going to come to any kind of understanding.'

'Well then, Mrs Cromwell, I must tell you that much as I would like to stay with you, I don't know whether I can please you and Mr James.'

'Why on earth not?'

Euralia hesitated. 'What I mean is, madam, I'm not sure that the kind of service I'm used to giving is what you will require. That is, perhaps I'm too settled in my ways to suit you and Mr James. I don't know whether it fits in with the way you wish to live.'

Casey was strangely touched. The poor thing was frightened, she realized. Under all that starched efficiency, she's the one who's scared to death. Probably feels like an inherited relic that nobody wants. 'I don't think you really know how we wish to live, do you? What makes you assume it will be all that different? You've known my husband all his life and you've seen something of me in the last five years. Do you think we're so terrible?'

'Oh, no, madam. Not terrible. But it would be different. You're very young and I am sure you have young friends. I know that my kind of world is passing. The way people entertain, that kind of thing. Even I know that most people today don't care so much about the conventional ways of running a house. I read a great deal, madam. And I can tell from the magazines that everything is much less formal than what I'm used to. It might be hard for both of us.'

'I'm still not quite sure I understand.'

'Let me put it this way, madam. Mr James's grandparents were quiet, conservative people. Like most of the others in this building. They had certain ways of doing things, certain friends who thought as they did. I mean no disrespect, but the late Mrs Cromwell talked a lot about your husband in her last days. She loved him very much, but she worried about his way of looking at things. She never gossiped with me, of course, but I know that she never understood his world or his friends. She always hoped that Mr James would follow his grandfather into the law. That he'd be active in the kind of charities his family favored. And,' Euralia hesitated, 'that he'd keep on seeing the kind of people he grew up with.'

Casey interrupted angrily. 'Also, I suppose, that he'd marry someone his grandmother considered more suitable? Someone born to that conventional life you were talking about?'

Euralia shook her head. 'Please, Mrs Cromwell, don't misunderstand me. I'm not a sophisticated person, and perhaps I shouldn't even presume to discuss these things with you. About Mr James and all that, I mean. I don't understand his work and neither did Mrs Cromwell. She just felt that he had gotten very far away from the life he grew up in. And I guess it worried her, her being such a sheltered lady. But one thing I do know, madam, she was very happy about you and Mr James. She used to say to me how glad she was that you had such a good marriage, even if it seemed strange to her, you two living in that little walk-up apartment and never seeing any of Mr James's old crowd.' Euralia stopped abruptly. She looked distressed. 'Forgive me for talking so much,' she said. 'I can't think when I've rattled on like this. You see, I just don't want to stay where

I don't belong. And I don't know whether I'm the kind of person to please you.'

For the first time, Casey felt as though she knew where she stood. Probably without realizing it, Euralia was trying to warn her that 617 Park represented a world unto itself. Dear God, she probably thinks we have orgies and wife-swapping! She actually believes all those wild things that are written about advertising men like Jim and ex-models like me. Poor thing. We must seem like immoral monsters.

'Listen, Euralia,' she said lightly, 'I want to thank you for your honesty. I believe that's the best trait in any human being. You are astute and very kind. But you're wrong about us. Sure, we have friends you might consider unconventional. They're not all Christians. And some of them happened to have been born with yellow skins or even black. And you're right; we probably will lead a freer, less rigid life in terms of set hours for meals and that kind of thing. But basically, we're not bad people or irresponsible ones. Lots of things will change. You're right about that, too. But the world is changing, Euralia, and sooner or later even people in this building will find that out. Meantime, if you want to stay, we'll respect your opinions, and we'll expect you at least to put up with ours. Under those ground rules, I think it can work. Of course, if you want to leave, Mr Cromwell will see to it that whatever his grandmother left you is supplemented by enough so that you can live comfortably. I'd like to have you here. But the choice is yours.'

She waited. After a moment, Euralia managed a diffident little smile.

'You're a fine young lady, Mrs Cromwell, and I'm grateful to you and Mr James. If you want me, I'll be pleased to stay. Perhaps I'm not too old to learn. I just worry whether you'll be happy in this building.'

'Don't worry about us. We'll be happy. If anything, maybe you should worry about the building. We might end up rocking the foundations.'

'They've been very solid for more than forty years. They won't give easily.'

Casey laughed. 'You know what, Euralia? Neither will we.'

* * *

As Jim had anticipated, a crash meeting in Tony Stewart's office was in progress by the time he arrived at SS&A's offices in the ugly skyscraper on Madison Avenue. As he started into 'the goldfish bowl', as the staff called the chairman's big room, Tony's secretary handed him a cup of coffee. When you had the first of your daily dozen cups in Tony's presence, you drank out of real china. Otherwise, it was a soggy paper container from the rolling wagon.

'There's more of this poison,' she said. 'And from the looks of those two, you'll be hollering for it.' She pointed to the newspaper on her desk 'You read Al Shriber this morning?'

Jim nodded. 'Green is not my normal complexion tone.'

'Stay loose,' she advised. 'Remember it's not the real world; it's only advertising.'

'Thanks, Mom. I'll try to hold that thought.'

Tony and Paul were in the 'conversation corner' of the office, a casual grouping of sofa, chairs and coffee table set apart from the big desk. Serious conferences always took place here. As though the informality of the setting made the deadly possibility of disaster less real. Tony and Paul were struggling to maintain a posture of calm. Jackets off, ties loosened, Gucci-loafered feet on the table, they looked like two suburbanites relaxing at the country club after a round of golf. You had to be one of them to know that every nerve-end was quivering with fear. You couldn't blame them. The agency's commission on an eight-million-dollar account would be nearly a million and a half dollars a year.

Jim slumped into a chair. 'Either of you know what the hell is happening?' he asked.

'That,' Tony Stewart said not unkindly, 'is *my* line. You're the managing supervisor on this one, Jim. We were hoping you'd have the answer. Christ, you've been practically living with Weinberg for months. Didn't you have an inkling of this?'

'Not a clue,' Jim admitted. 'Paul will tell you. We left there last week like fat cats. Has it been confirmed by the *Times*? Anybody talked to Al Shriber this morning? Where did he get the item?'

'He doesn't get to his desk until eleven,' Tony said, 'and there's no answer at his house. If it was one of the fly-by-night trade gossip sheets I wouldn't be so worried. But Shriber doesn't deal in rumours. Who's behind this, do you think, Jim? Weinberg himself?'

'Probably. He has a president and a battery of vice-presidents but the chairman makes all the important decisions. I don't get it. Paul will tell you that he was very high on the work we presented. As much as said that we had the business. Knocked himself out to praise the campaign. Said it was the best advertising he'd seen in his forty-odd years in the shoe business. That was Friday morning. And here it is Tuesday and it's a new ball game! Christ, I'll never understand this business. The longer I'm in it, the less I know.'

Tony looked at Paul Gordon. 'You were satisfied with the stuff we presented, weren't you, Paul?'

The creative director stretched his arms into the air behind his head, the long, sensitive fingers clasped. Gordon was the wonder-boy of the advertising world. At thirty-five he had a reputation for brilliant copy, bold art work, campaigns that caught the public's attention and sold the advertisers' goods. His advertising awards lined the halls of the agency. And perhaps best of all, in an industry of egomaniacs and con-artists, Paul Gordon's level-headed approach to his work, his honesty and lack of temperament combined with his genius as a creative ad man made him one of the four or five best-paid and most-admired members of his trade. When Paul said a campaign was good, it was good. And nothing that failed to meet his standards ever went out of the agency. Yet, ironically, his insistence on perfection kept SS&A from becoming a giant agency. He stubbornly refused to be dominated by clients, to do bad advertising even though it meant big commissions. In many cases, the agency was penalized for his honesty. They had lost accounts whose management tried to dictate the kind of advertising the agency should produce. It was to Stewart, Sutton & Atherton's credit that they preferred to remain relatively small and keep Paul Gordon. 'We want a creative director, not a whore-master,' Tony Stewart was fond of saying. Paul recognized the sacrifice and worked all the harder for it. Yet today he felt guilty about it. In a larger agency, the loss of an eight-million-dollar account would not be quite the catastrophe it would be at SS&A. Perhaps, he thought, if I'd presented more cornball, buckeye work to that bastard Lester Weinberg we wouldn't be in this mess. Maybe the advertising was *too* good. He realized that Tony was waiting for his answer.

'I was satisfied with the work we presented,' he said flatly. 'And, like Jim, I thought that Weinberg was, too.'

'Any of the others over there seem unhappy?' Tony asked.

Jim shook his head. 'No. But that doesn't mean anything. Nobody would disagree with the Old Man when outsiders were around. They'd wait to get him alone. Which is probably what

17

happened, though I sure as hell don't know who's trying to do us in.'

'Well,' Tony said, 'if the work was right and the chemistry seemed good, there's no point in our sitting around here this morning speculating on how it got screwed up. Let's find out first if there's anything to this rumor, Jim. And if there is, that'll be the time to regroup.'

The meeting broke up and Jim headed back to his office. He dialed Lester Weinberg's private wire, smiling ruefully as he did. That's how close to the account I thought I was, he told himself. I even have access to the chairman's unlisted office number. I wonder how many other agency guys are using the same hot line.

Weinberg answered immediately. 'Morning, Lester,' Jim said. 'It's Jim Cromwell.'

'Jim, boy! You're up and at 'em early. Not like some of those schlemiels who work for me. Can't get their asses in here before ten o'clock. How are you, kid?'

'I'm waiting for you to tell me,' Jim said. 'I got kind of a nasty shock with my coffee this morning when I read the ad column in the *Times*. What's going on over there, Lester? I thought you'd settled on SS&A. Did we goof someplace, or has Al Shriber got his wires crossed?'

Lester laughed. 'Take it easy, kid. No need to get excited. Fact of the matter is I meant to call you yesterday. Nothing's changed, really. It's only that some of our people thought we shouldn't rush into a decision. Thought we ought to interview a few more agencies. Just to be on the safe side, you know. We're not in all that big a hurry. Hell, our advertising's set for the next six months. I swear to you on my mother's grave, God rest her soul, that I was all set to sign. But what the hell, I said, if these wisenheimers around here need a little more reassurance that you're the best, what's to lose? Your stuff's terrific. Tell Gordon I said so. So we put off the decision a little while. Big deal. Take it from me, you're still the winner.'

'Can I take that as a firm commitment?'

'Well, now,' Weinberg hedged, 'I can't go against my people and say it's firm. But if you're a betting man, you could give odds.'

Son-of-a-bitch, Jim thought. He's playing with us. Something has come up. And as a betting man, I'll make book on the fact that it has nothing to do with Lester's executives. He's always gone it alone before. Why would he suddenly start listening to that bunch of yes-men now? He tried to sound very cool.

'If some of your people have doubts, maybe we should talk to them,' Jim said. 'Anybody you'd suggest? Any bases we haven't covered?'

Weinberg's phony heartiness set Jim's teeth on edge. 'No, no. You've done a great job, kid. Hell, you've talked to just about everybody in the joint except my wife.'

Intuitively, a bell rang in Jim's head. 'Your wife?'

'Oh, don't take that seriously,' Lester said. 'Just a figure of speech, you might say. I only thought of it because Gertrude's been getting a big rush from the wives of some of your competitors. One of them even got her on some cockamammie society charity committee. That Gwen Crawford – you know, her husband's a partner of Crawford-Thompson. She's been showing Gert the ropes. Gert's getting a kick out of it. You know dames. They get bit by the social bug. Nothing to do with business. Just a little fun for the missus. Don't even know why I mentioned it.'

Like hell you don't, Jim thought. That's the key to it. Crawford-Thompson's making a play for the account by having Gwen Crawford butter up Mrs Weinberg. To anyone in a rational business – meaning anything except advertising – such tactics would be unthinkable. But Jim had seen accounts change hands for more ludicrous reasons. He supposed he shouldn't even be surprised. To men like Weinberg, one agency was not all that different from the next. If Gertrude was bending Lester's ear every night with 'how darling Gwen Crawford is and what a great job her husband could do on Weinberg Shoes', it was not inconceivable that Lester might change his mind about SS&A, on the theory that peace in the family was more desirable than possibly superior advertising for his product.

In a split second, legends of similar insanities raced through Jim's mind. There was the big perfume account that departed one agency to go to an inferior one, just because the company's vice-president of advertising found a new Rolls convertible parked in front of his Scarsdale door one morning. And the fabric mill that deserted its agency of twenty years because the executive vice-president of the mill discovered that another ad agency owner could get him into a country club that had black-balled him for years. The stories were legion. In fairness, they were the exceptions rather than the rules. Some of them probably weren't even true. But they persisted in an industry where very often the clients were no more scrupulous than the agencies that pursued them.

19

This would not be the most reprehensible of such maneuvers if, indeed, it were true. It would be easy enough, and not even that unethical, to flatter the client's wife, with the certainty that she would be eager to repay the kindness. And it would not be that difficult to imagine Lester going along with Gertrude's wishes. Perhaps even he was flattered by the attention being paid to the Weinbergs. It was, after all, the only area that SS&A had not given thought to. Jim's dealings had been strictly professional. He had met Gertrude Weinberg only once, by chance, when she happened to drop by her husband's office. It had never occurred to him — to any of them — that an eight-million-dollar account could quite possibly go where the client's wife wanted it to go.

Time to regroup, Jim thought. I'll need Tony's help on this one. But not till I've had a chance to think it through. Meanwhile, it was important to maintain his attitude of sublime confidence as far as Weinberg was concerned.

Hating himself for it, he went along with the game.

'Well, I sure feel better now that I've talked with you, Lester,' he said. 'That *Times* piece gave us all a little scare.'

'Sure, kid. Relax.'

'I will. Talk to you soon.'

As he hung up the phone, Jim took a Gelusil. He was sure he was developing an ulcer. If he did, he'd name it after Lester.

*　　*　　*

When he left the office that evening, Jim hadn't told the others about his disquieting conversation with Weinberg. He'd stalled Tony and Paul, saying he'd not been able to get through to the prospective client. Tony had reached Al Shriber who confirmed that the item in his column came from 'highly reliable sources', a piece of information that plunged Tony and Paul into a state of despair. Still, Jim decided not to reveal, just yet, the game he was certain Lester was playing. Better to think it through, figure out a counter-attack and then present both problem and suggested solution to agency management. Fawning over clients wasn't SS&A's kind of thing. They'd always gotten new business on the strength of their reputation or their great presentations. But then, Jim reflected, they'd never before pitched an account to a rough diamond like Lester Weinberg or, apparently, a silly bitch like Gertrude.

Casey was home when he let himself into the apartment. For

20

the first time that Jim could remember, she was so involved in her own day that she completely forgot to ask anything about his. It was just as well. He wasn't ready to talk about it to anyone. Not even to Casey who'd often served as a useful sounding board, letting him spill out his business problems and clarify them just by putting them into words. Tonight he was grateful for the small talk about 617 Park. It kept him from thinking about Lester Weinberg.

Over their martinis, Casey filled him in on her first official visit to 14B. He complimented her on her handling of Euralia and expressed his pleasure over the outcome of the interview.

'Did you get hold of the super?' Jim asked.

'No. It was his day off. But I did meet one of our neighbors.'

'Oh?'

'I hadn't been in the apartment twenty minutes when a darling little old lady from across the hall rang the bell and asked if there was anything she could do to help me. Imagine. We've lived here five years and I've never met another breathing soul in the building.'

Jim held up his hand. 'Don't tell me. Let me tell you. Your darling little old lady is Miss Rosemary Murphy, spinster, age roughly sixty-five, inhabits apartment 14A with her spinster sister, Constance, and their classically matriarchal mother, Eileene Murphy, an antique widow-lady. Right?'

'On the nose. Obviously you know our floor-mates.'

'You'd better believe it. They've lived there since year one. I never met Mr Murphy. He went to his reward before I was born. Probably in self-defense. Good God, I'd almost forgotten about that trio of pious Irish harpies! Old Eileene must be ninety if she's a minute.'

'Ninety-four,' Casey said. 'And according to Euralia she's almost as physically agile and probably more mentally alert than you and I. She's on the board of the building, among other things. I didn't meet her or Constance, but Rosemary seemed adorable.'

'She's a nice lady,' Jim agreed, 'even though she's the resident snoop. That building is her life. She knows the dirt about every tenant. You won't get a package from Saks that Rosemary won't know about five minutes after it arrives. I'll say one thing for her, though. She's kind. Almost too kind. If you don't watch it, she'll be all over you like a tent. I guess the poor old girl needs some kind of outlet for her maternal instincts. It must be a helluva

21

life with that do-gooder, domineering mother and that dried-up sister.'

'Euralia says that she doesn't know how the building would get along without "Miss Rosemary". Apparently, everybody runs to her with their troubles.'

'Which she adores.'

'Probably.' Casey agreed. 'Anyway, she was very cordial. We had a cup of tea – if you're ready for *that*. And she told me about some of the other people in the building. That's quite a collection.'

Jim smiled. 'Okay, Mrs Leonard Lyons, I know you're dying to give me the run-down on our happy little group. Spill. Who else did Rosemary tell you about?'

'Well, she wasn't malicious about any of them, but I could kind of read between the lines. Like, did you know we have a real honest-to-God live-in celebrity? Antoinette Lawrence has apartment 8A. Remember her? The old silent film star. We've seen a bunch of her movies at the Museum of Modern Art. Only she's Antoinette Lawrence Stone now. Mrs Harry Stone.'

'Sure, I remember her from the movies *and* the building. Don't know her husband. She married him after I moved out. Who else?'

'There's a gorgeous Baroness. Teutonic-type. She's in 12A. Baroness Felicia Von Brennerhof. Terribly regal, I understand. Lives alone with a German housekeeper who speaks no English and cowers a lot.'

Jim nodded. 'Poor Frieda. I'm sure the Baroness beats her.'

'Then we have our own private shrink. Dr Richard Basil. He doesn't practice from the apartment. Has an office on Park Avenue. Also has a wife who tipples.'

'Tipples!' Jim roared. Suddenly he was enjoying himself hugely. Lester Weinberg seemed light years away. 'Honey, Louise Basil is a lush. She's bombed out of her skull every day of the year. I remember she used to crawl up to our floor at all hours of the night, yelling for Rosemary. Never could understand why old Eileene Murphy put up with it, but Rosemary used to take her in, let her cry her eyes out, sober her up and return her to that weird-o husband. They're in 8B, aren't they?'

'I think so,' Casey said.

'For God's sake, give Louise Basil a wide berth unless the doctor's around to handle her. Not that any of the others are to be cultivated, for that matter. Unless it's Elinor Simpson. As I recall, she's the world's funniest old party. Did Rosemary mention her to you? Mrs Edgar Simpson? A widow?'

Casey shook her head. 'Never heard of her.'

'Well, I guess Rosemary couldn't run down all thirty families in one sitting. On the other hand, there might be a little rivalry there. Elinor Simpson is chairman of the house committee and a member of the board. Sort of an unpaid housemother who looks after things like the decoration of the lobby and the upkeep of the communal roof garden. I think Rosemary's a little jealous. Probably thinks Elinor invades her territory. Anyway, old Elinor's swell. Likes a drink and even a good story, provided it's not too dirty. You'll like her. Pure Billie Burke with a touch of Helen Hayes. Anybody else?'

'No. Just our noble president, Mr André Dubois Livingston. He and his wife own 9B. That's where they hold the annual tenants meeting and the board meetings. We didn't talk about them a lot, but I gather they're very Old Money.'

'Stuffiest old goat in the world,' Jim agreed. 'Has that Harvard-Choate mumble. All stiff-upper-lip and old-school-tie kind of thing. Jesus, I think he's been president of the building since the day it opened. Runs it like a private club. No undesirables allowed. Pays very little attention to the building agents, Ridgely & Ryan. I remember he once told Grandmother that having an outside agent was pure nonsense. "Don't need the blighter at all. Only mess up a building. Try to bring in the wrong element if you don't watch them. That sort of thing." '

Casey laughed at his imitation. 'You're making that up,' she said.

'Word of honor. A direct quote. I'm sure the Livingstons still dress for dinner and have one small sherry before it's announced.'

The word 'dinner' brought Casey bolt upright. 'Oh, my God,' she said, 'look at the time! We haven't even eaten and I asked Paul and Mary to come by a little after nine!'

'The Gordons are dropping by tonight?'

'Yes. I talked to Mary this afternoon. She's dying to hear about the new apartment so I told them to come after dinner. I figured I'd be too worn out to do much about a meal tonight. Okay?'

'Sure,' Jim said. 'Paul didn't mention it today. Guess he didn't know about it until he got home.'

While Casey rattled the tiny kitchen pulling a hurried meal together, Jim made himself another drink and reluctantly thought about the Weinberg business. Maybe he'd have a chance to brain-

23

storm in with Paul tonight before they talked to Tony Stewart. They couldn't avoid the issue forever. Lester Weinberg, in all probability, would let things drift for weeks, even months, while his wife enjoyed the attention lavished on a woman whose husband was a heavy potential client. But sooner or later Lester would have to announce a new agency. And in the interim, SS&A could not afford to simply sit by and wait. Jim thought, as he often did, of how fortunate he was to have a man like Paul Gordon not only as an associate but also as his best friend. Professionally and socially, their minds worked alike. Or always had. Jim was not so sure how Paul would react to this kind of business problem which could not be solved by superior advertising. The answer might well be to fight back on the same battlefield; to outdo the other entries in the race for Mrs Weinberg's approval, if indeed that was the answer. It was a disgusting way to do business. But sometimes business called for primitive survival tactics. And for SS&A this was a matter of survival. Jim hoped Paul would accept that, even though it wasn't his cup of tea. Hell, he thought, it isn't any of our cup of tea to kowtow to a gullible *nouveau riche* female like Gertrude Weinberg. But if that's really what it takes, we'd better figure out how to do it. And do it better and faster than our less finicky competitors.

'Nice guys finish last. Thank you, Loe Durocher,' he said.

Casey stuck her head out of the kitchen door. 'What?' she asked. 'Did you say something to me?'

He had not realised he'd spoken aloud. 'Just wondered how you were coming along,' he lied. 'Do I have time to shower before dinner?'

'Sorry,' Casey said. 'I'm just about ready. It's not much of a meal, but you'll soon be rescued by Euralia. Take heart. You'll only have to live through a few more of my famous TV dinners. Then it's Cordon Bleu all the way!'

24

Chapter II

The friendship between Jim Cromwell and Paul Gordon had started when Jim joined the agency in 1966. The two men liked and admired each other instantly, and their wives had formed a friendship equally easy and secure. Despite the disparate backgrounds of the two couples, Jim, with his conservative, best-schools, WASP upbringing, and Casey, with her Midwest, middle-class origins, related happily to the attractive young Jewish couple who had been childhood sweethearts in Brooklyn and who continued to live in the neighborhood in which they'd grown up.

That, in itself, made them unusual. Paul's £75,000-a-year salary at SS&A could easily have supported a good East Side Manhattan address, a late-model car and private schools for his only child. It was part of their charm that they remained in a floor-through Brooklyn apartment, drove a four-year-old Ford and sent six-year-old Abigail to P.S. 62 on Flatbush Avenue. They were secure people, incapable of false values and blessed with a delicious sense of the ridiculous.

Even Abigail's name was an indication of their delight in whimsy. It certainly was not the kind of name a young Jewish couple ordinarily would give to their first daughter. She should have been Rachael, after Paul's mother. Or even Sarah, after Mary's. But to their parents' distress, the young Gordons had no deep religious convictions. They did not deny their Jewishness; they simply seldom thought about it. Neither of them had been to Temple for years, nor did they observe the Holy Days. And when it came to selecting a name for the baby, their impulses were creative rather than traditional. Before her birth, they had settled on two names: Abigail if it was a girl, Geoffrey if it was a boy. The decision had been, to them, a very simple and logical one: Gordon was such a nondescript surname that it screamed for a distinctive given one.

'What could be dumber,' Mary had asked in the eighth month of her pregnancy, 'than a name like Mary Gordon? It's as blah as Jean Smith or Lucy Brown. Let's don't do that to little what's-its-name.'

'Agreed,' Paul said. 'Paul and Mary Gordon sound like a recording team. Or made-up signatures at the bottom of a form letter. Let's call the kid something kind of New England primitive. Like the name you find on the back of old family portraits.'

So when it was a girl she became Abigail Gordon. And, to their mild astonishment, she had even turned out to look like her name. From birth she'd had pale blonde, Alice-in-Wonderland hair, fine delicate features, a skin as thin and fragile as porcelain.

'Where in God's name did *that* combination come from?' Paul had asked when he saw her for the first time in the hospital.

'Try not to be suspicious,' Mary had teased. 'Nobody in our family ever got knocked up by a G.E. refrigerator.'

They adored Abby and each other. They were pleased but unimpressed by Paul's success and their constantly increasing nest egg conservatively stashed in savings banks and non-speculative stocks. Through it all, they stayed loose. Relaxed, uncomplicated and utterly unpretentious, they enjoyed their comfortable life and their small circle of friends, which included the Cromwells.

Driving into Manhattan that evening, Mary filled in her husband on Jim and Casey's windfall.

'Casey says the apartment's sensational. Practically like a whole house, including a separate dining room with a working fireplace and three great big bathrooms. Boy, I didn't think they made 'em like that any more.'

'They don't,' Paul said. 'It's an old building, isn't it?'

'Um-hum. Belonged to Jim's grandparents. The apartment, that is, not the building.'

There was silence as Paul concentrated on maneuvering through the Third Avenue traffic.

'Funny Jim didn't mention it to me today,' he said. 'Of course, we were busy as hell, but we were together a lot. Maybe he's embarrassed about getting so far out of our class.'

'Some embarrassment,' Mary sniffed. 'It should happen to us, that kind of terrible humiliation.'

Paul glanced at her briefly. 'Would you like it to?'

'Do you mean would I like a swell co-op with a guest room

and a gigantic kitchen and all those goodies? Well sure I would. Why not? But don't tell me you have a secret millionaire uncle who's going to pop off and leave us one. I've met your whole family. They all came to the wedding, remember? And every damn one of them sent us a hand-painted bonbon dish.'

He laughed. 'You're a nut. A well-adjusted, beautiful, un-envious oddball.'

'So? Remind me to tell that to my head-doctor when I get one. Which may be sooner than you think. I have a feeling I'm going to go mad with envy when I see that apartment.'

Casey kissed them both warmly when they arrived, breathless, at the top of the three-flight climb to the Cromwells' apartment. 'Welcome,' she said. 'Come in and recover from the workout. Jim's just breaking out the ice.'

Mary collapsed on the couch. 'My youth has fled,' she moaned. 'I remember when I could take those stairs like a mountain goat.'

'You might try tapering off to three packs a day,' Paul said.

She made a face at him. 'Nag, nag, nag. Just because you've quit smoking you don't have to be so pious about it. I notice you're breathing a little heavily yourself, dear saint.'

'All right, you two,' Casey laughed. 'It won't be much longer. Pretty soon we'll be able to whisk you up to our new pad in an impressive walnut-paneled elevator driven by a man in white gloves. How's that for class?'

'Loathsome,' Mary said. 'If you weren't my dearest friend, I'd hate you. In fact, I may even manage to in spite of it.'

Jim came in from the kitchen, ice-bucket in hand. 'Hi,' he said, stooping to kiss Mary. 'I got extra booze. We'll need it to survive Casey's *House Beautiful* lecture. The lady is really hung up on the new place.'

'Aren't *you?*' Mary asked.

'Sure. But paint colors and matching curtains don't turn me on in quite the same way. That's woman's work.'

Casey pretended anger. 'See? That's how Women's Lib got started. You, James Cromwell, are a male chauvinist pig. Where is that share-and-share-alike stuff they keep writing about in *New York* magazine? You're supposed to participate in the things that involve both of us – up to and including the decoration of a new apartment.'

'Swell,' Jim said. 'Tell you what, Fanny Freedom, I'll swap you my account headaches for your domestic woes. Okay?'

'No deal,' Casey said.

Mary Gordon looked puzzled. 'What's that all about? Some kind of a house joke?'

'Would that it were,' Jim said. 'We got trouble at River City, otherwise known as Stewart, Sutton & Atherton.'

'I haven't had a chance to tell Mary about our double-dealing client,' Paul explained.

Mary looked at the three of them as though they were speaking another language. 'Okay,' she said. 'I assume that sooner or later you'll all tell me what you're babbling about. But don't worry about me. Patience is my best known virtue.' She turned to Casey. 'Let's let Batton and Barton talk shop, which is what they obviously are dying to do. We'll go in the bedroom and draw floor plans.'

As the two young women departed, Paul and Jim settled down to face their mutual worry. Jim finally recounted his phone conversation with Lester Weinberg. 'He was about as subtle as the proverbial sledge hammer. It's a sure thing that at least one other agency is wooing Mrs W. She could be a powerful influence on the decision.'

Paul shook his head. 'I can't believe it,' he said. 'Weinberg's a smart businessman. You'll never convince me that he'd base his choice on his wife's social ambitions. He's a tough old bastard. He'd tell her to go to hell.'

'I'm not so sure,' Jim said. 'A woman like that can make life miserable for a guy if she wants to. Besides, Gertrude Weinberg is at least twenty-five years younger than Lester. She's his third wife and he's nuts about her. Have you ever met her, Paul?'

Gordon shook his head.

'Well, I have. Once,' Jim said. 'Right after they were married. She's a prototype. Bleached blonde, overdressed, overjeweled. Playing the jet-set game to the hilt. She was his manicurist. That's how they met. She'd be a pushover for some nice, Christian agency president and his wife. They'd have the Weinbergs to dinner with impoverished royalty or get them a membership in a private club like Raffles or invite them to Southampton for the weekend. Gertrude would drive Lester up the wall talking about them. And finally, to shut her up and keep her happy, he just might decide to toss the account to Gertrude's friends. It's been done.'

'I hate to sound naïve,' Paul said, 'but what about the advertising? Even Weinberg said ours was the best he's ever seen.'

'And I'm sure he meant it,' Jim answered. 'But we're still running a risk. Weinberg doesn't really know from good advertising. He could figure that it doesn't really make all that much difference as long as his bloody shoes keep appearing on TV. Anyway, friend, I hate to say it, but we can't count on his appreciation of our quality. Or I should say *your* quality.'

'So what's the answer? There's no point in doing another campaign to show him. Or is there? Would it help to put together some crappy, harder-sell stuff? I know as well as you do how much this business means, Jim. If you think our campaign is over his head, I'll try to turn out the kind of junk he might understand – even if I throw up over every layout.'

Jim thought for a moment. 'No. I wish that were the answer, but I don't think it is. We'd better talk to Tony tomorrow. Maybe we can figure out a holding action. Entertain Gertrude a lot in the next couple of months. Try to fight fire with fire.'

'I wish I'd said that,' Paul said.

Jim laughed. 'A thousand pardons. I'm only a management supervisor. Allow me an occasional cliché, will you?'

Paul smiled. 'Sure. Trade you an old chestnut for a fresh drink. And let's knock it off for tonight, okay? Somehow I'd rather think about your new apartment than the office. Shall we join the ladies?'

They spent the rest of the evening talking about 14B. At midnight, Paul signaled his wife. 'Time's up, Cinderella. Back to your pumpkin in Brooklyn.'

'For an overpaid writer, you sure are lousy with metaphors,' Mary grumbled. 'That pumpkin is our geriatric Ford parked outside. But I've had a glorious few hours pretending I was going to live in The Palace.'

'Well, get your glass slippers shined, pal,' Casey said. 'I'm going to run your little feet off helping me pull that place together. How about lunch tomorrow? I'll show you the apartment and you can meet the formidable Euralia.'

'Love it. And maybe we can go to that mill-end fabric place on Forty-ninth Street. They have sensational . . .'

Paul interrupted. 'Wrap up the details on the phone in the morning, will you? We've got a baby-sitter waiting 'cross the river.'

Mary pretended to pout. 'See how unfair life is? The Cromwells are going to have a live-in lady, and they don't even *need* a baby-sitter. My mother was right. I should have married that rich dentist in Queens.'

When they were alone, Casey put her arms around her husband. 'You're worried as hell. I'd almost forgotten about the *Times* piece. It's that Weinberg business, isn't it? Was Paul any help? Does anybody at the agency know anything?'

He ignored the last question.

'In his own way Paul was terrific. It's a real sacrifice for him to offer to do some corny work if that would please dear Lester. But I'm afraid that's not the answer.'

'What is, then?'

'Honey, I honestly don't want to go into it any more tonight, if you don't mind. I'd rather think about the apartment. I'd even prefer to think about the Murphys, if you can believe that.'

She gave him a hug. 'I love you.'

'I know. For my money.'

'No, dope. For your beautiful soul.'

Jim burlesqued a leer. 'Little do you know how evil I can be. I can hardly wait to get into that building and shake up The System. All my intended victims are listed in a little black book. Soon they shall begin to see the error of their ways.'

'Beginning with Rosemary?'

'Oh, no. She'll be saved. But those devils she lives with will be among the first to feel my diabolical power.'

Casey pretended horror. 'You're going to reform the Murphys?'

'Why not? They're closest. Right across the hall.'

'And how, oh limb of Satan, will you do that?'

'Who the hell knows?' Jim said. 'Probably with shock treatments.'

*　*　*

Shock was an appropriate word for the reaction of Eileene Murphy and her elder daughter Constance when Rosemary reported on her first encounter with Casey Cromwell.

'She's planning to redo the apartment?' Eileene was astonished. 'Whatever for? Mrs Cromwell had it repainted not more than three years ago. And those marvelous antiques! Surely she's not going to get rid of all those fine old things!'

'She said that she wasn't sure, but she thought that she might prefer a more contemporary style,' Rosemary reported primly. Secretly, she was enjoying her mother's dismay.

'Then I suppose she'll want to redo the foyer on this floor, as well,' Mrs Murphy said. 'We'll just see about that. Her apartment is her own business, unfortunately, but the hall belongs to both of us. Mrs Cromwell and I agreed years ago on the way we wanted it to be. That's the way it is, and that's the way it will remain.'

'She didn't mention the hall, Mother,' Rosemary said.

'She will,' Constance chimed in. 'Mother's quite right. If she doesn't like antiques in her own house, she's unlikely to care for them in the entry.'

'Exactly,' Mrs Murphy agreed. 'But we'll deal with that soon enough. This is a bad start. A bad start. I'll tell you two girls in confidence that I had reservations about the suitability of young James Cromwell, but Mr Livingston didn't see how we could gracefully deny him the apartment. Perhaps I should have followed my instincts and made more of an issue of impetuous youth. But the others didn't seem terribly concerned. Now I'm beginning to be sorry.'

Rosemary spoke soothingly. 'Now don't get yourself all upset, dear. I'm sure we're anticipating a problem that won't arise. Really, she seems like a very sweet girl.'

Her sister snorted. 'How can you be so naïve, Roe? We know she was a photographer's model before she married James Cromwell.'

'What does that have to do with it?'

'Oh, really, you are impossible,' Constance snapped. 'What girl with breeding takes up modeling? I should think that even you could add up the ingredients: An ex-model married to an advertising man. For heaven's sake, can't you imagine what kind of life they're used to? I dread to think of the kind of people who're going to come swarming onto this floor! The board should have rejected them. You wait and see. They'll do nothing but disrupt this house.'

Firmly, Eileene Murphy intervened. 'All right, that's enough. I must say, I do share Constance's concern about our new neighbors. I smell trouble. On the other hand, Rosemary may be right. Perhaps we are jumping to conclusions too quickly. We'll simply have to wait and see how they behave. However, Rosemary, it's unseemly for you to go knocking on their door like some suburban housewife asking to borrow a cup of sugar. I'm sure you meant well, but the first thing they must learn is respect for privacy. And we must set the example. So please keep your distance until we know what kind of people they are. Heaven help us, we don't need another Louise Basil barging in at all hours of the day and night! I'm sorry for the poor soul, but we should never have allowed that to get started in the first place. We shall not make the same mistake again.'

31

'All right, Mother. But what about "Love thy neighbor"?'
'Don't be impertinent, Rosemary,' Mrs Murphy snapped.
'And don't be so dumb,' Constance added.
With that, they let the subject drop. Momentarily.

* * *

Apartment 14A was not the only one in which the imminent
arrival of the Cromwells was being discussed. In 18A, Antoinette
Lawrence Stone commented on it to her husband while he
struggled with the back zipper of her slightly-too-snug evening
gown. Harry Stone earned his keep as a dress zipper-upper and
social escort. Twenty-five years younger than Antoinette, he had
met the one-time movie star at Roseland where she and some of
her aging lady cronies, escorted by the perennial bevy of faggots,
had gone one night as a lark. Harry, an unemployed and un-
successful actor, had been there in the company of a faded old
lady who knew Antoinette. They were introduced and the great
Lawrence was instantly attracted to this still-handsome, forty-
year-old failure. Within six months they were married and Harry
moved into Antoinette's co-op.

He loathed his life, but took great pains to disguise the fact.
Antoinette was a caricature of the beauty she'd once been. The
famous black hair cut with Dutchboy bangs was heavily dyed
but worn in the famous same little girl style of the '20s. The
once petite figure now sagged in all the usual places, though
costly corsetting helped disguise much of the ruin. But worse
than any of this was the fact that Antoinette firmly refused to
believe that she was no longer the simpering sweetheart of the
silver screen. She spent her life, and most of her money, attending
balls and benefits, dragging an obedient, bored-to-death Harry
with her. For his part, Harry would infinitely have preferred
more evenings at home. He found Antoinette's friends stultifying
and her endless 'public appearances' embarrassing. But this, he
knew, was how he earned his keep. He was almost always attentive and charming to his wife, careful never to touch on a subject that would point up the difference in their ages, presumably
undisturbed by the fact that this was her fourth marriage and
his first.

Given his choice, Harry would have relaxed in an easy chair
most evenings, content to have a beer or two and watch television.
Regrettably, he had no such choice. Antoinette flatly refused to
have television in her home. It was, she pronounced in her pseudo-

32

society voice, a medium best suited to those whose only cultural interest lay in watching trained dog acts and detergent commercials. Harry knew differently. TV watching was a solitary pastime that deprived Antoinette of an audience. More importantly, he guessed, TV was synonymous in her mind with old movies. Antoinette would never watch one of her early films. She would never go to see them at the museum. God knows she would not want to see herself on 'The Late Show'. She would be destroyed by that young image of herself, comparing it with the reflection in her mirror. Antoinette wanted to be remembered, but only through a merciful haze of nostalgia – her own as well as others.

Struggling with the zipper, Harry was only half-listening to his wife's conversation.

'André sent off the letter of acceptance to James Cromwell yesterday,' she said. 'I suppose they'll move in before Christmas.'

'That's nice, dear.'

'Quite frankly,' Antoinette gasped, holding her breath as the zipper struggled to pass her rib cage, 'I'm not sure it's nice at all.' Annoyed with his demeaning task, for once Harry let some of his bitterness show through.

'Why not?' he asked sarcastically. 'You and his grandparents were great friends, weren't you?'

Antoinette ignored the implication. 'I knew them. Charming couple. But much older, of course. We were hardly contemporaries or even close friends. Judge Cromwell and I served on the board together. He was a great gentleman. Unfortunately, his grandson does not seem to enjoy quite the same reputation.'

Harry was still fighting the zipper. Godamn her, why can't she pass up just one of these evenings? Or at least get a maid to dress her.

'From what I hear,' Antoinette went on, 'the young Cromwells seem to have an appalling lack of taste and discrimination. Their friends, for example, are reputed to be somewhat odd.'

'Really?' Suddenly Harry was interested. 'How would you know that?'

'It's a very small world we live in, my dear. It so happens that Marianne Morgan has an apartment in the same building the Cromwells currently occupy. Some sort of dismal walk-up on Fifty-second Street. At any rate, the Cromwells live above her, and she tells me they're virtually Bohemian. All sorts of strange people coming in and out. Endless parties with the sort of guests who'd hardly be welcome in this house.'

Harry smiled to himself. He could imagine Marianne Morgan's

reaction to what was probably a young, swinging household. Marianne was Antoinette's vintage. They'd both been part of the early Hollywood scene, but she'd never really risen above the status of supporting roles. At seventy, though she pretended to have been a star, people knew that she didn't have a bean. She lived modestly but comfortably, thanks to the grudging support of a successful son-in-law. Perhaps through kindness, but more likely through condescension, Antoinette invited Marianne to tea every few weeks. Happily, Harry was excused from these afternoon visits which centered mostly around Antoinette's social life and The World That Was. During Marianne's last visit, Antoinette must have mentioned the new owners of 14B. And Marrianne, delighted to have some shocking gossip to contribute, must have painted a lurid picture of the Cromwells.

'I wouldn't take Marianne's comments too seriously,' Harry said. 'She hasn't approved of anybody since Irving Thalberg.'

'My dear, she never even *knew* Irving Thalberg. But she does know the Cromwells. Even if only at a distance. She tells me that after one of their parties the hall absolutely reeks of marijuana.'

'Seriously? But, tell me, how does a nice lady like Marianne recognize the smell?'

'Don't be nasty, Harry. Believe me, if they try that kind of thing here, I'll see to it that they're stopped. As a member of the board, I shall have my say.'

The zipper finally locked into place. Harry sighed with relief.

'I'm sure you will, dear heart. I'm sure you will.'

*　　*　　*

Four floors above, Baroness Felicia Von Brennerhof chose to discuss the same subject with her elderly German housekeeper. Frieda and the Baroness had an extraordinary old-world relationship. It was a kind of love-hate, royalty-peasant, masochistic-sadistic thing based on a mutual need which neither of them would admit. Frieda was terrified of Felicia while she simultaneously worshiped her. Felicia regarded Frieda with a protective condescension that smacked of feudal patronage. Only those brought up in pre-World War II Europe could have understood it. In one breath, the Baroness unmercifully abused her housekeeper for some minor offense – a speck of dust on a chandelier, perhaps, or a ball gown hung in the wrong place in the Baroness' endless rows of closets. A moment later, the two would be setting off together in Felicia's chauffeur-driven Bentley,

34

chummy as two friends and equals out for an afternoon drive. It was a way of life that had endured for more than twenty-five years. Almost since the day that the Baroness had fled Nazi Germany and arrived alone, mysteriously rich, in New York. She presumably divorced the Baron who remained in Germany. And she bought the apartment on Park Avenue, using her title and her hauteur to impress the board. Soon after the war she imported Frieda, making sure that the country-born woman learned very little English, insurance that she would not get grandiose ideas about American employment conditions and American domestics' wages.

In those first days of Felicia's arrival, there had been a certain amount of genteel speculation about Baroness Von Brennerhof. There were whispers that she'd been a Nazi spy, even that she'd been Eva Braun's closest friend. One rumor was that there never had been a Baron, but that her money came from her extraordinary sexual prowess, news of which had traveled quickly through the world of rich German industrialists. There was even a school of thought within the building that subscribed to the belief that Felicia had engaged in anti-Nazi activities and had escaped to this country with the help of a high official in the British Government.

Strangely enough, it was impossible to confirm or refute any of the rumors. All that was known for sure was that the Von Brennerhof title was a good but impoverished one. No one was certain about the Baron. There was one who still existed and was, presumably, separated or divorced from a beautiful woman who fitted Felicia's description. This meager information came from tenants with excellent European connections. But beyond this skeleton of fact, no one, in more than a quarter of a century, had been able to find out who Felicia really was or where she got her apparently considerable wealth. At sixty-five she was still a strikingly beautiful woman. She seemed to have an endless stream of attractive and suitable escorts. Her picture constantly appeared in *Town & Country* and her name in the gossip columns of the *Post*. Her apartment had that peculiarly wonderful air of expensive clutter that distinguishes really elegant European houses. She dressed beautifully, entertained impeccably and behaved with an arrogance that could change, when she chose, to an attractive and disarming simplicity. Her personalities were many and varied according to her audience. She had, for example, completely charmed André Dubois Livingston.

At her interview before the board, many years earlier, she had

spoken glowingly of 'this great, free world of America', profess-
ing her desire to live here always and admitting, a trifle sadly,
that her husband's insistence upon remaining in Germany had
been the primary cause of their divorce. As if to prove her
devotion to her new country, she never left it. She spent her
winters in Palm Beach, her summers in Newport and her
Christmas holidays in Santa Barbara. Though friends from
around the world came to visit her, she professed no desire to
leave her adopted land. In charmingly accented English she explained that for her Europe was a dead land. 'It does not interest
me,' she would say. 'Everything civilized is now in America – the
most superb food, the most elegant fashion, even the greatest
new art. One must simply know where to find them.'

Old Livingston had been so captivated by this cosmopolitan
creature that when an opening on the board came up five years
after Felicia bought her apartment, André asked if she would
consider serving as a director.

Felicia was appropriately humble and reluctant. 'Dear Mr
Livingston,' she said, 'I am honored. But I must say to myself,
"Am I capable?" After all I am only a naïve woman who knows
nothing about the affairs of business. It is a little frightening,
this great responsibility you offer. Can I truly be of assistance to
intelligent executives such as yourself?'

'You will be invaluable,' André assured her. 'After all, Baroness,
we need more than dollars-and-cents knowledge. We need board
members with taste and sensitivity. The running of a building is
not all business, you know. Much of it has to do with maintaining our high standards of service and in judging the suitability of
new applicants for ownership. In both these areas, you would be
rendering a great service.'

'Then, of course, I shall be delighted to do my small part.'

In the intervening years she had been as good as her word.
Almost too good. She was a rigid disciplinarian, reprimanding
any elevator operator with a soiled white glove or any doorman
with a spot on his uniform. These 'front men' loathed her.
'Bloody Nazi bitch,' they called her when they talked with the
'back men', the boiler-room attendants and service-elevator
operators. This group was sympathetic and grateful that they
escaped the Baroness' wrath, if only because she never saw the
behind-scenes staff.

To her 'royal privileges' she now added her own self-assumed
special rights as a member of the board. When she rang for the
elevator on the 12th floor she expected it to come immediately

and make no stops at other floors on the way down. When her car pulled up to the door, she required the instant appearance of the doorman, and God help the poor soul who had chosen that moment to go to the men's room.

Most of all, she was a ruthless inquisitor at the interviews with prospective purchasers. Many a rich and famous applicant found himself squirming under the cool scrutiny of Felicia's noncommittal eyes. If the applicant did not come up to her standards, socially, morally, religiously or professionally, the Baroness always succeeded in making the other board members see it her way. It was she who had, admittedly with some difficulty, convinced the others to reject a famous Jewish concert pianist 'because that endless practicing would drive us to distraction.' It was also she who turned thumbs down on the successful young Broadway star, Sally Morgan. 'Theater people,' she said, 'are notoriously irresponsible. No offense to you, my dear Mrs Stone,' she added quickly to Antoinette. 'We all know that this new breed of actress is quite different than the magnificent artists of earlier days.' And when Antoinette still showed signs of resisting, the Baroness played her trump card. 'Actually,' she said, 'my dear friend Jess Hargrove, the producer, did tell me that the lady's real name is Sarah Moscowitz. Not that it matters, of course.'

Her initial reluctance to serve on the board had been real. Livingston, Antoinette Stone and Eileene Murphy were crashing bores and she hesitated to get involved with them. But Judge Cromwell had a certain distinguished charm and Dr Richard Basil was an old friend. The sixth member of the seven-man board at the time she joined it was Bryan Rogers, an important newspaper publisher who, Felicia decided, might be useful to her in getting more of the publicity she adored. This had turned out to be pleasantly accurate.

Now, twenty years later, the board had changed very little. The vacancy created by Judge Cromwell's death had been filled by a woman named Elinor Simpson, a widow who had lived in 617 Park since the day it was built. Mrs Edgar Simpson was, if nothing else, amusing. She was bright, kind, cultured and given to saying deliciously flighty things. Even Felicia, who didn't like women, was tolerant of Elinor Simpson, in a detached, unthreatened kind of way.

On the whole, the Baroness was pleased to be on the board. She liked the sense of power it gave her, with 'life or death' decisions about applicants who often were richer or more intelligent or more famous than she. She adored being able to direct a whole staff of servants, which was the way she thought about the building's employees. On this morning, however, she was a little annoyed that there had been virtually no discussion about accepting the young Cromwells. Not that she really had any objection. It was just that she enjoyed the minute dissection of the private lives of most applicants. The young Cromwells had simply slid through on the credentials of his grandparents.

'We shall be having new people in 14B, Frieda,' she said when the housekeeper brought in her breakfast tray. 'Mr and Mrs James Cromwell will occupy his grandmother's apartment.' She spoke in German.

Knowing that some reply was expected, Frieda tried to sound interested. 'That's nice, Baroness. You know them?'

'No. I have never met them. Of course, I knew the senior Cromwells. The Judge was on the board. Before that, he was a very famous corporation lawyer.' For some reason, she spoke the last two words in English. Frieda looked puzzled.

'What is a "corporation lawyer", madam?'

Felicia sighed with annoyance. 'My God, you are an idiot. Do you know nothing? How can you have lived in this country for twenty years and not even understand English?'

The housekeeper did not answer. She would like to have said that she did not understand the language because the Baroness had very deliberately kept her from learning it. In the beginning, she had enrolled in night school to learn, but after she missed four consecutive lessons because of 'suddenly arranged' dinner parties, she gave up. Nor was she helped by the fact that the Baroness spoke to her only in German, mysteriously and confusingly interspersed, as now, with strange English phrases. Felicia ordered all the food by phone, dealt with all the household problems that required outside services. How could Frieda have learned English? No matter. Through her church friends she had discovered that in four years she could retire, collect the American Social Security and go back to live on the farm in Germany. Until that day, the Baroness would not know her plans. Frieda would continue to accept and bank the modest pay, endure the spare but adequate room and bath and the constant humiliation and infrequent kindness which her employer bestowed. She stood quietly by the bed while the Baroness attacked her melba toast.

'I approved young Cromwell, of course,' she said, 'though with questions in my own mind. He's in advertising, which is

38

a very risky profession. Fortunately, he has some family money. Also, it would have been awkward to take issue with the terms of his grandmother's will. What really disturbs me about the Cromwells is their youth. Both of them are only in their twenties. With that big apartment, they could decide to have a family. My God, all we need is perambulators in the lobby and a diaper service arriving every day! That's always the danger in selling to young couples. Imagine this building overrun with drooling, noisy little monsters!'

'Children can be lovely,' Frieda ventured.

Felicia snorted. 'A remark worthy of you. *Kinder, Küche, Kirche* – in whatever order you like, eh, Frieda? All very well for the German *Hausfrau*. Hardly suitable for a building of this character.'

Daringly, Frieda persisted. 'But Mrs Cromwell has no children now, has she? Perhaps they cannot have a family.'

'I'm not so naïve as to pin my hopes on "cannot". I prefer to trust in "will not". Oh, get out of here, stupid! I'd like some peace and quiet while I read my paper.'

The housekeeper gladly retreated. The Baroness was in one of her warmer moods this morning, but you never knew when the temperature would change.

* * *

In the apartments occupied by the other board members, there was less verbal speculation about the new tenants. After fifty years of marriage, the Livingstons had very little to say to each other about anything. André had already mentioned that 'Judge Cromwell's grandson had been accepted for 14B' and as far as the president and his wife were concerned it was a *fait accompli*, which did not lend itself to further discussion. The Livingstons' life was, and always had been, staid, peaceful and proper in every sense of the word. Their life style had remained virtually unchanged for half a century. Upheaval and unrest was something one read about in the morning paper, all very remote and deplorable, and far removed from their safe, secure, predictably comfortable world.

The Richard Basils spoke hardly more than the Livingstons, but for different reasons. When she was sober, Louise was like a ghost of a woman, wandering silently and unhappily through the apartment. When she was drunk, she screamed at Richard loudly and futilely, abusing him for his unfaithfulness, his prolonged absences. His ill-disguised disgust only increased her alcoholic ravings.

He answered this hostility with silence. Everything she said was true. Her drunkenness repelled him, and he refused to dignify any of her accusations with a reply. For that matter, there was little he could say. He had long been an adulterer, and though he took some care to be discreet about it, it was no secret from Louise. As for his prolonged absences, some were legitimate, others were not. He was an extremely successful psychiatrist and did, indeed; sometimes get evening calls that took him to a suicidal patient or to one recently hospitalized for shock treatments. For the most part, however, he spent as much time as he could with the woman he loved. A woman who was not, and probably never would be, his wife.

The more he withdrew from the unpleasantness of these encounters with Louise, the more her fury increased and the more heavily she depended upon the forgetfulness of drink. As a doctor, Basil knew that at times Louise was literally deranged. But he was not prepared to do anything about it. It had all begun so long ago. Airing it now would only cause a scandal – and to what end? He was emotionally incapable of recapturing what he had once felt for her. There was nothing to do now but go on with this sordid hidden way of life. He found his mental fulfillment in the world of medicine, and his physical satisfaction in the incredibly undiminished love-making of the woman who'd been his mistress for more than twenty years.

It was not surprising that he did not even mention the Cromwells to Louise. Though he served on the board of the building, he never discussed the activities of that august body at home. Any more than he spoke of the office or any of his other outside diversions. He was a solitary, unfathomable man. Clinically, he supposed he was not unhappier than most. When you spent each day listening to the real or imagined despair of other people, you developed more than a protective shell. You also learned to really do what you'd been taught as a child: To count your blessings. Fortunately for him, Louise was virtually a recluse. And, blessedly, on those rare occasions when they appeared together in public, she was quiet, sober and charming. It was, he supposed, as much as a man could hope for.

The two remaining board members did not spend time talking about the Cromwells for still other reasons. Bryan Rogers lay paralyzed with a stroke, unable to speak at all. And Elinor Simpson had no one to talk to in the lonely confines of 6B.

Edgar had been dead for five years and she missed him desperately. She had not become a self-pitying or disconsolate widow. On the contrary, she was as cheerful and appealingly bubble-headed as she'd always been. But Edgar's death left a void in her life that could not be filled by any number of friends or any amount of activity. She managed plenty of both, but at moments like these she allowed herself just a touch of depression. It would have been fun to discuss the new young owners with Ed. Even after all their years together, they had always found each other interesting companions, had never lacked, as so many long-married couples do, topics to explore. When she dined alone in restaurants these days, she looked with pity at the silent couples at nearby tables. You could always spot a long-married pair. They were silent eaters. She and Edgar had found each other stimulating conversationalists for forty years. He had teased her about her malaprops, adored her unconscious witticisms and made her feel needed and cherished. There was no substitute for that kind of happiness. And while she was grateful for the long years of it she'd had, she wished God had seen fit to let it go on a while longer.

She was unashamedly curious about the Cromwells. Like the others, she'd known the grandparents and liked them. And she was fully prepared to like this new generation and welcome the infusion of 'new blood', as she thought of it, into the staid confines of 617 Park Avenue.

She remembered when she had moved into the house as a bride. Even then, the atmosphere had seemed formidable. She wondered whether Mrs Cromwell would find it so. 'Casey', they called her. Elinor liked the sound of the name. It had a nice, peppy ring to it.

Chapter III

When Jim finally reported Lester Weinberg's telephone conversation to Tony Stewart the next morning, the chairman of the agency did not react with any particular surprise. Anthony Stewart had been in the advertising business longer than either Jim or Paul, though he was still a youngish man. In his late forties Tony had everything going for him – good looks, an impressive income and a brilliant business reputation. Four years ago his wife had left him to marry a solid type who came home at six o'clock every evening. And though Tony lived the life of that most enviable of all creatures, the eligible, successful, amusing bachelor, he was not really happy about it. He wanted to remarry. Not only because he preferred the more comfortable, less-demanding private life of the married man, but also because he felt that his two little girls would be better off if there was a woman around during the holidays that the court allowed them to spend with him.

Still, it was difficult, he knew, to be married to a man like himself. The agency consumed most of his energy, his thoughts and his waking hours. He was still ambitious, still driven. Endlessly energetic, Tony spent half his life on air-planes, visiting his out-of-town agency offices or his non-resident clients. His two partners, Sutton and Atherton, were sensible financial experts whose talents did not lie either in the direction of attracting new business to the agency or in creating the work that held them. Tony was the active 'front man' and Paul Gordon the creative star. With Jim Cromwell, they made a companionable and respected trio. Jim was the only young man Tony had found who showed signs of possessing talents similar to Stewart's own. Jim could attract clients and cultivate them, a vital asset for an agency. He had a way of sizing up a situation that was very like Tony's. And the chairman listened carefully now to his assessment of the problems with Weinberg. When Jim finished his recital, Tony nodded.

'I'm afraid you've pegged it,' he said. 'It's dirty pool, but God knows it isn't all that rare in our business. Particularly with a self-made, insecure type like Weinberg. What's your recommendation?'

Jim looked slightly sheepish. 'I wish I had a more brilliant suggestion, but the only thing I can think of to do is to play the same game as the competition. Entertain hell out of the Weinbergs. With concentration on la belle Gertrude. We haven't done any of that.'

'If you can't beat 'em join 'em, eh?'

'Paul Gordon would put you down for that cliché,' Jim laughed. 'His lip positively curled when I said, "Fight fire with fire". But I still think it's the only answer.'

Stewart was amused. 'We're not what you might call the repartee whiz-kids. I'm awed by Paul's originality, but I don't think this mess is going to be solved creatively. By the way, what did Paul say when you told him the situation?'

'He was great. As always. Even offered to do other campaigns if we wanted. I told him that I didn't think the advertising itself was the problem. It's damned good. and Weinberg knows that. I'm sure that Mrs W. is being snowed, and she's so impressed by all the attention that she's on Lester's back every minute. I think we just have to go in for the same. Only more so.'

'Agreed,' Tony said. 'How shall we start? Want me to give a dinner party for them at my house? I could get Suzy to play hostess.'

Jim hesitated. Tony's town house would impress Gertrude Weinberg. It was elegant, expensive and smoothly run by Stewart's Japanese houseman. The only thing wrong in the situation was Suzy. Tony's choice in women ran to young, beautiful creatures and Suzy was the youngest and most beautiful of all. Jim's instinct told him that Gertrude Weinberg would not welcome such competition. He was sure that she felt secure with – even superior to – the dowdy, well-bred agency wives who had been making friendly overtures on behalf of their earnest and ambitious husbands. He searched for a way to get this across, diplomatically, to his boss.

Tony was aware of the hesitation. 'You don't buy it?'

'Not exactly, Tony. I mean, I think it's a great idea to have a dinner for the Weinbergs at your house. Gertrude probably would flip out over it. It's just that, well, I have a hunch that she likes to be the belle of the ball. Probably outdresses and out-jewels those country-club types she's been running around with and thinks they're no competition. If I figure her right, she likes the female acceptance without the female threat. You know I love Suzy, but she's just so Godamn smashing.'

'And she's also so Godamn unmarried. Right?'

Jim grinned. 'Right. I could be way off base, Tony, but my other hunch is that the Gertrude Weinbergs of this world don't want their husbands exposed to all that unattached beauty. They don't even want the Lesters to get it into their heads that Bachelors Have More Fun.'

'In other words, if I had a nice, plain wife, it would sit better. I think you're right. So what's the plan? Do you want me to deal myself out?'

'Hell, no. Let's just start easy. I'm sure Gertrude *would* like to be entertained by you, the world's number one bachelor, with all your attention focused on *her*. She'd eat it up.'

'But wouldn't Lester have exactly the opposite reaction?'

'Not necessarily,' Jim said. 'If she's happy, he's happy. Why don't we start with the dinner at your house, but with a different cast? Just poor, lonely, charming you. Casey and me. Paul and Mary. And maybe round it out with that beast of a society columnist, Janet what's-her-name, who's a friend of yours.'

'Janet Chalmers? Jesus Christ, Jim, she's fifty-five, ugly as a toad and completely unpredictable. God knows what she might say!'

'All the better. Gertrude will be impressed by the name, fascinated by the outrageous behavior and out of her mind with joy when Janet writes up the dinner party *and* the guests in her column.'

Tony sighed. 'Okay. That's for openers. What next?'

'More of the same, with variations, I guess. We'll offer them a box at the opera, for instance.'

'Don't tell me. Let me guess. You happen to have a box at the opera.'

'Well, yes,' Jim said. 'That is, my grandmother did. I still have the subscription.'

'It figures. After that comes a Saturday night at the world's most restricted country club, lunch at The Knickerbocker, etc., etc., etc. And most of all, I keep my stable of sirens out of sight. Do I read you?'

'Perfectly. We have to buy time, Tony. Any way we can. Meanwhile, you and I will go on pursuing Lester on a man-to-

44

man basis. You should know him better, God help you. And we have to keep selling the agency to him while we're pumping social happiness into Gertrude.'

'Well, it's a long shot,' Tony said, 'but I guess it's all we have. I'll sent out the "pleasure of your company cards" for next week. Meantime, keep me posted on your conversations with Lester.'

'Absolutely. And thanks a lot, Tony, for not being offended. About Suzy, I mean. You know it's not personal.'

Tony shrugged. 'Never entered my mind that it was. Listen, pal, I know where my hang-ups are. I may be forty-eight years old, but emotionally I'm going on sixteen. I don't need an analyst to tell me what I'm trying to prove since my wife went off with that walking Dunn & Bradstreet. But that doesn't mean that my sex life ever interferes with my business judgment. And don't kid yourself for a minute that it ever will.'

Jim closed the door quietly. Tony Stewart would play his part perfectly. Now he'd have to cue the rest of the characters. That probably would not be quite as easy.

*   *   *

He started with the one closest at hand. Paul Gordon. As Jim had expected, Paul reacted with distaste to the wooing of the Weinbergs.

'It's a phony way to get a piece of business,' he said. 'Damn it, Jim, if our work doesn't stand up, we don't deserve the account. All this stuff about entertainment and impressing Gertrude Weinberg make us sound like some crappy little Forty-second Street ad shop. It really blows my mind.'

'I know,' Jim agreed. 'It's a new problem for me, too. But Tony's seen it happen before, and he goes along with the idea that this is the only chance we have. There's only one thing to keep in your mind, pal. A lot of people in this agency are going to be on the unemployment line if we screw up. The commission on eight million dollars' worth of billing can save the jobs of some of your best creative talent.'

'So be it. What do you want me to do?'

'At the moment, nothing special. Just alert Mary that you'll probably be on call for a dinner at Tony's next week. We'll have to play it by ear from there.'

'All right, I'll warn her. Provided I can find her. She seems to be spending most of her time with Casey these days. I don't know who's getting more of a kick out of fixing up that apartment, your wife or mine.'

'Don't knock it,' Jim said. 'It's better than if they'd decided to march down Fifth Avenue carrying banners for Women's Lib.'

*   *   *

Paul was right. Casey's determination to move into the co-op as quickly as possible was seconded with enthusiasm by Mary Gordon. The two of them drove themselves – to say nothing of a platoon of painters, paper hangers and upholsterers – to the edge of insanity. For both women, 617 Park became a fascinating challenge, a whole new world of luxury and status. Sometimes Mary felt a twinge of envy, but for the most part she was excited and happy for her best friend.

In those weeks, Mary was a godsend. She came over from Brooklyn nearly every day, arriving early and leaving just in time to be home when Abby returned from school. She and Casey stopped endlessly, delighted with the freedom to spend without guilt. They badgered workmen shamelessly, gossiped interminably as they lined closet shelves and arranged Jim's vast collection of books which he and Paul brought over in the Gordons' old Ford some days before the actual move.

Tony's dinner for the Weinbergs had gone well and had been given a chatty paragraph in Janet Chalmers' column. Casey and Mary talked about it as they worked. Gertrude Weinberg fascinated and repelled them.

'Silly bitch,' Casey said. 'She's the world's most vulgar, pretentious woman. Did you see how she played up to Janet Chalmers? All that crap about her Norell wardrobe and the house she and Lester plan to buy in Palm Beach! And he's so idiotically proud of her. Absolutely fatuous. That emerald-cut diamond must be twenty carats. She gets me crazy, that woman! And unfortunately it looks as though we're going to have to see a lot of her. I've always heard about "Jewish princesses" but I never thought I'd . . . ' Casey stopped in dismay. Somehow she never thought of Mary as a Jewess. She could have killed herself for her tactlessness, and her face registered her distress.

Mary laughed easily. 'Don't look so panic-stricken, for God's sake. Gertrude Weinberg would be just as repulsive if she was an Irish scrubwoman. I couldn't agree with you more. She's a horror. But for your information, she's not the classic "Jewish princess". Those are the little girls who've been brought up to believe that they're precious and special and very, very untouchable. This one, our gorgeous Gertie, had to claw her way from the manicure table to some degree of "respectability". She's the Jennie-come-lately Jewish matron. They make the princesses look like masterpieces of understatement.'

Casey was still remorseful. 'I didn't mean to sound like a rotten little prig. You know I've never cared what anybody is if they're nice people.'

'Of course I know that,' Mary said. 'Now will you forget it? And forget Gertrude Weinberg, too. That's business. This is fun. Especially since I see Euralia appearing with lunch. I'm starved.'

Like Mary, Euralia had turned out to be a treasure. Her capacity for hard work was unlimited and her knowledge of the building invaluable. She could always find George, the handyman, at a moment's notice. She knew where to run quickly in the neighborhood for curtain hooks, extension cords, picture wire and the thousand and one odds and ends that they seemed constantly to need. And unfailingly, no matter the state of chaos, Euralia appeared at one o'clock with two perfectly set luncheon trays for her employer and her employer's best friend.

As they attacked one of Euralia's tastefully arranged meals, Mary shook her head in admiration.

'Linen napkins for lunch, yet,' she marveled. 'Quelle swank! Why don't you tell her we could rough it with plastic mats and paper napkins?'

'Shush,' Casey said. 'I did that the first day and got told off very politely. "Paper napkins are only for kitchen use, madam," ' Casey mimicked. 'So I made some dumb remark about how of course I realized that, but I thought in the midst of all the work she might want to save herself some trouble. She just gave me that no-expression reaction and said that she was used to laundering the table linen daily and it really was no trouble at all.'

'Terrific. At least I know she's capable of a complete sentence. Up to now all I've heard her say is, "Yes, madam. No, madam. Thank you, madam." Not a very outgoing type, that one. But can she work!'

Casey agreed. 'She's fabulous. But I don't think I'll ever get used to this servant-mistress relationship. This business of "knowing one's place" gets under my skin. It just seems like an insult to human dignity. Not that dignity isn't Euralia's thing. God knows she'd make Queen Victoria look like Laurel and

47

Hardy. Still, that subservient attitude makes my flesh crawl.'

'Forget it,' Mary advised. 'That's the way she's used to operating. She's already given you the message that anything else would make her uncomfortable. If it suits her, be happy. You've got one of a vanishing breed there, kid. So, as we say in Brooklyn, "Enjoy!" By the way, any signs of life from your neighbors? What about little Rosebud across the hall?'

'Not a peep since the day we moved in. From her or anyone else. Do you think we've been blacklisted?'

'I doubt it. They're probably waiting for you to be formally ensconced. Then they'll appear in their little white gloves and leave cards on you.'

'I don't know.' Casey said uncertainly. 'You'd think that with all my coming and going I'd at least have caught a glimpse of somebody in the lobby or the elevator. But I haven't laid eyes on a living soul except the men who work in the building.'

'Yep, that is kind of odd. On the other hand, this ain't exactly the Pan Am Building. With so few tenants, one would hardly expect a traffic jam, especially during the day when the men are at work. Any kids going back and forth to school?'

'None that I've seen. I don't think there are any small children in the house.'

'Or puppies or pussy cats?'

'Beats me,' Casey said. 'But I guess I shouldn't complain. I'm an honest-to-God New Yorker, I suppose. Don't know who lives in the building and don't especially want to. It was the same on Fifty-second Street, now that I think of it. I didn't hobnob with a soul in the place. Anyway, it sure won't keep me awake nights. I'm just so pleased with the way this apartment is shaping up. You've been an angel, doing all this work. I really can't thank you enough, Mary.'

'My pleasure. In fact, it's a vicarious thrill. Some day I'm going to get old what's-his-name off his creative rear-end and see if we can't find a mansion of our very own. Brookly's okay, but I think we're growing out of it. Or should, anyway. So this is good training for the day the Gordons get out of the ghetto.'

'Wouldn't it be marvelous if you and Paul could get an apartment here?'

Mary smiled. 'Not marvelous, luv. Miraculous. Come on, Casey, you know this is a restricted building. They can't stop you from having a nice Jewish girl come to visit, but they sure wouldn't want their corporation to marry one.'

Casey was shocked. 'Doesn't that make you furious?'

48

'Not particularly. Paul and I don't care a lot for discrimination, but we know it exists and we're not terribly militant about it. Matter of fact, we've had blessedly little trouble with it. Maybe we don't "look Jewish". Or maybe it's because Gordon is the kind of who-can-tell name that could be anything. As opposed to Katz or Finklestein, I mean. Anyway, we don't go around looking for trouble. We don't push in where we know we're not wanted. To tell you the truth, in a nutty way I can sort of understand how people feel. There really are some terrible Jews. Like there are terrible anythings. Not that we're anti-Semitic. We haven't pretended not to be Jewish. We just don't make a big thing of it. It could crop up sometime, I suppose. Abby's liable to run into it one of these days. But meantime, we accept life the way it is. Not the way a lot of idealists wish it could be.'

'I wish I had your serenity,' Casey said.

'I'll let you in on a little secret,' Mary answered. 'I wish I had your apartment.'

*   *   *

By mid-December the Cromwells were installed in 14B and Casey was able to give their usual party for the 'waifs and strays' on Christmas Eve. It was an annual event with them, gathering together the people who had no families nearby, the people who found Christmas an introspective, lonely time. They asked about fifty of their friends, many of them Jim's associates from the agency. This year it was super-special, a combination Christmas Eve and housewarming, and Casey went all out to make it the best one they'd ever given. She and Euralia planned a lavish buffet and Casey hired a bartender and two extra waitresses. She packed the apartment with extravagant Christmas greens and found a tree that touched the top of the nine-foot living-room ceiling. In a moment of rashness, she even engaged a three-piece combo.

Jim, half-kiddingly, chided her for her extravagance. 'You're ruining me,' he said. 'It was enough of a shock when I got the employees' Christmas list. By the time I get through shelling out to fifteen guys, from the super to the relief man on the service elevator, I won't be able to afford a Christmas turkey, much less this bash. Christ, Christmas is getting to be a racket. We've only been in here two weeks and I'm handing out a fortune to a bunch of jokers who haven't done a thing for us.'

'That's not really true,' Casey protested. 'The men in the building were just marvelous to me while I was getting this place ready. And you know that everybody knocked themselves out to be helpful the day we moved in.'

'And you, Lady Bountiful, know that I tipped every one of those clowns heavily the same day.'

'True. But darling, it's Christmas.'

Jim looked around the room. 'How about that?' he said. 'You sure could have fooled hell out of me.'

The party was a huge, boisterous success. Everybody they'd asked came, and a few brought unannounced but cordially welcomed friends. The women were cheerfully and openly envious of the apartment. The men kidded Jim about his new affluence.

'You sure have made the big league, kid,' they said. 'Seven rooms in the Silk Stocking district! The whole Godamn ball of wax! Listen, if you play your cards right, we swear we won't tell the clients. Let 'em think you're still just a poor account joker trying to make a buck.'

Tony was there with a new girl, a six-foot Swedish beauty who, Casey speculated, couldn't be a day over twenty-two. The agency guys ribbed their chairman about his conquest and Tony took it good-naturedly.

'Just a bunch of jealous bastards,' he said. 'Want to get big blondes? Go open your own agency.'

Between Jim's wide contacts in the advertising field and Casey's brief but moderately successful career as a model, they knew a great many of the youngish people in fashion and the arts. Some of them were, to put it mildly, off-beat, but they were perfect guests – uninhibited, extroverted people who loved a party and adored a chance to show off. Even the unflappable Mary Gordon was stunned by the underground movie actress who arrived with her head completely shaved.

'Don't you just adore it?' the bald beauty asked. 'I think it's so sexy.'

Mary gulped. 'You bet. Yul Brynner always did give me goosebumps.'

Casey had to admit that some of the costumes were outlandish. They ranged from eccentric to elegant. A gay playwright, male, made a show-stopping entrance in a white chiffon jumpsuit with a full-length cape bordered in white fox. A department store owner's wife arrived in a toe-touching cape of deep black mink. It had begun to snow lightly, and Casey expressed concern that the woman's fur was more than a little damp.

'Rose, darling,' Casey scolded, 'why on earth are you wearing that beautiful new cape in this lousy weather?'

'Don't be silly, luv. Fur is perfect for the rain. After all, have you ever seen a mink carrying an umbrella?'

They poured in. The skinny young models in their see-through shirtwaists exposing breasts as flat as boys'. The magazine editors in their deliberately sleazy rayon shirts and pants covered with cheap rhinestone pins. 'Isn't it heaven?' one fashion editor asked Jim. 'I'm absolutely mad for the tawdry look, aren't you?'

They raved over Casey's Christmas tree which she had chosen to do in the most reverse-avant garde way, with old-fashioned decorations and yards of tinsel. 'My God,' a well-known writer screamed, 'that tree is so chic I could absolutely perish! I'm going right home and stomp mine to death!'

Casey laughed. 'Come on, Lee, you're putting me on. I'll bet you've got the most divine tree in town. How did you do it this year?'

'I'm ashamed to tell you. It's just yards of pearls and turquoise, with jade-green bows. Such a cliché compared to this! I do admire you, Casey. You can always spot a trend. A tree right out of *Little Women*. My God, it's *genius*!'

'What are you going to do next year, Lee?' somebody asked. 'Cover a pine with fat little Santa Clauses?'

'If he does,' Paul Gordon said, 'he'll have Cartier run them up in ruby jumpsuits with diamond beards.'

'You're all wrong,' Lee pouted. 'I wouldn't have that dirty old man in my house. What's *your* tree like, Paul?'

Mary chimed in. 'Ours isn't a Christmas tree, silly. It's a large Chanukah bush. We got dat ole-time religion, remember?'

Unconventional as it was, it was a good group. They kidded themselves and each other, kindly, without malice or condemnation. They accepted 'deviations from the norm' as the right of the individual, whether it was homosexuality or simply camp, designed to amuse the one who projected it in his clothes, his mannerisms or his conversation. They have a zest for life, Casey thought, that just doesn't happen anywhere else. She remembered one terrible Christmas that she and Jim had spent in Los Angeles. Some friends had invited them to the Coast, and for once they'd thought it might be fun to spend the holidays out of the city. It was horrible. Palm trees decorated with Christmas

51

lights and pink plastic Santas in sombreros on Wilshire Boulevard. They hated the fact that it was eighty-five degrees on December 25, and that their host in Beverly Hills had put fake igloos around the swiming pool. They cut short their visit and rushed back to New York in time for New Year. Casey remembered fondly that the streets of Manhattan were piled high with ugly soot-covered mounds of snow, and she loved them so much she wanted to jump out of the cab on the way back from the airport and romp in the dirty, symbolic mess. They'd laughed about it later. But they'd vowed never to be out of town again at this crazy, wonderful time of year. And it wasn't just geography, somehow. It was this mad mix of phony-unphony people who were gobbling up life with a kind of reckless drive.

As the evening wore on, Casey's happiness increased. She was a natural hostess who enjoyed her own parties, the magic ingredient for making other people enjoy them, too. Admittedly, from time to time she had a little pang of anxiety, wondering whether the music, the loud laughter and the endless opening and closing of the elevator door would ultimately bring complaints from the Murphys across the hall or from the unknown occupants in the apartment beneath them. She had been careful not to put coat racks in the foyer. God forbid that a carelessly hung overcoat should brush against the ancestral portrait which glowered over the delicate Chippendale table in the hall. She wondered who owned the portrait and the table. Mrs Murphy or Jim's grandmother? Those two had collaborated on the conservative decor. She must remember to ask Euralia. Not that she had any thought of changing it. The last thing she wanted was a confrontation with the Murphys over the look of their shared foyer.

Casey was a touch apprehensive, too, over the distinctive smell of pot which filled the air. Not that it was likely to creep out into the building. The thick old walls could contain the aroma of a thousand joints without the smell reaching any other apartment. The only 'stranger' who might notice it would be Euralia, and in all probability she would not know what it was. Even if she did, Casey thought defiantly, it was none of her damned business.

No, on the whole there was nothing to mar the perfection of her first party in her first real home. It was turning out to be a fun evening. Even Jim seemed relaxed and happy for the first time in weeks. Ever since that damned Weinberg thing began. Casey glanced at Jim affectionately. He had one arm

52

around a famous black fashion model, the other across the shoulders of a French *couturier* who had become the *enfant terrible* of Seventh Avenue. He was enjoying the evening as much as she was. Probably he had even forgotten how much it cost.

By midnight the party was in full swing. The noise was deafening. And Casey, straining desperately to hear what a slightly smashed copywriter was saying to her, was at first unaware that a newly arrived guest was trying to get her attention. She turned at last to look straight into the bloodshot eyes of a woman she'd never seen before.

'Excuse me,' the woman said, her voice slurred with liquor, 'but I'd like to introduce myself. I'm a neighbor. Name's Louise Basil. 8B. Married to a son-of-a-bitch doctor named Richard. Richard Basil. He's a shit.'

Startled, Casey groped for a polite reply. She tried to catch Jim's eye, but he was absorbed with his little group. Before Casey could answer, Louise Basil, weaving slightly, raised her glass to her hostess.

'Here's to ya, kid. Welcome to 617 Park. Hope you don't mind me bargin' in. I was all alone, see. So I decided to go visit my friend Rosemary. The one who lives across the hall. You know her?'

Casey nodded. 'Yes. Of course. Miss Murphy in 14A.'

'That's the one. The nice one. I go see her lots of times. Specially when that stinker leaves me alone.' Louise took another pull at her drink. 'Your name's Katherine, right?'

'Yes. They call me Casey. Casey Cromwell. That's my husband over there. The dark-haired man talking to the lady in pink.'

Louise focused her eyes in Jim's direction and nodded solemnly. 'He cheat on you much, Casey?'

This is ludicrous, Casey thought. What is this drunken woman doing in the middle of my living room asking me whether my husband is unfaithful? Helplessly, she tried to turn off the conversation.

'It was nice of you to come in, Mrs Basil,' she said lamely. 'You're the first of our neighbors I've met, except for Rosemary.'

'Sure. Rosemary. I was on my way to see her. Wanted to wish her Merry Christmas. Then I heard all the noise and your door was open so I thought I'd come by and be neighborly. Okay?'

'Of course,' Casey said. 'But isn't it a little late to be calling on the Murphys?'

'What time is it?'

'Just after midnight, I think.'

Louise considered this piece of information gravely. Suddenly she giggled. 'Don't know if it's the wrong hour, but it sure is the wrong night.'

'The wrong night?'

'Yep. Christmas Eve. The Murphys'll be at midnight mass. Wouldn't be home anyway. Not for a while. So, if it's okay with you, I'll just hang around and wait for 'em.'

Oh, Lord, Casey thought. She's right. The Murphys will surely arrive around one o'clock, just in time to get the full impact of this clambake. And all the time I was hoping they were asleep in their dear little beds. Well, no help for that either. Meantime, what do I do with Mrs Basil? Desperately she signaled Jim. This time he saw her and came across the room.

'Darling,' Casey said, 'this is Mrs Richard Basil from 8B. She was on her way to the Murphys, but they're at midnight mass.'

Jim shook Louise's hand cordially. 'Nice to see you again. Mrs Basil,' he said. 'It's been a long time.'

Louise looked confused. 'We know each other? Thought you just moved in.'

'We did,' Jim said. 'But I used to live here a long while ago with my grandparents. Judge and Mrs Cromwell. Remember?'

Louise thought deeply about that for a moment. At last her face brightened. 'Oh sure. Your granddad was on the board with my darlin' husband and the rest of those creeps. 'Scuse me. No offense. Didn't mean the Judge was a creep. Or was he?'

Jim laughed lightly. 'No. He was a nice old gent. He always spoke highly of your husband.'

'Then he didn't know him. Or else he really was a creep. Only people who can stand Richard are creeps.'

Casey interrupted nervously. 'May we get you something to eat, Mrs Basil? There's a buffet in the dining room.'

'Slice of lemon would be fine,' Louise said. 'Provided you serve it in a glass of vodka and soda.' She giggled. 'Don't care much for eating. Like drinking. A lot.' She looked around the room. 'Who're all these people? Friends of yours? Don't see any of our illustrious fellow tenants.'

'We haven't had a chance to get to know many of the people in the building,' Casey said. 'These are our friends. Mostly advertising and fashion people. Just the ones we love. And want to be with on Christmas Eve.'

54

Without warning, Louise began to cry. 'How cóme you're so Godamn lucky? How come you got so many people to love on Christmas?' Her tears increased. 'I got nobody. No friends. No children. No husband. Oh, people feel sorry for him. "Poor Richard. Tied to that crazy, boozed-up wife. What a terrible life for the wonderful doctor." That's what they say. They should know the real Richard Basil. The walking deep-freeze.' Her voice was getting louder and more hysterical. People standing nearby stopped their conversations, turned to look curiously at the little scene that suddenly was being played in their midst. Sensing their attention, Louise's tears just as abruptly ceased. She stepped up on a little footstool to raise herself slightly above the crowd.

'Listen, everybody,' she shouted. 'I love you. Do you hear? Everybody I love in the world is right here in this room! How about that? I love you because it's Christmas, and I don't even know your names. And you'll love me back, right? You will, won't you? I'm Louise Basil, and you have to love me. You have to!'

Jim stepped forward. Grasping her elbow, he tried to get her down off the footstool. 'Mrs Basil, please,' he said gently, 'let's go get a drink.'

Louise patted him on the head. 'Good boy. Good idea. Let's get lots of drinks. Say, I gotta great idea. Let's all go down to my place and hide till the doctor comes home. Then we can jump out and yell "Merry Christmas," and the first one who guesses what color lipstick is on his collar wins a prize!'

People were turning away now, embarrassed for her, trying to pick up the threads of their conversations. As she realized what was happening, Louise's tone changed again.

'No,' she pleaded. 'Don't leave me. Don't ignore me. Laugh at me. Hate me. But don't ignore me.' She began to sob again.

Gently, Jim helped her down from the footstool. He put his arm around her protectively. 'Let me take you home,' he said.

A polite voice beside him answered. 'Thank you, Mr Cromwell, but that won't be necessary. I'm Richard Basil. I'll take over.' He looked at Jim and Casey. 'There's no way I can adequately apologize for my wife's behaviour,' he said quietly. 'Thank you for being so kind. I hope we haven't spoiled your party.'

'Is there anything we can do to help, Doctor?' Casey asked.

'Thank you, no, Mrs Cromwell. I'm used to this, in one way or another. Fortunately, it's not usually so public. I had an emergency call, and when I came home and found her missing, the elevator man told me he'd brought her to this floor. I took the liberty of walking in unannounced. As, I gather, Louise did. I'll handle it from here. Again, I'm sorry. Good night.'

He led a sobbing but unprotesting Louise out of the apartment. Jim and Casey stood silent. In a moment, Mary Gordon joined them.

'It was nifty of you to provide a floor show,' she said, 'but I've already seen that movie. Next time, how about getting a belly dancer?' She made sure that her voice carried to most of the guests. Relieved, the others picked up their cheerful banter. The laughter began again, and the combo which had fallen silent during Louise's speech swung lightly into action.

'Bless you, buddy,' Casey said. 'You saved the day. My God, I just stood there like a wooden Indian! I didn't know what to say.'

'Honey, that outburst would have made Martha Mitchell speechless,' Mary said. 'What's with that dame, anyhow? I mean, I know she's loaded to the eyeballs, but do you think she's psycho? She sounded like an Arthur Miller reject. Listen, if this is how the upper crust carries on, maybe you and Jim had better eighty-six this Park Avenue scene and join Paul and me in Brooklyn. At least there the local drunks only sound off in the corner pub.'

Paul Gordon who had joined them broke in. 'Come on, let's forget it. The lady obviously has a problem that has nothing to do with us.'

Jim nodded. 'Personally, now I'm the one who needs a drink. Anybody care to join me?'

'Everybody,' Casey said.

*   *   *

It was close to 4 a.m. when the last guest reluctantly left. Their goodnights were loud, boisterous and, it seemed to Casey, surely audible to everybody in the building. Euralia began to collect the last of the glasses and empty the overflowing ash trays. Casey stopped her.

'Euralia, you're a dream,' she said, 'but for heaven's sake go to bed. It'll all be here tomorrow, I'm sorry to say. We can put the house back together then.'

Reluctantly, the housekeeper said good night and retired.

'She really is incredible,' Casey said. 'If I'd let her she'd be up another two hours getting everything cleaned up. I wonder what she thought of our first social evening. It must have been a blood bath for her, but I though she took it in stride, didn't you?'

'More than I did,' Jim yawned. 'My God, that was some bash. We must have used two cases of booze. And the added attraction of Louise Basil didn't do much to gladden my heart.'

Casey kicked off her shoes and flopped into a chair. 'The only thing we missed was a visitation from the Murphys. I was sure that when they got home from church they'd phone and tell us to shut up.'

'I'm kind of surprised nobody called the police,' Jim said. 'It was not what you'd call a sedate reception. Probably we got lucky. I'm sure a lot of people are away for the holidays.'

'Jim, what do you suppose really is wrong with Mrs Basil?'

'Who knows? Obviously she has a drinking problem that's a lulu. Maybe she has a mental problem, too. Unless you think the two are inseparable. Frankly, the less I know about it, the better I'll like it.'

Casey looked thoughtful. 'He's very attractive, don't you think?'

'Dr Basil? I suppose so. Not my type.'

Casey ignored him. 'What do you think he does that keeps her running up here to cry all over Rosemary?'

Jim yawned. 'How the hell do I know? All I hope is that she doesn't get the habit of dropping in on us the way she seems to on Rosemary. That I won't put up with, in case you have any thoughts of playing Big Sister to our live-in lush.'

'You know, that's odd, too,' Casey persisted. 'From what I've heard of the Murphys, I can't figure why that old tyrant of a mother would let Louise use her apartment like an upstairs branch of AA. Do you honestly think they'd have let Louise in at midnight if they'd been home?'

'All I can think at the moment is that if I don't hit the sack, I'll kill myself. Or you. Ready?'

Casey wearily rose to her feet. 'Yep. Just one more thing. Merry Christmas.'

'Same to you, Mrs Mesta. And by the way, in spite of our drunk and disorderly guests, the cigarette burns on the coffee table and a puddle of bourbon over there on your new carpet, you gave a helluva good party. You did us proud.'

'Thank you, sire,' Casey mocked. 'How ever were you lucky enough to get me?'

Jim was already halfway into the bedroom. 'Beats me,' he called back. 'I think you came as one of the fringe benefits from Blue Cross.'

* * *

On New Year's Day, Bryan Rogers succumbed to the stroke that had kept him lying immobile and mute for months. His death left the board with a vacancy to be filled, and immediately after the funeral André Livingstone summoned the remaining members to an emergency meeting.

'The board is empowered to name an interim member to replace our dear friend Mr Rogers,' he told them. 'Since our fiscal year does not end until April 30, this person would serve at least until the next annual tenants' meeting on May 1, at which time the owners will vote on the entire board and, of course, also on the election of the president.'

He waited, modestly, for the inevitable protest. It came, as expected, from Baroness Von Brennerhof.

'My dear Mr Livingston,' she said. 'I am quite sure that some of us are replaceable as board members and are quite willing to be at the mercy of the tenants' desires. But you are quite indispensable. There could be no question that you will remain president as long as you are so generous as to give your time and talent to the post.'

There was a murmur of polite assent from Antoinette Stone, Eileene Murphy, Elinor Simpson and Richard Basil.

'Very kind of you, Baroness,' Livingston said. 'I am deeply grateful for the confidence of the board. We are all entrusted with the responsibility of keeping our building a model of gracious living. However, the passing of Mr Rogers has sadly emphasized every man's mortality. All of us are active and vigorous,' he went on, 'but time takes its toll. That's why I believe we should consider the addition of a young member of the house to the board. It would serve us well, I believe, to have a dash of contemporary thinking in this changing world. But more importantly, it would begin to assure us continuity of control by those who comprehend and sympathize with our high standards.'

There was a pause as the other five tried to grasp the meaning of Livingston's somewhat convoluted speech.

'I gather,' Richard Basil said, 'that you have a nominee in mind for the vacancy on the board.'

58

Livingston nodded. 'I do, Dr Basil. Subject, needless to say, to the approval of all here.'

'And who might that be?' Eileene Murphy asked.

'I have been giving the matter great and serious thought,' Livingston said, 'and I should like to propose our newest and youngest tenant, Mr James Cromwell.'

There was a moment of shocked silence. Antoinette Lawrence Stone was the first to catch her breath.

'Mr Cromwell?' she repeated incredulously. 'I must say, Mr Livingston, *that's* an unexpected idea! Why, he has lived here only a few weeks and he's practically a child!'

'Quite true on both counts, Mrs Stone,' the president agreed. 'However, I think that he cannot be considered exactly an outsider. We all knew his grandparents. The Judge was one of our most respected board members for many years. We even agreed, if you recall, to dispense with the normal formality of a preliminary interview for Mr and Mrs Cromwell. I think we need have no fear that he is not a member of our own class, well steeped in our traditions.'

'But none of us has even met the Cromwells,' Antoinette said.

'Not precisely,' Richard Basil said. 'I met them briefly at Christmas. They seem like a very attractive and composed young couple.'

'What about you, Mrs Murphy?' Livingston asked. 'They share your floor. Have you any opinions?'

Old Eileene Murphy hesitated. 'I wish to be fair,' she said. 'I have not even seen these young people since they moved in. On the other hand, my younger daughter Rosemary has talked with Mrs Cromwell and seems favorably impressed with her. I do not think I could oppose Mr Cromwell as a board member, even though I am in no personal position to endorse him. I can only defer to your judgment, Mr Livingston.'

'Thank you,' André said. 'Mrs Simpson?'

'I like the idea of some new blood,' Elinor said enthusiastically. 'Don't know the Cromwells. I do know one thing, though, Mr Livingston. You're being very generous to say we're all so young and vigorous. My goodness, most of us are on the verge of becoming oblivious!'

Her audience looked puzzled. Finally, Richard Basil interpreted with a smile. 'I think you mean "obsolete", don't you, Mrs Simpson? Not that I agree with you about that, of course. I have seldom spent time in such attractive and stimulating company.'

Elinor waved a dainty hand. 'Oblivious, obsolete, who cares? The plain fact is that Mr Livingston has a point. None of us is going to go on until eternity. Let's get some of the young ones in here as the vacancies open up. I'm all for it.'

André looked around. 'Baroness? Your thoughts about Mr Cromwell?'

Felicia had been prepared to fight the idea until Antoinette opposed it. Anything that Mrs Stone was for, the Baroness Von Brennerhof was automatically against. And vice versa. 'I think it's a charming idea,' she said. 'It's only a four-month appointment, so we can get to know him. And, realistically, even if Mr Cromwell should unfortunately turn out to have unsuitable ideas, he is only one voice against six wiser heads.'

'Older heads you mean,' Elinor said.

Felicia glared at her. 'Fortunately, Mrs Simpson, the board has an enormous age range.'

Livingston intervened. 'Very well then, may I hear a nomination?'

'I nominate Mr Cromwell as an interim member of the board, pending the annual election by the stockholders next May,' Dr Basil said.

'Second,' Mrs Simpson said.

'All those in favor, please indicate by saying, "aye",' André said. The chorus responded. 'Those opposed?' Silence. 'Then as president I shall ask Mr James Cromwell to join us by unanimous invitation. Now,' he went on, 'is there any other business before the board?'

The Baroness raised her hand. 'Yes, a very important matter. Something must be done about the illegally parked cars which block our entrance. Most distressing. Why, the other afternoon when I came home from my golf game there was a strange car right in front of our door. I had to leave my own motor a good twenty feet from the canopy. I tell you, I gave the doorman a severe scolding.'

'I heard that you also gave the strange car a good whack with your eight-iron,' Elinor Simpson said.

The others laughed, but the Baroness was not amused. 'As a matter of fact, I did,' she said. 'Regrettably I made only a small dent.'

'Have you a suggestion of remedying this?' Livingston asked.

'I do. It is a simple and inexpensive matter to install a small ramp directly at the curb. This keeps an automobile from parking in front of the door.'

'Not a bad idea,' Eileene Murphy said with a flash of Irish humor. 'And it'll come in exceedingly handy when we all take to our wheelchairs, as Mr Livingston seems to think we're about to do.'

'Very well,' André said, 'I shall instruct Mr O'Shea to have such a device installed. Any other business before we adjourn? If not, I suggest that the next step is for me to immediately contact Mr Cromwell and offer him a place on the board. I should like to report to you all, and then schedule another meeting say, a week from this evening at six o'clock, here in my apartment, so that Mr Cromwell can be introduced. Will that be convenient or do you have other engagements on January eleventh?'

'Fine with me,' Elinor Simpson said. 'I could die tomorrow and never break a date.'

Courteously, Dr Basil escorted all the ladies to the elevator. Following protocol, the car went first to the 14th floor to deposit Eileene Murphy, dropped off the Baroness on 12, Antoinette and Richard on 8 and Elinor Simpson on 6. As the car made its measured way up and then slowly down again, the board stood stiffly in silence. One did not, after all, discuss internal matters in front of the staff.

Chapter IV

Casey answered the phone when André Livingston called. She couldn't get out of the habit of grabbing it when it rang, even though Euralia had discreetly suggested that this was part of a housekeeper's duties. It was another of those bits of domestic decorum that Casey kept forgetting to follow.

'Good evening,' the voice said. 'This is André Livingston. Is Mr Cromwell at home?'

'Just a moment. I'll call him.' Casey put her hand over the mouthpiece. 'Jim, it's Mr Livingston. *El Presidente!* Good grief, do you think it's a complaint about the party?'

Jim shrugged. 'It's a helluva delayed reaction if it is.' He took the phone. 'Hello, Mr Livingston. How are you?'

Casey tried to figure out the conversation from Jim's side of it.

'The board has *what*? Yes, of course, it is a surprise. Very flattering, sir, but I really don't know whether I can accept. Of course, I'd be glad to discuss it. Tomorrow? Yes, tomorrow would be fine. One o'clock at The Metropolitan. Right. Thank you, sir.'

'I'm dying,' Casey said when he hung up. 'What was that all about? Why are you meeting Himself? What have I done wrong?'

'Simmer down,' Jim said. 'What's giving you the guilts? Been putting slugs in the laundry machine?'

'Stop it, Jim. What's going on?'

'Nothing earth shattering. They want me to join the board.'

'The board of this building? You're kidding!'

Jim looked a little annoyed. 'What's so crazy about that? It's not the board of General Motors, for God's sake. It's only an apartment house. You don't have to be in Who's Who of American business to hold that kind of title.'

'You know I didn't mean it that way,' Casey said. 'I'm just

surprised because we're so new here and the other members are such old-timers. You needn't act like I've insulted your intelligence! I'm just amazed that they want somebody as young and snappy as you, that's all.'

Jim softened. 'Okay, okay. Let's don't have a fight about it. To tell you the truth, I'm a little amazed myself. But the whole subject isn't even worth discussing because I have no intention of joining the senior citizens. Good God, can you see me on the board with old lady Murphy and that goofy movie star and the phony Baroness? To say nothing of old marbles-in-the-mouth Livingston? Sorry, it's not my thing. No way.'

'But you are going to have lunch with Mr Livingston tomorrow?'

'Sure. I have to show that much courtesy. I'll be very polite. And very firm.'

'What if he really needs you, Jim? Maybe he realizes just what you said – that the board is made up of nothing but old types. He probably knows that they need vitality.'

'Then I applaud his good sense and wish him luck. But he can look someplace else for his shot-in-the-arm. I've got enough battles on my hands all day with the clients. Who needs more fights at home?'

'Speaking of which,' Casey said, 'what's with the Weinbergs? We've been blessedly spared their presence through the holidays.'

'Lester and Gertrude took the Christmas cruise on the *France*. They have a standing reservation every year for the biggest suite, the blackest caviar and the most choice seats at the Captain's table. But don't get lulled into a false sense of security, my love. They returned yesterday. It will be business as usual. In fact . . .' Jim hesitated.

'In fact what?'

'In fact, I've asked them here for dinner on the tenth.'

'Oh, no,' Casey moaned.

'I know it's a bore. But we're coming up on D-Day with that account. Lester can't wait forever to make up his mind about which agency he wants. We're still trying to stay in the running with everything we've got. Paul's done a whole new creative approach even though none of us thinks it's necessary. Like it or not, Casey, the decision is going to rest with Gertrude Weinberg. I'm more and more sure that the people she likes best are going to get the nod from the old man.'

'But Jim, we've socialized our heads off with the Weinbergs! Tony's already had a dinner party. You've taken Lester to lunch a dozen times. I've even gotten Mrs Adorable into the best places on Seventh Avenue to buy her clothes wholesale – as if she couldn't afford Bergdorf! My God, how much more can we do?'

'Listen, honey, I don't really know. But you can bet that whatever we're doing for Gertrude, our competition is doing more of it. I promise that the dinner here will be the last gasp. It was Tony's idea, actually. After our Christmas Eve party, he was so impressed with the house and the apartment and the whole atmosphere that he asked if we'd mind doing a little snobbish act for the Weinbergs. It's the kind of throw-away chic that just might impress them. Euralia. The white-gloved old retainer. All that crap. Anyway, I couldn't say no.'

Casey wanted to cry. 'Jim, that's less than a week away! Why didn't you tell me before. And who in hell will we ask? The Murphy ladies? The Baroness? Mr and Mrs André Dubois Livingston? Can't you just see it? The old-world social group making small talk with the shoemaker and his wife?'

'All right. Take it easy. Let's not get hysterical. We'll ask the Gordons because they're easy and the Weinbergs like them. Tony will come, of course. As for people in the house – despite your sarcasm – you could ask Mrs Simpson and the Basils.'

'I don't even know Mrs Simpson,' Casey snapped. 'As for the Basils, you have got to be kidding. After that Christmas Eve scene? He'd be okay probably, but what about her? We'd all be too embarrassed anyway. Jim, this is ridiculous. Forget the dinner. I'll have the Weinbergs here for a drink on the tenth. Just us and Tony and the Gordons.'

Jim shook his head. 'Won't do. I've already asked them for dinner. Black tie. Let's try it my way. I think Elinor Simpson would be tickled silly to come. And as for the Basils, maybe they'd like to make amends for that night. At least we know them. Sort of. We'll just have to take a chance that Louise will stay sober if her husband's around.'

'You are utterly out of your mind.'

'I know. And that's not a patch on what I'll be if we blow this account.'

*　　*　　*

The Metropolitan Club on East 60th Street just off Fifth Avenue remains as one of the last monuments to masculine arrogance. Its membership, private and all male, continues to

64

flick off Women's Lib like a speck of dust on the lapel of a correct dinner jacket. Ladies are allowed in to the cocktail lounge and the restaurant at the invitation of gentlemen members. Few come. The Metropolitan's ambiance is as foreboding and stern as its policies are rigid. Cocktails are served in the chilly, heavily marbled main foyer whose ceiling looms menacingly thirty or forty feet above the small tables, each of which is equipped with its own little bell to summon an aging waiter. The restaurant, reached through corridors of heavily carpeted halls hung with dour oil paintings of early, founding members, is reminiscent of the dining rooms of long-gone Saratoga hotels. The food is heavy, surprisingly inexpensive and thoroughly inedible. It has no appeal to active young members. But that is of no consequence. There are no active young members. Nor many new applications. Even though a few of the sons and grandsons of the wealthy men who founded the club seek membership as a token gesture to The Family, they never grace the premises. The club is old. The building is old and reeks of long-discarded attitudes and vanishing values. It is a sad, stuffy place.

As he entered it to keep his luncheon appointment with André Livingston, Jim could not recall ever having set foot in the Metropolitan before. Even his grandfather had preferred the Knickerbocker, equally social and infinitely less depressing. Though that, too, Jim reflected, was merely a matter of degree.

André was waiting for him at one of the bare little tables in the foyer. His host had already ordered scotch with no ice and was sipping it comfortably, obviously at home and happy in these familiar, austere surroundings. He greeted Jim cordially, gave the table bell a little ping and relaying Jim's order for an extra dry gibson with a twist.

'Well, young man,' he said, 'it's nice to see you again. Good of you to come.'

'My pleasure,' Jim lied. 'How have you been, Mr Livingston?'

'Fine, my boy. Very fine indeed. Haven't told you personally how happy we are to have you and your wife living in 617. Enjoying it there?'

'Very much, sir. The apartment is perfect and Casey has gotten a big kick out of fixing it up.'

'Casey? Family name?'

Jim smiled. 'No. My wife's name is Katherine, but everybody calls her Casey. Because of her initials. K.C.'

'Glad it doesn't stand for Knights of Columbus,' André said, amused by his own feeble joke.

Jim managed a halfhearted laugh. Jesus, this was going to be some lunch to get through. Imagine sitting on a board with this old fool. He decided to get the crucial question out of the way fast.

'Mr Livingston, I want you to know that I'm very flattered by your request to join the board, but I'm afraid I must beg off.'

The shaggy gray eyebrows arched in a silent question.

'You see,' Jim plunged on, 'I just don't think I could give it the time it requires. Or deserves. I have a very demanding job, sir, and I honestly couldn't promise to be available for the meetings.'

'Dr Basil and I also have demanding jobs,' André said coldly, 'but we manage. I find it hard to believe that the life of an advertising man is more grueling than that of a doctor on call twenty-four hours a day.'

It was hard to refute that one. André was not going to be easy to brush off.

'I appreciate that,' Jim said, 'but I guess I'm just not a joiner, Mr Livingston. I've never gone in much for group activities, committees, that sort of thing.'

'In that case, I find it odd that you should live in a co-operative apartment. By the very nature of its name, it is a joint venture. If all the owners chose to shirk their responsibilities, the building could not operate, now, could it?'

Jim suddenly was annoyed. Whether at Livingston or himself he was not quite sure. There was a vestige of truth in what the old man was saying, but it was twisted, the way a skillful lawyer rearranges the facts to his own purpose. André knew damned well that not every owner participated in the policy-making activities of the building. It was simple mathematics. There were only seven board members versus thirty-five apartments, most with more than one occupant. Seven people really made the decisions for approximately seventy. The rest of them had only a once-a-year chance to express approval of the board's actions at the annual tenants' meeting. Or – unheard-of idea – disapproval. Jim had to smile. André was making it sound as though 617 Park was a commune. It was, in fact, much more like a benevolent dictatorship.

'I certainly don't want to shirk my duty, sir,' Jim said gravely. 'It just seemed to me that the house is full of people who would welcome a chance to serve on the board. People who'd enjoy having something to make demands on their time. Whereas for me, it would be a bit of a hardship.'

André used the most unnerving weapon: Silence. For a few seconds Jim waited for him to answer. When he did not, Jim plunged on compulsively, feeling more and more like he was pleading a schoolboy's case before the headmaster.

'Anyway, Mr Livingston. I'm so new in the building that I don't think I'd be a great addition. I really don't know anything about the way it's managed or its financial condition or what's needed for the future.'

His last word provoked a reaction. 'The future,' André said, 'is perhaps the single most important reason why I want you on the board, young man. And please note that I said "*I* want you on the board". Your nomination was approved unanimously but, I will tell you, not wholeheartedly. Some of our members had serious doubts about your suitability. Your experience and quali-fications. But I feel strongly that we need younger people coming on to the board. To help us be aware of what is called "changing life styles", I believe. You see, many of our owners foolishly assume that we can continue to live as we always have, with the same service, the same comforts, all for the same money. We need realistic people on our board who will be able to speak forcefully and convincingly when certain unwelcome problems arise, as they inevitably will.'

Jim's curiosity was aroused. 'Unwelcome problems?' he re-peated. 'What kind of unwelcome problems?'

Livingston knew he had him.

'In confidence, Cromwell, our tenants are not prepared to face certain facts of life. Costs are rising. Taxes are going up. Our staff is unionized now and we will have a new contract to negotiate this coming year. All these things cannot be handled under the present circumstances. We will have to increase our maintenance charges or decrease our services. Probably both. We may have to investigate replacing our manned elevator with a self-service one. These things are going to distress most of our tenants. They will not want to hear about any change in their way of living. Not in terms of less service. And certainly not in terms of increased cost of living. I will need help in putting through some new policies. And, between you and me, I am looking for board members who will bolster the decisions that I know the house will have to make. Not that I like these steps any better than the rest will, mind you. But I know we can't run away from them, and I'll need support in getting them accepted.'

'And the present board won't back you?'

'I didn't say that. Dr Basil understands these matters as well as you and I do. But the ladies, bless 'em, do not have a keen grasp of business. They've not had to grapple with economics, you see. Oh, they will ultimately go along with whatever I tell them is necessary. So will all the tenants. But my task will be easier if I have board members who are more conversant with financial problems.'

'But surely,' Jim said, 'there are other men in the building who could serve the same purpose for you.'

'Probably,' André agreed. 'But we have very few *young* men. Most of the tenants are older people, retired in many cases. They may understand the need for change, but they will be more likely to try, even vainly, to cling to the old ways. When a person gets along in years, he tries not to think that things are changing. One denies it, just as one denies the thought of one's own mortality. Most of us would like to retain the status quo in all things. Our gentlemen tenants are, for the most part, at that point. Getting their support would be almost as difficult as convincing the ladies that some drastic upheavals may be forthcoming.'

Jim made one last effort. 'But what about the management people – Ridgely & Ryan? Surely they could help you explain these ideas to the board and the individual owners.'

Livingston's expression was pure distaste. 'Fools and incompetents,' he said. 'Never wanted an outside management company to begin with. Only accepted them because the tenants thought they would lighten some of the work load for me. Nonsense. All they do is come around once a month, take a look at the building and charge us six thousand a year for the privilege. Outsiders. Understand nothing about our kind of building. Have to instruct them myself about everything. No, I can't look to Ridgely & Ryan, nor to that idiot Carl Paterman who's supposed to be their representative for our house. The man's completely insensitive. My boy, 617 Park has flourished since before you were born. It's like a family business. Does better under family control. And that,' André said, 'is precisely why I want the board to remain firmly within the control of people who understand our "family". You are the next generation of it. I think you have an obligation to participate in the continuity of its direction.'

Jim had to admit that Livingston was articulate and convincing. Even that he made a certain amount of sense. Jim could imagine that André would, indeed, need all the level-headed help he could get if the changes he indicated really had to be made. And without knowing much about it, Jim could see the handwriting on the wall. The building had not levied a maintenance increase in years. With rising costs they must by this time be running dangerously close to the red. Oh, what the hell, he thought, how much time can it take. Maybe I'd better get in there and keep an eye on my investment before that bunch of well-bred ding-a-lings runs the house into bankruptcy. He smiled admiringly at André Livingstone.

'I understand why you are such a successful attorney,' Jim said. 'If you're this persuasive in front of a jury, I'd sure want you for my lawyer.'

Livingston acknowledged the compliment with a nod. 'Used to have a good time at that kind of thing. Don't do it much any more. Let the young partners do battle in the courtroom now. But I still enjoy it.'

'Well,' Jim said, 'I guess you've gotten the verdict you wanted in this case. If you need me on the board, sir, I'll do my best.'

'You've made a wise decision,' André said. 'I'm delighted. Truly delighted. And I'm sure the board will be, once they get to know you.'

Jim smiled at the somewhat left-handed compliment. André seemed unaware of the slightly condescending remark.

'There's a special board meeting on the eleventh. Six o'clock. My apartment. Can you make it?'

Jim consulted his pocket calendar. 'Looks okay from here,' he said. 'Although I'm sure my secretary will go into shock. It will be one of the few times I've ever left the office that early.'

Livingstone couldn't resist making a final point. 'See? Your new duties do have a personal benefit. They'll let you get home at a respectable hour now and then. Never could understand why people can't get their work done by four-thirty or five o'clock anyway. All these late hours you young men put in seem ridiculous. Makes me suspect you're wasting a lot of time during the day. Or else you're not very well organized. Nine-thirty to five should be more than enough time to accommodate the work of any executive, it seems to me.'

'No disrespect, Mr Livingston, but you obviously have never worked for an advertising agency. We spend all day with our clients. Then we do our own work after those same nine-thirty-to-five guys have gone home.'

'Silly business, I'd say.'

Jim laughed. 'Believe me, I agree with you.'

'Good philosophy,' André said. 'Keep agreeing with me and we'll get along just fine. Now how about a spot of lunch?'

They took the elevator up to the dining room. It was a typical club lunch: heavy, inexpensive and nearly inedible.

* * *

That evening Jim returned home to a snappish, nervous wife. Instead of her warm welcome, she gave him a quick almost reluctant little kiss and immediately busied herself making him a pre-dinner drink. Jim accepted it with thanks.

'Tough day?' he asked.

'You and your Godamn clients.'

'And just what does that mean?'

Casey sighed. 'What that means, my love, is that I've spent this whole bloody day arranging your precious dinner party for the Weinbergs. Including, I might add, calling a couple of complete strangers and inviting them to the festivities. I never felt so silly in my life.'

'Well, how did you make out?'

'To my complete and utter surprise, I seem to have batted a thousand. Mrs Simpson didn't even have to look at her date book. She accepted straight off. And Louise Basil said she'd have to check with the doctor, but as far as she knew it was fine with them.'

'Now, that wasn't so bad, was it?' Jim asked. 'By the way, was our resident alcoholic sober when she accepted?'

'I presume so. But it was only ten o'clock in the morning when I called. I still won't vouch for her at eight o'clock at night.'

'It'll be okay,' Jim reassured her. 'As long as Basil is with her, I'm sure she'll stay under control. What about the Gordons?'

'Mary said they'd be glad to be sacrificial lambs. Did you check with Tony?'

Jim nodded. 'Yep. He sent you his love and his thanks. He was tickled that we're doing it.'

'I'm glad *somebody* was pleased,' Casey said.

'It's important, Casey, or I wouldn't ask you.'

'I know,' she said. 'I'm being a real drag. Sorry. I seem to be making everything a crisis these days. Maybe I'm just tired. Between moving and the holidays and the Christmas party, I guess I'm bushed. My basic disposition is showing. I seem to be a walking bundle of nerve ends. So consider that an apology, okay?'

'Sure. By the way, I have a piece of news that might please you more. In spite of my big speeches this morning, I did an about-face at lunch and told Livingston I'd go on the board here.'

'You didn't! What brought that on?'

'I'm not sure, exactly. Partly his persuasiveness. Partly the realization that you were very ESP. Seems he does want younger tenants taking a more active part in the building management, and he doesn't have a hell of a lot of them to choose from. But mostly I said yes because it's pretty clear that this house is going to have to make a lot of changes, and I don't feel entirely comfortable having them decided by a bunch of old crocks like Mrs Murphy. Livingston is Methuselah's grandpa himself, but he knows there needs to be a lot of tightening up around here and he can use all the support he can get. That's really why he wants me: To help him sell the old folks on the New American Way of Life.'

'He must have been very convincing,' Casey marveled. 'When you left here I'd have given a million to one that you were going to say no.'

'And your odds would have been right. But when I listened carefully to the old boy it came out like a plea for help. Anyway, I don't think it'll be all that much trouble. Might be interesting, in fact. And it wouldn't make me mad to have a voice in some of the things that are going to affect the value of our property. To say nothing of the amount of money it will cost us to live here.'

'It's going to get more expensive?'

'Probably. They've got to cut expenses and increase revenue, all at the same time. Neat trick. It won't help Livingston win any popularity contest in this building, I'll tell you that. And he knows it. But he also knows it's necessary. So I'll do what I can to help. We go into action at the next board meeting on the eleventh.'

'Assuming you survive our dinner party on the tenth,' Casey said.

'Hey, right. That's good timing. We'll have two of the board members here the night before the meeting. Give me a chance to get to know them a little.'

'When they meet your friends the Weinbergs you might be off the board before you're on it.'

Jim spread his hands, palms up, in a helpless gesture. 'What

71

can I tell you?' he said. 'Nobody's perfect.'

That evening, Livingston dutifully rang up each of the board members and gave them the same report. 'I thought I would let you know that Mr Cromwell has accepted our invitation to join the board,' he said. 'He will attend the meeting on the eleventh. I'm sure you're as pleased as I.' The reaction to his announcement ranged from enthusiasm to chilly acceptance. Elinor Simpson was clearly delighted.

'Lovely,' she said. 'They sound like such a nice, warm young couple. Why, do you know, Mr Livingston, that Mrs Cromwell invited me to dinner on the tenth? Such a friendly attitude for new tenants.'

Richard Basil was quietly pleased. 'Glad to hear it," he told André. 'He should be very helpful when we put the bad news to the board. And I daresay he can make quite a strong contribution at the tenants' meeting as well. Seems a sensible fellow. Louise tells me we're asked there for dinner next week. I'll have a chance to look him over before the meeting.'

Eileene Murphy was already in bed when Livingston called, but Constance and Rosemary simultaneously picked up the extension phones. 'I hope you're making the right choice,' Constance said coldly. 'All we've seen of our neighbors is a raucous group of friends going to their Christmas Eve party. The noise went on until three in the morning. So far they don't give the impression of solid, mature people. But hopefully Mr Cromwell has a more serious side to his nature.'

'I'm sure he'll be just fine, Mr Livingston,' Rosemary chimed in. 'His wife is a delightful girl. I don't think my sister means to give the impression that we are disapproving. After all, we really can't judge people by one holiday party.'

'Speak for yourself, Rosemary,' her sister snapped. 'I can judge by any standards I choose.'

Antoinette Lawrence Stone's well-trained voice did not completely disguise her distress. She had been hoping that James Cromwell would refuse. 'Thank you for letting us know right away,' she said. 'I am afraid that we may be making a rather impulsive decision, but I shall, of course, be open-minded about Mr Cromwell's abilities.'

André's final call, to the Baroness, soothed his mounting irritation. 'I am sure, as always, that you have led us to the proper conclusion, dear Mr Livingston,' she said. 'No doubt we will all find it stimulating to have this young man in our midst. I feel so sorry that the presidency keeps you so hard at work, even in the evenings. But whatever would we do without you? Bless you for taking the trouble to call. You are a gentleman of great consideration.'

Charming woman, the Baroness, he thought as he hung up the phone. Not prickly like Antoinette. Nor defensive like Constance Murphy. Not even vacuous like Elinor Simpson, agreeable as that lady always was. He was content with his choice and somewhat gratified by his performance at lunch. Cromwell had arrived at the Club determined to refuse the appointment and he, André Livingston, had skillfully maneuvered him into accepting it. I may have passed my three score and ten, André thought, but I haven't forgotten the tricks of my trade. For the first time in the history of the house, Livingston anticipated dissension in the ranks. He was comforted to have captured what he believed would be a strong and vigorous ally.

*　*　*

The ally spent the next few days worrying about his business. He gave no more than a passing thought to his new role as a board member. The up-coming difficulties of the building, which had intrigued him into becoming a part of its policy-making body, were low on his priority list of problems. They had no relationship to the struggle to get the Weinberg Shoe business safely into the competent and needy hands of Stewart, Sutton & Atherton.

He made it a point to see Lester Weinberg nearly every day. If the chairman was unavailable for lunch, Jim managed to squeeze himself onto the man's calendar for a few minutes chat, twice arriving at Lester's office at 8.30 with coffee and Danish, like some high-priced office boy. He also made it a point to be on very friendly terms with Weinberg's secretary, Becky Rothman. And through her, he kept tabs on the pursuit of Gertrude Weinberg by the rival agencies.

'Mrs W. is now having her hair done by Mr Kenneth *himself*,' Becky told him one morning. 'How do you like that? Mere mortals are occasionally allowed into that salon, but only the Jackie Onassises and Barbara Paleys of this world get their hair bent by the great man in person. Mrs W. sure is making it into the big time.'

Every scrap of information about Gertrude, no matter how seemingly trivial, was of interest to Jim these days.

'No kidding.' He gave a low whistle. 'How'd she manage to work that?'

'Mrs Crawford got her on the preferred list,' Becky said. 'You know. Her husband owns Crawford-Thompson. They're pitching the account, too.' Becky pretended innocence. She knew damn well the game that was being played. And while she was rooting for Jim, she couldn't help getting a kick out of dropping these little, unnerving pieces of news that she knew added to his anxiety.

Lousy dame, Jim thought, meaning Becky rather than Mrs Crawford. She's like all the rest. Gets her kicks out of watching the advertising big shots squirm. Gives her a feeling of power. Probably compensates for her $7,500-a-year salary. Still, Becky could be as helpful as she was irritating. The more SS&A knew about the tactics of the enemies, the better position they were in to counterattack. He hid his irritation under his profession cool.

'Mr Kenneth turning Mrs W. into a Gloria Guiness type?'

Becky smiled. 'Well, she seems to think so. She goes to the salon every morning, even if it's only for a comb out.' The secretary paused. 'And Mrs Crawford usually goes with her.'

Jim pretended indifference. 'Nothing like a great hair-burner to keep a woman happy,' he said casually. 'Those guys have replaced dress designers as the new status symbol – socially and professionally. They seem to turn up in all the name-dropping columns these days.'

'Yeah,' Becky needled. 'And so does Mrs Weinberg.' The buzzer on her desk rang. 'You can go in now, Jim,' she said. 'And don't spill the coffee.'

Lester greeted him with his usual phony joviality. 'Jim, boy! Good to see you! Hey, what's that? Coffee and Danish? Now that's what I call friendship. Humility, even. How many guys would come by with breakfast for a hard-working pal? Particularly guys who make forty, fifty thousand dollars a year, right? You're the best, old buddy. What's new?'

Jim watched with disgust as Lester wolfed down the prune Danish (his favorite) and took long, long pulls at the coffee. Christ, what am I doing here pandering to this terrible old bastard? You're trying to lock up eight million dollars, he told himself. That's what you're doing here. He managed a casual smile.

'What's new is that you still haven't looked at the new campaign Paul Gordon has put together,' Jim said. 'Listen, Lester, the guys at the agency have been burning the midnight oil to come up with some new stuff to show you. It's great. When can we make a presentation?'

Lester looked surprised. 'New campaign? Who asked for a new campaign? I told you I thought the other one was the best advertising I've ever seen. What the hell are they working on more stuff for?'

'They'd be glad to stop,' Jim said quietly, 'the minute you indicate that we're the new agency of record. But until you give us the word, we have to assume that you're not entirely happy with the work.'

Lester looked hurt. 'Now, Jim, what do you want from me? I've told you it's practically a firm decision.'

'What I'd like from you, Lester, *is* a firm decision.' Jim tried not to press. Force was not the strategy to use on Weinberg, but this cat-and-mouse game was getting under his skin. 'I don't know why you're keeping us dangling like this if you really *have* made up your mind. Trouble is, I don't think you have.'

The chairman leaned back in his oversized swivel chair and assumed the closest thing to a boyish look that his dark, fleshy face could manage. He gave a little laugh.

'Listen, pal, I'll level with you. You're a married man. You know the score. Life is beautiful at home while Gertrude is getting more attention from high-toned people than she's ever had in her whole life. Okay. I admit it. I'm buying as much of this peace on earth as sound business judgment will allow. So hate me. But while these jokers are kissing Gertrude's behind and thinking they're getting to me by doing it, I'm using them to enjoy the first pleasant moments I've had since my honeymoon. For the first time in her life, Gertrude feels important. Powerful. Like one of those Beautiful People I keep reading about. It's a pile of crap. I know it and you know it. But what the hell, Jim. If I can use these clowns, and they're suckers enough to go along with it, why not? Believe me, when I come up to the deadline, I'll put my money where the talent is. Not where Gertrude thinks it is.'

Jim wanted desperately to believe him. He had no choice but to believe him. Still he knew he was not hearing the straight truth.

'Okay, Lester,' he said. 'I understand. You don't really have to make an official announcement for another couple of months. Gertrude can keep on being the darling of Madison Avenue if that's what makes her – and you – happy. But if that's really the way it lays out, why don't we sign the contract today and

75

keep the whole thing hush-hush? I swear to you, nobody will know we've got the account except you, Tony, Paul and me. But we'll feel a helluva lot better knowing it's settled.'

Lester appeared to be considering that. 'You know I'd do that in a minute, Jim, except for one thing. When more than one person knows a secret, it stops being a secret. I know you believe that there wouldn't be leaks, but I wouldn't feel comfortable taking that chance. Why don't you and your guys just relax? It would take an act of God to knock you out of this ball game. Play along for your old pal Lester. Have a little trust. We're gentlemen, aren't we?'

'I've always gone on that assumption. But honest to God, you're giving us a hard time.'

Weinberg laughed easily. 'Don't worry about it. I'll probably never have such a break again. You can't really blame me for taking advantage of it, can you? I don't change agencies every day, you know.'

'Thank God for small favors,' Jim said. 'All right, Lester, if that's the way it is, that's the way it is. I believe you're a man of your word.'

'And you're a man of discretion. So let's keep this conversation strictly between us, huh? I mean, what I said about secrets still goes. I've told you the truth. But you're the *only* one who knows. So hang in there. It's important. I mean it.'

The significance of his words did not escape Jim. He could not tell even Tony that Lester was verbally committed, for fear that Tony would slip and let Weinberg know he knew. They'd all have to live through this childish game a while longer. Jim only hoped Lester was leveling with him.

'Guess I'd better get back to work,' Jim said. 'And let you get a few things done. I appreciate your confidence, Lester. And I give you my word that I'll respect it.'

'I know you will. You got breeding. That's why I like you. Oh, by the way, Gertrude's thrilled about dinner at your house. She's nutty about those old Park Avenue apartments. Dying to see yours. Who else is coming?'

Only Lester would have the chutzpa to ask for the guest list. 'The Gordons and Tony. And we've asked a couple of people who live in the building. A very nice lady named Mrs Simpson and a Dr Basil and his wife. He's a psychiatrist.'

'A shrink?' Weinberg clutched his head. 'Oy-veh. That's the one thing Gertrude hasn't thought of. Next thing you know I'll be on the hook for fifty bucks an hour.' He laughed indulgently.

'I don't imagine the doctor will be pitching for new patients,' Jim said coldly. 'And from what I know of Gertrude, if she'd ever considered analysis, she'd be in it by now.'

'Yeah,' Lester said, 'I think you got something there. Not much gets by that little lady. Especially if it's expensive.'

'See you on the tenth. Casey and I are looking forward to it.'

'Same here. And remember, kid. This morning is just between us. For the time being, of course.'

'Of course,' Jim said.

'Meantime, take the heat off those poor devils at your shop. Don't have to tell 'em why. But I don't need to look at any more campaigns. I'm satisfied, baby. You know that.'

'Fine. That's the best news I've had in quite awhile.' I only wish, he thought, that I really believed it. On the way out he gave Becky a wink and a confident, jaunty smile. He hoped she'd report both to the boys at Crawford–Thompson.

Chapter V

Dressing for the dinner party at the Cromwells' gave Gertrude Weinberg a small problem. But it was the kind she was learning to like. In these past few weeks of her 'new life', as she thought of it, she had spent many hours wondering what to wear to the teas and luncheons and fashion shows to which she suddenly was being invited. Gertrude had no education, no background, no frame of genteel reference. But she was not a stupid woman. She'd been smart enough to land Lester and clever enough to keep him fascinated. By the same token, she was bright enough to know that she was being used by these snooty advertising people who were all over her with their invitations and their phony professions of friendship.

Gertrude got a kick out of letting them believe she was buying their snow jobs. It amused her to know privately that it really was she who used them. It was her own little secret. Even Lester, poor fatuous boob, thought she was taking it seriously. Gertrude was, in fact, enjoying the attention. But more importantly she was learning how to act in 'better circles'. Women like Gwen Crawford and Casey Cromwell were serving as teachers, paying for her to learn how to be at ease in new social situations, what to order in restaurants and how to dress appropriately and smartly for any occasion.

In the beginning, she'd been scared to death and had made a million mistakes. But she was a quick study. She'd already grasped the fundamentals of acceptance in this group. Her hair style had gone from bleached bouffant to frosted chignon. The ornate, overtrimmed dresses had been replaced by simple, elegant clothes for day and evening, all of them bearing labels that said 'Norell' or 'Trigère' or 'Galanos'. She had even traded in the jewelry she'd selected immediately after her marriage to Lester.

The jazzy acquamarine and emerald 'matched sets' of earrings, pin and ring had given way to discreet gold and diamond pieces, all related but none exactly the same in design. She'd learned that a sable-lined poplin raincoat was more elegant than a blond mink. And she'd given her mink stole to her sister who didn't know enough not to wear it.

Proper dressing had been relatively easy to learn. Even though, as tonight, she had to think carefully about the suitability of what she put on. It would not do to be overdone for a small dinner party at home. On the other hand, it was important to look chic and rich. She settled for a black Trigère dress with long sleeves and a high neckline. Her only jewelry would be a heavy gold Cartier chain with a diamond-and-ruby-encrusted gold cross. No earrings. And only her diamond wedding band. Gertrude smiled as she fastened on the necklace. What would Mama say if she saw her nice little Jewish girl with a cross around her neck? Not that it had religious significance. It just happened to be the status ornament of the season.

No, it hadn't been difficult for Mrs Weinberg to affect the outer trappings of simplicity. All you had to do was watch and study the other women and have enough money to go to the right hairdressers and buy the right fashion labels that meant automatic social security. What was more difficult were the intangibles – some of which Gertrude recognized and some of which, regrettably, she did not.

She did not realize, for example, that her voice was Bronx-nasal and grating, and that she made constant grammatical errors. She was unaware that her eating habits were close to repulsive, though she knew that she was still sometimes uncertain about which fork to use and invariably got confused about placing a fingerbowl on its doily to the upper left of her desert plate. She sensed that she had to watch her unconscious use of obscenities, though she comforted herself by remembering she'd once heard that 'only a lady can say "shit" and get away with it'.

All in all, Gertrude was pretty well satisfied with the progress she'd made in the past few months. She'd come a long way from the sexy, obvious manicurist who'd gone to bed with Lester and then said 'no' until he divorced his third wife. She was good in bed and Lester was lousy. But no matter. Her secret was that she made him feel that he was the greatest thing since Casanova. Gertrude smiled at the new Mrs Weinberg in the full-length mirror of her bedroom in the big apartment on Central Park

West. You've come a long way, baby, she hummed, and you've still got a long way to go.

She went into Lester's room to see how nearly ready he was. Lester refused to sleep in his own room but at least he consented to dress in there which was a blessing. She could no longer bear the sight of his sloppiness, the discarded underwear dropped in the middle of the floor, the wrinkled business suit thrown across the unused bed, the jumble mess of money and keys and credit cards tossed on the dresser. Thank God there was a maid to pick up after him. At least she could retreat to her own frilly bedroom with its gold-satin chaise and Carlin Shop accessories. Gertrude had not yet learned about the delicate, understated chic of Porthault sheets and pillow cases at two hundred a fifty dollars a pair. The day she did, Lester would spend even less time in her bed.

Lester was struggling with his black tie. He preferred the ready-tied ones, but Gertrude would no longer allow him to wear them.

'How ya doin'?' she asked.

Lester gave an angry tug at the offending accessory. 'Fuckin' tie,' he growled. 'Never will learn how to do the Godamn thing.'

Gertrude sighed. The Transformation of Lester was not an easy thing. 'Here,' she said. 'Let me do it. We're already late. Not that I'd dream of arriving on time, but there *is* a limit, Lester. We have to go all the way across town.' She made a quick, deft bow. She was used to dressing – and undressing – men.

Lester patted her bottom. 'Thanks, honey. We won't be all that late.' He looked at her questioningly. 'You don't look very dressed up for such a big night.'

Gertrude regarded him with pity. 'Poor Lester,' she said, 'you're so smart about some things and so dumb about others. This ain't – I mean isn't – a charity ball we're going to. It's a little dinner at home. And I'll tell you something else, buster. Every dame in that room will know that this dress cost eight hundred bucks.'

His glance traveled downward. 'For Christsake, Gert, you're not even wearing Weinberg shoes!'

'You bet I'm not. I wouldn't own a pair of those crappy twenty-dollar numbers! Boy, that's just like you! Expect me to put on a Trigère dress and a Cartier necklace and wear cheap junk on my feet!'

'They may be cheap junk to you,' he mumbled, 'but don't

80

forget one thing, baby. If we didn't sell millions of 'em you wouldn't be wearing thousand-dollar goy crosses around your beautiful little neck!'

She punished him by refusing to speak to him all the way to Park Avenue. She sat very straight beside him in the back of the Cadillac, her face a mask of silence, haughty disdain. Gertrude's anger always made Lester miserable. As they pulled up to the door, he took her hand.

'Forgive me, sweetie,' he said. 'I'm just a big old fool. You look beautiful.'

She condescended to return the squeeze of his big hand. 'Forget it,' she said. 'You look pretty swell yourself.'

Lester's relief was visible. As the doorman approached, he gave the building a quick glance. 'This don't look like much,' Lester said. 'Hell, it's a crummy-looking lobby. Makes ours look like Buckingham Palace.'

The newly informed Mrs Weinberg disagreed. 'The trouble with you is you don't know class when you see it. It's like the Crawfords' building. Kind of shabby-rich. Not all crystalled up with a bunch of chandeliers.'

Lester shrugged. All this was over his head. As they waited for the elevator, he pointed to the simple Adams chairs which flanked the small fireplace. 'Get those chairs,' he whispered. 'Jesus, wouldn't you think in a place like this they'd be able to afford upholstery?'

A butler, hired for the evening, admitted them and relieved Gertrude of her new, floor-length sable coat. Casey, in a pink crepe hostess gown, came out of the living room to greet them, Jim close behind her. They ushered the Weinbergs in to meet the other dinner guests who already had arrived.

'You know Mary and Paul Gordon and Tony Stewart, of course,' Casey said. 'Mrs Simpson, may I present Mr and Mrs Weinberg? And Dr and Mrs Basil, Mr and Mrs Weinberg.' Introductions were acknowledged all around, drinks served to the new arrivals and Euralia passed a tray of canapés. Gertrude looked around with what she hoped was cool interest.

'What a charming apartment,' she said to Casey. 'So, uh, old-world.'

Casey smiled. 'We love it. In fact, it's changed our whole lives. You know, when Jim and I moved in I had every intention of replacing his grandmother's things with our own furniture. The kind we had in our old apartment. But as it began to shape up, I felt more and more that these rooms called for softer shapes and more mellow woods. So the furniture is pretty much the way it was. With a few of our own things added, of course. But somehow, the building has a dignity of its own. I almost felt that it rejected the intrusion of our contemporary stuff.'

'You mean you didn't have a decorator?' Gertrude asked.

This time Jim answered. 'No, *ma'am*,' he said emphatically. 'I can't stand the idea. Fortunately Casey agrees. I don't want to live with somebody else's taste. Rather take a chance on our own.'

'And quite right you are,' Elinor Simpson chimed in. 'What Mrs Cromwell says is most interesting. It's strange how a building like this almost dictates the decor of its individual dwellings. You see, Mrs Weinberg, I've lived here most of my life and I know nearly all of the apartments quite well. It's fascinating how so many of them have this same kind of restful and very personal charm.'

In spite of herself, Gertrude looked impressed. She turned to Richard Basil and gave him one of her subtly seductive smiles. 'What about you, Doctor? Do you and Mrs Basil go along with that?'

'Indeed we do,' he said. 'I'm afraid that many people find all of us here rather stuffy types. Mrs Weinberg. We seem to tend to a tribal sameness.'

Lester gave a hearty laugh. 'Well, now, Doc,' he said, 'as a big-time shrink, doesn't that strike you as a little sick?'

There was an embarrassed silence which Richard quickly covered. 'No,' he said seriously, 'not at all. This is more likely to indicate a healthy awareness of one's true self and a security that comes from knowing the convolutions of one's own personality.'

Jim Cromwell was amused. He was sure that Basil was making up a lot of nonsensical double-talk, having fun at the expense of Weinberg, perhaps getting even for that unfortunate reference to a 'shrink'. In any case, the Weinbergs were eating it up. They probably thought they were having an 'intellectual conversation'.

Gertrude perked up. 'Oh, you're a psychiatrist, Dr Basil? How fascinating!' She turned to Louise. 'It must be terrific to have him come home and tell you all the crazy things people say to him all day, Mrs Basil. Boy, the secrets you must know!'

As Jim had predicted, Louise was on her good behavior. She had accepted only one glass of sherry and was nursing it through the cocktail hour. This was a far different lady than the drunken, maudlin creature who'd blundered into their Christmas party.

Louise smiled kindly at Gertrude's gauche question.

'Unfortunately for me,' she said, 'Richard never discusses his patients. Doctors' ethics, you know. Not that I don't sometimes wish they weren't quite so ethical. It would be fascinating to hear some of the secrets, but wild horses couldn't drag them from Richard.'

'Well, that's comforting,' Gertrude said archly, 'in case I ever need that kind of help.'

'I'm sure you never will, Mrs Weinberg,' Richard said.

'Brother, that's the best news I've had all day!' Lester boomed. 'Prices you fellahs get, no wonder you can afford big apartments on Park Avenue!'

'Darling,' Gertrude said, 'let's not discuss money, shall we?'

Casey and Mary Gordon exchanged glances. The Weinbergs were utterly impossible I think I'm going to commit suicide, Casey's look said to Mary. I wouldn't blame you, Mary telegraphed back silently.

At dinner, Gertrude, seated on Jim's right with Dr Basil beside her, was obviously enjoying herself. She flirted blatantly with Richard, a ploy that unnerved Casey but seemed to have no effect upon either Louise Basil or Lester Weinberg. Probably the former no longer cared, Casey thought. And the latter was either too insensitive to notice or too sure of Gertrude to be concerned. Seemingly, none of the others at table seemed perturbed by Mrs Weinberg's outrageous behavior. Tony remained his suave, self-assured self. The Gordons made light, polite talk. And Mrs Simpson proved to be as delightfully frothy as Jim had painted her. Considering the incredible ingredients, Casey decided, it was not as big a mess as she'd feared. The dinner was perfection and the service flawless. Still, she was relieved when the meal ended and she rose to lead the oddly assorted troup back into the living room for coffee. At least there could be only an hour or so more of the Weinbergs. And after that, Casey swore to herself, it would be many a day before she'd let them set foot in 617 Park again.

Gertrude, a little drunk from cocktails and the wine at dinner, stopped Casey at the doorway of the living room.

'Listen Casey. You don't mind if I call you Casey, do you?'

'Of course not. I thought we were on a first-name basis long ago, Gertrude.'

'Right. Well, listen, Casey, I gotta go to the john, and I thought maybe you'd show me around the apartment a little at the same time. We're gonna redecorate our place, and I think your taste is swell.'

Casey could not help feeling pleased. 'Of course,' she said. 'Let me just settle the others in and I'll be glad to give you the tour.' She asked Mary to pour the coffee which Euralia had brought in on the big silver tray, then excused herself and joined Gertrude. She took her first into the master bedroom and waited outside the bathroom door while Gertrude went in.

'You can come in with me,' Gertrude called. 'Plenty room. Biggest damn can I ever saw! Makes ours look like an outhouse.'

Standing outside the door, feeling ridiculous, Casey declined the invitation. 'I'll just wait here for you,' she said. Then, feeling that something more was called for, she added. 'That's one of the nice things about these old buildings. The bathrooms are really spacious. Of course, Jim and I did quite a bit of remodeling. The fixtures were the original ones.'

After an inordinately long period of time, Gertrude re-appeared. She had refreshed her make-up and, all too obviously, put on more of her expensive, hideously heavy perfume. It was the newest scent, the hundred-dollar-an-ounce choice of women who not only wanted to look like money but smell like it as well. The perfume was over-whelming. The ultimate vulgarity. And typical.

'Okay,' Gertrude said cheerfully. 'Let's have the twenty-dollar tour.'

As quick as she could, Casey led her through the two guest rooms and baths. Gertrude admired the delicate antiques and the carefully chosen new wallpapers and fabrics. Despite her own modest background, Casey had inherent good taste. She had done it beautifully, following her instincts for warm, inviting colors and comfortable, well-planned arrangements. Gertrude was visibly awed by the fact that it had been done without professional help.

'Gee, kid, you oughta open up your own business,' she said. 'It's a helluva lot better than some places I've seen done by fag decorators.'

'Well, thank you,' Casey said. 'I don't know whether it's as chic as it might be, but it suits us pretty well. Sorry I can't show you the rest of the house, the kitchen and butler's pantry and Euralia's room and bath, but I'm sure they're cleaning up in there. We'd probably be trampled to death. Maybe some other time,' she lied. 'I really love the kitchen. We had everything built in. It's a real luxury after trying to cope with a kitchenette for five years.'

Gertrude nodded. Kitchenettes were a frame of reference with which she could associate. Maybe this Casey wasn't so high and mighty after all, in spite of her antiques and her family silver. Privately, Gertrude thought the apartment was pretty square. But her sharp little mind told her that is was Class. And more than anything Gertrude wanted Class.

'Say, Casey, when we start redoing our joint, would you help me? I mean, I think I gotta have a decorator because I just don't have time to shop around for stuff. But would you give me your opinion sometimes? I don't want some fruity guy to go off half-cocked and make a mess of it. I'd sure appreciate it. Specially since I think you and I have the same taste.'

God forbid, Casey thought. But anything for The Cause. 'Of course I'll help if I can,' she said. 'I'm flattered that you like what I've done. Incidentally, *I* had a lot of help, too. From Mary Gordon.'

Gertrude looked surprised. 'No kidding! You mean that little broad from Brooklyn knows about stuff like this? I thought her husband was the arty one in that family.'

'He's a fantastic creative director,' Casey said, getting in a plug for the agency. 'But Mary's equally talented in other ways.'

As they rejoined the party, Gertrude managed to seat herself near Richard Basil again, 'Tell me, Doctor,' she said, 'do you have your office here in the building?'

Before he could answer, Elinor Simpson spoke. 'No, Mrs Weinberg, we don't have any professional apartments in this building. But Dr Basil does serve on our board of directors. And by the way, we are so happy to be in the home of our newest board member tonight.' She turned to Jim. 'I haven't really had a chance to tell you, Mr Cromwell, how pleased we are that you've agreed to serve. Mr Livingston phoned to give us the good news.'

'I second that,' Dr Basil said. 'I'm counting on you, Jim, to give André and me some moral support. We have a tough time with these ladies. They'll still outnumber us four to three,' he laughed, 'but at least we'll go down swinging.'

Elinor Simpson pretended disapproval. 'My goodness, Doctor,' she said, 'you make us sound like a quartet of orgies!'

Paul Gordon choked on his brandy. I've got to remember that one, he thought. Bless her funny little heart, she means 'a quartet of ogres.'

'Anyway,' Elinor went on, 'it's a good thing we *are* strict. You know there are two apartments for sale in this building right now, and you'll be counting on us to do the screening of the new applicants. You men never take time to check into the backgrounds the way we do.' She wagged her finger at Jim. 'Now just you remember that, young man. It's one of the most important functions of the board. You'll see.'

'Two vacancies?' Jim asked. 'I didn't know that. It's unusual, isn't it? As I remember from the old days, it was a rare occasion when one of these apartments came on the market.'

'Yes, it was,' Elinor agreed, 'but unfortunately we are losing more and more of our original tenants. A lot of us are getting along in years. But as my dear husband used to say, "If you don't want to grow old, you have to die young." Anyway, the good Lord has taken two of our families.'

'To that big co-op in the sky,' Paul Gordon said facetiously.

'Exactly,' Elinor said with delight. 'What a charming way to put it, Mr Gordon! Yes, I'm sure Bryan Rogers has found a new 12B, and dear Mrs King is probably happy in another 6A somewhere up there. Such a beautiful way to think about it! I shall find it very comforting when I leave 6B to know that my neighbor is already there waiting!'

Her cheerful enthusiasm completely charmed the group. All, that is, except the Weinbergs. Lester and Gertrude looked completely bored by this flight of fancy. Lester busied himself lighting another of his illegal Cuban cigars and Gertrude concentrated with a frown on her left index finger which, dammit, showed a slight chip in the dark-red polish. She thrust the offending hand under her gold mesh evening bag and went back to staring seductively at Richard Basil. For a moment there was quiet. Then, surprisingly, Lester also turned his attention to Basil.

'What do these apartments go for, Doc? Say, one the size of this?'

'It's hard to say, Mr Weinberg,' Richard answered. 'It depends a great deal on the condition of the apartment. Some, I'm afraid, are in a rather deplorable state of neglect. And also, of course, there's the question of whether the owner is anxious for a quick sale. Sometimes when there's an estate involved and the family does not wish to live in the building they're anxious to dispose of it to get rid of the monthly maintenance charge. That, of course, continues, whether or not the unit is occupied. As an average, though, to answer your question, I'd say that most apartments like this one are sold for around a hundred thousand dollars.'

'Peanuts,' Lester said. 'With a price that low, you must have a helluva high maintenance charge. Isn't that the way it goes with co-ops? Either a high purchase price and low maintenance or a cheap buy and a high monthly bite?'

'In some cases,' Dr Basil said, 'I guess that's correct. Fortunately, in this building the monthly costs are quite reasonable. At least at the moment.'

Because the conversation had taken on a faint tinge of business, Lester Weinberg was suddenly interested. All that stuff about 'big co-ops in the sky' had left him cold. But money was another matter.

'So what do you call "reasonable"?' he asked.

'Well, again,' Basil said, 'it depends upon the size of the apartment. That determines the number of shares the owner holds in the building. And each share denotes a monthly charge.' The doctor obviously was not anxious to tell Weinberg how much the Cromwells paid in maintenance. Jim found himself getting angry at the gross inquisitiveness of his boorish 'guest of honor'.

'Since you're so interested, Lester,' Jim said coldly, 'this size apartment carries the largest number of shares. And the maintenance is six hundred dollars a month. For seven rooms. Okay?'

Lester pretended not to notice the chill in the air. 'Six hundred for this spread? You're stealin' from the poor! Why I'm paying twelve-fifty a month rent for our place. And no tax deduction at the end of the year like you get. You got it made, kid. Of course, I don't mean to be offensive, but our building's got a helluva lot more glamour to it. Big lobby, for instance. I like that. Makes you feel like you're coming home every night to the Fountainbleu. Right, Gert?'

His wife gave him a pained smile. 'I think we ought to be going, Lester. It must be getting late, and these gentlemen have to get to work in the morning.'

Weinberg gave a snort. 'Honey, I don't know about the doc, but don't worry about Tony and Paul-baby. I got a feeling they don't show up at that agency before ten, eleven o'clock. Not Jim, of course. Damn if he's not a beaver! You know he sometimes hops into my office before nine? Hope you appreciate him, Tony. You got a real, Grade-A gent there. You better watch out or I'll steal him for my own organization. Or maybe,' Lester said slyly, 'get him into some other agency where he can handle my account.' He laughed. 'Don't get up-tight, Tony. I'm only pulling your leg.'

'Come on, Lester,' Gertrude said. 'It's time to leave.' She turned to Casey. 'Thanks for a gorgeous evening. I hope you meant what you said about helping me with the apartment.'

'Of course,' Casey said. 'Whenever you're ready.'

The others rose to their feet as the Weinbergs did. There was a polite exchange of thank-you's and good nights all around. As the door closed, Jim looked anxiously at Casey.

'What was that last crack of Gertrude's about your helping her with an apartment?'

Casey sighed. 'God help me, she thinks we have the same taste. She's planning to redecorate and wants me to give my opinion. That's all I need. To get involved with that terrible bitch. Enough is too much, James. I don't have to go that far, do I?'

Jim groped for words. He would have liked to have told her that of course she didn't have to get involved with Gertrude in that or ony other way. But he was so deeply committed to getting the Weinberg account that he would now go to almost any length to bring it in. He hated himself for the professional whore he'd become. When Lester had made that patronizing speech about him, Jim had wanted to punch him in his big mouth, tell him to take his Godamn eight million dollars and give it to somebody else. But he hadn't. And he wouldn't. Any more that he'd reassure Casey that she didn't have to cater to Gertrude Weinberg. My God, Jim thought, the things you have to do these days to keep afloat. And for what? To be able to afford a Park Avenue address and a full-time maid? Or was it more that that? Was Lester Weinberg's account a kind of weird challenge that he and the agency simply could not resist? Were they playing a game without rules? Or were the rules laid down by the competition? It's a crazy world, Jim thought. And I'm letting things get out of proportion. He realized that Casey was still waiting for an answer. All he could give her was evasion.

'Let's jump off that bridge when we come to it,' he said. 'Maybe Her Imperial Highness will be too busy in Bergdorf to ever get started on the apartment.'

For the first time in their marriage, he saw disappointment in Casey's eyes. It was not the answer she'd hoped for. At this moment he was not the man she'd married. But she said nothing. She didn't have to.

There was a message from Tony Stewart waiting for Jim when he got to his office the next morning. Contrary to Lester Weinberg's disparaging remarks of the evening before, the chairman of Stewart, Sutton & Atherton usually was one of the first executives in the building and he was waiting, now, to talk with Jim and Paul Gordon.

'Nice party,' Tony said when Jim walked into his office. 'Casey's terrific. She's really taken to the new apartment, hasn't she?'

'Like the proverbial duck,' Jim agreed. 'She's quite a girl. You'd think she'd been giving sit-down black tie dinners all her life. Funny. She was scared to death of the whole setup before we moved in. Now I think I'd have to blast to get her out of it.'

Tony nodded. 'Women like that kind of thing. No matter how much they talk about being "liberated", running a house still comes naturally, I guess.'

Jim smiled. 'Well, Casey isn't exactly scrubbing floors or ironing my shirts on the kitchen table. But I know what you mean.' He wondered where this conversation was leading them. Tony was not given to small talk during business hours. This gentle preamble was leading up to something. Paul Gordon, already seated on the sofa, obviously thought so, too. He had a faintly quizzical look, as though his reaction matched Jim's own. They both watched curiously as Tony, jacketless, strode restlessly up and down the length of his office. He's the only man, Jim thought irrelevantly, who can look elegant in his shirt sleeves. Of course, the Turnbull & Asser shirt and the Van Cleef cuff links don't exactly hurt the image.

'Okay,' Tony said finally, 'here's the way the Weinberg thing lays out. Lester is no dope. He's got to pick a new agency pretty quick. He likes our work. But Gertrude's putting the heat on him to consider her new buddies. Any problems with that?'

Jim considered telling the other two about Lester's almost firm commitment but decided against it. He wasn't sure that it was real. But above that, even, he had given his word to Weinberg to say nothing, and he couldn't risk even an inadvertent slip from the other two – a thing that could destroy Lester's confidence in him. So he merely shook his head in answer to Tony's question. 'Not so far,' he said.

Tony looked at Gordon. 'Paul?'

The creative director moved uncomfortably in his seat. 'I guess not. If you're really sure he likes the work. We have a couple of new campaigns on the drawing board, just as backups, you know. Maybe I'm naïve, but if he really thinks the advertising is all that good, I can't believe the other consideration will sway him.'

'Unfortunately, most clients don't see that simple rationale as clearly as you do,' Tony said. 'The life of an agency man would be a helluva lot easier if they did. No, Paul, I'm afraid this one is out of your hands. The creative work is great. You've delivered your part of the deal.' He paused for emphasis. 'From a work standpoint, at least.'

The last sentence did not escape Jim. 'What other standpoint could Paul be involved in?' he asked.

'I'm not sure,' Tony said. 'But let's leave that for a moment. Let me finish my recap of the Weinberg *cause célèbre*. We know that Weinberg's being cute. Just how cute, we're not sure. What we do know is that we've matched our competition's courtship of Gertrude so far. At least I think we have. Up to and including taking her into our homes.'

'Except mine,' Paul said wryly. 'Do you think we might touch her heart by offering a homely little Kosher dinner in Brooklyn? Maybe it would bring back loving memories of her childhood.'

There was an embarrassed pause. Paul instantly regretted his flippancy. 'Sorry,' he said. 'That was childish. I forgive you both your pure Aryan backgrounds. Maybe I even envy them. Anyway, forget it. What's the next step, Tony?'

The chairman hesitated. 'Maybe this is going to sound crazy, but I've got a hunch. I watched Mrs W. pretty carefully last night. She was eating that Park Avenue atmosphere with a spoon. Notice how she cut Lester off when he began to sound off about how much snappier their Central Park building was? Gertrude is the deadliest kind of female – smart, rich and socially ambitious.'

'No argument,' Jim said. 'So?'

'So what would be the greatest coup we could pull? The one that really would top anything the competition has been able to do? I'll tell you what it would be,' Tony said. 'It would be getting Mrs Lester Weinberg a super-social address. One that just plain money can't buy.'

Jim began to sweat. The implication was clear. 'Like,' he said, '617 Park Avenue, for instance?'

'Give that man a cigar,' Tony said. 'Right on, Jim. That's exactly what I've been thinking ever since last night. If we could get the Weinbergs into your building, we'd have Gertrude's eternal gratitude, probably closely followed by Lester's account. Make any sense to you two?'

Jim exhaled slowly. 'As an idea? Terrific. As a practical move it's a hopeless dream. About as realistic as The Man of La Mancha. No way, friend. I'm not proud of it, but I live in a restricted building with a capital R. To my certain knowledge, they've never accepted a Jewish tenant. And I doubt that I'll live long enough to ever see it happen. The Weinbergs would have about as much chance of getting into 617 as Billy Graham has of becoming Pope. Not that I don't think Gertrude wouldn't love it. I agree that it really could be the clincher. But it won't work. Not with *any* Jews. But especially not with the Weinbergs, who are about as obnoxious and obvious as any I've ever seen.'

For a moment, he had completely forgotten Paul Gordon's religious persuasion. Suddenly he realized he must be insulting his best friend. Awkwardly, he tried to make amends.

'Jesus, Paul,' he said, 'I'm sorry. You know I don't mean you. I'm making a stupid generalization. I apologize.'

Paul waved off the apology. 'Nobody knows the facts of life about obnoxious Jews better than those Jews who think *they're* not obnoxious,' he said easily. 'And you're one thousand per cent right, Jim. This kind of housing discrimination is not exactly a deep, dark secret. Everybody knows about it. I'm surprised that you don't, Tony.'

'I do,' Tony answered. 'But I also think there must be a way around it. It's not only immoral, it's illegal. Everything but fattening. Look, this is the twentieth century and we're more than half-way through it. This kind of crap has got to go – along with all the other kinds of racial bias.'

'Of course it has,' Jim protested, 'but we're not going to wish it away. That building I live in has hard-and-fast rules. We're not going to change 'em, no matter how smart we think we are.'

'I'm not sure,' Tony said slowly. 'Let me ask you a question. If they accepted one Jew, they'd have no basis for turning down others, would they?'

'Damned if I know,' Jim said. 'Anyway, the question is academic. They're never going to accept the first one, so you can forget the next steps.'

'But what if they didn't know they were accepting a Jew until it was done?' Tony persisted.

Paul Gordon spoke up. 'Come on, Tony, what are you driving at? I have a sneaky feeling this has something to do with me. If so, let's have it.'

91

'All right,' Stewart said, 'it does have something to do with you. According to what I heard last night, Jim, there are two apartments for sale in 617 Park. What if Paul got one of those apartments, thereby shattering their sacred precedents?'

Jim looked bewildered. 'I hate to sound dense, Tony, but Paul is Jewish. He'd never be accepted. Forget his desirable character-traits, his financial ability, all those things. They'd blackball him because of his religion. We've just gone over all that.'

'You're missing the main point,' Tony said. 'There's no reason they have to know about his religion in the beginning. Let's tick off the points in his favor. One: He doesn't "look Jewish" — if you'll forgive that unfortunate turn of phrase, Paul. Two: Gordon is a name that could be anything. Three: He's already met two of the board members who liked him and his wife. Four: He's your best friend and you are now a member of the governing body of that building.'

'And five,' Paul interrupted, 'you are presuming that he will subscribe to a lie. Which, sorry, he will not.'

'I was afraid you'd feel that way,' Tony said, 'and I can't help but admire you for it. But, frankly, I think it's pretty damned unrealistic. If you want to stand on your high and mighty principles about strict adherence to the truth, I can't do anything but applaud you for it. On the other hand, I think you have a helluva lot to gain from this. A great apartment, for one thing. You know Mary would love it. And so would you, I suspect. That's the purely materialistic side. On the idealistic side, you'd be helping to blow a rotten system sky-high. You know that this kind of discrimination stinks, Paul. Anything anybody can do to punch holes in it is a good deed in a naughty world.'

'Oh, cut it out, Tony,' Paul said. 'What do you think I am? A babe-in-the-woods? Sure we'd like a better apartment. Sure I'd like to help knock discrimination in its ugly head. But we all know what you're really concerned about. You want me to be the device that opens the door to Jews in general but the Wein-bergs in particular. You're a smart guy, and I love you like a brother. But this time you've gone too far. Sorry, friend, I won't be used that way. It turns my stomach.'

'Eight million dollars' worth?' Jim asked quietly.

'Yeah, pal. Eight million dollars' worth.'

'Hold it,' Tony said. 'Look, Jim, if Paul feels this strongly, his principles are worth more to me than an eight-million-dollar account. Okay, let's say it was a dumb idea to try to get Paul in under false pretenses, announce it later and hope that the board would soften up enough to accept another Jewish family. Forget it. Leave Paul out. The idea of an apartment for the Weinbergs is still a good idea. So let's pursue that one. We know it's illegal to refuse a sale because of a man's religion. But how illegal? I mean, how much can they make it stick?'

'I'm not sure,' Jim said. 'But I'll find out. Not,' he added, 'that I'd look forward to having the Weinbergs as neighbors, but you're on target about making a crack in the Christian Curtain. I'm for that. And less loftily I'm with you about it being a clincher with the Weinbergs. Gertrude would sell her soul to get off the West Side. And if I know that lady, she's probably aware that it's damn near an impossibility for them to buy into our kind of building.'

'Good enough. Check it out, will you?' Tony said. 'And, Paul, I'm sorry to have suggested the other thing. I do admire you. And I envy you. You haven't let a sticky business situation get in the way of your personal ethics. You can be proud of that. I mean it.'

Paul didn't feel proud at all. He felt confused. His emotional reaction was sincere: he wouldn't pretend to be something he was not. But he had an unhappy feeling that he was letting down his fellow workers. Not just the two who were his friends but the dozens who would be looking for jobs if SS&A didn't get this important piece of business. How important *are* your so-called principles? he asked himself. And why do you feel so guilty about the stand you've taken? But he had taken it, vehemently. And there was no backing down now. All he could hope was that Jim would figure some other way to get the Weinbergs into 617 Park. There was no guarantee that Tony's first idea would work anyhow. Maybe, he thought hopefully, Lester and Gertrude wouldn't even be interested in an apartment there. But his common sense told him that Tony had correctly zeroed in on an area that could be the deciding factor. If SS&A made it possible for the Weinbergs to crash WASP territory, what in the world could the competition do for an encore?

'I'm sorry,' Paul said. 'I guess I'm letting everybody down.'

'Forget it,' Tony said again. 'Let's see what Jim can come up with. Hell, it's easier for us, Paul. We're not emotionally involved.'

'Right,' Jim agreed. 'Let me go to work on it. I don't know where to begin, to tell you the truth, but that's my problem.

93

Tonight I attend my first board meeting. Maybe I'll get some idea of which way the wind blows. Not that I'm putting much faith in the liberal attitude of our ruling tenants, but if the rest of them are half as amiable as Mrs Simpson and Dr Basil, maybe we can make some headway.'

'I think you also need more background,' Tony said. 'There's a helluva nice guy who heads the Committee Against Racial Discrimination. It's a national organization with headquarters in New York. I've been thinking about them since we started to talk. They probably have rooms full of information on all kinds of discrimination, including housing. Why don't you give him a ring, Jim? Name is Lazarus, I think. Saul or Sam, something like that. I think he'll remember me. We worked on a Fair Employment Committee about six months ago.'

'Good thought,' Jim said. 'I'll call him right away. Try to get back to you later in the day.'

As they left Tony's office, Paul looked miserable. 'Why do I feel like such a Judas?' he asked Jim. 'Tony's first idea was good, even though there's no guarantee that it would change anybody's mind about the Weinbergs. And I can't deny that an apartment like yours would have a lot of advantages for the Gordon family. What in hell's wrong with me, Jim? I've never given a damn about formal religion one way or the other. What made me come on like a rabbinical student?'

'Some things are just born in you, I guess,' Jim said. 'You reacted from the heart, not the head. Look, Paul, don't eat yourself up about this. We'll solve it somehow. And if we don't, just between us I still think Lester's going to come through with the account. I can't believe he won't. This will only be extra insurance if we can swing it.'

Paul shook his head. 'I don't know. My gut instinct says it could be just the thing we need. And Tony's right. The only way it would, have a remote chance of working is if I agreed to go along with his first idea. Without that, I think you're a dead duck. But dammit all, Jim, I still can't buy it.'

'Okay, okay,' Jim said soothingly. 'Relax. Put it out of your mind. Or if you can't, talk it over with Mary tonight. She'll agree with you, I'm sure. And don't get some stupid idea that your decision will make any difference in your relationship with Tony or me. You know better than that.'

'Yeah,' Paul said. 'I just hope those kids on the employment line never find out who helped put them there.'

Jim had his secretary call Sam Lazarus. He sounded like a very relaxed guy.

'I've got an easy morning,' he said when Jim explained briefly what he was after. 'Why don't you hop over right now and I'll tell you anything I can.'

Within fifteen minutes Jim was on his way to the appointment.

Chapter VI

Sam Lazarus worked in a little rabbit-warren of an office behind a desk overflowing with papers and pamphlets and press clippings. He extended a friendly hand and then leaned back in his swivel chair, giving Jim a cordial but curious look.

'Well, now, Mr Cromwell,' he said, 'what's this all about? And how's Tony Stewart, by the way? Nice fella, I recall.'

'Tony's fine. Sent you his regards. He thinks you're a nice fella, too.'

Jim was relieved. Sam Lazarus was going to be pleasant to deal with. Jim had been afraid he was going to meet some stern, overbearing zealot, all hung up in the crusade for equality. Instead, this youngish guy was apparently as loose as he was dedicated. He decided to play it straight with Lazarus. In a few sentences he outlined the problem, explaining the agency's previous tactic to get the account and ended with their latest idea of getting Weinberg into a restricted building. He didn't reveal the address. And he deliberately omitted the idea of sneaking in the Gordons under false colors. That, he decided, was now irrelevant. And probably Lazarus would react to it with the same distaste that Paul had.

'And so,' Jim concluded, 'what we need now are facts. How serious is the racial discrimination problem in housing? And what, if anything, can we do about it vis-à-vis this present situation?'

By way of reply, Sam dug into an untidy pile of newspaper clippings and came up with a one-column story from the New York *Times*. He handed it to Jim. 'You can read the details later if you like,' he said, 'but let me capsule if for you. A rich Jewish businessman named Irving Mayer tried to buy a $150,000 co-op on Fifth Avenue and now claims that the building turned down his application for no reason except that he is a Jew.

Actually, it was the board of directors of the building who turned him down on behalf of all the tenants. In spite of the fact that the attorneys for the owner of the apartment – in this case an estate – were perfectly willing to sell to Mr Mayer. Got it so far?'

Jim nodded.

'Okay,' Sam said. 'Now this happens all the time. And in ninety-nine per cent of the cases, the Jewish applicant just takes it and shuts up. Goes and buys himself an apartment in one of the new buildings where, I'm glad to say, this discrimination seldom seems to apply. But Mayer is a different breed of cat. He has decided to fight it. He's not used to losing. He's got money and muscle and enough of the street-brawler in him to bring the whole ugly mess out in the open.'

Jim was getting interested. 'How does he go about that?'

'His first step is to file a complaint with the New York City Commission on Human Rights. Then the Commission, on Mayer's behalf, goes to court for an injunction against the corporation – which means the building itself. In addition, they name not only the corporation but the real estate company that manages the building, the broker who had the apartment listed, the agent who works for the broker and each individual member of the co-op's board. It's just a damned good thing that the estate and its lawyers were in favor of selling to Mayer or he could include them too. How's that for a keg of worms?'

'Incredible!' Jim said. 'What happens now?'

'In this particular case, the judge of the State Supreme Court who's hearing the complaint has continued the "stay" that the Commission on Human Rights has asked for. In simple language, that means that the apartment in question cannot be sold to anybody except Mr Mayer until the case is finally settled. And that, friend, could drag on for months. Maybe years.'

'So,' Jim reasoned, 'in the meantime the estate is wild because they have to go on paying the maintenance while they're stuck with an apartment that they legally cannot sell to anybody else. Correct?'

'Exactly. The heirs are yelling bloody murder and the board will not budge an inch. What do they care who pays the maintenance? They're fighting for their pure, unsullied, Aryan lives. And there's more. You see, Cromwell, this violates federal, state and city statutes. If the alleged discrimination is proved, there could be damages levied against the directors of the building as

97

well as the building itself. The broker could have his real estate license revoked. And we already know that the apartment is "posted", which means that it has an ugly sign on the door saying that it cannot be sold or rented to anyone until the matter is settled. Very embarrassing, no?'

Jim flinched. 'Good lord, with all that at stake, how can the building hold out?'

'Well, the real hold-outs are the members of the board. My guess is that they're such fat cats that they're willing to gamble on paying damages. But more likely they're betting that Mayer hasn't got a chance of winning his case.'

'Do you think he has?' Jim asked.

'Private opinions? I doubt it. This kind of discrimination is almost impossible to prove. Especially when the building is in a position to afford a lot of high-priced lawyers. Officially, CARD — that's my organization — is one hundred per cent behind Mayer, of course. What's happened to him is wrong. Dead wrong. And we're prepared to help him every way we can. But off the record, I'm glad I'm not betting next year's salary on his winning his case.'

Jim shook his head. 'It's not only wrong, it's disgusting. Tell me, is there a lot of this kind of thing? Discrimination, I mean. I've always had an idea that only a handful of buildings still practiced it.'

'Frankly, we can only guess at how much goes on,' Sam said. 'As I told you, most people who experience this kind of prejudice are too hurt or too embarrassed to report it. Most of them don't even know they have legal recourse. Or wouldn't go through the time and expense of using it if they did know. Of course, there are a few hopeful signs. A handful of people, like Mayer, aren't going to take this lying down. The publicity he generates might serve to scare a few bigots, even if he loses his case.

'And we're getting information from other sources, too,' Sam went on. 'From time to time we get tips from some brokers who dislike the practice as much as we do. They'll tell us, strictly on the Q-T, which buildings are off limits to Jews. Of course, if they're ever faced with it officially, they'll deny it to the sky. But we know that a lot of real estate brokers have coded cards, tagged files and other secret devices that flag their people not to show a Jewish applicant an apartment in certain buildings. Naturally, their instructions come from the building agent or the building. Or both. And we also use the Reverse Directory, though it's not always possible to get an accurate picture from that.'

'What's the Reverse Directory?' Jim asked.

'It shows the names of everyone living in a given building. By address and with a listed telephone. We can pick out any particular house and look at the names of the occupants. If there are no obviously Jewish names on the list, the building is immediately suspect. Of course, you can't always tell about a house just by looking at the occupants' names. In fairness, sometimes there are Jewish tenants whose names don't identify them as Jews. And on the other side of the coin, there also are buildings who have their "token Jews", one or two families in a building of ninety units, maybe. But it's enough to keep us from seriously investigating. There's also the dodge of renting a professional apartment to a Jew. A doctor, usually. He doesn't really live there and doesn't own the apartment, but his name shows up on the list of occupants which helps to make everything – you should pardon the expression – Kosher.'

'It's fantastic,' Jim said.

Lazarus smiled. 'It may seem fantastic to you, but actually I'm amazed that it isn't worse. Does that surprise you?'

'A little,' Jim said. 'What do you mean?'

'Look at it this way. Most of this discrimination doesn't represent the building as a whole. At least, that's my personal conviction. You see, the board is empowered to make these decisions without consulting the whole body of tenants. I'm not sure they'd get away with this stuff if applicants were voted on by the building as a whole. Which gives me hope that there are fewer bigots than the co-op picture might lead us to believe. You see, Cromwell, my experience indicates that this intense discrimination exists primarily among a small and powerful group of men and women. The kind who practice it in their social and business lives as well. There usually are one or two ringleaders on every board who carry the others along with them. And I'll bet you dollars to doughnuts that those ringleaders all belong to restricted country clubs, or run businesses where no Jew is part of the top management echelon. My theory isn't completely conjecture, of course. I've personally run down cases where one of those biased bastards will go as far as sell his shares in the building to a Jewish front man who will vote the shares for him. How do you like that for a neat little cover-up?'

'You mean another Jew would be party to a setup like that?'

'We don't have any proclaimed saints in our religion,' Sam

said. 'We're just human beings. And some people, whatever their religion, will do anything for money.'

Sam's voice did not betray any hint of condemnation, but Jim suddenly felt uncomfortable. He was doing something phony for money, too. He knew in his heart that the Weinbergs didn't really belong in 617 Park. Not because they were Jews. Just because they were incapable of relating to the kind of building it was. Yet he was trying to pull a fast one to further his career which was, no matter how you tried to rationalize it, linked with money. Still, this was the stance he'd taken at the agency. There was no turning back now.

'All this is quite a revelation,' Jim said. 'Hell, I know that Jews have a tough time buying into some buildings. That's why I came here today. To find out more. But I didn't believe it was as complicated and difficult as you describe.'

'For whatever it's worth,' Lazarus said, 'Jews don't have the toughest time of the minorities. They're like third on the list. Blacks and Puerto Ricans have a harder time even renting decent living quarters in this town. As for co-ops, of course, forget it. And Italians have nearly as much trouble as Jews.'

'No Irish prejudice any more?' Jim asked, thinking of Mrs Murphy.

'Afraid I'm not an expert on the Irish,' Sam answered. 'But I can tell you some other people who have a helluva hard time buying apartments. Diplomats, for one. They find it nearly impossible to get into good buildings.'

'You're kidding.'

'Not at all. They're frequently rejected on the basis of the fact that they have "diplomatic immunity" which conceivably could allow them to get away with more than the average citizen. Also they entertain a lot, which most staid houses don't like. Latin diplomats, in particular, are discouraged because of their late dining hours. Many houses take a dim view of dinner parties that begin at ten or eleven at night.'

Jim was speechless. Lazarus was enjoying his little lecture. This was his favorite subject, and he was always pleased to have an audience. He continued to speak, easily and matter-of-factly.

'Then there are theatrical people,' he went on. 'They're taboo because their profession is considered unstable, to say nothing of the fact that they are notorious for keeping odd hours and giving noisy parties. People in big government jobs have a hard time buying in because the building might be picketed, or newsmen and photographers might be hanging around. Union leaders haven't a prayer because they're constantly threatened by assassins and therefore have to have a lot of bodyguards hanging around, cluttering up the lobby.

'Also on the unwanted lists,' Sam continued, 'are families with small children. Obvious. They play games with the elevators or race around the halls with their scooters, skates and sleds. And divorced women are unsuitable because they're considered financially risky. I've never quite figured out why single women seem to have a slightly better chance. Maybe the theory is that a single lady can earn her own living but a divorcee may lose her alimony through death or indiscretion. Anyway, Cromwell, as you see, Jews aren't the only ones who have a hard time getting into co-ops. They just happen to be the group that my organization is particularly interested in.'

'Are you making any headway?' Jim asked.

'Oh sure. Quite a bit. We're learning more every day about the problem. A while back, we compiled a list of nearly a hundred and forty New York buildings consisting of approximately four thousand apartments, most of them on the East Side. We asked these buildings to have their representatives meet with us to discuss the problem. At the same time, we sent a letter to the principles of the major real estate firms that act as managing agents for these buildings. The list was based on a diversification of apartment houses – those built prior to World War II as well as the newer ones. Some were accused of acts of discrimination and some weren't. Same with the agents. What we were after was a cross-sample of information.'

'And what did you get?'

Sam Lazarus smiled cynically. 'Just about what you'd expect: everything in the book. Some people never answered at all. Some were co-operative, apparently anxious to be helpful or maybe scared to death. Quite a few referred the letter to their attorneys. And a handful were decidedly unfriendly, even hostile. But we finally did have a meeting with a number of presidents of co-operative buildings and some of the representatives of the agents. Naturally, everybody pleaded innocence. Oh, they did admit that discrimination might exist in some buildings. Never their own, of course. But even so, they took the position that discrimination was considerably diminished due to the passage of anti-discrimination laws, the creation of government agencies like the city and state Human Rights Commission and the quote excellent efforts of the Committee Against Religious Discriminations unquote. And on and on. All that garbage. They had to admit that some applications were rejected, of course. But never, according to them, on the grounds of race, color or creed.'

'So what do you do now?' Jim asked.

'Now we turn over to the appropriate government agencies our files on those buildings that either failed to co-operate with us in the study or that appear to engage in "tokenism" or "exclusion". We'll do the same with the files on the real estate management firms that appear to be balky. The appropriate agencies, by the way, are the New York State Commission on Human Rights, the New York City Commission on Human Rights and the United States Attorney's office.

'After that, we'll recommend legislative changes. For example, we think the government agencies should have the names of all applicants who try to buy apartments and should find out whether they are accepted or rejected. If they're rejected, why? Also, we think that anyone who is turned down should be given the reasons in writing if he so desires. And finally, we hope to broaden the anti-discrimination laws to make it illegal to discriminate in this area against persons because of their sex, occupation or the fact that they have children. You see, Cromwell, we do also worry about divorcees, actresses, diplomats and parents, Jewish or not.'

Jim looked thoughtful. 'It's strange,' he said. 'Most people are worrying about housing for the poor. You're concerned with housing for the rich.'

'That's putting it a little strongly,' Sam said, 'but in a sense you're right. Just because people are prosperous doesn't mean that discrimination against them is any less terrible than it is against people with very little money. Sure, the rich man can go rent something else where the poor one may be on the street. But the principle of freedom of choice is the same. It's just as bad to deny a Jew who can afford it a hundred-thousand-dollar apartment as it is to refuse to sell a ten-thousand-dollar house in a white neighborhood to a black man who can meet the mortgage. In some ways, it's almost more serious. Because the people who are making those decisions which affect the rich applicant are usually people in positions of community leadership. They, of all people, should be intelligent enough to know better. And they do. They know damned well they are violating federal, state and city laws, and they arrogantly go ahead with it. I can find more excuse for the poor little ten-thousand-dollar home-owning schnook who hasn't had a chance to reason out his prejudices than I can for these educated bigots. The co-op clique, as I call it, is deliberately driving financially eligible people out of our town. That's not only bad for people, it's ruinous to the healthy economy of New York City.'

'You sure are going to shake up a lot of boards of directors,' Jim said. 'I can imagine what's going to happen if they have to legally justify every blackball when, for years, they've had carte blanche.'

Lazarus nodded. 'By the way, that's crucial to the plan. We think that one of the things that's blocking progress is that the same people serve on the boards of these buildings year after year. Their prejudices don't lessen. They probably increase with age, the way all human characteristics become magnified. We know it's tough to get younger people to serve on the board of a co-op. It's a bloody bore. But we think it could help do away with a lot of the problems if there was a time limit to service, a constant rotation of board members so that the power didn't stay in the same hands for decades.'

Jim got to his feet. 'I've taken an awful lot of your time, Mr Lazarus,' he said. 'And I can't tell you how much I appreciate all the information you've given me.'

'It's my pleasure – and my job. By the way, would you mind telling me which building your firm is trying to get your Jewish client into?'

Jim hesitated. '617 Park Avenue.'

Sam picked a file out of his bottom desk drawer, ran a finger down a long list of addresses. 'What do you know? That's one of the buildings on the suspect list. Seems to me you're in a position to do a good deed for three groups of people.'

'Three? I'm not sure I follow you.'

'Well, you'd make the Weinbergs happy, right?'

'Yes.'

'And you'd make your agency happy.'

Jim nodded. 'Check. But what's the third?'

Lazarus smiled grimly. 'Number three could be the biggest group of all – the 617 Park Avenue Corporation, its agents, Ridgely & Ryan, its representative Mr Carl Paterman and its seven-man board of directors. Believe me, Cromwell, you're skating on thin ice. And you seem like too nice a guy to take a cold bath.'

Right after lunch, Jim reported his conversation with Sam Lazarus to Tony and Paul. They listened, as Jim had, with amazement and disgust, but of the two Paul's reaction was most

103

violent. His anger was instantaneous and his voice highly charged with emotion.

'Sons-of-bitches!' he exploded. 'Who do they think they are – some kind of privileged, untouchable, superior breed? The bloody arrogance of them! Hell, everybody knows there's still discrimination against Jews. It's wishful thinking to believe that much has changed since Laura Hobson wrote *Gentlemen's Agreement*. But I doubt that many people know that prejudice is this deep or this widespread. I sure didn't. It isn't just Jews they're against, it's everybody who doesn't fit their tight little standards of acceptability. It's a conspiracy, all right. Very subtle. Very neat. People. How rotten can they be?'

Tony gave Jim a knowing look. Then very deliberately he pretended to be surprised by Paul's outburst.

'I don't know why you're behaving like an Italian tenor,' he said. 'This can't come as a surprise to you, Paul. Oh, sure, maybe the game's a little rougher than we imagined, but it's the same game. There are just more players sitting in on it than we knew.'

'You better believe there are,' Paul snapped. 'Maybe they wouldn't accept *you*, Tony, if you tried to buy into one of those hundred and forty buildings. You're a bachelor, divorced, presumably a swinger. How would you like to be turned down by a delegation of stiff upper-lip snobs who don't consider you their equal?'

'I'd hate it,' Tony said simply. 'But I wouldn't accept it without protest. I'd do anything I could to beat them at their own game. Even lie, if I had to. Because I'd be on the side of the angels.'

His insinuation was clear. If Paul went along with Tony's original idea, he might be able to break a precedent in 617 Park. He'd have to cheat, something he'd never done in his life. But what chance does an honest man have in a crooked crap game? Outside, the gray January sky was already turning toward its early winter darkness. Jim would have to leave soon to make the six o'clock board meeting at the apartment. Paul felt both of his co-workers looking at him without expression. They could go ahead with their second plan, to try to get the Weinbergs into the apartment without Paul's co-operation. Or they could use the very valuable weapon that Paul conceivably could provide. They were waiting for his decision. He tried desperately to sort out his feelings. Nice guys though they were, Paul did not delude himself that breaking down prejudice was their primary motive in this complex affair. It figured in, of course. But they could not feel as insulted as he did. Their first thought was the Weinberg account, as it had been from the start. He didn't blame them. He knew how important it was. Still he felt betrayed. They were playing on his emotions. He was aware of that. And they knew he was aware. Earlier today he had been firm in his rejection of Tony's attempt to involve him. But now, with the ugly facts laid bare by Jim's report, he knew that he had to change his mind. Not only for the good of the agency. For his sense of decency. In a funny way, he had to lie for his own self-respect.

'Okay,' he said ruefully, 'I'll go along with your scheme, Tony. Mary and I will apply for 6A. We'll phony it up with the background and the references if that's what it takes. What a screwy world. I may turn out to be the first crooked crusader in Jewish history.'

Jim's sigh of relief was almost audible. After his talk with Lazarus, he'd almost given up any hope of getting the Weinbergs into the building. But now maybe, just maybe, Paul's co-operation would make it possible. It was, Jim knew, a sacrifice. He understood the conflicts within his friend. And he recognized that the decision was as much for Paul's own sense of justice as it was for the future of Stewart, Sutton & Atherton.

Tony was openly jubilant. 'That's terrific! You've made a good decision, Paul. Not only for us but for yourself and for a lot of other people. Okay, let's go to work. What's the next step, Jim?'

'Hang on a second,' Paul said. 'I'm a big hero, but, assuming I get accepted, how do I know I can even afford to buy the apartment? These things are cash deals, aren't they? Where will I get a hundred thousand bucks to plank down for a co-op?'

'Don't worry about it,' Tony said. 'First, the asking price is never real. They always end up knocking at least twenty-five per cent off the original. So let's say you can get the place for seventy-five thousand. We'll finance you. The agency, that is. Let you pay it off over the next ten years, if you like. And make you a much better interest rate than you can get from a bank. No problem. My God, compared to the money we'll make on the Weinberg business, it's what Mrs Simpson probably would call "a mere bag of shells".'

Jim laughed. 'You're right, Tony. Seventy-five grand is "a mere bagatelle" in all this. But don't go too fast. We do have to get Paul in there, even if he has the money. And if we succeed, let's not count on it doing the trick as far as the Weinbergs are concerned. I mean, it's an ingenious plan, but we still only have an idea to go on. Nothing more.'

'I deal in ideas,' Tony said. 'That's my business. So are hunches. I consider this one of my more brilliant concepts, and I intend to take a positive attitude about its chance of success. I advise both of you to do the same.'

'Would you like to run through that number for my wife?' Paul asked. 'It suddenly occurs to me that I'm making a major commitment without even finding out how Mary feels about it. There's always an outside chance that she might not be willing to be the sacrificial lamb. I know she'd give anything to own an apartment like Jim's, but the lady has principles, you know. I'm betting she'll buy the idea, but I can't be sure until I talk to her. She could chew me out pretty good for this phony deal I've agreed to.'

'I doubt it,' Jim reassured him. 'Mary's as honest as you are, but she's probably a helluva lot more realistic. She may not like the way we have to go about it, but you know damned well that she'll be one delighted female when she hears she's probably going to get that great apartment. And I know that Casey will be out of her head with joy. So you see, pal, you're doing us a personal favor, too. It'll be great to have you two in the building.'

'All right,' Tony said, 'enough of the mutual admiration bit. To go back to my earlier question, Jim, now that we've settled the money problem what's the next step?'

'I'll find out tonight at the board meeting who's the person Paul should talk to. Then, if Mary agrees, he can make an offer, and if it's satisfactory to the estate, his application will come up for review by the board. Don't worry,' he said, 'I'll see that things move fast. I'm well aware that this is only move number one in this complicated chess game. And I know we've only got a few weeks to maneuver the whole operation. It won't be easy on a number of fronts, including the time element.'

'All of a sudden I'm grateful to Weinberg for stalling,' Tony said. 'About his final decision, I mean.'

'Don't worry about him,' Jim said. 'He'll play his little game as long as he can. We already know that. But once I get the first real glimmer of hope, I'll dangle that bait in front of him. He doesn't really have to choose a new agency quite as soon as we've been leading him to believe. With the advertising all prepared, he could wait three months and still be in plenty of time to place his full schedule. I'll be sure he knows that when the time is right.'

'If it ever is,' Paul said morosely.

'Oh, for God's sake go home and talk to your wife,' Tony said. There was affection in his voice. 'You've got big news, man.'

'Sure,' Paul grumbled. 'I can hear me now. "Hello, honey, how'd you like to lie about your family and your religion and phony up some references so you can live in a nice restricted apartment that wouldn't take you if they knew the truth?" Now that's designed to make a guy feel like Mr Wonderful!'

'You're making it sound a lot worse than it is,' Jim said lamely.

'I know, Pollyanna. It's all in a good cause, right?'

'Several of them,' Tony reminded him. 'Don't forget to make that clear to Mary.'

'That's right,' Jim agreed. 'And don't forget one other thing, Paul.'

'What's that?'

Jim smiled mischievously. 'When you tell her, don't forget to duck.'

* * *

On the subway to Brooklyn, Paul spent his time wondering what Mary's reaction would be. He thought she'd be happy. He was ready to concede that women were, as Jim had pointed out, usually more 'practical' in matters such as these. And he knew that Mary would revel in the comfort and spaciousness of the apartment. Still, she was even less of a hypocrite than he. They had often talked about people who faked their way through life by pretending to be richer or smarter or more social than they really were. Mary had nothing but scorn for Jews who changed their names, the Greensteins who became Green or the Herschfelds who became Hart. Both of them had been almost patronizing about these Jews who tried to 'pass' in a prejudiced world. Now Paul realized that possibly these people's motive was not shame but a realistic recognition that their Semitic origin was keeping them from something they wanted or needed. Just as Paul's was. For all I know, he thought, 'Gordon' may well have started out as Gorkovich or Greenberg somewhere back in the past. Maybe I, too, had ancestors who found it easier to blend into the New World by shucking the appellation of the Old.

Mary was surprised when he let himself into the apartment.

107

'Hey, it's only five-thirty!' she said. 'What happened? The building burn down?'

'Barely had time to get your lover out the back door, right?'

'You bet,' Mary laughed. 'If I've told that grocery boy once I've told him a million times, "Get going by five o'clock in case my husband comes in early!" We nearly blew it this time. Seriously, Paul, how come you're home at this ridiculously civilized hour?'

He explained the day's developments to her. Beginning with his first rejection of Tony's plan and ending with his change of heart when he heard the extraordinary facts that Jim had discovered.

'I don't know how you feel about it,' Paul said. 'And I'm sorry to have half-way made such a big decision without consulting you. But Jim and Tony said you'd be pleased. And practical. Are you?'

Mary had listened attentively to the long, involved recital, trying to sort out the realities from the emotional considerations. She understood and shared the struggle that was going on within her husband. Of course she wanted the apartment. But even so, under normal conditions she would have rejected the proposition out of hand. These, however, were not normal conditions. The very life of the agency could hang on their decision. Her realistic nature told her that this was more significant than the small blow against prejudice that their gesture might deliver. She suspected that, perhaps unconsciously, Paul knew this, too. He was very likely rationalizing his desire to help the agency by deluding himself that he wouldn't be party to such deception merely for the sake of business. He had to believe that he was fighting injustice as well. It was important for him to believe that. And Mary would not disabuse him of that belief. He was waiting for her answer. She had to phrase it just right for his peace of mind.

'Pleased?' she echoed. 'You bet I'm pleased! I'm more than pleased. I think I'm as proud of you as I've ever been in my life. It couldn't have been easy to do what you did, Paul. We've never made a big thing of religion, either of us. But we've never been ashamed to admit that we're Jews. Of course, we've been lucky. We've never had an important reason to deny it. I mean, a reason that really could contribute to a saner world. Okay, now we have one. What's a little dissembling if it means beating these bastards at their own lousy game?'

'Funny,' Paul said, 'that's exactly the phrase Tony used:

"Beat 'em at their own game." Somehow it has a more believable ring coming from you.'

'You mean, "Big Chief may speak with forked tongue but loyal squaw tell truth"?'

'Something like that, I guess. Anyway, honey, it's okay with you? Really okay? We'll have to lie our heads off, you know, in that application and in the personal interview before the board. Sure it's worth it?'

'I'm sure,' Mary said firmly. 'For an apartment like that I'd swear that my grandfather was Cardinal Spellman.'

Paul was almost pathetically relieved. 'That's the sensible side in you coming out. Well, then, that's it. Jim's paving the way, hopefully, at the board meeting tonight. By tomorrow, if all goes well, we should be able to make an offer for the apartment.'

'Incidentally,' Mary said, 'you haven't told me the price.'

'They're asking a hundred but they'll probably take seventy-five.'

Mary gulped. 'Seventy-five-thousand dollars? That's not exactly grocery money. And I know that buying a co-operative is a cash deal. We'll have to sell everything we own.'

'No we won't. The agency will finance it for us over a long term. We don't have to touch any of our savings. We'll be able to repay the loan, with interest, out of my salary.'

Mary looked bemused. 'Tony was that anxious, huh?'

'Yes,' Paul said quietly, 'he was that anxious.'

* * *

The door of 9B was open when Jim arrived promptly at six o'clock for his first board meeting. He walked into the Livingstons' apartment expecting it to be a duplicate of his own five stories above. To his surprise, there were great differences. Not only in decor, but in actual physical layout. André Livingston who came forward to greet him in the foyer noted his puzzled look and guessed immediately at the reason.

'You're amazed that all the apartments on the same line aren't identical, isn't that so, Jim?'

'As a matter of fact, I am. I'd expected all the B apartments to have the same arrangement.'

André smiled genially. 'That's one of the charms of our building,' he said. 'In the days when they were putting up houses like this, every purchaser could look at the plans and specify his own preferences to a great degree. You'll find that on every floor there's an element of difference in each unit. It's one of the few "custom-made co-operatives' left in Manhattan, I'd guess. Too bad. My wife says that apartment houses are like women's fashions these days: No more made-to-measure styles. All mass-produced with a thousand copies of each. Pity. Hate regimentation in any form. Whether it's clothing or co-ops. Well, enough of that. Come in and meet the others.'

Except for Dr Basil, Jim was the last to arrive. Of course it figured. The other members were all ladies, none of whom had an engagement more pressing that a hair appointment. André made the introductions all round. 'May I present Mr Cromwell, our newest board member,' he said. 'Mrs Stone, Baroness Von Brennerhof, Mrs Murphy, Mrs Simpson.' The first two acknowledged the introduction with a cool, polite nod. Eileene Murphy gave Jim an appraising look.

'So this is my new neighbor,' she said.

'I'm delighted to meet you at last, Mrs Murphy,' Jim said courteously. 'My wife has the nicest things to say about your daughter.'

'Hope she hasn't been troublesome,' Eileene said. It sounded as though Rosemary was a five-year-old child.

'On the contrary,' Jim replied. 'Casey says she's been most friendly and helpful.'

Mrs Simpson's warm greeting was in striking contrast to the others. 'Mr Cromwell and I already know each other,' she said. 'Welcome aboard. Or should I say "to the board"?'

'I'm sure Dr Basil will be here momentarily,' Livingston said. 'And I understand you two also have met.'

'We have indeed.' Richard Basil strode in. 'My apologies, ladies and gentlemen. Hello, Cromwell. Nice to have you with us.'

The meeting was called to order. The president made a somewhat long-winded, overly formal speech extolling the virtues of their newest board member. He reminisced about Jim's grandparents, exaggerated Jim's prominence in the advertising world and generally succeeded in reducing his subject to a state of acute embarrassment and his audience to a period of utter boredom. During Livingston's pronouncements, Jim was uncomfortably aware of the Baroness. Her carefully made-up eyes never left Jim's face except to exchange brief and apparently knowing glances with Dr Basil. Richard's expression was noncommittal, but Jim somehow sensed a special rapport between these two. He remembered Sam Lazarus' words earlier that day. 'There usually are one or two ringleaders', Sam had said. Jim had a peculiar feeling that Felicia and Richard filled the roles in 617 Park. There was nothing tangible. Just an unspoken communication that he seemed to pick up. It was eerie. Casey would call it ESP, Jim thought. Personally, he'd never held with that stuff. Yet he couldn't shake the feeling that there was a conspiratorial atmosphere. But over what he couldn't imagine.

'And that,' Livingston was saying, 'is the major item under "old business". Oh, yes, Baroness, I trust you notice that the ramp has been installed in front of our door.'

Felicia nodded. 'I'm delighted that for once our decrepit superintendent got something done in reasonable time. Heaven knows he's slovenly in nearly everything else. Too old, I fear, to continue much longer. I believe we must soon look for a new superintendent, Mr President. Mr O'Shea is no longer capable of competent management.'

Eileene Murphy sniffed. 'Ridiculous!' she said. 'Mike O'Shea isn't too old to handle his job. He does it very well. Always has.'

Jim was amused. He supposed that from the vantage point of a vigorous ninety-four, Mike's eighty-five years seemed a tender age to Mrs Murphy. The Baroness was right, of course. O'Shea should be retired. Even Jim had noticed the increasing carelessness that had begun to pervade the building. Apparently Antoinette Stone had noticed it, too.

'Much as I hate to disagree with Mrs Murphy,' Antoinette said, 'I must admit that Baroness Von Brennerhof does have a point. Several disquieting things have come to my attention, Mr Livingston. And I believe they should be pointed out to Mr O'Shea.'

'What kind of things?' André asked.

'Well, twice now I've smelled liquor on Charles. He's the afternoon elevator man,' she said parenthetically to Jim. 'And it seems to me we're having increased absenteeism among the staff.'

'There are other things even more disgusting,' Felicia said. 'My housekeeper reported, only yesterday, a serious breach of etiquette on the service elevator.'

Elinor Simpson looked at her inquiringly. 'My goodness, what happened?'

Felicia managed to blush delicately. 'It is a bit difficult to discuss in mixed company,' she said, 'but to put it bluntly the handyman's trousers were slightly ajar.'

André Livingston looked shocked. 'Good Lord! Can't have that kind of thing! Mrs Simpson, as chairman of the house committee will you be good enough to speak to Mr O'Shea about these matters?'

'All of them?' Elinor asked nervously.

André reconsidered. 'No, on second thought, I'll speak to O'Shea myself. It wouldn't do to have you discussing such things with the superintendent. I'll see to it. Rest assured. It will give me an opportunity to talk with O'Shea. Size him up. See whether he really is ready for retirement. Give you a report about that. Shocking. Really shocking. Good man, O'Shea. Probably been here for thirty years.'

'Forty-four, to be precise,' Eileene Murphy said. 'I distinctly remember that we engaged him a year after the building opened. He's been very loyal. I don't think we should rush into a change until we're sure that it's absolutely necessary.' She glared at Felicia.

The Baroness merely shrugged. 'I am content to leave the judgment in Mr Livingston's capable hands,' she said. 'But I am sure that he will find our superintendent failing badly. Too bad, of course. But we must not let sentiment interfere with the efficient operation of the building, must we?'

'No, of course not,' Livingston agreed. 'Mrs Simpson, does the house committee have a report for this meeting?'

Elinor brightened. 'Yes, indeed.' She began to read from a piece of paper. 'I am pleased to report that we have replaced the leaking intake steam-pipe valves and improved the insulation of the boiler room. Mr O'Shea was very clever about it. The Garsons are very pleased.'

Richard Basil addressed himself to Jim who was looking thoroughly confused. 'To bring you up to date, Cromwell,' he said, 'the Garsons have the ground floor apartment and up until now the heat from the boiler room just below them has made the place damned near unlivable. They've screamed their heads off at every tenants' meeting for the last five years. Can't say I blame them. Don't know why they didn't notice it before they bought, but they didn't. Anyway, I'm glad to hear it's been remedied. Nice work, Mrs Simpson.'

Elinor smiled modestly. 'Poor souls, I'm glad we could help. They've been so discouraged they've been trying to sell. But everybody who comes to look is practically overcome with heat frustration.'

I must start jotting down Elinor's malaprops, Jim thought. Paul can add them to his collection. Mrs Simpson was still consulting her notes.

'There's one more thing,' she said. 'We really must do something about the water tower on the roof. It's warped and leaking and I think there's a defective steam valve there, too, which must be fixed to keep the water from freezing. I don't know whether Mr O'Shea can take care of this. We might need recommendations from Ridgely & Ryan about professional engineers. Does the budget provide for such repairs, Mr Livingston?'

'The budget provides for very little, unfortunately,' André said. 'In fact, I fear that at some time in the near future we might have to talk seriously about the expenses of the building. We may even have to insist upon a maintenance increase or other measures.'

'Good heavens, I hope not!' Antoinette sounded distressed. 'You know how that so many of our owners are older people on fixed incomes. They simply couldn't afford a rise in rent! I'm afraid we'd have more apartments going on the market than we have-now!'

'Now, now, Mrs Stone, let's not become prematurely alarmed,' André said soothingly. 'We simply must realize that the possibility is there.'

He's going to chicken out for this meeting at least, Jim thought. Probably postponing the inevitable. I see what he means about the ladies on the board. Looks like they really run the show here.

'Any other new business?' Livingston asked.

'Just one thing,' Jim said. 'In line with Mrs Stone's statement about empty apartments, I believe I have an excellent prospect for 6A, and I wonder how he goes about making application for the purchase.'

Livingston hesitated. 'You consider him an appropriate candidate?'

'Very much so, sir. He's my closest friend as well as a business associate.'

'Then I'm sure he'd be desirable. Why don't you wait after the meeting and discuss it with me? No use taking up these good people's time while I outline the routine procedure. Agreed?'

'Certainly,' Jim said.

'If there is no further business, I will entertain a motion for adjournment,' the president said.

113

'So move,' Richard Basil said.

'Second,' Antoinette echoed.

'The meeting is adjourned,' Livingston pronounced. 'Thank you very much, ladies and gentlemen. You will be notified when the board meets again.'

Jim stayed behind after the others left. 'About your friend,' André said. 'Married?'

'Yes, sir.'

'Children?'

'One little girl. A very well-mannered, quiet child.'

'Hmmmm. We normally shy away from families with small children, Jim. Can be very disruptive, you know.'

Jim smiled. 'I understand. But not this one, Mr Livingston. Abigail Gordon is six years old going on thirty-two. She has more poise than most adults I know.'

'Gordon? That's the family name?'

'Yes. Paul and Mary Gordon. A delightful couple. He's the creative director at my advertising agency. Brilliant. And highly responsible. I think you'll like them very much.'

'Gordon, hmm? Used to know a very capable judge by the name of Harold Gordon. But he was, uh, not one of us. Don't suppose your friend is a member of the same family, is he?'

Jim stiffened at the implication. 'No, I don't think any of Paul's family are judges.'

'Well no need to get into all that until we see his application. Now, what you want to know is how he goes about it, right?'

Jim nodded.

'Confidentially,' André said, 'the way an outsider would approach it would be through our building agents, Ridgely & Ryan. But since you're family, I will tell you in confidence that your friend can go directly to the King estate. Have him get in touch with Sullivan, Whetherbee, Botsford and Beene. They're the attorneys for the estate. If he works directly with them, the owner can cut out the brokerage fee and reduce the price. Make the whole thing move faster as well. They're on Wall Street. Tell them I suggested it.'

Jim jotted down the name of the law firm. 'Thanks very much,' he said. 'I'm sure Paul will appreciate the advice – and the saving.'

'Your friend seen the apartment yet?'

'No,' Jim admitted, 'but it sounds exactly like what they've been looking for. Can Mike O'Shea show it to them?'

'Yes. Any time.'

'They'll probably come tomorrow,' Jim said.

'Good,' André said. 'Hope it works out, my boy.'

'So do I, sir,' Jim said fervently. 'So do I!'

Chapter VII

On the morning of January 12, Paul and Mary Gordon, accompanied by the Cromwells and escorted by Mike O'Shea, made a solemn tour through 6A and pronounced it acceptable. It needed work, of course. But Mary was delighted. And even Paul, despite his lingering misgivings, had to admit that it was like a comfortable six-room house. Jim phoned the estate's attorneys and found that the partner they would deal with was Willard Beene, the youngest member of the firm and apparently the one delegated to handle the least important transactions. Jim and Paul left their wives to deal with measurements in 6A while they took the subway to the law firm's Wall Street offices.

On the way downtown, Paul seemed cautiously optimistic. 'Maybe this whole thing is a blessing in disguise,' he said. 'It will be great for Mary and Abby to have a nice place to live. Not that there's anything wrong with Brooklyn.'

'It's going to work out fine,' Jim assured him. He did not mention Livingston's not-too-subtle query about 'Judge Gordon'. 'All we have to do now is haggle a little over price and get the application. By the way, you'll have to supply references. Three social and three business. But I don't see any problem there.'

Paul raised an eyebrow. 'Social? That could be tough. We haven't been invited on the Onassis yacht in at least six months.'

'Let's not get touchy,' Jim said. 'It isn't the first time in your life you've been asked for references.'

'True. But they've always been straight business credentials. The ones that normal people are used to giving.'

Jim sighed. 'Well, that part's easy anyway. You can give our esteemed chairman of the agency, your bank and whatever stockbroker you use.'

'What do you have in mind for the debutante division?'

'You can use me, for one,' Jim said. He paused.

'Do go on,' Paul said. 'Or if you can't think of any other acceptable people, how about my giving our client, Abe Levenstein, the Kosher Wine King, for the second? And we could always count on Mary's rich brother-in-law, Irv Schwartz, for the third.'

Jim ignored the sarcasm. 'I was thinking more of somebody like George Hiller,' he said, mentioning the name of a mutual friend who published fine-art books and was the product of a well-known Boston family.

Paul looked a litle ashamed of himself. 'Good idea. And I could ask Lucy Wilding. Might be a good idea to have at least one woman on the list.'

'Lucy Wilding? The Texas oil heiress? I didn't know you knew her. She'd be great. The lady philanthropist of the world. Where did you run into her?'

'Mary worked with her on a committee. Something to do with young drug addicts. She took a fancy to Mary and we've seen her quite a few times. I think she'd be glad to be one of my "respectable" references.'

Jim was delighted. 'That's perfect. You never cease to surprise me. How many other big-shot friends have you been holding out on me?'

'Oh, a few,' Paul said airily, 'but unfortunately you wouldn't be acceptable to them. They're Jewish.'

'Thanks a lot,' Jim said.

'Don't mention it. With a little luck you might break into Our Crowd. I could help you out with your non-WASP references.'

Jim cringed. 'Do we have to go into this again, Paul? You know how I feel about it. I just want you to get that apartment, that's all.'

'Is it? I'm not sure. You're liable to get carried away with all this pioneering crap. The Big Bigot Buster, that's you. Next thing you'll decide that Mary and I should have a boy so he can grow up to be the first Jewish astronaut.'

'Hey, that's right,' Jim said. 'Now that I think of it, there's never been a Jewish astronaut, has there? I wonder why not.'

Paul shook his head. 'Simple, meathead. Nothing wrong with the idea of Jewish spacemen. It would be their mothers. Can't you just picture Mrs Rosenbloom telling her son the astronaut to be sure to call her the minute he arrives safely on the moon?'

* * *

The meeting with Willard ('Call me Bill') Beene went even more smoothly than Jim had expected. The attorney was clearly anxious to sell the apartment and with only momentary hesitation, agreeable to the offered price of seventy-five thousand dollars cash. He was amenable to dealing directly with the purchaser since his client also benefited by cutting out the agent's fee. And if he had any doubt about Paul Gordon's suitability, he gave no sign of it.

'I'm sure the family will be delighted, Mr Gordon,' he said. 'And may I tell you, you're getting an excellent buy. You're lucky that all the King heirs already own co-operatives. Otherwise, I'm sure one of them would occupy 6A himself. So. We'll start drawing up the papers. We'll require a cashier's check, of course, in the full amount. And you know you'll have to be interviewed by the board. But that's only routine.'

'What about the application?' Jim asked.

'Have one right here, as it happens. Fill it out tonight, Mr Gordon, and we'll submit it to the building. I see no reason why you shouldn't take possession very quickly. Could be tomorrow as far as I'm concerned, but I suppose there'll be a slight delay while the board arranges to meet. I won't deny that I hope it's before February 1. The estate is not anxious to pay another month's maintenance. Can't say I blame them.'

'Perhaps I can help hurry it along,' Jim offered. 'I live in the building and serve on the board.'

'Excellent!' Beene said. 'Be most helpful if you could. Well, gentlemen, I'm sure everything will be in order. We'll need to check your business references, Mr Gordon, but I foresee no problem. You will get the application back to us promptly?'

'Absolutely,' Jim said. 'And thanks very much, Bill, for your co-operation.'

'Yes,' Paul said. 'Thanks.'

'Not at all,' Beene said, shaking their hands warmly. 'It's been a pleasure talking with both of you.'

In the corridor, Paul looked with amusement at his friend.

'I'm glad that good old Bill found it a pleasure talking with both of us,' he said. 'Personally, I felt like Charley McCarthy. Every time I opened my mouth your voice came out. What's with you, anyhow? Were you afraid I'd come on like the Yiddish Art Theater?'

'I'm sorry,' Jim apologized. 'I'm afraid I did monopolize the conversation. I didn't realize it at the time. Guess I was just compulsive, I was so damned anxious to see this deal go through.'

'*Everybody* seems anxious to have this deal go through,' Paul said. 'And everybody also seems to have his own little axe to grind. Mary wants the apartment for the apartment's sake. Tony wants us to have it for the clout it might give us with the board. Old marbles-in-the-mouth Beene, the friendly attorney, wants us to take it off his clients' hands. And you. Why are you so steamed up? Do you really give a damn about cracking this prejudice thing; or are you, like Tony, strictly using the Gordons as stepping stones for your onward-and-upward climb to success?'

Before Jim could answer, Paul slapped him on the shoulder. 'As your friend, I advise you to take the Fifth. Don't answer that question. It might be self-incriminating. And if it is, I don't want to know about it. Let's push on and get the whole damned business wrapped up.'

They went back to the agency and told a well-satisfied Tony Stewart that the first hurdle was behind them.

'Now,' Paul said to him, 'all I need is some petty cash. About seventy-five thousand dollars' worth if you have it handy.'

'As good as done. You guys go ahead with the application and I'll take care of the financial end.'

Filling in the application proved to be something of a trauma for Paul. It was an enormously detailed, probing document and some of its questions called for answers which could only be flat lies. They could not, under these circumstances, give the true name of Mary's father – which was Martin Silverstein. Nor could they tell the truth about Mary's mother's maiden name which was Mary Goodman. A distortion was also in order when the questionnaire called for Paul's mother's maiden name which had been Rosenberg. Paul gritted his teeth.

'Got any creative ideas?' he asked Jim.

Jim tried to pass it off lightly. 'We'll just take a little poetic license,' he said. 'Let's see. Mary's maiden name can become Silson instead of Silverstein. And her mother's maiden name can be Goodbody. As for your mother's maiden name, how about Rowan, instead of Rosenberg? What do you think?'

'I think it stinks. But I suppose if you're going to be a hooker, the *degree* of prostitution isn't all that important. Go ahead and fill it in.'

Their biggest problem, even worse than the fake names, came at the point where the application asked for 'Religious Affiliation'.

' "Protestant" okay?' Jim asked tentatively, pen in hand.

'No, Godamn it, it is not okay!' Paul yelled. 'You push too far,

119

Jim! Phonying up everybody's family names, trumping up a lot of Establishment references – that's not bad enough? Now you want me to pretend to be High Church of England, for Christ's sake?'

'What do you want me to write in this space?' Jim's voice was quiet.

Paul swallowed hard. 'It's not like I follow my religion, you know.'

'I know.'

'It's just that, well, I've never had to deny what I am. It's not a very pretty feeling.'

'I'm sure.'

For a few seconds there was quiet in the room. Then Paul said, 'What would happen if I just said "agnostic"? That isn't exactly a lie. I'm not sure what I really believe in. I mean, I do believe in some kind of power, so I'm not an atheist.'

'Seems reasonable to me,' Jim said. 'Let's settle for it.'

The rest of the questions went easily. And the personal reference were wrapped up with a few simple phone calls. The only uneasy moments came when Paul told George Hiller and Lucy Wilding that the Gordons were not going to mention their religion. Neither seemed surprised or concerned. They both promised to write glowing references immediately. By four o'clock in the afternoon, the application was on its way by messenger to the offices of Sullivan, Whetherbee, Botsford and Beene. Tony checked in to say the money was ready any time Paul needed it. Now all they could do was wait.

* * *

The waiting time was even shorter than Jim had dared hope. Five days after the application went in, Paul received a call at his office from André Livingston. Could he and Mrs Gordon come in on January 20 to meet some of the directors of the building? Say, about six o'clock? Paul assured him politely that they could. He immediately phoned Mary.

'Big announcement,' he said. 'The Nuremberg trials are set for six o'clock on the twentieth.'

Mary's response was pure female. 'What on earth will I wear?'

Paul laughed. 'Sackcloth and ashes might be appropriate. Lacking that, it probably should be some little Peck & Peck number. Isn't that where the Four Hundred go for their tweed skirts and cashmere sweaters? Hell, how do I know what you

120

should wear? You always look good to me.

She did, indeed, look charming when the Gordons presented themselves at apartment 9B promptly at the appointed hour.

'I'm as nervous as a cat,' Mary whispered as they waited for the door to open. Paul squeezed her hand reassuringly.

'Nothing to be nervous about,' he said.

'Then why is your palm so clammy?'

André Livingston greeted them cordially. 'Mr and Mrs Gordon? Do come in. Nice to meet you. I'm André Livingston.' As he had with Jim, he presented them to the board members, receiving the same response: Mrs Murphy, Mrs Stone and Baroness Von Brennerhof acknowledged the introductions coolly, Elinor Simpson and Richard Basil mentioned having met them before and said pleasantly that it was nice to see them again. Jim shook hands with Paul, rather formally, and gave Mary a quick little kiss on the cheek. He also managed an encouraging wink.

There was an awkward moment as everyone found a chair. Mary opened her bag to get a cigarette, noticed that no one else was smoking and decided against it. She closed her purse with a snap that sounded like a firecracker in the silent room. Finally, Livingston spoke.

'We have before us your application to purchase apartment 6A, formerly occupied by Mrs Winston King. Her heirs, through their attorneys, have requested permission to sell the premises to you. I presume, Mr Gordon, that you and your wife have inspected the apartment and found it to your liking?'

'Yes, we have,' Paul said. 'It suits us very well.'

Jim spoke up. 'As the board may know, Mr and Mrs Gordon are my very dear friends. Not that they need my recommendation, but I would like to say at this time that they will be very desirable owners.'

'We have all read the application, Mr Cromwell, and we have received impeccable social and financial references including your own,' André reminded him. 'But of course we are always happy when the prospective purchaser is well and personally known to one of our present tenants.' It was unmistakably a mild rebuke. Jim flushed like a chastened schoolboy. 'Perhaps some of our board members would like to chat with Mr and Mrs Gordon,' Livingston continued. He looked inquiringly around the room.

Antoinette spoke up. 'I believe you now live in Brooklyn? I'm not familiar with that address. Is it in The Heights?'

'No,' Paul said easily. 'The Heights is a bit more fashionable

121

than our area.' Make of that what you will, he thought.

'But our section is really lovely,' Mary said nervously. Paul could have kicked her. Don't grovel, he thought. For God's sake don't grovel!

'Then why do you want to leave it?' Antoinette asked.

Paul spoke quickly before Mary could answer. 'Very simple, Mrs Stone,' he said. 'This apartment is more spacious and infinitely more convenient to my office. Beyond that, we think it is desirable to own property, and Park Avenue happens to suit us better than Westchester.'

'Quite right,' Elinor Simpson agreed. 'My dear Edgar always said that one should have invested in electronics in the fifties and aerospace in the sixties. I'm sure if he were alive today he would say that real estate is the best investment for the seventies.'

Jim looked at her in amazement. She really was the most extraordinary woman. One minute she talked like a helpless matron and next like a security analyst. God bless her, he thought. At least she's on our side.

'Mrs Gordon, I note that your maiden name was Silson. Is that an English name?' The question came from the Baroness.

Mary hesitated. Stay with it, Jim pleaded silently. He was thankful that the question of origin had been put to her rather than Paul who looked dangerously tightlipped at this point.

'Silson may have been an English name somewhere back,' Mary said. 'I don't really know. You see, my family has been here for many generations, but we've never really gone to the bother of tracing the family tree.'

Jim could have applauded. It was a deft answer and, miraculously, not even a lie. Mary had not said that her name was Silson. She had just talked about the name itself. And added that neat little barb about not bothering to check on genealogy, as though such nonsense was beneath her.

'I also notice,' the Baroness went on, 'that you have a small child. I am very fond of children, but, to put it bluntly, I do not think this building lends itself well to raising them. I am told that there are no adequate private schools in the neighborhood. Or do you propose to send her to public school?'

The note of condescension did not escape Mary. She smiled sweetly at Felicia.

'How very clever of you to be aware of such things, Baroness,' she said. 'Fortunately, that presents no problem. Abigail goes to private school in the city now. Friends' Academy. The Quaker school, you know. I shall continue to take her there each morning as I always have. If anything, it will be more convenient than it's been in the past.'

It was a barefaced lie. Abby went to public school in Brooklyn, Jim knew, and he hadn't heard anything about enrolling her in Quaker school in Manhattan. Anyway, what difference? Mary was carrying this off beautifully. Much better than Paul who sat in almost sullen silence.

André Livingston looked at the others. 'Mrs Murphy? Dr Basil? Anything you'd like to ask?' They shook their heads in negative reply. 'Very well, then,' André said, 'we will get back to you very shortly with our answer.' He rose, dismissing the Gordons. 'It was good of you to come. I hope we will be seeing you again.'

Jim walked to the door with them. 'Go on up to our place,' he said quietly. 'Casey's waiting. I'll join you as soon as the returns are in.'

It took only a few minutes for the board to approve the sale of 6A to Paul and Mary Gordon. The question of religion never came up, though Jim had feared that Mrs Murphy might frown on 'agnostics'. And in the brief discussion that followed, no one, not even the Baroness, could find anything serious enough to make them withhold their approval. Livingston finally said he would give the verdict to Sullivan, Whetherbee, Botsford and Beene and would notify the Gordons in writing that they were welcome to live at 617 Park Avenue.

Jim dashed upstairs with the good news. They broke out a bottle of champagne and toasted the fact that they would be neighbors. For a little while they managed to forget what was behind it all. Gertrude and Lester Weinberg were a million miles away from their thoughts. It was only unfortunate that they couldn't stay there.

*   *   *

The speedy, effortless acceptance of the Gordons was almost too good to be true. Within three days the same kind of 'welcome' letter that the Cromwells had received was being savored by Mary. The cashier's check had been delivered to a beaming Bill Beene and the actual certificate of ownership turned over to Paul at the formal closing ceremony. He now possessed 150 shares of stock in the 617 Park Avenue Corporation, along with, as he said to Mary, 'one hell of an obligation to Tony Stewart' in the form of a long-term loan.

For her part, Mary was sublimely happy. The untruths they had told to get 6A became, in her mind, 'little white lies' that hurt nobody and benefited her family. When she thought of them, which was seldom, she was almost proud that they had put one over on the narrow-minded, class-conscious board. They might never know that they'd been fooled, but that did not lessen her satisfaction. She knew that her performance at the interview had really turned the trick, and she couldn't help feeling just a little smug as she went about getting the apartment in shape.

Now, with the roles reversed, it was Casey who was a tireless and invaluable aid to Mary. It was, to some extent, a scene replayed except for Euralia's part in the picture.

'Are you going to get a live-in housekeeper?' Casey asked.

Mary looked startled. 'We haven't discussed it, but I doubt that we will. Not now, anyway. I'm spending an awful lot of money on the apartment, and while we're paying off the loan I don't think we need that extra expense. Mattie will still come in twice a week for the heavy cleaning, the way she did in the other place. She's grumbling a lot about the trip from Brooklyn, but she'll stick. It isn't every day a cleaning lady from Flatbush Avenue gets promoted to Park. She's probably bragging her head off about "the rich folk" she works for.'

'Makes sense,' Casey agreed. 'And I'm sure that Euralia would baby-sit for you if you needed her. She's crazy about you and Abby.'

'She is? She sure does a good job of hiding it. I mean, she's always polite, but I never felt any overwhelming surge of affection.'

'And you never will from that one,' Casey laughed. 'Nevertheless, it's true. She does like you. Believe it or not, I think she even likes Jim and me. She doesn't say much, but you can tell.'

'It's worked out well, hasn't it?' Mary said. 'Remember how apprehensive you were about Euralia?'

Casey nodded. 'And if anything, she was more frightened of us. Yes, it seems to be working out okay at home. I just wish things were as easy for Jim at the office. That Weinberg mess is driving him out of his mind.'

'Which reminds me,' Mary said. 'Heard anything from lovable Gertrude since your dinner party? Lord, that seems like a hundred years ago! So much has happened so fast! If anybody had told me two weeks ago that I'd be in the middle of fixing up my own co-op, I'd have told them they were certifiable!

Anyway, what about Gertrude? Has she surfaced?'

'Not a ripple, thank God. Not even so much as a thank-you note. Not that she'd know enough to send one. I'm only grateful that she's either given up her plans to redecorate their apartment or forgotten that she asked me to help her with it.'

'Don't count on Mrs W. forgetting anything,' Mary warned. 'One of these days she'll be on the phone asking you to okay some *faux*-French furniture she's picked out. Bet you it'll be Miami-Beach-Rococo, too.'

'Bite your tongue,' Casey said. 'Don't wish that one on me. I'm a rotten wife, I guess, but I'll tell you the truth, Mary. I almost hope the agency doesn't get the Weinberg account. If they do, we're both going to have to put up with Lester and Gertrude, and I can't think of a worse fate than spending time with those awful people.'

Mary looked solemn. 'I don't know,' she said. 'I'm afraid that not getting the account would be a worse fate. From what Paul tells me, the future of the agency damned near depends on it. I think it's really serious, Casey. Much more than I thought in the beginning. At first I just had the idea that it would mean firing a few people if they didn't get the account. Not that that's a very happy idea, but it does happen all the time in the agency business. Lately, though, I get the impression that there's more riding on the Weinberg thing than just personnel. SS&A has made an enormous investment in the cost of presentations. Much more than any agency should to get a new piece of business. And from what I piece together, now there's a kind of industry prestige thing involved as well. So many good agencies are after Weinberg that the one who gets him is really going to be known as the "hot shop". Paul says if they land this one, then two or three other big accounts probably will come in automatically. Maybe even bigger accounts than Weinberg. It could be the difference between their being a nice, medium-sized agency and a giant.'

'I didn't realize that part of it,' Casey said. 'Jim just hasn't wanted to talk about it.' She looked troubled. 'If you're right – and I'm sure you are – it's more serious than I thought. Because it could also work in reverse, couldn't it? I mean, if they don't get the Weinberg account, they not only won't get other new business, but I suppose they could even lose some of the ones they have. Is that possible?'

'I'm no expert,' Mary said, 'but I should think it's very possible. Clients are really demented. When they think an agency is hitting its stride, they all want to be one of the accounts in the shop. As soon as there's a smell of failure, they're like rats deserting the sinking ship. They all want to be with "the winners" even if it doesn't make sense for their companies. Paul says that most companies never take into consideration the kind of things that a particular ad agency is good at. They think if an agency has been successful in increasing sales of an itty-bitty automobile they can do the same for a teeny-weeny lipstick. And it ain't always so. Anyway, that's where we are. If SS&A gets the Weinberg Shoe account, you can make book on the fact that they'll probably have a refrigerator company and a famous deodorant maker begging them to take their business. And if they blow it, as you said, they may have a hard time hanging on to some of their present accounts, dumb as that rationale is.'

'I wish Jim had explained this to me,' Casey said. 'If I'd known how much was at stake, maybe I could have helped somehow. Even if it meant following up with Gertrude.'

'I'm sure he didn't want to worry you,' Mary said. 'Anyway, nothing dire has happened yet. Lester's still cogitating. And Paul says they haven't given up by a long shot. Never underestimate those fellas. Especially Tony. Would you have believed that he could have convinced my honorable husband to tell those whoppers so we could get this apartment? That's all part of the Weinberg caper, too, you know.'

'What are you talking about?'

'Didn't you know? The secret-Jewish Gordons in 6A are merely paving the way for the overtly Jewish Weinbergs who may apply for 12B. We're supposed to be the live-in prejudice smashers. The theory is that if they took one "chosen family", they'll accept another.'

Casey looked stunned. 'It's not true,' she said. 'It couldn't be. My God, Mary, you know the Weinbergs couldn't buy into this building!'

Mary shrugged. 'I'm not even sure they'd want to. But wouldn't it be a master stroke if the agency said the magic words that opened the possibility to them?'

'And if they applied and were rejected? What then?'

Mary shrugged. 'I haven't gotten that far. Not even sure that Tony or Jim has. Look, Casey, I'm sorry I brought this whole thing up. I just assumed you knew about it. Paul will kill me if he finds out I've discussed it, so don't say anything, will you?'

'Not even to Jim?'

'No, please, not even to Jim. He'll tell you himself in time, I'm sure. He probably just doesn't want to upset you. I doubt that Paul would have told me if he hadn't had to explain why we were trying to buy into this restricted building.'

'All right,' Casey said, 'I won't say anything. I promise. But it's the world's wildest scheme! How ever do they think it can work?'

'I prefer not to think about it,' Mary said. 'The possibilities are too horrendous. Either way.'

*　*　*

In his private moments of fact-finding, Jim was dubious about the Weinbergs' chances of moving into 617 Park. Yet if the agency did not come up with something just this dramatic, the account would almost certainly get away from them. And that, as Mary had accurately explained to Casey, could have repercussions far beyond the loss of a single piece of business. He'd stalled talking to Lester about the still vacant apartment as long as he possibly could. He was just postponing what he rationally knew was a long shot. Now Tony was pushing hard and Jim had run out of excuses. The Gordons were safely in possession of 6A. With that miracle so easily accomplished, Tony's confidence was greater than ever. Where once Tony had admitted it was a gamble, he was now convinced it could work.

'We've cracked the prejudice thing in your building,' he told Jim. 'There's no way they could refuse another Jewish family.'

Jim tried to make him face reality. 'Don't you believe it,' he said. 'The Gordons got in through a fluke. You keep deliberately forgetting that the building doesn't even know yet that they're Jewish! But nobody would be able to fool the board about the Weinbergs. And even when they discover that they've taken in one non-Christian family, it might really get their backs up. There's no way to predict the reaction, Tony. My feet are getting colder all the time. I'll tell Lester about the Gordons moving in, but I'll have to warn him that he might not be accepted.'

'Do you think that's wise?' Tony asked.

'Damned if I know any more what's wise. But I still know what's stupid. We've got to be realistic, Tony. Getting Lester's hopes up for nothing might do us more harm than never mentioning it to him at all. Of that I feel absolutely certain. The best I can do is provide the entree and let him take his chances, promising I'll help every way I can. He'll either appreciate it or throw me out on my ass.'

'It's your baby,' Tony said. 'Play it like you see it.'

Great, Jim thought bitterly. All of a sudden it's my baby. Which means that my personal future is at stake in this thing. If we strike out, it'll be my fault all of a sudden. And I wasn't even the one who thought of this cockeyed scheme in the first place. He remembered Tony's flip remark to the men who'd kidded him about the blonde at the Cromwells' Christmas party. 'If you want big blondes, go open your own agency,' Tony had said. This was a kind of remote parallel: if you don't want to follow the boss's orders, go open your own business. He'd talk to Lester at lunch today. They had a date at Le Mistral, a semi-chic restaurant on Fifty-second Street where a lot of agency men took clients. Maybe some of the competition would see him there with Weinberg. It might rev up the rumour that SS&A had the account buttoned up.

Lester was twenty minutes late arriving at the restaurant. Jim was slowly drinking a weak Bloody Mary. This was not a martini lunch. He needed to be clearheaded when he dangled the elusive apartment bait in front of his elusive prospective client.

'Sorry,' Lester said, heaving his bulk onto the banquette. 'Gertrude called just as I was leaving the office. Dames! She spent half an hour telling me about some fag that she thought she'd hire to redecorate our apartment. Like I cared who she gets as long as I can have at least one room that doesn't look like some queen did it. A man needs a place where he can dump cigar ashes on the rug and sit a drink down without worrying that it's going to mess up some Godamn priceless old antique.'

Jim felt the hope of reprieve. If Gertrude was going ahead with her plans to redecorate Central Park West, that could mean that she'd have no interest in Park Avenue. Jim prayed that that would be the case. If so, he'd get credit for the thought if not the deed. If the Weinbergs couldn't care less about the co-op, Gertrude would still be flattered by the idea that she could live there if she chose to.

'So Gertrude's about to redecorate?' Jim asked casually. 'She mentioned to Casey that she might. In fact, she asked Casey to help choose some of the things.'

'Yeah,' Lester said, 'Gert's been on my back about how out-of-style our place is. I finally told her "okay already, if it'll make you happy, go ahead and fix it up!" Not that I see anything wrong with it.'

Jim took a deep breath. 'Ever think about buying instead of renting?'

128

'One of these co-ops, you mean? Like yours? Could be. Like I told the doc the other night, seems to me you can pick 'em up pretty cheap. And I guess with the tax deduction it's a good deal, huh?'

'Well, it has its disadvantages, too,' Jim said. 'You do tie up a certain amount of capital in the purchase. And of course any improvement or repairs are strictly out of your own pocket instead of a landlord's.'

'Penny-ante stuff,' Lester said. 'That part wouldn't bother me. And if you could get into the right building, it might be a damned good investment. Better than tossing all that dough into rent every month with nothing to show for it. Gertrude thought your place had real class. Fact is, though, Jim, I wasn't that red-hot for it. Looked a little run-down to me. The building, I mean. But she said that was high society stuff.' He laughed. 'That's what she gets from running around with all those snooty broads. I hardly see her these days.'

Jim's stomach tightened. It was no accident that Lester had let him know that the pursuit of Gertrude continued. Nor that the competition's strategy still might work. It was now or never, he thought.

'If Gertrude liked our building so much,' he said, 'what would you think about making an offer on an apartment there? The Gordons just bought 6A, but I believe that 12B is still on the market.'

Lester looked surprised. 'Paul Gordon got in the building? I thought he was one of us.'

'If you mean is he Jewish, the answer is yes.'

'I'll be damned. I'd have bet a bundle that your building was restricted.'

'Restricted?' Jim asked innocently.

'Get off it,' Lester said. 'You know damned well what I mean. No niggers, no wops and no Hebes. Everybody knows the town's full of co-ops like that. I sure thought yours was one of them.'

Jim hesitated. 'Well, I won't deny that they're pretty stiff about okaying applications, but Paul and Mary didn't have any trouble.'

Lester seemed fascinated with this piece of sugar-coated information. 'What did his apartment go for?'

'I think they were asking a hundred. But he got it for seventy-five,' Jim said.

'What's the price tag on the other one – the 12B setup?'

'I'm not positive,' Jim hedged. 'I think they're asking a

hundred and twenty-five. It's one room bigger than the Gordons'.'

'So they'd probably grab ninety and run like thieves,' Weinberg said. 'Interesting. Maybe we ought to take a look at it. You're a big-shot there, Jim. How do we get to see it?'

Jim's momentary hopes began to disappear. Lester was almost too quick to snap at the suggestion. As though he'd been waiting for it. Jim felt the sweat at the back of his collar. The way out he'd have been relieved to find wasn't there after all. Lester was waiting now for an answer to his question.

'Actually, the building agents, Ridgely & Ryan, are supposed to show all vacant apartments,' Jim said. 'But in this case, I'm sure I can get the super to show us through.' I'd better, Jim thought. He knew that Ridgely & Ryan would stop the Weinbergs cold. One of those little flags that Sam Lazarus mentioned probably would pop up the moment they saw Gertrude and Lester. The agents would know better than to allow anybody like the Weinbergs to get as far as looking at the apartment, much less allowing them to make application for it. Jim was sure the building agents had very specific instructions from the corporation about this.

'Great!' Lester said. 'How about first thing tomorrow morning? Think you could make arrangements by then? I'd like to look at it right away, just in case. Wouldn't want to start a lot of redecorating in our apartment if we had any thought of moving.'

'I'm sure I can arrange it for tomorrow,' Jim said. 'I know it's empty. The man who owned it died a few weeks ago. He was a widower. Lived alone. There's just one thing, Lester . . .'

'What's that?'

'I don't know exactly how to put it, but there is something in what you said earlier. About the building being restricted, I mean. I hate to admit that it's so, but I have to be honest with you. Even if you applied, it wouldn't be fair not to warn you that you might be turned down by the board.'

'What the hell are you talking about? You just finished telling me that Gordon didn't have any trouble.'

'I know. But there's something I didn't tell you. He faked the answers on his application. The building has no idea that he's Jewish.'

Weinberg thought about this for a moment. Then he roared with laughter. 'Well, I'll be Godamned, that's a hot one! You mean those high and mighty neighbors of yours got a Jew in

130

their midst and don't even know it? And you probably helped, didn't you? You knew that Gordon could pass on his looks and his name. But Weinberg – that's another story! Hell, I couldn't fool anybody if I changed my name to Rockefeller and had a nose job to boot! What are you, Cromwell, some kind of a nut? Why did you bring the whole thing up in the first place? What kind of game are you playing?'

'No game, Lester,' Jim said. 'You're right. I never thought for a minute that you could fool anybody about what you are. But I didn't plan that you'd try. If you and Gertrude want that apartment, you have as much right to it as the Astors or the Whitneys. Human decency says so. The law even says so. I don't know if you can make it, but you've never run away from a fight in your life, and neither have I. I warn you that there could be a fight. And we might damned well lose it. But if you're game, I am.'

'You mean you'd go to bat against all your cronies if you had to? For Gert and me? It doesn't make sense, Cromwell. Or is this some kind of scheme to make me feel obligated to you?'

'I'll level with you, Lester,' Jim said. 'I'm not going to deny that the agency would hope you'd be grateful if we helped you get into 617 Park. But we know there's no guarantee that you'll get the place, or that we'll get your business if you do. You don't play that way. And we wouldn't expect you to. No, what I said before still goes. If you like that apartment and can afford it, you're entitled to it. But I couldn't let you think that all you had to do was walk in with your check in hand and take over.'

He could see that Weinberg was taken off-guard. Even impressed with Jim's frankness. Lester wasn't buying it all the way, but Jim knew that his forthrightness had hit the mark.

Weinberg shook his head. 'You're either the dumbest bastard I ever met, or the most honest. In either case, it seems to me you've got more to lose than I have.' He looked meaningfully at Jim. 'Personally *and* professionally, if you get what I mean.'

Jim smiled. 'Maybe I'm not so smart, but I sleep well. So what's the answer? Do you still want to look at the apartment?'

'Sure. Why not? All I can get is snubbed. And when you've come up the way I have, that's not exactly a brand new experience. Set it up for ten tomorrow. I'll try to get her ladyship out of the sack by then. And you'll have a good excuse for getting to the office late. After all, you'll be working on new business, right?'

'Hopefully,' Jim said. 'Anyway, it's a date.'

131

'I still think you got rocks in your head. In fact, I'm so sorry for you that I'll break a rule and pay for lunch. How about that?'

'They'll never believe it at the agency, but I accept.'

Chapter VIII

Contrary to what he'd told Lester, Jim didn't sleep well at all that night. At three in the morning he was still tossing and turning, punching his pillow and smoking cigarettes in the dark. In the other twin bed, Casey shared his wakefulness in silence. Finally she snapped on the bedside light and propped herself up against the headboard.

'If you're going to thrash around all night,' she said, 'you might as well talk about it.'

'About what?'

'Whatever's on your mind. It must be a hefty problem if it keeps *you* from sleeping. It's Weinberg trouble, isn't it? Jim, why didn't you tell me about this convoluted plot to get the Gordons into the building? I didn't know how the Weinbergs figured in until Mary told me. I promised her I wouldn't let on I knew. In fact, I was kind of sore that you hadn't seen fit to take me into your confidence. Why didn't you?'

'I guess I was afraid you'd think I was nuts.'

'Well, you're right there,' Casey snapped. 'Of all the wild schemes I ever heard of! I should have known there was something odd about Paul and Mary's move. I never asked how-come the Gordons made it, but I did wonder. I figured you must have done a little fancy twisting of the truth and fooled the board. But the Weinbergs! How on earth did you ever think of that?'

Jim sighed. 'Call it panic. Grasping at straws. Whatever you want. Look, Casey, I'm not copping out, but Tony can be very persuasive. When he gets all fired up with an idea, you find yourself believing that maybe it *can* work. Even when the rational part of you keeps warning that it won't. I've been through the Godamndest series of reactions on this one. First I said to myself, "Why not? The law says that discrimination is illegal, but this building will get around it somehow unless we can make them break the precedent without knowing it." That's when we decided to sneak the Gordons in.'

'That was Tony's original, brilliant idea, right?'

'Yes,' Jim said, 'but I talked myself into believing it. I even helped talk Paul into believing it.'

'And then?' Casey asked.

'Then I went into Phase II. Knowing that even if we broke the news about the Gordons, it wouldn't make a damn bit of difference as far as the Weinbergs were concerned. I knew we'd been kidding ourselves. I was desperate to do something so impossible that Lester would be eternally grateful. And at the same time I was convinced that it wouldn't work.'

Casey looked puzzled. 'But you could have backed out even then, couldn't you? Weinberg had no idea of this master stroke you'd planned.'

'Sure we could have. And that would have been the time. But once the Gordons slid through so easily, Tony was full of confidence and Paul was looking forward to letting the board know how they'd been taken. So I went into Phase III.'

'I'm afraid to hear,' Casey said wryly.

'You should be. Your husband is an unrealistic jerk. I was too chicken to tell Tony we should drop it. Even at that late date. But all I said was that I'd tell Lester about the apartment and warn him that he might be turned down. What I was secretly, stupidly, hoping was that he and Gertrude wouldn't be interested in buying here. Well, I tried that one on for size at lunch today.'

'And?'

He and Gert will be here at ten o'clock in the morning to look at 12B.'

'Swell.'

'You bet. With my luck they're going to love it. And make an offer on it. And be turned down. And then, so long Weinberg Shoe biz. Jesus, I've always known how dumb guys can be when they're running scared, but my case-history is one for the books! How could I keep trying to fool myself this way? Even Weinberg thinks I'm nuts. He said so today.'

'Did you tell him about the Gordons?'

'Sure. And he recognized in a second that one thing won't necessarily affect the other.'

'Then why is he even coming to look if he doesn't think the building will accept him?'

134

'I guess he can't believe that I'm not holding out some important piece of ammunition. I don't know what he believes. But he must assume I have something up my sleeve or I'd never let him go this far. Or else he's crazy enough to think that he might just fight the battle of the bigots and win. How the hell do I know what he thinks? I don't even know what I think any more. Except that I'm the world's champion idiot!' He gave his pillow a savage jab.

Casey came over and sat on the edge of his bed. 'Okay, idiot, you haven't been very realistic, I'll grant you that. But it isn't the end of the world. You're not the first guy who got himself all embroiled in something out of sheer desperation. That doesn't make you the all-time dummy. For Pete's sake, Jim, you're not alone in this. Tony Stewart is supposed to be a bright man. And Paul's no slouch. They went along with it the same way you did.'

'Not the same,' he said. 'They don't know this house the way I do. I'm sure they don't really believe how deeply these people feel about "undesirable tenants". No. I'm the one who should have called it off long ago. I knew better. They were working on theory, but I've seen it happen too often in this building – thumbs down on the *non*-Christian in *this* arena.'

Casey felt sorry for him. 'Look, let's stay with Phase III. The only graceful, face-saving way out of this mess is to make the Weinbergs not want the apartment. I can help. I'm sure 12B is a disaster area, and I'll come along in the morning and point out every lousy aspect. If they hate it, you get A for effort and no harm done. At least Lester will know that you tried to do something special for him. That might be enough to save the account and all's well.'

'Now don't *you* start kidding yourself,' Jim said. 'One in the family is enough. What I've got to think about is what happens if they try to buy it. I'll have to put them in touch with the estate who'll probably be so anxious to unload it that they'll take the application, the same way the Kings' lawyer did. Then what? Are you ready for that application and that interview? I'll have to be one of the references. Not that I give a damn what anybody in this building thinks about me, but when he's rejected I'll sure as hell get a busy signal whenever I try to call Lester. By comparison to the agency and me, Crawford-Thompson will look like Jesus and the apostles rolled into one.'

'If they did get as far as an interview, do you think anybody on the board would vote for them?' Casey asked.

135

'Are you kidding? What have I just been talking about? Oh, Elinor Simpson might go along. Period. Livingston would swallow his dentures and Mrs Murphy would go to church and pray for my soul. Antoinette would swoon. As for the Baroness, I've already had reports of her past anti-Semitic performances. I remember some of the stories Granddad used to tell. And she has Richard Basil in her back pocket. He'll go whichever way she does. You know,' Jim said irrelevantly, 'there's something between those two.'

'You mean like a love affair?'

'Maybe. Anyway, there's so much electricity, the room crackles.'

Casey went back to her bed. 'Try to get a little sleep. I promise you that the Weinbergs will hate 12B. By tomorrow night we'll be laughing our heads off over this. I'll put on a great performance in the morning.'

Jim buried his face in his pillow. 'And I'll nominate you for an Academy Award.' Somehow he felt better for having admitted his blunders. In a few minutes he was asleep. It was Casey who lay awake the rest of the night, worrying.

*　*　*

At ten o'clock the Cromwells were waiting in the lobby for the Weinbergs. They had borrowed the key to 12B from Mike O'Shea, deciding it was better if the super did not meet them. He was as gossipy as an old woman, and there was no point in letting him get into conversation with the prospective buyers and report on them, in advance, to anybody in the house.

The long black limousine pulled up a few minutes after the hour and the Weinbergs emerged majestically. They looked smashing. Lester's dark Chesterfield was beautifully tailored and the Black Homburg, though a little overdone, did give the impression of solid prosperity. Gertrude had learned her fashion lessons well. The famous sable-lined raincoat covered a black pants-suit by Dior, and the Mark Cross shoulder bag with its statusy MC initials gave just the right air of casual indifference. Gertrude's highly made up face had just the proper amount of 'natural look' and the streaked hair was pulled back simply and tied with a black and white Givenchy scarf. If only they never had to open their mouths, Casey thought, you could take them anywhere. Unfortunately, speech patterns were not like dress patterns. You couldn't alter them to fit the wearer.

After brief greetings, the Cromwells escorted them to 12B. Thank God it was too early for the Baroness to be stirring, Jim reflected. All they needed was her appearance from the other apartment on that floor. In all this, he had forgotten that Felicia occupied 12A. If it wasn't so terrible, it would be funny to think that the Weinbergs might be seeking occupancy right opposite the woman who would most violently oppose them.

Casey noted happily that 12B was in even worse condition than 6A had been. During Bryan Rogers' prolonged illness the place had been inhabited by a slovenly housekeeper and three shifts of uncaring nurses. In those months the apartment must have been virtually untouched. The windows were filthy and a thick layer of dust covered everything. In the kitchen the old linoleum had started to peel up off the floor, and the grimy range and refrigerator must have been at least twenty-five years old. Dusty 'portieres' hung at all the doorways and the outline of a crucifix recently removed from above Bryan Rogers' bed stood out as the one clean spot on the walls of the master bedroom. Casey was sure that Gertrude would be appalled. Only someone with great imagination could picture the place as it could look with a little simple painting and cleaning and some relatively minor repairs. And Gertrude was not a woman of vision.

'Holy cow,' she said now, 'what a dump! They got some nerve asking over a hundred grand for this place! The layout's the same as yours, Casey, but you'd sure never know it!'

Casey managed to look distressed. 'It is dreadful,' she agreed. 'I had no idea it was in such awful condition. It would cost a fortune to put it in shape.'

She chose exactly the wrong words. Anything that cost a fortune had an irresistible appeal to Gertrude Weinberg.

'Yeah,' she said thoughtfully, 'it sure would. But that's one thing Lester and I don't have to worry about, do we honey? You know, it kind of shocked me at first, but I guess you're right, Casey. If you spent enough dough on it, it might turn out to be a drop-dead place! Look at the size of these rooms, will ya? Makes our joint look like a doghouse.'

Jim and Casey exchanged nervous glances. Gertrude was getting more enthusiastic by the minute. 'Look, Lester, this room would make a swell den for you. Just the kind you always said you wanted. It's even got a fireplace you can toss your cigar butts in.' She was walking rapidly around the apartment now. 'The kitchen's a mess, that's for sure. But I've seen some terrific setups in *House & Garden*. We could rip the whole thing out and put in those new wall ovens. I've been wanting to do that anyway, but our kitchen isn't big enough. This one is.'

Lester looked dubious. 'I don't know, Gert. It's the worst mess I ever saw. Look, if you want to buy an apartment, I got no objection. Been thinking it over, and it makes sense to buy instead of rent. But not this. Why buy a broken-down place when we can afford to go into one of those big new modern buildings? Hell, if you like the neighborhood there's a co-op going up right in the next block. Why don't we take a look at that?'

'Yes,' Jim said, 'that does make sense. I'm with Casey. I had no idea that this apartment was as run-down as it is. I'd have been too embarrassed to show it to you if I'd known. I think Lester's idea is a good one. You probably could choose a new apartment from plans and have any alterations done while it's in construction.'

Their resistance only heightened Gertrude's determination. 'Who wants to buy in a new building? The walls are so thin you can hear the johns flush in the next apartment. Besides, Lester, I told you the first night we came here that this is class. Everybody I've told about Casey's apartment says it's one of the best buildings in the city. I'm surprised anything is for sale here. Even Gwen Crawford says its THE address in New York. Her husband's president of Crawford-Thompson Agency,' she explained unnecessarily to Jim.

'I know,' Jim said. 'I understand they've been very hospitable to you and Lester.'

'They're dolls,' Gertrude said. 'We've been to their apartment lots of times. But even Gwen says she'd rather live here. I bet she'd grab this in a minute if she knew about it.'

Once more, Casey tried to sound a discouraging note. 'Do you think it's big enough for you? Compared to some of those apartments on upper Fifth Avenue, this one really isn't all that spacious, you know. It's only seven rooms. Maybe you need twelve or fourteen if you and Lester really are serious about buying a co-op.'

Gertrude laughed. 'Honey, if there's one thing I've learned, it's the difference between quantity and quality. If all we wanted was space, we could take over a floor of the Hilton. No, I think it's about time the Weinbergs went in for elegance. People know we got money. I want 'em to also know we got style.' She looked appealingly at her husband. 'Buy it for me, Lester? Pretty please?'

Lester looked inquiringly at Jim.

'It's not quite that easy, Gertrude,' Jim said. 'As I explained to Lester, they go through quite a rigmarole here about accepting new owners.'

'I don't get it,' Gertrude said. 'If we got the money, who's to say we can't buy the apartment?'

'Unfortunately, the board of directors has the right to veto any sale,' Jim explained. 'And sometimes they have some pretty weird reasons for refusing to okay a new tenant.'

Gertrude looked belligerent. 'Are you trying to tell me we wouldn't pass inspection? What's the matter, we're not good enough for 'em? They think being in the shoe business is dirt or something? Or maybe I need a fancy boarding-school background to make it?'

'Hold it,' Lester interrupted. 'Jim hasn't said we can't buy the apartment. He's just said that you don't go in and pick up one of these things the way you do a diamond at Tiffany's. As I understand it, we'll have to apply, give references, all that kind of crap. Nobody says we'll be turned down. Jim's just telling us what we'll have to do.'

Somewhat mollified, Gertrude managed an apologetic smile. 'I'm sorry, Jim,' she said. 'I didn't mean to carry on so. What have we got to worry about anyway? Lester owns a big business. He's a respected member of the community. Gives all kinds of dough to charity. What could bother your high-busted board of directors?'

As Jim groped for an answer, Lester cut in.

'It's called the Jewish problem,' he said bluntly. 'Some buildings are "restricted". Like some country clubs and hotels.'

Gertrude squinted at him from beneath her fake eyelashes. 'You're just saying that, Lester, because you don't want the apartment. So what if they do have some kind of allergy to Jews? The Gordons got it, didn't they? And you're the one who told me that there's nothing money can't buy. Well, let's see you do it.'

'That's not the point,' Lester bluffed. 'Hell, if I couldn't put the fix on somebody down the line to get up in here, I'd be ashamed of myself. I can do it, all right. But who wants to? God Almighty, Gert, what's such a big deal about this building? Screw 'em. We can buy something that'll make this look like a split-level in Jackson Heights! Come on, let's get out of here.'

Gertrude didn't budge. 'This is the apartment I want,' she said.

139

'Well, you can't have it!' Lester bellowed. 'Now let's go!'

The Cromwells stood by in embarrassed silence. 'Look, Gertrude, he's right,' Jim said finally. 'Lester's always gotten anything he wanted. I'm sure he could get this apartment the same way. But his point is a good one. Why try to move into a house that's full of prejudiced people? Besides, it's not that great. The shape it's in, you'd practically have to gut it and start over. If you want to buy an apartment, I'm sure Casey would be glad to go looking with you. There are hundreds of other buildings just as good as this one. Better, even. Why don't you shop around before you make up your mind? After all, this is the first co-op you've looked at. You're liable to find half a dozen you like better.'

'No dice,' Gertrude said. 'You're a fine one to talk. Who got us over here in the first place? We didn't come running to you, chum. What's the matter, Jim?' she asked shrewdly, 'you afraid we'll get turned down and Lester'll be so mad he won't give you the account? Now you just listen to me, all of you. I like this place. It could be a knockout. And if you don't get it for us, Lester, I'll make your life so miserable that you'll have to buy the whole damned building and evict everybody in it! As for you, Mr Cromwell, let's see you put *our* money where *your* mouth is!'

She flounced out the door and rang for the elevator, leaving the three of them speechless. Lester was the first to recover.

'I guess we got that message loud and clear, didn't we? Okay, genius, what now? The little lady's made up her mind, and believe me she's not kidding. If I don't get this apartment for her, I'll never hear the end of it. Right now, the mood she's in, she wouldn't settle for the White House. And she's got a point, Cromwell. You started it. Now let's see you finish it up neat and tidy.'

'I'll do my best,' Jim said. 'Call you later.'

'I'll be waiting. But not very long.' He tipped his hat to Casey and followed his wife into the elevator.

As Jim and Casey closed the door to 12B, the door to 12A opened and a trimly dressed Baroness appeared. She greeted Jim with unusual cordiality.

'Mr Cromwell! What a pleasant surprise to see you on my floor.' She looked inquiringly at Casey.

'Uh, Baroness Von Brennerhof, may I present my wife?'

Felicia extended her hand. 'Madame, I am delighted. You are

140

as attractive as your husband. Tell me, what brings you two down here so early in the day?'

Jim hesitated. 'One of my clients is interested in buying the Rogers' apartment,' he said. 'Unfortunately, it's in dismal shape.'

'Quite,' the Baroness agreed. 'So sad. Poor man. He had nothing but servants about him for months. I'm sure the premises must be dreadfully neglected. Are your friends interested?'

'I'm not sure,' Jim lied. 'They want to think about it.'

Felicia gave a little laugh. 'We do seem to be attracting a great number of your friends, don't we? First the young Gordons and now the — what did you say their names were?'

Casey interrupted hastily. 'Please forgive us, but we must dash. Jim's expecting a call from the Coast. In fact, it was due five minutes ago, darling! You take the elevator, Baroness. It will be quicker for us to dash up the back stairs. So happy to have met you.' She grabbed Jim's hand and almost literally pulled him through the service door toward the back stairway. They ran up the two flights like frightened burglars. At the top they stopped, breathless, and simultaneously collapsed with laughter.

Jim leaned against the wall, shaking with amusement despite his anxiety.

'If I've ever seen a Keystone Cops exit, that was it!' he said. 'Nice going. You saved the day.'

'I'm sure she's still standing there with her mouth open,' Casey giggled. 'She must think I'm a maniac.'

'At least you got us out of a sticky spot. Even though it's only a temporary reprieve.'

They rang the back doorbell and Euralia let them in. She looked startled and somewhat disapproving to see them making their entrance through her kitchen.

'We're fugitives from justice, Euralia,' Jim said. 'Hide us quickly!'

The housekeeper looked blank. 'Mr Stewart telephoned while you were out,' she said. 'He'd like you to call him immediately.'

Jim nodded. 'Probably wants to know how we made out with the Weinbergs,' he said to Casey. 'Sorry you lost your Oscar.'

* * *

Through Mike O'Shea, Jim tracked down Natalie Rogers Spear, Rogers' married daughter and sole heir. It was the only way he could think of to start. There was no point in discussing this sale with Livingston or with the building agents. He'd be through as soon as he mentioned the name Weinberg. His only hope was that Mrs Spear would be so anxious to unload the apartment that she'd at least accept Lester's application. As it turned out, he was exactly right. When he phoned, she fairly oozed helpless charm.

'I just don't know about these things, Mr Cromwell,' she said, 'but I'm sure if these are friends of yours, they must be lovely people. I'm afraid, though, you'll have to call my lawyer. He's taking care of it for me. His name is Binky Coleman. He's a darling.'

'How do I get in touch with him?' Jim asked.

'Well, now, let's see. It's noon. You probably can find him at the University Club.'

'Maybe it would be better if I called him at his office,' Jim said. 'He does have an office, doesn't he?'

'Why of course he has an office,' Mrs Spear replied indignantly. 'It's Coleman & Prentiss. He's Coleman.'

'Binky Coleman? Is that who I ask for?'

She laughed. 'I see what you mean. No, he's Robert Coleman, of course. I'm just so used to saying Binky. He's a very dear old friend. Used to be a beau, in fact. But that doesn't really matter to you, does it?'

'Thanks, Mrs Spear,' Jim said. 'I'll get in touch with him.'

'His number's in the book. His office is somewhere at the end of the earth. I can't remember where.'

Five'll get you ten it's Wall Street, Jim thought. I seem to be in a rut. All I do lately is take the subway to moldy old law offices. But when he looked up Coleman & Prentiss he was relieved to find that their offices were at Forty-eighth and Park. He waited until 2.30, rang up Binky Coleman and made a date for four o'clock.

To his surprise, Coleman was a youngish, easygoing attorney, the antithesis of the supercilious Bill Beene with whom Jim and Paul Gordon had negotiated. Coleman's office was bright and airy, done in pure contemporary style. It looked more like Tony Stewart's than it did like the sober den of a rich man's lawyer. Binky immediately put Jim at ease.

'Like a drink?' he asked.

'No thanks,' Jim said. 'A little too early for me.'

'Me, too,' Binky replied, 'but to tell you the truth you look like a man who could use one.'

Jim smiled. 'That's about right. I've got a problem. Did Mrs Spear tell you what it's all about?'

Coleman looked amused. 'Natalie never knows what anything's all about, bless her little heart. But I could do a little reading between the lines. As I got it, you have a friend who wants to buy her late father's apartment. So far, so good. What's the hang-up? Is he short of cash?'

'Quite the contrary,' Jim said. 'He probably could pay for it out of his change pocket. The problem is his name's Lester Weinberg.'

'Oh,' Coleman said slowly. 'You're right. You've got a problem.' He looked searchingly at Jim. 'You seem like a bright guy, Cromwell. Surely you know the taboos in that building. Not that I approve of them, mind you. But we're both aware of the situation. What I can't figure is, knowing that, why would you try to get a Jewish friend into a situation where he could be humiliated? What are you, some kind of a champion of the underdog or a Human Rights agent in disguise?'

'Neither,' Jim said. 'I'll give it to you straight, Mr Coleman. Then you'll have to decide whether or not to accept Weinberg's offer. Incidentally, I'm sure he'll pay the asking price, even if he feels obligated to haggle a little. I only mention that in the hope of influencing your position.'

Jim told the lawyer quickly and succinctly the whole strategy, beginning with Tony's idea and ending with a description of the morning's meeting. When he got to the part about himself and Casey running up the back stairs, Binky Coleman threw back his head and shouted with laughter.

'I'd have given a lot to have seen that,' he said. 'I know the Baroness, naturally. Used to see her now and then when I was taking Natalie out. A terror, that one. Pleases me to hear of somebody getting the best of her, even for a minute.' Then he sobered. 'But the main issue is what to do about all this. I'm anxious to get rid of the apartment for Natalie. And I have no hang-ups about the religion of the buyer. I don't think Natalie has either. But we still face that board. Honestly, I think we'd both be wasting our time if we even presented them with this application. I'd do it in a minute if I thought we had a prayer of success. But why go through the motions when we both know the Weinbergs will be turned down faster than you can say Felicia Von Brennerhof?'

'It's possible we could fight it,' Jim said. 'We both know that this kind of discrimination is illegal.'

'Sure,' Binky said. 'So's a poker game in your living room. But who's going to prove you were playing for money? I really doubt that a case would stand up, even if it got that far. It's a dangerous game you're considering, Cromwell. Better think about it before you get in too deep.'

'I can't get in much deeper than I am now.'

'Let's leave it this way,' the lawyer said. 'I'll speak to Natalie and try to make her understand the ramifications. If she agrees, we'll accept Weinberg's application. Maybe you can swing it since you're on the board.'

'But you doubt it,' Jim said.

'You do have a gift for understatement. We could end up with a nasty court fight that would generate all kinds of publicity. I don't think you or your agency would want that, any more than my client would. Worst of all, prejudice is damned hard to prove. We'd probably lose even if we took it to court. I'll give you my honest, unqualified opinion. If you can't get the board's approval, I don't think you stand a chance in a legal fight. Much as I hate to lose a prospective buyer, I'd strongly recommend that you forget it.'

Jim thought about that for a moment. 'But you will accept the application if Mrs Spear agrees?'

Coleman nodded. 'In the interest of justice and money, I'll go that far. But I wish the odds were better.'

Jim rose to leave. 'I'm very grateful to you for your help,' he said. 'I'll do a little more talking with all the people involved and maybe we can come to some sensible decision.'

'Good luck. Hope you make it.'

'Me, too,' Jim said. 'But damned if I know how.'

* * *

'Do just what you said: play it straight,' Tony Stewart advised when Jim reported the latest developments. 'There's no other way. Weinberg knows the score. Even if he gets turned down, he'll have to admit that we did everything possible. After what you told me about this morning, I'm coming around to the view that he might even be glad if he can't get the apartment. Sounds like he doesn't want it anyway. I think you did right to spell it out for him, Jim. If he wants to apply and take his chances, that's up to him. At least we tried.'

Jim looked worried. 'I suppose you're right,' he said, 'but even so, Gertrude really shook him up this morning. I didn't like the way he pointed the finger at me. He was sore as hell that I'd gotten him into this in the first place. I have a terrible gut-feeling that he expects me to deliver. Or else.'

Paul Gordon who'd been silent through the conversation suddenly joined in. 'Maybe I'm crazy,' he said, 'but I have the feeling that we've gotten off the track here somewhere. If memory serves me, the whole object of sneaking the Gordons into that building was to smash a precedent. Remember me, Gordon, the non-goy guinea pig? I think I can quote you almost word for word, Tony. "If they accepted one Jew they'd have no basis for turning down others." Is that pretty close to what you said a few weeks ago?'

'Yes,' Tony said, 'I think that's about it.'

'Then I'm bewildered,' Paul went on. 'I thought the main point of getting Mary and me into 617 Park was to use us as an object lesson when the Weinberg case came up. Now it's come up. You'll excuse me if I seem a little simple-minded, but isn't this just what we anticipated? Weinberg wants in. The board has already accepted one Jew. Ergo, they have no reason to refuse a second. Right? Wrong?'

'Both,' Jim said. 'Right, originally we did think your acceptance would give us a stronger position when Weinberg applied. Wrong, the house doesn't know you're Jewish, but I don't think now that it would help to tell them.'

Paul shook his head as though to clear it. 'Wait a minute. Let me get this straight. Do you mean you're not going to tell the board that we're Jewish? Then what the hell was the whole point of the lying and cheating we went through in the first place? Jesus, I never cared about living in that building enough to go through that unless I thought it had a point. I thought I was doing something good for equality and the agency. You two made me feel obligated to do it. Now you're telling me that it was a dumb idea and meaningless? Oh, boy!'

'Simmer down,' Tony said, 'and let's get this in some kind of order. Everything you've said is right, Paul. That was the original plan. But, like Jim, now I'm not sure that it has the muscle I thought it had. Not enough, anyhow, to turn the trick for the Weinbergs.'

'Wait a minute, Tony,' Jim said. 'Let's not panic again. Maybe Paul's right. Maybe you both are. What Paul says is true. We did hope to prove something by getting him into the building. And we proved it. With no knowledge of his religion, he was easily accepted by the board. At this point we can only hope

145

that makes a case for accepting people on their own merits. We have to present the Weinberg application to the board now. And if they refuse it, then we'll tell them that they have already accepted a Jewish tenant. It's a slim chance but our only one. I guess I'm still hoping for miracles, but how can we quit now?'

'Wishful thinking, old boy,' Tony said. 'I've had second thoughts. All that the Gordons and the Weinbergs have in common is religion. I realize that now. There's a considerable difference in appearance, deportment, background, a dozen other things. Hell, if Lester showed up dressed like St Francis of Assisi they wouldn't let him live under their roof!'

'Still,' Jim said stubbornly, 'it is our only hope. I can't say I have much faith in it, but Paul's right. If we're not going to use the only weapon we have, why did we bother to get it? Maybe we were carried away, but we're committed now.'

'Amen,' Paul said. 'We've got to use it. Otherwise, it's no contest. Besides,' he said, 'this is the moment I've really been waiting for. All the time I was telling those whoppers, I kept thinking what pleasure it would be when they found out they'd been had. You're not going to deprive me of that, are you?'

Tony and Jim exchanged smiles. 'Okay, Paul,' Tony said. 'For whatever it's worth, you'll get your revenge. Jim, you'd better get to Lester and tell him that the estate probably will accept his application.'

'Will do,' Jim said. 'But not till tomorrow. For today I've had it. I am in no mood to face Lester Weinberg. Once every twenty-four hours is enough. Frequently, too much. Before we all start switching positions again, I'm going home and have a drink with Casey. Several, probably.'

*   *   *

When he let himself into 14B, Jim found that Casey was already having a drink. But not alone. Elinor Simpson was perched cheerfully in Jim's favorite chair, sipping a small glass of sherry. A comfortable blaze was crackling in the fireplace and the creamy shaded lamps gave the room a soft, warm, welcoming look. It was like stepping into another world, Jim thought gratefully. One far removed from ad agencies and law officers and stupid career problems.

'Oh dear,' Elinor said when she saw him. 'It must be late! Do forgive me for staying so long, Casey. I was having such a pleasant visit I quite forgot the time! I'm sure Jim would like to

146

relax without outsiders around. Poor men, they work so hard. The least we can do is provide them with peace and quiet when they come home, isn't it? I know dear Edgar always wanted some time to unwind when he came home from the office.'

Jim laughed. 'You'd be a failure in Women's Lib, Mrs Simpson. You're much too considerate of us male chauvinists. After all, we're exploiting you, haven't you heard? Using you as sex symbols.'

Elinor blushed. 'What nonsense,' she said. 'I haven't been a sex symbol since Lillian Russell's day!'

'Not so,' Jim said gravely. 'The word is that you're the glamour girl of 617 Park.'

Elinor was enjoying the by-play. 'As a matter of fact, that's quite true,' she said. 'I'm considering going to a publisher to see whether I should write my armoires.'

Casey broke up. 'Mrs Simpson, you're delicious!' She turned to Jim. 'Mrs Simpson has been asking whether I'd like to help her on the house committee. They're planning a lot of improvements. Like the roof garden. We've been saying how nice it would be if we could extend it to all sides of the building instead of just having that little patch of green in the middle. You know, maybe put lounge chairs up there next summer so the tenants could have a place to sunbathe.'

'Sounds like a good idea,' Jim said. 'Who's on the committee now?'

'I'm the chairman,' Elinor said. 'Or is it chairlady? Anyway, I represent the board. Then, of course, there's Rosemary Murphy. She's just wonderful..Such devotion. My goodness, I don't know what we'd do without her. She really needs help, and I'm afraid I'm very naughty about doing my full share.'

'Are there just the two of you?' Jim asked.

Elinor hesitated. 'Well, no, Mrs Basil also is a member, but she's not very well, you know. She has her bad days. Such a sad little thing.'

'If Casey wants to join the committee, I certainly have no objection,' Jim said. 'Not that I could stop her if I did! She's one of those liberated females, Mrs Simpson. Does exactly what she likes.'

'And I'd like very much to join your committee,' Casey said.

'Oh, I am pleased!' Elinor chirped. 'It's just like the board. I was so happy to see your dear husband become a member of that. It's lovely when young people are willing to take on responsibilities. So many of them don't seem to care about any-

147

thing these days. Heavens, all that smoking out of pots or whatever they call it. I can't think where it will all end.'

'You flatter us,' Jim said. 'We're practically middle-aged. In fact, after a day like today I feel that I'm a weary old man.'

'Nonsense, dear boy. Nobody's old any more. I heard a delightful thing the other day. Someone told me that when dear Ruth Gordon reached her seventy-fifth birthday her husband said that she'd never grown *old*, she'd merely grown *up*. Now wasn't that a nice thing for him to say?'

'It was a lovely thing for him to say,' Casey agreed. 'I hope Jim will be able to make the same statement about me.'

'Now I really must be going,' Elinor said. 'Thank you for the sherry, dear, and for your wonderful co-operation. You'll contribute so much to our lovely building.'

Casey saw her to the door. When she returned to the living room Jim was in his own chair. He seemed deep in thought.

'Tough day, huh?'

He nodded. 'You were there at the beginning of it. That was a French farce if I ever saw one.'

Casey began to laugh all over again. 'I swear I'll never forget the back stairs. It was priceless!'

'If you think that was funny, wait till you hear her reaction to the Weinbergs' application for the apartment opposite hers.'

'You mean they're really going to apply?'

'I'm afraid so. I haven't talked to Lester since this morning, but I think I've got the go-ahead from the Rogers estate to accept their application.' He described his meeting with Binky Coleman and the subsequent talk with Tony and Paul. 'So we're just going to tackle it head-on, I guess,' Jim said. 'When the board kicks up a fuss about the Weinbergs, we'll spring the surprise about the Gordons.'

'And when that gets you nowhere?'

'Who knows? I suppose Weinberg could sue everybody if he chose. His rejection would be illegal.'

'It's ugly,' Casey said. 'I feel sorry for Mary, too.'

'Mary? Why Mary?'

'I don't know, Jim. She's different than Paul. He'll get a kick out of thumbing his nose at the snobs in this building. But Mary really loves it here, and its bound to be unpleasant for her when the news gets out.'

'For God's sake, Casey, you're beginning to sound like a bigger WASP than any of them! What's more, I think you're underestimating Mary Gordon. You can't make me believe that she'll be ashamed when people find out she's Jewish. She was in on this from the beginning. And the whole name of the game was to outmaneuver the Establishment. Are you really trying to tell me that now she'll be upset?'

'You bet that's what I'm telling you,' Casey said. 'And you know what else? I wouldn't blame her! She went along with this game of "let's pretend" for the sake of you and that agency. Okay, she did her duty. Now she'll have to live with people who know she's an out-and-out liar!'

'And under the circumstances that's so terrible?'

'It sure isn't so pretty,' Casey said. 'It's easy enough for Paul. He goes off to work every day and never sees anybody in the house from one month to the next. But Mary's in the laundry room, and running in and out shopping, and taking Abby back and forth to school. She sees more people in one day in this building than Paul sees in a year. Isn't it conceivable to you that she could find that embarrassing?'

Jim didn't answer.

'And the worst part of it is,' Casey went on, 'that it's all so pointless. Even when you tell the board that the Gordons are Jewish, it probably isn't going to make an ounce of difference as far as the Weinbergs are concerned. You said that yourself.'

He knew she was right. But they'd come too far to turn back. 'All right, Casey, so I accept what you're saying. What would you have me do? Leave the Gordons out of it entirely? Are you *that* sure of what it would do to Mary?'

She relented. 'No, of course I'm not that sure. But you're not sure that it would help anything to unmask them, either. Jim, there must be some other way of getting the board's approval.'

'All suggestions will be gratefully received,' he said. 'I'm fresh out of ideas.'

'Maybe you could talk to some of the board members in advance,' Casey said hopefully. 'I mean, what if you tried to explain that it's *illegal* to discriminate, even if they don't think it's immoral?'

'Casey, you know I can't do that now,' Jim said wearily. 'Appealing to their so-called better natures would be ridiculous. But even if I tried to reason with the holdouts, I could only do that *after* they'd mixed the application, not *before*. Right now it would be like sending up a red alert.'

'I guess you're right,' she conceded. 'It's all so unfair! Good Lord, don't you think any of those people have something in their past they'd like to hide? What are they, paragons of virtue?

It makes my blood boil that they can sit there so smugly and decide who may and who may not live in this building. God knows I'm not in love with the Weinbergs, but I'd take 'em any day over the Baroness!'

Jim rose wearily. 'Let's knock it off for now, okay? I'm going to take a shower before dinner. And after that I don't want to do anything more mind bending than watch the boob-tube. "Ironside" is on tonight, isn't it? I wish I were as smart as Raymond Burr. He solves tougher problems than this and *he's* in a wheelchair!'

Chapter IX

Determined to put his doubts aside, Jim went through the preliminary steps of trying to get the Weinbergs into 12B. A call to Binky Coleman early the next morning established that Natalie had agreed to accept their application. The lawyer still took a jaundiced view of the whole matter. He did, however, send a messenger to Jim's office with an application for Lester to fill out. As soon as it arrived, Jim called Weinberg. There was no answer on the private wire so he dialed the company and got Weinberg's secretary.

'Hi, Becky,' he said. 'Is he there?'

'Would you believe it, it's ten-thirty and no sign of him. First time in twelve years he hasn't beaten me into the office. I can't imagine what's happened to him. Must be a lulu, whatever it is. I didn't turn on the radio this morning. Did they by any chance declare World War III?'

Jim shared her surprise. But he was more curious than alarmed. 'Probably had a barber's appointment or something he forgot to tell you about,' he said. 'When he comes in, have him give me a ring, will you? It's very important that I see . . . '

'Hold on a second,' Becky said, 'the ten o'clock scholar has just walked in. I'll put him on.'

When he came on the line, Weinberg's voice was less than cordial. 'Morning,' he said. 'What's up?'

'Becky and I thought you'd been kidnapped,' Jim said. 'Anything wrong?'

'Oh, no,' Lester said sarcastically. 'Nothing's wrong. My favorite pastime is staying up all night listening to Gertrude yell at me about that Godamn apartment. She didn't shut her big mouth until four o'clock this morning. First time in twenty-five years I've slept through the alarm. Now, what's *your* good news?'

'The lawyer for the Rogers' estate has sent over an application

151

for you to fill out. They'll accept your offer for 12B.'

'Terrific. Very big of ther....'

'Seriously, Lester, whether you know it or not, it's the first step. I mean, the owners can always refuse an offer.'

'I should be so lucky,' Weinberg growled. 'How much they asking?'

'Just what we expected. A hundred and twenty-five thousand. Cash.'

'Offer 'em a hundred.'

Jim sighed. 'Look, Lester, if you want to bargain, you'll have to do it directly. But I suggest you don't.'

'Why the hell not? Everybody knows the asking price isn't for real.' Lester paused. 'Oh, I get it,' he said. 'They're doing me a real favor just to let me apply, is that it? So I better be a good boy and not make waves about the price. Now that's cute!'

'Cute or not,' Jim said, trying not to sound annoyed, 'that's the way it is. You know what's involved here. For God's sake let's not make it any tougher than it already is.'

Lester was an irascible man and, this morning, a tired one, but he was not unreasonable.

'Okay, okay,' he said. 'I'll roll over and play dead about the price. Screw the twenty-five thousand. Gertrude will just have to get along with one less sable coat next winter. What do they want to know on the application?'

Jim explained about the background questions and the references. It was like reliving the Gordon scene, except that this time there was no point in fabricating the answers to the social or ancestral inquiries nor to the one about religion. 'Use my name as one of your personal references, if you like,' he said. 'And I'm sure you'll have no trouble coming up with a couple of other people who'll say nice things about you and Gertrude.'

'And it would help if they weren't Jews, right?'

He may be a boor, but he's not stupid, Jim thought. 'Use your own discretion,' he answered.

Lester couldn't resist one final barb. 'Well, it may not be too hard to get some nice genteel blessings,' he said. 'I'm sure Gwen Crawford would be de-lighted to do that favor for Gert. And Becky's got a drawerful of letters from protestant ad agency presidents who'd be happy to oblige.'

In spite of the childishly nasty dig, Jim couldn't even feel angry. If Lester wanted to keep threatening, well, let him. Poor bastard. In his own way he hates this as much as Paul Gordon did. He has to have some outlet for his anger. So let him take it

152

out on me. We're the ones who put him in this spot.'

'I'll have the application on your desk within thirty minutes,' Jim said. 'When it's ready, call me and I'll get it back to Coleman & Prentiss, the lawyers for the estate.'

'And then what?'

'They'll submit it to the board of 617 Park.'

Lester laughed. 'Who'll probably run for the smelling salts, huh?'

'I'm going to do everything I can to see that that doesn't happen,' Jim said quietly. 'If they refuse you, they'll take my resignation as well.'

'I don't know whether to kill you or marry you,' Lester said. 'After last night you couldn't be a bigger pain in the ass than Gert, but I wish to God you'd never started all this.'

'I know. Let's just wait and see what happens.'

As he hung up, Jim realized that none of his conversations with Weinberg even touched on advertising any more. It was clear that that decision would be made only after the housing crisis was settled.

* * *

The notice of a special board meeting in the building came as no surprise to Jim when he received it a week later. Livingston gave no agenda, but Jim was certain that the Weinberg application had been received and would be acted on in this special session.

When the group gathered in Livingston's living room, Jim noticed unhappily that the full complement was present. He had hoped that the Baroness would be in Palm Beach. Without her there might have been a faint hope of getting Basil on his side, and with Elinor Simpson's support the decision could at least have been deadlocked. Damn her, Jim thought, looking at Felicia. What's she doing here, anyhow?

'Nice to see you, Baroness,' he said civilly. 'I thought you always spent the winter in Florida.'

'I do, Mr Cromwell. In fact, I leave tomorrow. To tell you the truth, I had planned to leave yesterday, but when I received the notice of this special meeting, I thought it my duty to delay my departure.' She smiled charmingly at André. 'In fact, I telephoned our president to see whether it was important that I be here, and he assured me that it was.'

'That's quite true,' André said. 'I feel very strongly that when we are discussing the sale of an apartment, the ladies on the board are the ones to be listened to. The Baroness was gracious enough to postpone her trip so that she could participate in the meeting. We are deeply indebted to her. And to you all, of course; for responding to this rather hastily called session.'

Jim was getting bad vibrations. Not that he'd hoped for good ones, but instinct told him that it was going to be an even worse debacle than he feared.

'I suggest we keep this very informal,' André said. 'And, for reasons which shall become clear to you, may I ask that everything said here tonight be off the record as well?' Satisfied, Livingstone produced a familiar looking piece of paper.

'We are in receipt of an application for the purchase of apartment 12B,' he said. 'This unit, carrying one hundred and seventy-five shares of stock in the corporation, is currently owned by Mrs Natalie Rogers Spear, daughter of the late Bryan Rogers. Through her attorneys, Coleman & Prentiss, Mrs Spear has accepted an offer of one hundred and twenty-five thousand dollars for the apartment.' He underlined the next sentence. 'Subject, of course, to the approval of the purchaser by this board.'

Antoinette Lawrence Stone turned surprised eyes on the president. 'That's a very good price for that apartment,' she said. 'I've seen it, and I must say it is not in very good condition. Mrs Spear was clever – or perhaps fortunate – to get such a generous offer. It does make one feel encouraged about the value of one's own apartment. Not that we have any intention of selling, of course. But it's reassuring to hear that the unit commands such a high price.'

'A surprisingly high price, it seems to me,' Felicia Von Brennerhof said. 'Do tell us, dear Mr Livingston, who is willing to give Mrs Spear so very much money for that apartment?'

André cleared his throat. 'The prospective purchasers are a Mr and Mrs Lester Weinberg, currently residing at 240 Central Park West.'

An ominous silence filled the room. Again, Felicia spoke.

'Weinberg?' she repeated. 'Did I understand you correctly, Mr Livingston? Lester Weinberg?'

André nodded. 'Yes. The gentleman owns a large shoe manufacturing company, I believe.'

Felicia continued to probe. 'And this shoe salesman wishes to move from Central Park West to our building? But it is preposterous!'

'What's preposterous about it, Baroness?' Jim asked quietly.

154

Before Felicia could answer, Antoinette Stone chimed in. 'You must understand, Mr Cromwell,' she said, 'that the board is charged with a heavy responsibility. Our duty is to see that the most desirable people live in our building. This is very important if we are to keep up the value of our own apartments.'

'I still don't see what that has to do with the Weinbergs,' Jim said.

Livingston interrupted. 'I think you all should know that the applicant has given Mr Cromwell as one of his personal references.'

'Has he indeed?' Felicia said. 'That's extremely interesting. Is he a dear friend of yours, Mr Cromwell?'

'Not a dear friend, Baroness. A business acquaintance. However, my wife and I have entertained Mr and Mrs Weinberg in our home. In fact, Mrs Simpson and Dr Basil met them there one evening.'

Elinor Simpson looked flustered. 'Yes, of course. I remember now. They seemed like very nice people. Very down to earth.'

Richard Basil said nothing. Finally Felicia challenged him. 'And you, Dr Basil. Did you, too, find them "very nice people"?'

Richard almost visibly squirmed under her cold, steady stare. 'I don't wish to offend Mr Cromwell,' he said, 'but I can't honestly say that I was taken with them. Not exactly offensive, you understand. But Mrs Weinberg seemed a bit loud. And he was what one might call a diamond in the rough.'

Felicia looked at his disdainfully. Obviously, Jim thought, she expected a more forceful criticism. Still, Basil's comments could hardly be taken as a recommendation. Jim felt his indignation rising.

The Baroness casually lit a cigarette. 'I'm sure that none of us wishes to be unfair either to Mrs Spear nor to these Weinbergs,' she said. 'But on the basis of their previous residence and Dr Basil's considered judgment, I should like to recommend that Mrs Spear entertain applications from other buyers.'

'I think that's very sensible,' Antoinette said.

Jim was suddenly violently angry. 'Mr President,' he said, 'if the Baroness thought the idea of the Weinberg application was preposterous, then I can only say that this drawing-room scene we're playing is incredible! You asked us at the beginning of the meeting to keep everything off the record. Well, what I have to say can go on the record. The proposed rejection of the Weinbergs has nothing to do with their previous address nor with Dr Basil's condemnation. It is very simply that Jews are not welcome in this house. This board, with one or two exceptions, is monstrously anti-Semitic. And anyone who denies that is guilty of flagrant abuse of the truth!'

Felicia ground out her cigarette. 'I presume, Mr Cromwell, that your remarks are directed primarily at me, since I've been the only one here with enough courage to recommend the rejection of these people. Very well. I will answer you. If you wish to call it anti-Semitism, you are free to do so. I do not give it that name, but I do not deny that I am unalterably opposed to the admission of Jews into this building. Perhaps you have never seen a ghetto, Mr Cromwell, but I have. A disgusting collection of noisy, clannish, emotional people whose only aim is to spread their own greedy, conniving way of life over as much of the world as they can. Are these the kind of people you want as fellow tenants, Mr Cromwell?'

'Even if I agreed with your overly dramatic picture of Jews, which I do not, I would hardly say that the admission of the Weinbergs would transform 617 into a ghetto, Baroness!'

'Would you not, Mr Cromwell? Well, let me tell you something, sir. You are quite wrong. If this board accepts your Weinbergs you will next present us with the Levys and the Cohens and the Greensteins. A charming and desirable building will become a beehive of noisy activities. I have seen those people in Germany, Mr Cromwell. Their huge families, their endless holidays, their vulgar wedding receptions and Bar Mitzvas. Overdressed women. Cigar-smoking men. Precocious, flamboyant children. Perhaps you are willing to live in such an atmosphere, but I am not!'

Jim was stunned. He had expected resistance, but he was not prepared for this fanatical outburst. Before he could reply, Livingston spoke.

'Please, ladies and gentlemen, let us try to keep our tempers,' he said. 'I would like to hear from some of the other members of the board. Mrs Murphy, have you an opinion?'

The old lady raised her head proudly. 'Mr Livingston, I'm ancient enough to remember the days when Irish Catholics couldn't live in certain parts of this city. When they were unable to get decent jobs. When they were treated like the dirt in which they grew their potatoes in the old country. I remember my own father being called "shanty Irish" and "pig in the parlor Irish". Of course,' she said with a twinkle, 'that was before he became quite rich. After that, we were known as "lace curtain Irish". Now it's true that I don't like certain kinds of people. I have my prejudices, too. I'm against rowdy people. And immoral people. Vulgarians of any kind. And I'd vote against having them in this building. But it seems to me that all we know about Mr and Mrs Weinberg is that their religion is different than ours. Well, sir, mine is different than yours, but we get along, don't we?'

My God, Jim thought, she's going along with me. I can't believe it. Then, as quickly as his spirits were raised, they were dampened.

'I must say, however,' she continued, 'that though I don't feel as strongly either way as the Baroness or Mr Cromwell, I don't think we should be hasty about this. Can't say I'm for the Weinbergs or against them. Never met them. I believe they're at least entitled to an interview. If we meet them and find them objectionable, that's time enough for a rejection.'

'Mrs Stone?' Livingston asked.

Antoinette was just as much against the Weinbergs as Felicia was, but she tried to preserve the appearance of gentility at all cost. When she answered, her voice was mild, even conciliatory.

'I do have to agree with the Baroness. I'm dubious about these applicants, but for a different reason. I don't think they'd be happy here. They appear to be from a different world, and I'm sure they'd find the adjustment terribly difficult. Besides, the West Side is lovely. Every time I go to Lincoln Center I think how charming it would be to have one of those old apartments overlooking Central Park. I'm sure, Mr Cromwell, that your friends would be foolish to give up what they have and move into strange surroundings.'

Mr Livingston turned to Elinor. 'Mrs Simpson? Your feelings?'

'I think Mrs Murphy made very good sense,' Elinor said. 'My gracious, how can you reject people you've never met? It just wouldn't be fair. I vote that the Weinbergs be invited for an interview.'

'What about you, Dr Basil?' André asked. 'A professional opinion might be helpful to us.'

Richard looked very serious. 'I could hardly give a professional opinion of the Weinbergs based on one social evening,' he said. 'However, at the risk of generalizing, I feel duty-bound to say that I treat many patients of the Jewish persuasion. Over-all, they are indeed inclined to be highly emotional, even volatile as a group. And they are, as everyone knows, extremely clannish. In fairness, history has forced them to become so. Yet it is un-

157

deniable that they cling together, preferring their own people, even resisting intermarriage. On the whole, while I certainly have no anti-Semitic feelings, I am inclined to think that we might do well to discourage the beginnings of a sect within the building.'

Why you bloody quack! Jim thought. What a bunch of hogwash! How intellectual out-and-out bigotry can be made to sound when it's mouthed by a professional man. Jim still had his two trump cards: The anti-discrimination laws and the Gordons. But something told him that it was not yet time to play them.

'So,' Livingston said, 'let me now see where we stand. Mr Cromwell, Mrs Simpson and Mrs Murphy are in favor of granting the Weinbergs an interview. Baroness Von Brennerhof, Mrs Stone and Dr Basil think an immediate refusal is in order. Under our by-laws, as president I must cast the tie-breaking vote.'

Jim held his breath.

'I feel that these are, in all likelihood, not desirable owners. However, we would be remiss in our duty to them, to the Rogers' estate and even to half of our board if we did not extend the courtesy of an interview. Therefore, I shall vote in favor of an appearance by Mr and Mrs Weinberg before this board on, shall we say, next Wednesday evening at this same hour?'

'But what about my departure for Florida?' Felicia protested. 'Really, Mr Livingston, this is most inconvenient and, if you'll forgive me, a stupid waste of time. We all know that the final answer will be against these people. It is most inconsiderate of you to ask me to stay another week just for a pointless interview.'

'We could try to manage without you,' Jim said pointedly.

'You'd like that, wouldn't you, Mr Cromwell?'

Jim merely smiled.

'You do bring up a question, Baroness,' André said. 'I'm sure the board hates to inconvenience you further. Perhaps we could arrange the interview sooner. Could you all make it in three days' time instead?'

Jim hated the idea. He'd hoped for a little more time to rehearse the Weinbergs, but maybe it was just as well not to prolong the inevitable. He nodded along with the others.

'Jim, I wonder whether we might impose on you to get Mr and Mrs Weinberg here on Friday evening? Do you think that's possible?'

'I'm sure it will be.'

'Good,' Livingston said. 'I hope you will bear with us a few more days, Baroness.'

Felicia shrugged. 'I seem to have very little choice. I will be here on Friday, but I wonder if the Weinbergs will. After all, that should be their night in Temple, shouldn't it?'

In spite of his anxiety, Jim had to smile. He knew that Lester and Gertrude hadn't set foot in church since they were children.

'I'm sure the Lord will forgive them,' he said gravely. 'After all, they are His Chosen People.'

*   *   *

It was not the fact of Felicia's opposition that surprised Jim. He had anticipated that, but he was unprepared for the bare-fanged vehemence of it. The Baroness' temper was no secret to anyone who'd ever gotten within close range. But her violent outburst against Jews combined with her German background was enough to give even an insensitive observer food for thought. Then there was her domination of Richard Basil. With every encounter Jim became more convinced that a strong bond existed between these two. Maybe, as Casey had suggested, it was a love affair. With Basil's predilection for extra-marital activity, it was easily possible that he and Felicia were, or at some point had been, involved. In any case, her control of Richard was obvious.

His first act the next morning was to call Lester and confirm the Friday evening interview. Weinberg sounded unhappy.

'What'll they ask us?' he wanted to know.

'They'll be polite,' Jim said, 'but I have to warn you that it will be tough going. I won't kid you, Lester, the board is split about the decision. We have a couple of fanatics who are highly Aryan-oriented. I'm afraid they'll try their damnedest to keep you out.'

'Any of them on the take?' Lester asked. 'It'd be worth a couple of thousand to change their minds.'

Jim was amused by the idea of the Baroness being offered a bribe. Wouldn't she love that, he thought. It would be the perfect piece of damaging evidence.

'No way,' he said. 'These aren't the kind of people you can buy off, unfortunately. We'll just have to play it by ear. The best thing you and Gertrude can do is be yourselves. Nice and easy and relaxed.'

'Meaning we should keep our big mouths shut as much as possible, right?'

'Well,' Jim said diplomatically, 'if I were you I'd let them do most of the talking. Just answer their questions briefly. Be friendly but not overanxious. After all, you don't have to justify anything.'

Lester snorted. 'Except our existence.'

Jim felt sorry for him. 'Stop that,' he said. 'Hell, you could buy and sell the whole crowd!'

'Okay. Anything else?'

'Just a couple of other things. Your allies are Mrs Simpson and me. Mrs Murphy and Mr Livingston are uncommitted. The rest are pretty much in favor of the blackball.'

'Sounds like lousy odds,' Lester said.

'I told you they weren't great. But you've won on long shots before, haven't you? And one more thing, Lester . . .'

'Yeah?'

'Tell Gertrude to play it very conservative. A little black dress. Not much jewelry. You know.'

Lester merely grunted and hung up. Jim knew that Weinberg thought he was being patronized. And Jim felt ashamed of himself. Because no matter how you looked at it, Weinberg was right.

During the morning his mind kept returning to the Baroness. The Mystery Woman. According to Casey, who got all the gossip from Rosemary, nobody really knew much about Felicia's background. The conflicting rumors about her life before she came to 617 Park persisted after all these years, unverified and intriguing. Did she, as gossip had it, flee from the Nazis? Was she one of them who got out in time? Had there ever been a Baron? Where did she get all her money and jewels? How did she travel so extensively, live so luxuriously with no visible means of support? Intrigued for no reason that he really could explain, Jim wandered down to the office of Joe Kauffman, vice president of SS&A's International Division. The agency had twenty-five small offices overseas, and Kauffman was in charge of all of them, including the one in Berlin.

When Jim arrived, Joe was dictating in fluent Spanish. He waved Jim to a chair and finished his letter. Then he dismissed his secretary and gave Jim his full attention.

'Morning,' he said. 'Something I can do for you?'

'I've got a funny request, Joe. Is there any way we can do a quiet check on a lady who claims to be a Baroness and a German refugee?'

'Depends,' Kauffman said. 'This is an advertising agency, not the CIA. Who's the lady?'

'Her name's Felicia Von Brennerhof. Baroness Von Brennerhof. She's been living in this country since, I'd guess, around 1943. Nobody has a very clear picture of how she got here in the middle of the war or what the circumstances of her departure were. Is there any way we can find out, maybe through the Berlin office?'

Joe considered the problem. 'This have something to do with the agency?'

'No. It's strictly personal. Wait a minute, I guess you could say it has to do with the agency. We're trying to help one of our prospective clients buy an apartment in my building. It would be a big feather in our cap if we could get it for him. And the Baroness is probably going to block it because she hates Jews.'

'Oh, the Weinberg thing,' Kauffman said. 'I heard about that at the water cooler.'

'You don't miss much, do you?'

'Listen, friend, when you're wheeling and dealing in twenty-five countries you get in the habit of filing away every piece of information that comes your way. Besides, you've been in the agency business long enough to know that there are no secrets. Hell, you can find out more in the men's room than you can at a stockholders meeting.'

Jim smiled. It was unquestionably true. He never ceased to be aghast at how quickly news traveled through the agency. As with all big companies, the grapevine was well to think that half of the place didn't know about the Weinberg problem.

'As for checking on your Baroness,' Kaufman went on, 'that might not be so easy. If she's been here going on thirty years, any records could well have been lost. Particularly any that existed in Germany during the war. I'll be glad to have the Berlin office try to run down whatever they can, Jim. But it might take some time.'

'That's the other problem. I don't have any.'

'What's your deadline?'

'Friday evening.'

Kauffman jumped out of his chair. 'Friday evening? *This* Friday evening? You gotta be off your head! This is Thursday morning, pal. Which means it's Thursday afternoon in Berlin. For Christ's sake, Jim, we couldn't run down the records of Adolf Hitler in a day and a half! Look, I'll be glad to help if I can. But your timing is ridiculous.'

Jim nodded. 'I know. You're right, of course. It was a stupid idea. Anyway, I'm just fumbling in the dark. I don't even know what I hoped to find out, or how I could use whatever information I got. Forget it, Joe. It was a dumb request. That's what comes of pushing the panic button.'

'I'll still ask the office to go to work on it if you want me to. But even if they come up with anything, it sure won't be in time. Want me to try anyhow?'

'No. It's silly. Thanks anyway, Joe.'

'Good luck on the account,' Kauffman said. 'Sorry I couldn't help. If you'd gotten to me sooner I might have been able to find out something you could have used.'

'Maybe,' Jim said. 'But it probably wouldn't have made any difference.'

He wandered back to his office disconsolately. His desk was overflowing with correspondence, reports and unanswered memos. The sight of this neglected mountain of paper work reminded him that he had spent practically every minute of the past weeks worrying about the Weinberg account. Meantime, his current clients were being sadly neglected. Bad executive procedure, Jim old boy, he told himself. While you're chasing this will o' the wisp, the money makers you already have could get away from you. Better start mending the fences that are already there. After all, he still had two other big accounts to watch over. He called each one in turn and made lunch dates for Thursday and Friday. It was not only good business; it would also help to keep his mind off of Friday evening.

* * *

While Jim was making his 'duty calls' from his office, Felicia, propped up in her quilted, king-sized bed, was also busy on the telephone. She was still seething with rage over the board meeting of the night before. She had anticipated a quick rejection of the Weinbergs, and the unexpected fence straddling of some of the members filled her with annoyance and frustration. She mentally reviewed her allies and her enemies, as she thought of them. Richard was no problem, of course. He would go along with anything she demanded. Cromwell, on the other hand, was completely hopeless. A born troublemaker. One of those young, unrealistic, so-called 'liberals'. It had been a bad mistake to take him on the board. In her own way, Elinor Simpson was just as bad, although in Felicia's opinion she was nothing more than a silly, misguided old fool. Obviously, Elinor was taken with Cromwell. She was sickeningly motherlike about him. It was highly distasteful.

So there remained the other three to be won over. Felicia was certain that in the end André Livingston would revert to his inbred conservatism and vote against the Jews. Antoinette Stone seemed to present very little problem. A flattering phone call would unquestionably insure her allegiance. The one who really worried Felicia was Eileene Murphy. Disgusting old woman. It was obscene that she was allowed to remain on the board. The woman was senile. All that nonsense about the persecution of the Irish. Felicia did not believe for a moment that Mrs Murphy would welcome the Weinbergs despite all that noble talk about discrimination against her own kind. But Eileene was ancient and unpredictable. She might be even feeble-minded enough to go along with Cromwell and Elinor Simpson. Or, Felicia suspected, wicked enough to do it just to annoy the Baroness.

In any case, Felicia consoled herself, there was nothing to worry about. Even if Mrs Murphy defected, there would still be four of them voting against the Weinbergs. She had only to make sure that Antoinette was in the right camp. She looked up the Stones' number and dialed.

Harry Stone answered. He had just finished doing the breakfast dishes, a task that made every day start on a sour note. When he had married Antoinette, he'd had no idea that she was far from rich. He thought he was about to become a luxuriously kept man. After all, when Antoinette was at her earning peak in films, taxes were virtually non-existent. He was sure that she had salted away a fortune. Unfortunately, he made an error in judgment. Antoinette had enough money to maintain the apartment and to dress herself and Harry for the endless charity balls and theatrical benefits they attended. She did not have enough money to pay servants. They had a cleaning woman twice a week. And in the absence of domestic help, Harry found that his duties as a husband and escort also included those of personal maid, chief cook-and-bottle-washer and, as now, telephone-answerer.

'Stones' residence,' he said.

'Mr Stone? Felicia Von Brennerhof here. I do hope I'm not disturbing you.'

'Not at all, Baroness. I was just going over the stock quotations. The market is worrisome these days.'

Felicia smiled to herself. Everyone knew that Harry Stone had no job, but they went along with the pretense that he

163

'dabbled in The Street'. Silly Antoinette, she thought. If she had to buy herself a husband, she might at least have found one with more finesse.

'You men are so intelligent,' Felicia sighed. 'How fortunate dear Antoinette is to have someone like you looking after her affairs. I do hope, dear Mr Stone, that you are also giving her the benefit of your rational thinking about other matters as well.'

'Other matters?'

'The board meeting last night. I presume she discussed the unpleasantness with you? So distressing. I'm sure she is as emotionally distraught as I at the thought of such unfortunate tenants.'

Harry had no idea what Felicia was talking about. Antoinette rarely discussed the board meetings with him. Her regard for his intelligence was on a par with his admiration for her charms.

'Just a minute,' he said. 'Let me get Antoinette. Nice talking with you, Baroness.'

'Lovely to talk with you, Mr Stone. We must get together when I return from Palm Beach.'

He put his hand over the mouthpiece. 'It's that crazy broad Von Brennerhof,' he said to Antoinette. 'She's carrying on about the board meeting and unfortunate tenants. What happened? Is Sammy Davis, Jr, moving into the neighborhood?'

Antoinette took the phone, waving him away impatiently.

'Good morning, Baroness. Yes, I agree. Most distressing. As I said last night, it would be extremely awkward. No, I've not changed my mind. Why should I? Of course I shall be opposed. It's the only sensible course to follow. Not at all. Nice of you to call.'

For a moment after she put down the receiver, Antoinette sat staring at it.

'What the hell was that all about?' Harry asked.

'Such an upsetting thing. A Jewish couple is trying to buy the Rogers' apartment. And they're friends of the Cromwells, which makes it doubly embarrassing.'

'So that's what's gotten Her Majesty up before noon, is it? What's the matter? She afraid you'll let 'em in and turn this sacred building into Tel-Aviv Towers?'

'It's no laughing matter,' Antoinette said. 'Not that there aren't a great many very attractive Jewish people. Heavens, the theater is full of them. I've worked with many marvelously talented members of the Hebrew faith. Even become friendly with them. But inviting that sort of thing into one's own building could be quite another matter. I'm afraid they'd feel very uncomfortable. Being the only ones, I mean.'

'Get off it, Toni,' Harry said. 'What you mean is that you'd feel very uncomfortable having to share the same elevator with Jews.'

She bristled. 'How dare you! How can you be so crude?'

'It's a crude subject. But you're going along with the Baroness, aren't you? At least, that's what I gathered from your end of the conversation. Can't blame you, I guess. Bucking the Baroness would be like running head on into a Panzer division.'

Antoinette bristled. 'I assure you that no one intimidates me. Including Felicia Von Brennerhof. No, my decision has to be based on what I think is best for all concerned. I don't think we'd be doing these people a favor letting them move in here.' She paused. 'But perhaps I have no right to make this decision for both of us. It is *our* apartment, Harry. What's your feeling?'

He shook his head. 'Oh, no you don't,' he said. 'Don't use me to justify your guilts. This isn't *our* apartment, it's *your* apartment. I just came along with the fourteenth Samba at Roseland. Damned if I'll let you make me party to your prejudices, Antoinette. Anyway, we already know how you're going to vote, don't we? Why waste time discussing it?'

'That's very unfair of you,' she protested. 'I'm only thinking of those people.'

'Like hell you are,' Harry said. 'You're doing what comes naturally – thinking of yourself. You might kid the world, but you can't sell me that Lady Bountiful act. With you, it's pure, concentrated self-preservation, nobly disguised. Keep your chin and your property values up, I always say. What do you always say?'

Antoinette turned her back on him and walked out of the room without answering. Harry began to read the *Times*. It was true that he was going over the stock quotations. Right over them to the sports page.

* * *

Satisfied with her conversation with Antoinette, Felicia toyed with the idea of calling Eileene Murphy and then abandoned it. To hell with that old fool, she thought. It's not worth my time and effort. We can win without her, now that I know Antoinette's vote is safe. Instead she dialed Richard Basil's office. It was five minutes before noon. He would have dismissed his last patient of the morning. A good time to reach him. His nurse put the doctor on as soon as Felicia announced herself.

'Can you come in for a drink tonight?' Felicia asked without preamble.

'I suppose so,' Richard said. 'Anything special on your mind?'

'If you mean romance, dear doctor, I think I'll let you wonder about that all the rest of the day. Do you find that exciting?'

'I always have. Does that make you happy?'

She was feeling frivolous, now. Pleased with herself. 'Quite happy. After all, I am getting to be a very old lady. Is it possible that I still please you?'

'As extraordinary as it seems, you are still the sexiest woman I know.'

'Dear, dear,' Felicia mocked, 'I do hope your nurse is not listening in.'

'She's gone to lunch. Shall I come to you for lunch?'

'A delicious idea, but I think cocktails are better. After all, you must have patients this afternoon. You'd have to rush. And I loathe being rushed. Come early so we can have lots of time.'

'My last appointment is four o'clock today. I'll be there by five-thirty. Can you wait?'

Felicia laughed. 'The question is, can you?'

*   *   *

Richard had known Felicia too long and too well not to suspect that she was up to something. The deliberately seductive conversation was designed to do more than set the stage for an assignation. Not that she had to work hard at rousing him. He was constantly amazed that she remained so exciting. Past sixty, the body was as perfect as it had been when he first knew her at thirty. And it still exerted the same magic over him. She was a fantastic woman in every way. She could be as soft as a kitten, as expert as a courtesan and as steely as a lion tamer. She had been all these things to Richard over the years. And she still was.

When he arrived at her apartment that afternoon his suspicions were confirmed. The 'tea-gown' – Felicia abhorred pants or even pajamas in any form – was invitingly low-cut and provocatively sheer. The scent of her perfume was everywhere. She'd worn it always, Richard remembered. Even in those long-gone days when the expensive French scent was nearly impossible to come by. It was part of her, like the famous oversize star

166

sapphire ring she was never seen without. The stage, Richard thought with amusement, was exceptionally well set. He wondered what his role was today.

Felicia made him a drink and kissed him as she handed him the glass. 'I sent Frieda to the movies,' she said. 'I cannot understand why she adores them so. She barely comprehends a word of English.'

'Maybe she understands more than you think,' Richard said.

The Baroness shrugged. 'No matter. As long as we have privacy. Are you tired, *liebhaber*? You seem very quiet.'

'I'm catching my breath,' he said. He gave a little laugh. 'You know, we didn't plan it very well when we moved into this building. Twenty years ago I didn't mind walking up four flights to see you. But these days I have a hunch that it's probably going to kill me.' His reference was to the fact that in order to avoid suspicion, Richard always got off the elevator on his own floor, the eighth, and took the back stairs to her twelfth floor apartment. How many times I've made that climb, he thought. And what a ridiculous picture it would be to an outside observer: The aging lover painfully climbing all those stairs to see his paramour, a dashing lady of sixty-plus. 'You know, there's some talk that we may have to install automatic elevators in the building,' he said. 'That's one motion I'll vote for with enthusiasm.'

Felicia frowned. 'If you do, I'll oppose you. It's a perfectly horrid idea. All those nasty little pushbuttons and no operator! It would be like living in an office building.'

'You may have to learn to accept it one day soon,' Richard said. 'We need to reduce operating expenses. The cost of everything is constantly going up – including union wages for those operators you love so much. Anyway, my love, what will you choose: automation or my first heart attack?'

'Nonsense,' Felicia said. 'You're as beautiful and virile as the first day I set eyes on you.' She caressed the back of his neck gently. 'But let's not talk about the past. I'm far more concerned about our immediate problem. Richard, dear, we must make absolutely certain that those Weinberg people do not get into this building.'

Ah, he thought. So that's the subject for today. He pretended surprise. 'The Weinbergs? Why should that concern you? It seemed pretty obvious last night that the vote will go against them. We're just going through the motions of an interview. There's no chance they'll make it.'

'I'm uneasy about it,' Felicia said. 'I called Antoinette Stone this morning and she has agreed to vote with you and me. But I won't rest until I know that André and Mrs Murphy are on our side as well.'

'For God's sake, Felicia, you know they'll never vote for the Weinbergs. Livingston wouldn't knowingly accept a Jew in this building any more than he'd take a Harlem drug pusher! He was just playing the benevolent patriarch last night. Trying to look as though he was being fair and impartial. Probably thought he had to put on an act for Cromwell. As for Eileene Murphy, I'll bet she was making the sign of the cross inside her head the whole time she was spouting off about Irish discrimination. You can't possibly take either of those two performances seriously! I know Elinor Simpson will go along with Cromwell. But that's the end of it. The vote will be five to two. Now will you relax? It seems to me you're making an awfully big thing of this.'

'That's very strange talk, coming from you,' Felicia said angrily. 'You seem to have developed a very short memory, Richard. Or have you been out of Germany so long that you've forgotten? Yes, I am indeed making a very big thing of this. If I could arrange it, I would never see or hear of the Jewish race again as long as I live. I would erase them from the world. And with them, all memories.'

Richard was quiet. 'What a curious conversation this is,' he finally said. 'What an odd reversal of roles.' He took her hand. 'All right, dear, what do you want me to do?'

'Speak to André, please. I don't think it would look very well coming from me. But I'm sure he'll talk openly to another man. All I want to know is that you're right. That he doesn't plan to let down the barriers. He'll tell you, Richard, I'm sure. And then I can put my mind at ease.'

'Why André?' Basil asked. 'Why not ask me to talk to Eileene Murphy? She seems the riskier of the two, if you happen to think either one is a risk.'

'I thought of asking you to approach her,' Felicia said, 'but I think André is a better choice. As I said, you can talk to him man-to-man. He's not a senile old fool like that woman upstairs. Besides, my dear, wouldn't you find it a bit awkward invading your wife's territory? She does seem to be very close to the Murphys, doesn't she? Their foolish sympathy for her might produce just the wrong effect. If Eileene felt it her matriarchal duty to punish you on Louise's behalf, your solicitation of her support could — what's the word — backfire.'

168

'You've thought this out very carefully, haven't you?' Richard said.

'If I did not think things out carefully, I would not be here today, my darling. Nor, probably, would you.'

Richard sighed. 'You know I'd do anything in the world for you, but I firmly believe that going to Livingston is unnecessary. It might even be dangerous. He could wonder why I'm so anxious.'

'But you will do it, won't you?'

'If it makes you happy,' he lied. 'I'll try to get to him before Friday.'

The French clock chimed six times. 'Such a lovely romantic hour,' Felicia said softly. 'What a pity to waste it.'

Wordlessly, Richard pulled her to her feet. With the familiarity born of many such encounters they went slowly into her bedroom.

Chapter X

While Felicia and Basil were behind the closed doors of 12A, the Cromwells were dressing for the theater. Jim had called Casey late in the day.

'I'm depressed as hell,' he said. 'Let's do something cheerful this evening. How'd you like to see the new musical at the Wintergarden?'

'Love it. Paul and Mary went last week and said it was a smash.'

'Okay. I'll pick up a couple of seats.'

'Do you think you can get them on such short notice?' Casey asked. '*New York* magazine says the scalpers are getting seventy-five dollars a pair. I'm sure we don't want to go for that.'

'Don't worry about it,' Jim said. 'After what I've gone through for this agency lately, they owe me an evening of relaxation. I'll put the tickets on the expense account. It's known as a fictitious evening with a non-existent client.'

'You'd be shocked if somebody else in the agency did that.'

'Not at all. My expense accounts have been too low lately anyhow. Bad precedent. Makes you hated by your co-workers. Their padded swindle-sheets look suspiciously fat by contrast. I'm only doing them a favor. It's a seven-thirty curtain, so be ready on time.'

'And you get home early enough to make it,' Casey said. 'I'll have Euralia fix a snack to hold us over and we can have supper somewhere later, okay?'

'Fine. We'll live it up. I might take you to the Copacabana like a visiting fireman and drink champagne out of your slipper.'

Casey was delighted to hear him in such a good mood. He'd been so down lately, worrying about the agency and the Weinbergs. A fun evening would be good medicine for him. Like the old days, she thought wistfully. Sometimes she was almost sorry

170

that they'd moved into 617 Park. It seemed to have changed their whole lives, and not wholly for the better. Jim had become more tense and pressured. First there'd been that thing with the Gordons getting into the building. She understood his tension better now that she knew all the subterfuge it involved. But even that hadn't seemed to work out well. These days she actually saw less of Mary than she had when her friend lived in Brooklyn. And when they were together it was as though there was a strain between them. Mary loved her apartment. But Casey kept having the feeling that she wasn't really welcome there. Perhaps, she thought, Mary's subconsciously blaming Jim for urging them to take it under false pretenses. Maybe she feels self-conscious about faking her way in. And it will be worse if Jim tells the board the truth about the Gordons. She hoped he wouldn't. But she knew that on Friday evening he'd have to use any ammunition at hand to try to force the Weinbergs' acceptance. She tried to shake off her distress. After all, the Gordons went into this thing with their eyes wide open. Nobody held a gun at their backs. Still she felt now that all of them would have taken back the events of the past few months if they could. Including the Cromwells' own move to 14B. It was a great apartment, but it made her feel old and staid and heavy with responsibility. I believe I really was happier in that dumb walk-up on Fifty-second Street, she told herself. It was like that old Joe E. Lewis gag. 'Money can't buy everything; it can't buy poverty.' What a screwball I must be, Casey thought, wanting to be 'poor' again. But we *were* happier.

Jim got home at six o'clock, triumphantly waving two seats, tenth row center.

'I'm impressed,' Casey said.

'You're supposed to be. More importantly, you're even ready! I'll hustle and change so we can have that drink and snack before we leave.'

He was knotting his tie when the doorbell rang. They looked at each other in surprise. 'Unexpected callers?' Jim said. 'There's a forbidding sign in the lobby saying "All Visitors Must Be Announced". Who could that be?'

They could hear Euralia talking at the door. The voices sounded excited, even alarmed. Curious, Jim went out to see. Rosemary Murphy was in the entrance hall. She looked frightened. When she saw Jim, a look of relief crossed her face.

'Oh, Mr Cromwell, thank heavens you're home!' she said. 'I just didn't know what to do! I think she's gone crazy, and I'm all alone with her!'

'Calm down, Miss Murphy,' Jim said. 'Who's gone crazy? What's the trouble?'

'It's Louise Basil. She came up about an hour ago. I've never seen her like this. She's a wild woman! Raging drunk and running around smashing things in our apartment. I can't control her. I've been trying for an hour and it's just getting worse. Can you help me? My mother and sister are both out for the evening and I'm terribly frightened. I'm afraid she's going to kill me. Or herself.'

'Have you tried to reach her husband?'

'Oh yes, I sneaked into my room and called, but he doesn't answer anywhere. He's left his office and he's not in his apartment. His answering service said they'd have him call as soon as he checked in but that was at least forty-five minutes ago. I hate to ask you, Mr Cromwell, but can you come over?'

'Of course,' Jim said. 'We'll both come.' Casey nodded.

As soon as they walked into 14A, they saw that Rosemary had not exaggerated. A smashed lamp lay beside an overturned table in one corner of the living room. An empty Vodka bottle had been thrown with deadly acuracy at the mirror over the fireplace and jagged bits of glass were scattered over the mantel and the hearth. Louise Basil faced them defiantly from the center of the room. She looked like a wild animal. Her hair was disheveled and the flushed face was contorted with anger. The housecoat she wore was spotted with blood. Evidently she had cut herself during her rampage. She was breathing heavily and she did, indeed, look as though she'd gone out of her mind.

Jim approached her curiously. He kept his voice low and calm. 'What's wrong, Mrs Basil? Are you ill? Can we help you?'

Louise backed away. 'Don't come near me!' she screamed. 'You come near me and I'll kill you! See?' She waved a large kitchen knife. 'I can do it. But first I'm gonna kill him.' Her voice became sly. 'He'll be here. You'll see. He knows where to come looking for me when I'm not home. And when he comes, I'll kill him.'

Jim stalled for time. He tried to sound reasonable. 'But why here, Mrs Basil? Why in Rosemary's apartment? If you want to take your husband's life, why didn't you just wait for him to come home?'

Louise laughed. 'You're a very stupid man, Mr Cromwell. All men are stupid. You don't understand. I have to have a story for the police.'

Jim kept talking quietly. 'A story for the police? What kind of a story? Look, why don't we sit down and you tell me about it.' He motioned Rosemary and Casey out of the room and they withdrew to the hall.

'I'm going to call the police,' Casey whispered to Rosemary. 'Is there a phone I can get to without her noticing?'

'In my bedroom over there,' Rosemary said. Cautiously, Casey started to cross the hall. Louise noticed her.

'Stay where you are, Mrs Casey Cromwell,' Louise called. 'I don't want anybody to move until I explain to your stupid husband what I'm going to do. You two should listen, anyway. I'm very, very proud of this plan. Been thinkin' about it a long time now . . . ' Her voice wavered.

'Now you don't really want to do it, do you?' Jim said gently. 'Please, Mrs Basil, come and sit down. I'm very interested in your plan. It must be extremely inventive.' He walked closer to her. Casey held her breath. At any moment, this poor mad woman could stick that knife right into Jim. But Louise allowed herself to be led to a chair. The fight seemed to have gone out of her. She even permitted Jim to take the knife out of her hand. 'Why don't we all have some coffee?' Jim said. 'I'm sure Rosemary would be glad to make us some.'

Louise shook her head. 'Don't want coffee. Want another drink. Want to tell you about my plan. You think I'm bad, don't you? He makes everybody think I am. But I'll show 'em. I'll show 'em who's really the bad one in this family. Bad, bad, Richard. Always been bad. Every Nazi was bad, isn't that right, Mr Cromwell? They killed millions of people, didn't they? Remember that? Richard killed a lot of people. Now I'm going to kill Richard.' She smiled slyly. Her voice dropped to a whisper. 'I'm going to tell the police that I was so afraid of him that I came up here to hide. I'll say he came looking for me, and as I was running he smashed all the furniture. I'll say I had to kill him because he was going to hurt Rosemary. I figured it out very carefully. If I kill him here, Rosemary can be a witness for me. That's why I can't do it in my own apartment. Need a witness. For the police. They'll believe Rosemary.'

Jim took her hand. 'It's all right,' he said soothingly. 'It's all right now, Mrs Basil. We'll take care of you. You don't have to stay with your husband. But you couldn't kill anyone. You know that.'

Louise laughed. 'Oh, you're wrong, Mr Cromwell. I could kill Richard. I should have done it years ago, when I first found out what he was.' She looked at Rosemary who was clutching Casey's

173

arm. 'Why don't you tell him, Rosemary?' she said. 'Tell him everything about Richard. You know it all. You're the only one who does, except me and Richard and his lying bitch of a Jewish mistress downstairs. Why don't you tell Mr Cromwell, Rosemary?' she pleaded. 'You'll have to tell it all to the police anyway. That's the way I planned it.'

Jim looked at Rosemary who stood mute and trembling in the doorway. She opened her mouth but no words came out. She was clearly in a state of shock. Casey put her arm around her, reassuringly.

'I don't think Miss Murphy is able to tell us your story,' Jim said. 'She's very concerned for you. We all are. Give me the name of your doctor and I'll call him. Then we'll see that you have a nice rest. You'll be fine tomorrow.'

His calm, kind words seemed to bring Louise back to reality. Suddenly she seemed sober and completely sane. 'No,' she said wearily, 'I don't need a doctor. I'll go home now and wait for Richard. Don't worry. You're right. I won't kill him. I should, but I won't.' She spoke to Rosemary. 'I'm sorry about this. The damage I did. I'll pay for it. You tell your mother that I'm sorry.' She looked back at Jim. 'It happens once in awhile,' she said. 'I get these terrible pains in my head and I take a few drinks to make them go away and then sometimes I can't control myself. Rosemary knows. That's when I come up here.' She looked around the room. 'But this is the worst I've ever been. I'm so terribly, terribly sorry.' She began to cry.

'You're in no condition to be alone,' Jim said. 'Take it easy for a few minutes, Mrs Basil. We're your friends. Just relax. Isn't there anything we can do for you. Something we can get you?'

She looked at him gratefully. She was calm and pathetic now. The raging creature of a few minutes earlier had disappeared. 'You're a nice man, Mr Cromwell. I'm sorry I said you were stupid. I'm sorry I said those other things, too. About Richard being a Nazi. And about his Jewish mistress.' She gave a helpless little laugh. 'They're true, of course, but who cares except me? Ancient history, that's what it is. You two were children when it all began. That's hard to believe. Makes me realize I've lived a whole lifetime with a man who never wanted me, just used me like he uses everybody. Except her. She's the only one who's ever been able to handle him.' She looked at Rosemary and Casey. 'You're lucky, both of you,' she said. 'You've got a nice husband who loves you, Mrs Cromwell. And you Rosemary, should get down on your knees every night and thank God for sparing you

174

from a degrading, disgusting marriage like mine.'

Her audience maintained an embarrassed silence. Jim and Casey were bewildered by these half-revelations. Only Rosemary understood. Sympathetically, she approached Louise. 'Now that you're yourself again, maybe it would do you good to talk about it,' she said. 'You can trust the Cromwells, dear. Perhaps they can advise you what to do.' Louise started to protest, but Rosemary stopped her 'Wait,' she said. 'Think about it. All these years you've had only one inexperienced old maid in whom to confide. I've tried to help you, Louise, but I know my limitations. My whole life has been spent in a very narrow little world. An old-fashioned one with a very strict code of morals. I have realized for a long time that you need professional help. But you've told me that Dr Basil would never permit that. So maybe God has worked in His own way tonight. Maybe He meant you to become involved with Mr and Mrs Cromwell just so you could tell your story to people who understand such things. Tell them about your life, Louise. Rid yourself of the burden. Maybe what you need is to purge yourself. Make a confession. It will help.'

Jim was amazed by Rosemary's almost clinical approach. He would never have dreamed that she had such insight. And he was admittedly curious about Louise's references to her husband and the 'Jewish bitch downstairs'. Yet a basic sense of decency made him try to squelch Rosemary's suggestion. Whatever Louise's story was, it wasn't right for her to reveal it to strangers. Especially in this highly charged atmosphere. With the best intentions in the world, Rosemary was putting her friend into a dangerous position. Louise might also, Jim sensed, be giving him and Casey more information than it would be comfortable for them to have.

'I'm not sure that Mrs Basil should do that,' he said. 'She's distraught now, and it's not the best time for her to talk. Why don't I take her home, and if some time she thinks it would help to talk things over with Casey and me, we'll be glad to listen and do anything we can. But not tonight. She's had a bad few hours. Let her think it over and decide later.'

'No,' Louise said steadily, 'Rosemary's right. I've been a hell of a burden to her. Saddling her with all my problems and swearing her to secrecy. She's entitled to get out from under. And she's right about something else. As comforting as it's been to tell her everything, she isn't equipped to help me handle it. It's been unfair and selfish of me to expect solutions from her. It's true that she had suggested psychiatric help and I'd welcome it. But

175

Richard won't stand for the idea of my going to an analyst. Afraid the word will get out among his colleagues, I suppose.

'I'd really like to tell you what this is all about,' she continued. 'Not because I want to shift the problem to you. Anyway, I don't *think* that's the reason. But you're entitled to know. You got involved in a nasty scene trying to help Rosemary and me. I think I owe you an explanation.'

Casey and Jim exchanged helpless glances. 'You don't owe us anything, Mrs Basil,' Casey said. 'We're glad we could help. And your problems really are none of our business.'

'I suppose that's true,' Louise said. 'But I'd appreciate it if you'd listen. There's a lot in what Rosemary said. Maybe I need to get some things off my chest. Kind of clear the air. Would you mind terribly?'

'Of course not, if you're sure that's the way you want it,' Jim said.

Louise leaned back in her chair, surprisingly composed. 'It started with Richard and Felicia in Germany,' she said, 'many years before I came into the picture. In 1939, Richard was a young doctor in his late twenties. He was one of those beautiful Aryans who were the backbone of the Nazi movement. He was bright, dedicated to Hitler and he rose very fast in the Party. At one time he was the third-ranking psychiatrist on the Führer's personal medical staff. But I didn't know that until much, much later. At any rate, he had been a long-time lover of Felicia's. She's a few years older. Her real name is Rosenwald. Comes from a rich, upperclass Jewish family. There's never been a title. The Baron is fiction. As far as I know, she's never been married. She simply took the Von Brennerhof name – which she knew was a good one – and the title – which was impressive – when she finally got to the United States. But to go back, Richard and Felicia had known each other for years and had been desperately in love. Or I suppose,' Louise said ruefully, 'as much in love as two egomaniacs can ever really be. They had planned to marry as soon as Richard established a good practice. Then, of course, the Hitler thing began and Richard got very caught up in it.

'He knew he could never marry a Jewish girl, but in his own way I suppose he loved her and used his influence to protect her and her family. I think, to give him credit, *he* cared more about her family than *she* did. She hated them for being Jewish. For what they had done to her by making her one of them. Instead of feeling part of their persecution, she became more anti-

176

Semitic than Richard. She even,' Louise said slowly and disbelievingly, 'turned in her own father. Told the SS troops about his anti-Hitler activities. She tried everything to ingratiate herself with the Nazis,' Louise shuddered. 'Could I have a glass of water, please?' she asked.

'Of course,' Jim said. 'Look, Mrs Basil, do you really want to go on with this?'

Louise nodded. 'Yes, it's important for me. And maybe it's important for you, too, to know what kind of evil people there are in this world.' She took a swallow of water and continued.

'Finally, about 1943, Richard realized that he couldn't save Felicia much longer. By then millions of Jews had been exterminated and the frenzy was out of control. He managed to get her to Portugal, and as a refugee she eventually got to this country. Needless to say, she left with all the family jewelry and paintings. Enough to keep her comfortable for a lifetime. She sold some early on and still sells a diamond now and then when she needs a sizeable amount of cash.'

'What about her family?' Casey asked.

'She left her mother and sister behind. They died in a concentration camp. The same one, ironically, of which Richard was in charge at the time. But by then he didn't care. His precious Felicia was safe, and he was so deeply involved in the Nazi credo that all Jews were enemies to him.

'The plan had always been that when Germany won the war he would get permission for Felicia to rejoin him. He was confident that in a victorious Germany he could appeal to Hitler to make this exception, especially in view of Felicia's "loyal activities" on behalf of the Nazis. You see, among other things, she was busy propagandizing anti-Semitism in the States. An activity, Mr Cromwell, which, as you may have heard, has never ceased.'

Jim did not answer. But many things were coming clear to him now. Felicia's outburst about the ghettos. Basil's obvious devotion to her. It was beginning to add up.

Louise sighed. 'As we know, things did not work out as planned. At the end of the war Felicia was comfortably settled in New York, in this very building. But Richard was in danger of being found out and tried as a war criminal. That, regrettably was where a very naïve eighteen-year-old girl named Louise O'Brian came into the picture. My father was a colonel in the American Army, and we were sent to Berlin as part of the occupation forces. Things were in great turmoil in 1945. Everybody

177

was denying that they'd had anything to do with Hitler or the Nazi Party. And many of them were very convincing. Especially Dr Richard Basil. I met him, I thought by chance, in a coffee-house. And I fell madly in love with him. Of course it was all planned, but I was too inexperienced to know that. He told me that he had worked for the underground all through the war, that he had helped Jews to escape Germany and that he'd had to pretend sympathy for the Nazis in order to survive.

'I was, as they say in cheap novels, "blinded by love". I believed him and when he asked me to marry him I accepted. My father hit the roof, of course. But Richard and I got to Switzerland and were married. As the husband of an American citizen he was able to get to this country. And as the son-in-law of an American Army officer, my father saw to it that his record was discreetly lost. We came here and soon after bought this apartment. Richard passed his examinations and set up his medical practice. I was a year before I knew about him and Felicia. When I found out, he told me the whole story. Everything. And laughed in my face.'

'Why didn't you divorce him?' Casey asked softly.

'I'm a Catholic, Mrs Cromwell,' Louise said. 'Even if I'm not a very good one. I had my religion and I had my pride. I couldn't admit to my father that I'd been such a fool. Or that all the dangerous, illegal things he did for us were not worth the risks he took.'

Another piece of the jigsaw clicked into place in Jim's head. The religious bond explained Louise's attraction to Rosemary and, more importantly, explained why Mrs Murphy put up with her constant, troublesome visitor. Talk about the clannishness of Jews, Jim thought. Is there any group more self-protective than Catholics?

'It's still going on,' Louise said. 'The affair with Felicia. They're tied together by their secret. Sometimes I almost think that Richard would like to break it off, but he's afraid she'd destroy him. After all, she's the only one who knows about his background. Except me. He knows that I'd be too ashamed to give him away and let the world know what a gullible fool I was. And even though my father's dead now, I still have an obligation to protect his reputation. So I drink. And sometimes, like today, I think I go a little mad. I know I can't fight Richard, so I think about silencing him. Forever.'

Casey came over and put her arms around Louise. 'You know, Mrs Basil, I don't think you're afraid to expose him because of

178

your own pride or your father's reputation. I think in spite of everything you still love him.'

'You're wrong, Mrs Cromwell,' Louise said. 'How can you love a man who doesn't love you? Who's told you he only married you to save his skin and be near the woman he really loves? He's with her right now, you know. Just two floors below us. As he's been nearly every day for almost twenty-five years. There's a love affair all right, Mrs Cromwell. But it's not mine.'

'Sorry,' Casey said. 'But I don't believe you. I mean I don't believe that you don't love him. You could ruin him if you wanted to. After all, as you said, it's ancient history. It couldn't matter to you or your father now. But you won't use it. Doesn't that say anything to you?'

Louise smiled. 'Yes. It says that I'm the biggest damn fool that ever lived.'

Jim cleared his throat nervously. 'This may be an inappropriate question, Mrs Basil, but if the doctor is so sure that you won't give him away, why hasn't he divorced you and married the Baroness – or whatever she is?'

'He can't take that chance. He can't really be sure that in some drunken rage or in some sober moment of contrition, like this, I won't tell the world what he was. And that would finish him as a doctor. No.' Louise said, 'we three live in an eternal triangle. As you can see, it is slowly killing me. Funny. It doesn't seem to trouble the other two. Perhaps it's their European background. The idea that a mistress is a perfectly acceptable, even an expected, thing. I've never learned to live with that. And I don't suppose I ever will. Someday I probably will kill Richard. Or myself. Or both of us. Someday there won't be any nice, sympathetic people around to stop me. Anyway, I am grateful that you let me talk. Rosemary was right. I needed to tell someone. And I just know, instinctively, that everything I've said will never leave this room. I think I knew that when I began to talk. I am right, am I not?'

'Of course,' Jim said. 'You can count on it. But I do think you should follow Rosemary's advice and see a psychiatrist before the awful things you predict really do happen.'

'Maybe,' Louise conceded. 'Rosemary keeps trying to get me to go to Confession. Maybe I should. Apparently I need to talk. God knows I have little enough chance at home.' Once again she stood up. 'Rosemary, I don't know how you'll explain this to your mother. Probably a variation of the truth is the only way.

179

She knows how drunk I get. Tell her I smashed up the place, but I'll pay for it. No need to tell her the rest. About the knife and the Cromwells and all.'

'No need at all, dear,' Rosemary assured her. 'Are you quite certain you're all right? Shouldn't one of us take you home?'

'I'm fine,' Louise said. 'And thank you. All of you.'

The other three stood quietly until they heard the elevator come and go. Rosemary looked distractedly around the room.

'Let me help you clean up a little,' Casey offered.

'No, no,' Rosemary said. 'I'll do what I can before Mother comes home. I've taken enough of your time, but I am so very grateful. I don't know what I would have done if you hadn't been here, both of you. Poor soul. I don't know what will become of her. It's all so sad.' She began to carefully pick up pieces of glass. 'Well, I suppose the Lord will provide.'

'He'd better,' Jim said to Casey when they were back in their own apartment, 'or 617 Park will wake up one morning and read about an axe murder on the front page of the *Daily News*.' He glanced at his watch. 'Well, unless you want to catch the second act of that show, we might just as well forget our big evening at the theater. It's eight-thirty.'

'Who needs theater?' Casey asked. 'Tennessee Williams would have a hard time topping that script we just heard. Jim, do you think it's true? Or do you suppose she's stark, raving mad?'

'I'm afraid I believe her. It's too far out for anybody like Louise Basil to invent. Explains a lot of things, too. My God, what I could do with that information! All I'd have to do is hint to Basil and Felicia about what I knew, and the Weinbergs would be in like their name was Flynn!'

Casey was horrified. 'Jim, you wouldn't! We promised!'

'What kind of rat do you think I am? Of course I wouldn't. But you have to admit that it's some temptation. I could solve all my problems just like that.' He snapped his fingers.

'Yes, you could,' Casey agreed. 'But you'd have a bigger problem.'

'What's that?'

'Alimony. Who needs a squealer for a husband?'

He pretended to think it over. 'I guess you're right. I can't afford to support two households, so we'd better stay married. But come to think of it, if I don't get the Weinberg account I may not even be able to afford one. Does that make a difference?'

'I'd rather live in a Central Park tree with an honest bird than share a gilded cage with a stool pigeon,' Casey said. 'Your lips are sealed, and don't you forget it.'

'Yes, ma'am,' he said meekly. 'My lips are sealed.'

*   *   *

On the Friday that the Weinbergs were to be interviewed by the board, Al Shriber's advertising column in the *Times* carried another small, disquieting paragraph. Mary Gordon read it as Paul was dressing to go to the office.

'Did you see the item in Shriber's column this morning?' she asked.

'No. Haven't seen the paper. What does he say?'

' "Shoe Company Still Foot-loose." That's the heading. "Reports that Weinberg Shoe has chosen a new agency were denied today by Lester Weinberg. The company did confirm, however, that its choice had narrowed to two Madison Avenue biggies. Insiders are wondering whether Tony Stewart or Mike Crawford is the Cinderella in this slipper-y situation." '

'Godamn bastards,' Paul muttered.

'Who? Weinberg, Tony or Mike Crawford?'

'All of them,' Paul said. 'All I wish is that the suspense would end. One way or another.'

'It probably will tonight,' Mary assured him. 'The Weinbergs come up for their examination by the board.'

Paul didn't answer.

Mary hesitated. 'Does Jim plan to tell the board about us? To help get the Weinbergs in, I mean?'

'Damned if I know if he does or he doesn't,' Paul said. 'I thought that was the whole purpose of sneaking up past the board. But the last conversation we had sounded like Tony and Jim now have serious doubts as to whether it would even help to let them know they already have Jews in residence. Why? Would you mind if he did?'

'No, not really, I guess.'

'You don't sound very positive. What's happened to you all of a sudden? You never cared before whether people knew we were Jewish. How come you're so touchy about it now?'

'I still don't care. For us,' Mary said. 'I'm just thinking about Abby. I'd kill the first so-and-so in this building who made a crack to her.'

Paul sighed. 'Now who'd do that? The elevator men? You're being silly. Nobody's going to say anything to that child. Even

181

if they wanted to, they wouldn't have a chance. She never goes in or out alone. You're always with her.'

'I know. I'm making a noise like a mother tiger. It's just that I hope we haven't done something that will bounce back and hurt her.'

'It's a great time to think about that,' Paul said.

'I thought about it before, but it seemed so important for us to buy in that I tucked it into the back of my mind. Now that it's a possibility it scares me.'

He gave her a penetrating look. 'Is Abby the real reason you're worried about the exposé? Or are you afraid that life will be so unbearable here that we'll have to move?'

'It's the real reason,' Mary said. 'Honest to God. I'm not married to this apartment. There are plenty of others just as good. I won't deny that I prefer Manhattan to Brooklyn. But since we've made that break I could pick myself up and move to another address. I just won't have my kid picked on. You can count on that.'

He smiled. 'Baby tigers have fathers, too, you know. If there's the first sign that Abby's being hurt, away we go. Okay?'

'Of course. As if I didn't know.' She kissed him. 'And speaking of away we go, it's almost ten o'clock. You don't want dear Lester to call and not find you in the office, do you?'

'He'll never call today. He's probably home rehearsing his lines for tonight.'

'A lot of good that will do him,' Mary said. 'If I ever saw a show that was destined to close in New Haven, this is it.'

* * *

The Weinberg interview was not as bad as Jim had feared. It was worse. From the moment Lester and Gertrude walked into Livingston's apartment, the smell of disaster was more overpowering than Gertrude's perfume. For one thing, they had chosen to ignore Jim's advice about dress. Incredibly, they were in full evening clothes at six o'clock in the evening. Lester even had a boutonniere. After the introductions, there was a pregnant pause. The board members stared at the Weinbergs who feigned nonchalance. Finally, Jim decided it was up to him to break the ice.

'Perhaps we should get on with this, Mr President,' he said. 'Obviously, Mr and Mrs Weinberg are going on somewhere after the meeting. And I'm sure the board members have engagements as well.'

Lester waved his hand expansively. 'Don't worry about us,' he said. 'Take your time. We're in no rush. Just thought I'd take Gert to dinner at "21". Those captains get plenty from me. They'll hold the table till we get there.' He smiled confidently. 'We thought we ought to celebrate. It's a big night.'

'Celebrate?' the Baroness asked. She looked pointedly at Gertrude's low-cut gown. 'It must be a very festive occasion. May I ask what you're celebrating?'

'Well now, Mrs Von Brennerhof,' Lester said, 'didn't you celebrate when you bought your apartment? I admit maybe it's a little premature until you give us the nod. But the way I look at it, we're here. Right? So you must be interested in us. Heck, everybody knows that these interviews are just to get acquainted. I do the same thing when one of my people at the office hires somebody to work for him. It's a matter of courtesy to say how-do and welcome him to the group.'

Jim winced. So this was how Lester had decided to play it. All confidence and bravado, as though the deal was signed, sealed and delivered. Jim didn't know what else he expected. Lester coming on low-key in any situation just wasn't in the cards.

Livingston politely cleared his throat. 'I'm afraid it's not quite the same thing, Mr Weinberg. We take our interviews very seriously. You are quite right. We have, of course, studied your application and find your financial rating more than adequate. However, there is more to buying a co-operative apartment than cold facts and figures. We are like a family here. We want to make certain that all the members are congenial. You see, we'd like to feel as certain as possible that you'd be as happy with us as we'd be with you. That is the true purpose of this meeting.'

Lester looked impressed. 'Is that a fact?' he said. 'We never heard that from other people who bought apartments. Always thought it was a matter of routine. My friend, Jim Cromwell, tells me he never had an interview at all.'

'That was a bit different,' André said stiffly. 'Mr Cromwell inherited his apartment. His grandparents lived here for many years. Besides, sir, most of us knew him, at least by sight.'

'Okay,' Lester said jovially. 'Now you know us by sight. What can we tell you?'

Elinor Simpson spoke up timidly. 'We'd like to know a little about your interests, Mr Weinberg. Yours and your charming wife's. Do you have hobbies?'

Lester laughed. 'Sure. Mine's making money and Gertrude's is spending it.' He waited for the appreciative chuckle which did not come. Suddenly his voice became serious. 'I don't have a hobby, Mrs Simpson. Hobbies are for when a man retires and takes up stamp collecting or those whatcha-call-it high-priced books – first editions. I'm not ready to kid around with that kind of thing. I've got a business to run.'

Elinor smiled. 'And a very nice business it is, Mr Weinberg. I've bought a great deal of your footwear over the years. It's excellent quality.'

'Nothing but the best,' Lester beamed. 'Let me know next time you need shoes. I'll get 'em for you wholesale.'

'I have a hobby,' Gertrude volunteered suddenly. 'I've been doing some work with The Girls Club of New York. My friend, Gwen Crawford, got me interested. She's Mrs Michael Crawford. Her husband owns one of the biggest advertising agencies, Crawford-Thompson.'

'The Girls Club?' Elinor repeated. 'Oh, my dear, that's very worthwhile. They're dedicated to helping underprivileged girls, aren't they? What do you do – help out selling things in their Thrift Shop? Or do you actually teach those poor unfortunate little things how to cook and sew?'

'I haven't done any of that,' Gertrude said. 'But I do send them all my discarded clothes to sell in the shop. Lester gets a big tax deduction for it, too. It's called a charitable contribution.'

'Perhaps you belong to other organizations,' Antoinette Stone suggested coldly. 'A garden club, possibly? Or The Junior League?'

Gertrude shook her head. 'The only garden I could work in would be Central Park. We don't even have a terrace. Not that I'd want one. They're terrible. Track all kinds of dirt into the house every time somebody goes out on it. As for that other thing, The Junior League, I guess you have to be a society girl to belong to that, don't you? Anyway, Mrs Stone, I'm just too busy. Being married to Lester is a full-time job. He's so fussy. Always wants me to look just right. Do you know I have to go to Kenneth every single day? Between that and lunch and maybe playing a little canasta, I just don't know where the time goes. And I'm a very particular housekeeper. Lord, the help you get these days! These colored girls think they're as good as you are! Seems like I have to fire one every week.' She turned to the Baroness. 'You have that trouble, too?'

Felicia smiled. It was not a pleasant smile. 'Fortunately, no,' she said. 'My housekeeper has been with me for years.'

Gertrude nodded. 'That's the only answer. I'm going to do that, too. Get a white live-in. Maybe a couple, though I guess that little room isn't big enough for two even if they're married.'

Jim felt his world falling apart. The Baroness did not pursue the matter. She didn't have to. The Weinbergs were writing their rejection letter as surely as if they were dictating it themselves. Even Lester seemed to sense that the atmosphere was growing increasingly tense.

'Let's give somebody else a chance to talk, Gert,' he said. 'Seems to me these people must be interested in more important things than your household problems.'

'Quite right, Mr Weinberg,' Richard said. 'Perhaps you'd tell us a little of your background. Where you were born and educated, that kind of thing.'

Jim saw Lester stiffen. He hesitated, as though he was deciding whether or not to answer. 'Born right here in New York, Doc,' he said finally. 'I'm sure you don't know the section, but you've probably heard of it. It's called the Lower East Side. My parents were Polish immigrants, rest their souls. Arrived here without a dime. Papa never made more than twenty-five bucks a week in his whole life. Funny,' Lester went on, 'he was a shoe salesman in a store on Houston Street. He was so proud that his Lester grew up to own a whole damned shoe business. Thank God he lived to see it. Used to say it was proof that anything could happen in this country. That everybody had a chance, no matter how low-down they started. Education? We couldn't afford that. I was pushing dress racks on Seventh Avenue when I was twelve. Fourteen hours a day for fifteen bucks a week. Yep, it's a great place, the U.S. of A. By the way, Doc, where do you come from?'

'I don't think that's germane to the question,' André interrupted. 'It is not Dr Basil who's being interviewed here, Mr Weinberg.'

'True,' Lester agreed. 'But you said something earlier about this being like a family. About how we should all be happy with each other. Congenial, I think it was. Well, how do we know we'd be happy with you if all the questions are one-sided?'

Score one for Lester, Jim thought. Not that his well-put question would serve any purpose except to further antagonize this group. Thinking of Louise's story, it was almost eerie that Lester had chosen to inquire into Basil's background. It was pure coincidence, of course. But for a moment Jim thought that Weinberg might have been doing a little investigating on his own.

Mrs Murphy used her cane to signal for attention. 'I can't help but wonder, Mr Weinberg, why you and your wife chose to apply for 12B. From all you've said, I would assume that your tastes would run to something bigger and more grand. More in keeping with your life style. Your wife has already mentioned that the servants' quarters seem quite inadequate, for one thing. And I'm sure,' she added dryly, 'that there are many buildings more convenient to Mr Kenneth's. We understand that you have offered a very high price for the unit. Does this house hold some special attraction for you?'

Lester began to look grim. 'Let me tell you something, Mrs Ryan . . .'

Jim interrupted. 'Mrs Murphy, Lester. Not Mrs Ryan.'

'Same difference,' Weinberg said. 'Anyway, Mrs Murphy, with all due respect to your age, I think you're out of line. My wife and I have seen an apartment we like. The owner is willing to sell. We can afford to buy. And for cash. Not even through one of these new co-op bank mortgages they just signed into law. Now if you think I've got some special reason for wanting in, then say so. I'm getting a little fed up with this polite third degree. We've answered your questions and some of them are pretty damned personal. You know all about my bank balance and my character. What have we left out – my latest X-rays?'

'Take it easy, Lester,' Jim said. 'I'm sure the board doesn't mean to make this sound like an inquisition. As Mr Livingston told you, all applicants are questioned like this. None of the members has any doubt of your sincere wish to live in 617. They merely want to make sure that you'll be happy here. After all, that's in your best interest, too.'

Before Lester could answer, Felicia spoke. 'I'm sure, Mr Cromwell, that the applicant realizes these questions are in the best interest of *all* the owners. Not merely the board which represents them. I have something to add, if I may.'

'Of course, Baroness,' André said.

She looked coldly at Lester. 'Mr Weinberg, I am not one to mince words. It has been my experience that a tenant is not happy in a building unless he is living among people who have shared his background and who continue to share his daily interests, his politics and, of course, his convictions. Listening to this interesting exchange, I am convinced that you would find this building neither convenient, as Mrs Murphy mentioned, nor really suitable to your needs in other ways. I think you would be making a great mistake coming into an atmosphere which is so

186

foreign to your beliefs in all areas. We would do you a great disservice to allow you to expose yourself and your wife to a world that concerns itself with teachings diametrically opposed to your own. At best, I think you would find us all quite boring.'

Jim braved himself for a roar of rage from Lester. Instead, the voice that came from the great dinner-jacketed hulk was as steely as the flat pronouncements made by the Baroness.

'I will not ask you to elaborate on those statements,' he said. 'I understand them perfectly, and I'm sure my wife does, too. But I'll tell you this. We have sat here and been patronized by damned near every one of you. You've tried to make us feel like we were asking for a handout. Begging to be taken into your private little circle. You've said that the building isn't suitable for our needs, that we wouldn't be happy living here. But you're afraid to come right out with the one thing you don't want: Jews living under your precious roof. You were scared to say that, weren't you? You had to look for other excuses. Like where I was born and what Gertrude does with her spare time. But that wouldn't have mattered if we'd been the right religion, would it? If I wore a cross instead of a Star of David, you might just manage to overlook the fact that we're not in the Social Register, wouldn't you? What did you let us come here for in the first place? You were just covering yourselves, weren't you? In case I turned out to be one of those rotten kikes who decided to make trouble, you could always plead innocence. You can always say that you gave us our interview and decided that we were "incompatible", isn't that the way it goes? Well, we'll see about that. For your information, we've got some pretty stiff laws in this state about discrimination. And they're getting stiffer.'

André Livingston interrupted. 'There's no need to be so angry. Mr Weinberg,' he said. 'The board is simply trying to do its duty with as much consideration for you as for the tenants it represents. I see no need to invoke the threat of legal action here. The board has not even had a chance to vote on the matter of your application. In forty-five years, 617 Park Avenue has been above reproach, sir. We have nothing to cover up, and I resent your implications.'

'*You* resent?' Lester's voice was louder now. 'That's really funny. You don't know what resentment is all about! Who do you think you're kidding? Everybody knows about this building and a hundred like it. Off-limits to Jews. Let one in and there goes the neighborhood! I knew all about you before I ever walked in here. But in a dumb way I thought maybe some idea of the real world was getting through to you. No chance. You're going to have to have it rammed down your throats. And I'm just the guy who can do it!'

He strode to the door, a trembling-lipped Gertrude trailing in his wake. Jim followed them, helping her into her coat. As they waited in silence for the elevator, Gertrude began to cry.

'How could you let this happen?' she asked Jim. 'You must have known what they'd be like.' She turned to Lester. 'And you. You're so smart. How could you expose us to such an awful scene?'

'For Christ's sake, Gert, I just was trying to get you what you wanted,' Lester said miserably.

'What was that? Insults? Is that what I wanted?'

Jim felt six inches high. 'I'm terribly sorry, Gertrude,' he said. She stepped into the elevator. The tears were running down her face. 'It's a little late to be sorry, isn't it?'

Jim walked slowly back into the apartment. The other board members were wordless, but their faces told the story. Eileene and Antoinette looked righteous, Felicia smugly triumphant. Richard Basil wore his usual, noncommittal mask. André seemed troubled. And Elinor Simpson was visibly upset.

'Oh, dear,' she said, 'what a dreadful scene! Those poor things. They seemed so happy and confident at the beginning. I'm afraid we hurt them terribly. Goodness, nothing like this has ever happened before. Not in all my years in the building!'

The Baroness looked angrily at Jim. 'Possibly because no one has ever tried to force people like that on us before,' she said. 'I shouldn't worry too much, Mrs Simpson. Brooding over those thick-skinned people is simply sentimental drivel. My only regret is that this entire episode was a waste of time. I hate to say "I told you so", but we all knew from the beginning that we were simply going through a pointless exercise. It was a ridiculous inconvenience.'

What an unspeakable woman you are, Jim thought. In view of what he now knew about her, the Baroness seemed more than ever a monster. He recalled Louise Basil's story in every detail. How can a Jew feel that way about other Jews, he wondered. But he could not betray Louise, not even to punish Felicia and Basil. Not even to reverse the inevitable verdict about the Weinbergs. With an effort of will, he remained silent. André Livingston seemed to be lost in thought. Finally he spoke.

'I must warn you that this situation could be more serious than perhaps you realize,' he said. 'Mr Weinberg is not only a very angry man, he is also a rich and powerful one. He could make trouble.'

'What kind of trouble?' Antoinette Stone asked.

'There have been cases,' André answered, 'where a rejected Jewish applicant took his case to court, claiming religious bias. I don't recall anyone ever winning one, but they can be long, drawnout affairs, involving expensive legal fees and bad publicity. There is the possibility that Mr Weinberg could sue the corporation.'

Jim saw his last chance. 'Mr Livingston is quite correct,' he said. 'Mr Weinberg could sue. Not only the corporation, but each of us board members individually. What's more, nothing's to say that he might not win.'

Antoinette gasped. 'I can't believe it! Are you telling me that we have no right as building owners to reject people we don't consider suitable? What are we living in – a Communist state?'

'On the contrary, Mrs Stone, we are living in a democracy,' Jim said. 'Laws are designed to provide equal rights for every citizen. Including,' he could not help glancing at Felicia, 'Jews.'

Felicia remained unperturbed. 'I think perhaps you are trying to frighten us, Mr Cromwell,' she said. 'And I, for one, am not easily intimidated. You see, I do recall that these Weinbergs applied under your sponsorship. I am not surprised that you would go to any lengths to force us into accepting them – even an attempt to terrorize us. One ugly incident like this does not change my mind about the Weinbergs or any other like them. Why don't we dispense with this idle speculation and call for a vote?'

'Before we do that,' Jim said, 'I'd like to hear from the other members, if you have no objection, Baroness.'

Eileen Murphy answered him. 'Perhaps I should speak first,' she said, 'since I was one who was strongly in favor of an interview as the only fair way to judge the applicants. Now that I have met them, my conscience is at rest. I can say that their vulgarity, rather than their religion, is sufficient cause to refuse them.'

'In other words,' Jim persisted, 'if they'd been attractive, cultured people, you'd have voted for them in spite of their being Jews?'

Eileene nodded. 'Yes, I would. And I believe that some of the others would, too, if the Weinbergs had been well-bred, well-spoken people.'

'Do you agree with that, Mrs Stone?' Jim asked.

'Of course. We are not bigots, Mr Cromwell. What Mrs Murphy says is absolutely right.'

'Then I take it that you don't object to the fact that you already have one Jewish tenant?'

'What are you talking about?' Felicia snapped.

'The Gordons, Baroness. Paul and Mary Gordon whom you accepted for 6A. You had no idea, did you, that you were allowing Jews to live under the same roof with you? And we haven't really seen 617 Park turn into a ghetto as you predicted, have we? We've already broken our "restricted" precedent because you were tricked into it.' He turned politely to Antoinette and Eileene. 'Forgive me, ladies, but I don't believe a word of what you said a moment ago. Your prejudice had determined your decision long before you met the Weinbergs. It would have been the same with the Gordons if you'd known they were Jewish. You're charming women, but you're terrible hypocrites. How relieved you must have been when the Weinbergs turned out to be such earthy people! Because that's all they are: kind, well-meaning, self-made people who haven't had the advantages of your education or your cultural background. If you accepted the Gordons, you have no right to refuse decent people like the Weinbergs. This building already is open to Jews.'

Felicia was scarlet with anger. 'You are dispicable, Mr Cromwell,' she raged. 'How dare you be party to such a shabby trick? You encouraged the Gordons to lie, to insult us all, to make fools of this building and this board! I'm sure you fancy yourself a great liberal, a high-minded champion of the underprivileged. Well, you're a fool and a cheat! You got away with it once, but not this time!'

Richard Basil interrupted her tirade. 'Just a moment, Baroness,' he said. 'You are quite right in reproaching Mr Cromwell for his blatant dishonesty. But it changes nothing. In fact, as I see it, it is precisely the ammunition we need if Mr Weinberg is so foolish as to try to take us to court. Thanks to Mr Cromwell, we are in a perfect position to refute any charges of racial discrimination. How can we be accused of bias when we already have Jewish tenants – the Gordons – living here? Your little scheme has boomeranged, Mr Cromwell. You rather outsmarted yourself, didn't you?'

'Very discerning of you, Doctor,' André Livingston said with relief. 'Of course that's the answer! As long as we can show that we have accepted a minority family in the building we cannot lose our case. Even if Mr Weinberg decided to be unpleasant

190

about it, this is ample evidence that people are accepted or rejected on the basis of their personal qualifications, not their religion.'

Jim was stunned. Both his trump cards had failed. Backfired. The board he'd hoped to sway first with the threat of legal action and, as a last resort, with the revelation about the Gordons, had used both weapons against him. What a naïve fool I am, he thought angrily. His only consolation was Sam Lazarus' cynical reference to 'token Jews'. If Weinberg decided to sue, the Court might well decide that the Gordons were merely 'tokens'. He was sure that Lester's lawyers would recognize that fact and use it. If they let him, Jim would testify and so would Paul Gordon. Probably they could get some impressive statistics from Sam Lazarus' lists as well. By God, he thought, Weinberg still could win this. Jim dimly heard the president calling for a vote on the application.

'Those in favor of acceptance?' Livingston asked.

Elinor Simpson and Jim raised their hands.

'Opposed?'

Four other votes were cast.

'The majority of the board has ruled against this application,' André said. 'Mr and Mrs Weinberg will be so notified, as will Mrs Natalie Rogers Spear and her attorneys, Coleman & Prentiss.'

Binky Coleman will be disappointed but not surprised, Jim thought. Neither, for that matter, will Lester Weinberg.

Chapter XI

Casey was waiting anxiously when Jim came back after the disastrous board meeting. He filled her in on the results and then retired to the 'study' – the third bedroom which they had turned into a combination den and office for him.

He called Tony Stewart at home and gave him the bad news. Tony took it philosophically. 'We knew the deck was stacked,' he said. 'Don't let it throw you. You did your best. Nothing to be gained by losing any more sleep over it. We'd better start worrying about the clients we *have*. We've practically ignored them to concentrate on Lester.'

'Do you think Lester will file a complaint?'

'Probably. You'll get a reading on that when you speak to him.'

'I won't be able to reach him until tomorrow,' Jim said. 'He's taking Gertrude out to dinner. At least, that was his original plan. But she was so upset that they might have called off the evening. I could try him at home tonight.'

'I wouldn't,' Tony advised. 'Better give Lester – and yourself – a chance to cool off. Call him in the morning. Spoken to Paul?'

'No. I thought I'd speak to you first. I'll get to him now. By the way, Tony, I'm going to resign from the board.'

Stewart considered that. 'I guess that's the only thing you can do. It'll be sticky enough for you living in the house, much less having to face that group on a regular basis.'

'It isn't only that,' Jim said. 'Except for Elinor Simpson, they're a rotten bunch. I didn't want to go on that damned board in the first place. I'm glad to have a good reason to get off.'

When he and Tony hung up, Jim called Paul Gordon and repeated the story. Paul's first comment almost echoed Jim's thoughts.

'Looks like we're not cut out for the Madison Avenue match-game. From now on, we'd better leave the tricks to agencies like Crawford-Thompson. Our bag is advertising. I guess this should be a lesson to us. If we can't get an account on the basis of good work, we might as well forget it.'

'No way I can argue that,' Jim admitted. 'Seems like we blew it all the way around. Or I did, at least. You know, I had to tell them about you and Mary. And they even managed to use that against me.' He explained Basil's interpretation and Livingston's agreement. 'Sounds like they'll use you to *disprove* discrimination if Weinberg does go to court.'

'Good. Let 'em. I've never been a "token Jew" before.'

'But what about Mary? Won't she be upset?'

'Don't worry about Mary,' Paul said. 'Or anything else connected with that building. We've got bigger problems. Like finding a piece of business to replace the Weinberg billing we'd counted on. If you must have something to fret about this weekend, it'll be a helluva lot more productive to spend your time thinking about getting a big, new account. By the way, when does the jury send Lester the official verdict?'

'Livingston will write him a letter, but I plan to call him tomorrow.'

'Good luck. Thank God I decided to be a creative director. You poor account bastards really get the short end of the stick. I wouldn't want to be chewed out by Weinberg, even over the telephone.'

'Chewed out' was putting it mildly, Jim thought when the conversation ended. Lester would be in a monumental rage. And with good reason. He'd been thoroughly insulted. A man like Weinberg didn't forgive that. He'd probably never want to hear the names of Stewart, Sutton & Atherton again, much less hire them to do his advertising. Slowly Jim began to write his letter of resignation to André Livingston. That would not be a surprise either. He couched it in polite terms, merely saying that the pressure of business made it impossible to devote sufficient time to the board and offering his best wishes for the continued success of their activities. It was a polite and phony note which, he knew, would be accepted with relief. As he was finishing it, the phone rang. His first thought was that it must be Lester, but when he picked it up he was surprised to hear the voice of Elinor Simpson.

'Oh, dear,' she said, 'I'm so terribly sorry, Mr Cromwell. You must be dreadfully upset. And your poor friends the Weinbergs! Is there anything I can do?'

'It's kind of you, Mrs Simpson, and I really appreciate your support, but I'm afraid there's nothing any of us can do now.'

'A nasty business,' Elinor said. 'For the first time in all my years here, I'm really ashamed of my neighbors. You know, Mr Cromwell, they're not really very nice people, are they?'

'Well, they do leave a little to be desired.'

'Perhaps your friend should be glad they weren't accepted.'

'I hope they'll feel that way,' Jim said doubtfully.

'It's rather like the thing my mother used to say about people who didn't appear at parties.'

'What was that?'

'Mother was very philosophical,' Elinor said. 'When guests didn't show up, she used to simply shrug and say, "Well, if they don't come, they don't have to leave." Now that's something to think about, isn't it, Mr Cromwell?'

Jim laughed. 'It certainly is, Mrs Simpson. For all of us.'

* * *

Elinor's somewhat oblique analogy was strangely comforting to Jim next morning when he called Lester. For all her vagueness, she was extraordinarily perceptive. Even if the Weinbergs had been accepted, they might not have stuck it out. The ambiance of 617 Park just wasn't what they were used to. They would have been bored with it halfway through the decorating. They needed grander surroundings, a more obviously affluent atmosphere, Jim told himself. And then wondered whether he was brainwashed by what had been said the night before, or whether he was simply trying to cushion the blows that Lester certainly was prepared to deliver.

Gertrude answered when he called at eleven o'clock on Saturday morning. She was cool and curt, giving Jim no time to offer his apologies. As soon as she heard Jim's voice she put Lester on the line.

Weinberg brushed right past the formalities. 'If you've called to say you're sorry, Cromwell, forget it. It'll take more than a few words of regret to block that scene out of my mind. Damn it, Gertrude bawled her head off half the night, poor kid.'

Jim cringed. 'I am sorry,' he said again. 'I'd do anything in the world to make it up to you, Lester.'

'Sure you would,' Weinberg said sarcastically. 'Anything to keep from losing the account.'

'No. Honestly. It isn't that. I really mean it. I knew it might be rough, but I wouldn't deliberately have subjected anybody to that kind of embarrassment. And that's the God's truth, Lester, I'll swear to it on a stack of Bibles.'

'That's exactly what you may have to do. I've been on the phone for the last hour with my lawyer. We're filing a complaint with the city Commission on Human Rights first thing Monday morning. You got any idea what that means?'

'A slight idea,' Jim said.

'Well, in case you don't know the facts, let me spell it out for you. We're charging that anti-Semitism is the reason we've been turned down. The Commission, on my behalf, will go to court for an injunction against the 617 Park Avenue Corporation and every individual member of your Godamn board of directors. I'm only sorry that we didn't go through Ridgely & Ryan on the deal so we could include them, too. Same for that what's-his-name, Binky Coleman. We can't touch him or Mrs Spear because they didn't block the offer. They were a helluva lot smarter than the rest of you.'

Jim was not surprised. Sam Lazarus had prepared him for this. Ridiculously, he tried to head Lester off.

'Aren't you being a little premature?' he asked. 'After all, you haven't had word that your application was turned down, have you?'

Lester laughed coldly. 'Haven't I? You better believe I have. A letter from your cold fish Livingston arrived an hour ago. Hand-delivered yet. All very polite. And full of some crappy excuse about "incompatibility" whatever that means.'

They must have drafted the letter after I left the meeting, Jim thought. They didn't waste any time. The Baroness probably wanted to make sure it was written before she caught her plane to Palm Beach.

'I don't know what to say, Lester. All I can offer as evidence of my apologies is the fact that I've resigned from the board because of the way you were treated.'

Weinberg snorted. 'You *have* resigned? Or you *will* pretty damn quick now that you know you could be involved? It won't make any difference, you know. You were on the board when they turned us down. You're still personally liable.'

'That's unworthy of you,' Jim said quietly.

Lester had the good grace to sound ashamed. 'Sorry. I guess

195

it is. I don't really blame you, Cromwell. In fact, I've already told my lawyer that you and that Mrs Simpson should be stricken from the complaint. I know you were for us, and that nice lady was the only decent one in the bunch. But it was pretty dumb of you to get me into this. Makes me wonder how bright a businessman you really are. You and Gordon and Stewart.'

'You have a right to wonder,' Jim admitted. 'It was a bad error in judgment. I appreciate your keeping Mrs Simpson and me out of this, Lester. You're right. We did vote for you. It was five to two.'

Weinberg merely grunted.

'One more thing,' Jim said. 'Paul and I are prepared to testify or give depositions for you, if that's the way it works. It's the least we can do.' He hesitated. 'I hope you don't misunderstand what I'm going to say, but is all this worth it? I mean, do you still want the apartment after what you went through last night?'

'You don't know me very well, do you? You bet I want it. More than ever. I'll let you in on a secret, Cromwell. I may never even move into that building. I might just let the apartment sit there empty. Keep it as an investment, maybe. Real estate in that area has got to increase in value. Or maybe I'll sell it to some other nice "desirable Jew" like Paul Gordon. But so help me, I'm going to buy 12B if I have to go all the way to the United States Supreme Court to do it. Those bastards aren't going to get away with this kind of thing.'

Jim felt a new respect for Weinberg. It wasn't just a personal status thing with him, after all. He felt deeply about it, with all his latent racial pride. Good for him, Jim thought. Even if we don't get the account, I hope he makes it.

He spoke the last thought aloud. 'I hope you make it, Lester.'

'I think I will,' Weinberg answered. 'And even if I don't I'll throw enough of a scare into those fake aristocrats so they'll never pull this on anybody else.' He hung up abruptly.

I don't know what I have to feel good about, Jim thought, but all of a sudden I like the human race again. Some of it, anyhow.

* * *

When he got into the office on Monday morning, there was a message to call Joe Kauffman. Instead, Jim went over to see the head of the agency's International Division. 'What's up?' he asked.

'Remember that run-down you asked for on your girl friend the Baroness? Well, I got some stuff from our boys in Berlin. Didn't think they'd be able to move so fast, but they've come up with quite a dossier.'

'I'm sorry you went to all the trouble,' Jim said. 'I should have told you Friday that I didn't need it anymore. I accidentally stumbled on the whole story through another channel. Hope I didn't make a lot of unnecessary work for you or your guys in Germany.'

'That's okay,' Joe said, 'I haven't read anything this juicy since they stopped publishing *Confidential* magazine. That's some lurid female you got there! Didn't know you were hob-nobbing with Nazi ladies of easy virtue, old man.'

'Nazi ladies?' Jim repeated. 'You've got it mixed up. Actually, she's Jewish, though she doesn't admit it. Had to be gotten out of Germany by her Nazi boy friend.'

'Not the way I read it,' Kauffman said. 'Just the other way around. Your little friend, Felicia, was using her lily-white Aryan body to get what she wanted out of all the German brass. According to this report, she was making it with everybody except Hitler. In fact, she was even trying for him, rumors of his virility to the contrary.'

'I don't get it,' Jim said. 'Something's screwy. If she was so in with the big boys, why did she leave Germany? It doesn't make sense.'

Kauffman shook his head. 'It makes plenty sense if you've ever heard of a lady called Eva Braun. They were buddies for a while, until little Eva caught on to the fact that the Baroness had big eyes for the Führer. Then, kerput went Felicia. The Baroness scooted for her life, leaving behind a bewildered Baron and, presumably, a raft of bereft lovers. She had enough money and enough pull to get the hell out of the country. She divorced the Baron in Mexico. Came to New York a while later and bought the apartment in your building.'

Jim was getting increasingly confused. 'You sure about these facts, Joe?'

'Pretty sure. At least, as they say, my sources are unimpeachable.'

'Did your sources mention anything about a Richard Basil?'

Kauffman leafed through a sheaf of notes in front of him. 'Yeah. That's an odd one. She met Basil in Mexico. Seems he was a German refugee, too. With an even better reason for running. He's a Jew. Got out one jump ahead of Buchenwald, from what it says here.'

'Anything more on Basil?'

'Not much. Wait a minute, there is something. It says here that Basil brought his German-Jewish wife with him to Mexico. Name's Louise. Evidently they were trying to get to the States. Felicia managed to get them in somehow. They stayed in Mexico a year after she left and then came East. Hey, the Basils live in your building too. What the hell is all this?'

Jim shook his head in confusion. 'Damned if I'm sure now,' he said. 'All I know is that somebody's either a liar or a lunatic. Or both.'

Kauffman tossed the notes across the desk. 'You're welcome to this stuff if you want it. Some of it makes pretty good bedtime reading. You must introduce me to the Baroness one of these days. Preferably when my wife's out of town.'

Jim took the information back to his office. Joe was right. Felicia's list of conquests read like the Who's Who of International Diplomacy. No wonder she'd been able to escape. Contacts like that, even in wartime, must have been far reaching. Could have enabled her to get Basil into the States without too much trouble as well. If so, no wonder he was clearly in her debt. The good doctor might even be here illegally. Probably in love with her, too, if the report of her charms was even half true.

In many ways, the report from Berlin made a lot more sense than Louise Basil's version of the story. It also meant that Louise was either paranoid or a half-crazed alcoholic. She had reversed every fact. If this dossier was to be believed, she and Basil were both German Jews, and all that fantasy about her American Army officer father was pure fabrication. As was Richard's background. And, of course, Felicia's. What else was a lie? Maybe Richard wasn't even a doctor, for all anybody knew. No, that's not possible, Jim told himself. He couldn't pass his exams and maintain a prominent practice all these years without having the proper credentials. He supposed it would not have been difficult to have his background kept confidential because of possible reprisals. But why did Louise Basil put up with his abuse and his unfaithfulness? If there was no father to protect, no Catholicism to consider, why hadn't she divorced him long ago? Or vice-versa.

At least, Jim thought, I can understand Felicia's anti-Semitism. It was ironic that he should be able to accept it more readily under these conditions than he could when he thought she was a traitor to her own people. And it was understandable that Basil would go along with the discrimination thing to please Felicia if he did, indeed, literally owe her his life.

Jim was no longer sure exactly what he believed. In a way, it had been easier to see the Baroness as an anti-Semitic Jew. More plausible to accept Louise's story than this one. She had been so convincing, so pathetic about her betrayal. Now, Jim realized, he was unconsciously accepting this new set of facts from an anonymous source. The actions of Richard and Felicia were clearer in this light. It was Louise who had become the mystery woman.

He tried to push the whole thing out of his mind and concentrate on his work. What difference did any of it make now? Weinberg had been rejected and Weinberg was going to sue. It would make a messy newspaper story and the background of this odd triangle could only add to the sensationalism. He was right back where he was on Friday night. Worse. Even if he brought out Basil's real background, he would only be pointing up more evidence of non-discrimination in 617 Park. There would be two Jewish families in residence, a fact which any judge would probably find even more favorable to the building. Yet the question of Louise nagged at him. The story she'd told had been so believable, the performance so convincing that he couldn't wholly believe it was without a vestige of truth. Whether she was lying or not, he still felt an obligation to protect her.

It occurred to him suddenly that even without his help the story might come out. If he knew Weinberg's lawyers, they would make extensive investigation about everybody in the building. If it had been so easy for SS&A's Berlin office to get the story on the Basils and Felicia, why would it be any more difficult for Weinberg's bird dogs? My nest of WASPS has turned out to be a hive of hornets, he thought. And we haven't begun to feel the sting.

* * *

For the next ten days an ominous silence settled over 617 Park Avenue. Livingston had not replied to Jim's letter of resignation from the board. Presumably he had expected it and accepted it without further comment. Confirmation of this acceptance was received third-hand from Rosemary Murphy, who confided to Casey that Mrs Murphy had briefly mentioned Jim's resignation and the fact that they would probably not choose a replacement until the next annual tenants' meeting in May.

'I do hope that scene in our apartment with poor, dear Mrs Basil didn't have anything to do with Mr Cromwell's leaving the board,' Rosemary said.

'Not directly.'

Rosemary looked worried. 'You haven't told anyone, have you? About that night, I mean, or all those things that Louise said?'

'Of course not,' Casey said. She chose her words carefully. Jim had told her the result of the Berlin investigation with its complete contradiction of Louise's story. Perhaps Rosemary would inadvertently give them a clue about the truth. 'Louise said that you'd heard the facts many times before,' Casey went on. 'Tell me, has she ever varied the details?'

'I don't understand,' Rosemary said. 'Why would she vary the details? My goodness, nobody would tell fibs about such things, if that's what you mean. You couldn't ever make up such an awful life if you wanted to!'

'I didn't mean that Louise was making it up,' Casey said. 'Not deliberately, anyway. I just wondered, well, if she might not be unbalanced. Even for a drunk, that performance in your apartment was pretty wild. Smashing things and waving a knife around. You must admit, Rosemary, that she seemed out of her mind. Perhaps she's not clear any longer about what happened twenty-five years ago. That's all I meant.'

'Oh, she's clear all right,' Rosemary said. 'She's told me that story a hundred times. And always the same.'

'Have you ever met any of her family?'

'No. I don't think she has any family left. I believe her father was the last. And he died some years ago. In a Veterans Hospital.'

'What about Dr Basil?' Casey persisted. 'Does he have relatives?'

'None that I know of. At least I've never heard Louise mention any.' Rosemary looked suspicious. 'I'm sure I don't know what you're driving at. Seems to me you think Louise is either crazy or a liar. But what difference that could make, even if it were true, is beyond me. Poor, tortured soul, she has enough problems with the drink. It doesn't seem very Christian of us to suspect her of other weaknesses, does it?'

'Of course not,' Casey said reassuringly. 'But on the other hand, if Louise is seriously ill, mentally that is, she could harm herself one of these days. Or she could harm you, Rosemary. I was scared out of my wits the other night. Thank God we were home, or who knows what might have happened to you.'

'Louise wouldn't hurt me,' Rosemary said. 'I'm her only friend.'

'But if she's mad . . .'

'She is not mad,' Rosemary stated positively. 'And she's not going to harm anyone. The Good Lord will see to that.'

Casey gave up. 'I hope you're right. Just promise me you'll be careful. Don't let her in if you're alone in the apartment, okay?'

'I can't promise that,' Rosemary said. 'Where would the poor thing go? I only wish I could get her back to the Church. I'm sure if she'd return to her religion, it would be her salvation. I've talked to Father Flanagan about her, but she refuses to see him. Maybe one of these days she'll change her mind. I do hope so.'

Score another point for the boys in Berlin, Casey thought. If they've got the right dope on this trio, Louise can't very well go back to a religion she never had. She'd need a rabbi, not a priest, and then what would old Eileene Murphy think of the 'fallen Catholic' she's tolerated?

When Jim came home that night, she told him about the conversation. Like him, she now felt that Louise's story was whole cloth. And also like him she saw nothing to be gained by making the knowledge public. 'Rosemary doesn't doubt Louise for a minute,' Casey said, 'but then why should she? We didn't either until you got that report from Berlin. Louise is a good actress, you have to say that for her.'

'Either that or by now she does believe the story herself,' Jim said. 'I think she probably is deranged. It would help explain why the good doctor doesn't dump her. Even if she's certifiable, he doesn't need that kind of publicity in *his* business. As for her, where would she go if she was sane enough to leave him? As far as I know, she isn't equipped to support herself. And if she was the one who walked out, she'd probably end up with no more than eating money. Anyway, I've had the Basils and Felicia and the whole bloody crew right up to *here*. All I want now is for Weinberg to sue them all. And collect.'

Casey looked thoughtful. 'It isn't going to make living here very pleasant for the Gordons. Or for us.'

'They're not going to love us here whether he wins or loses,' Jim said. He began to sort through the morning mail which Casey had left for him on the desk. There were the usual appeal-for-funds letters from charities, two of them from mysterious post office boxes asking for money for an unknown African mission and an unrecognized child-care center. There are some sweet rackets going on, Jim thought absently. I wonder how many suckers support these 'welfare agencies' which probably are fronts for a con man with a printing press in his basement. He passed over the gift catalogues from artsy-craftsy mail-order houses. God forbid you should ever order anything from a mail-order ad. Once you did you magically got on twenty different lists and were bombarded by offers of indescribable junk. He put the legitimate charity requests and the bills to one side. At the bottom of the pile was a hand-delivered letter with the return address, '617 Park Avenue Corporation.' He read it curiously.

'How come you didn't open this letter from the house?' he asked Casey.

'How come you think I open letters addressed to you?' She read over his shoulder. 'What do you think that's all about?' she asked. 'A special tenants' meeting next week? I thought the annual one was in May.'

'It is. That's why this one is billed as special. And I've got a damned good idea what it's probably all about. Must be to inform the owners that the corporation is being sued by Weinberg. What else would be urgent enough to precipitate a special meeting?'

'So he's really going through with it,' Casey said. 'I don't know why, but all along I've had the feeling, or maybe the hope, that it was a bluff. It's hard to picture Lester as the "injured party" in any situation.'

'I'm glad he's doing it. You would be, too, if you'd seen how they humiliated him at the interview.'

'Don't get me wrong,' Casey said. 'I'm not sorry he's suing. But even after you told me what he said, I never really believed it would get this far.'

'Usually it doesn't. That's why the practice continues.'

'I can go to this meeting, can't I?' Casey asked. 'The letter was addressed only to you.'

'That's only secretarial routine. Like the monthly maintenance bill. Sure you can go. In fact, you're supposed to. This is a meeting for all tenants.'

Casey smiled. 'It'll be my first look at the whole troupe. And theirs at me. Makes me feel like a debutante.'

Jim grinned back. 'Some coming-out party,' he said. 'As the wife of the most-hated man in the house, they'll probably receive you with all the warmth they'd give a coiled cobra. Anyway, it won't be dull. I can promise you that.'

Casey looked at the letter again. 'Next Wednesday night. Eight o'clock. I think I'll call the Gordons and ask them to have a bite with us before we go. By the way, does Paul know about the Berlin information?'

'Naturally. So does Tony. We're all in this together.'

'But they don't know the first story, Louise's version, do they?'

'No. And no reason they should. At this point none of that mess seems relevant anyhow. Besides, I promised I wouldn't say anything, and I like to think that in spite of being an advertising man I have *some* integrity left.'

'I'll remind you of that when Ralph Nader gets around to investigating Madison Avenue,' Casey teased.

* * *

On the evening of the special tenants' meeting, the Cromwells and the Gordons arrived together at Livingston's apartment and quietly took their seats at one end of the living room which had been set up with rows of folding chairs.

'Looks like they expect a full house,' Mary whispered.

Jim nodded. 'They'll get it. I'll bet this is the first time they've had a special tenants' meeting since they gathered to celebrate the untimely passing of Franklin Delano Roosevelt.'

Casey looked around with interest. It was hard to see the decor because the furniture had been pushed against the walls to accommodate the temporary seats in the center of the room. What she could see, though, was enough to reflect the 'shabby gentility' of the Livingstons' home. The chintz couch and wing chairs were just worn and faded enough to reflect the security of the long-time rich. Family portraits flanked a fine old Chippendale mirror over the fireplace, and the unyielding Hepplewhite side chairs were as prim and proper as the people who owned them.

The assembled tenants were even more interesting. Most of them were strangers to Casey and her group. She had never even seen these faces in the elevator or the lobby. It was a fascinating assemblage of older people, some of them barely able to navigate to the spindly chairs. Here and there a 'middle-aged' couple like the Basils received the geriatric panorama, but it was obvious that the Cromwells and the Gordons were the youngest families in the house.

Louise Basil nodded remotely to Jim and Casey. She looked pale and subdued, as she always did when Richard was around.

Watching her, Casey had the feeling that she had imagined the scene in the Murphy's apartment. This almost mouse-like creature bore no resemblance to the raging, destructive mad woman they'd encountered, nor to the pitiful creature who'd later spun her tale of grief and deception. Mrs Murphy made a late and majestic entrance, leaning heavily on a silver-headed cane. She, too, nodded coolly at Jim as she took the comfortable armchair which had been reserved for her.

Only Elinor Simpson came over to greet the young quartet cordially. 'How pretty you look!' she said to Casey. 'And dear Mr and Mrs Gordon, how very nice to see you again! What a pity we can't have meetings like this more often. At least we'd have a chance to visit with our neighbors.'

Jim couldn't help smiling. If an air-raid alert sounded, he thought, Elinor Simpson would find it a wonderful reason for the whole group to have a reunion in the boiler-room bomb shelter. Still he marveled at her unshakable cheerfulness. Perhaps she hasn't heard about the law suit, he decided. Or maybe she's already learned that the two of us have been stricken from the complaint. He spied Antoinette Stone in the sea of familiar faces, but when he made a gesture of greeting, she pointedly looked the other way. He was startled to see Felicia in a prominent chair at the front of the room. She must have flown back from Palm Beach for the meeting, Jim realized. That promised to add a little spice to the whole affair.

In front of the heavily draped windows a small table and two chairs had been set up. Richard Basil occupied one and André Livingston stood beside the other. The president now called for attention, gently rapping a small gavel to quiet the gathering.

'Ladies and gentlemen,' he said, 'it was good of you to come to this special meeting of all tenants. I think most of you know that I am André Dubois Livingston, president of the corporation. Beside me is Dr Richard Basil, a member of the board and our secretary. He will take the minutes of this meeting which later will be distributed to all owners.

'We shall dispense with the usual role call of shareholders as this is an extraordinary session and will require no casting votes. It is, if you will, an informal and informative meeting to acquaint you with a most unpleasant situation that has arisen and of which your board thinks you should be apprised.'

There was an attentive, almost respectful silence as they waited for Livingston to continue.

'As you know,' he began, 'all of you own shares in the 617

Park Avenue Corporation. These shares vary in number according to the size and value of your apartments. You are, in effect, property owners on one of the most select and desirable avenues of New York City. And as property owners, you have entrusted an elected board of directors with the heavy responsibility of protecting the building that houses your investment.'

Very neat, Jim thought. He's paving the way for full support of the board. Making the owners fearful that something might happen to decrease the value of their co-ops.

'In the past few weeks, a unique and painful situation has arisen,' André went on. 'As you probably are aware, when an apartment in this building is put on the market, the applicants desirous of purchasing it are interviewed on your behalf by your board. It is our obligation to see that prospective owners are not only financially qualified to purchase and maintain the unit, but that they are compatible with the other families in the house. We take this responsibility very seriously, knowing that a rash or careless acceptance of the wrong sort of people can seriously damage the image – and ultimately the desirability and value – of these premises. Are there any questions so far?'

Harry Stone raised his hand and was recognized by The Chair.

'I should just like to say, Mr President, that I believe I speak for all the tenants in offering our thanks to the board for its untiring efforts in this area. Since my wife serves with you, I am well aware of how many hours all of you spend on our behalf.'

What a lap dog Harry Stone is, Jim thought. That's a well-rehearsed speech if I ever heard one. Antoinette apparently has turned to directing now that she's too old for acting.

Livingston smiled modestly. 'Thank you, Mr Stone. On behalf of the board, I can tell you that we are glad to do our duty as we see it. Your recognition of that fact is deeply appreciated.' He paused. 'Very well then, let me continue with the matter at hand. Your board has, on various occasions, refused permission for owners to sell to persons whom the board considered unsuitable. Until now, we have suffered no recriminations from this exercise of judgment nor wreaked any hardship upon the parties involved. Regrettably, we are now faced with our first unpleasantness as a result of a well-considered decision. It is my duty to give you the background of this problem and to appraise you of the immediate situation and the possible consequences.' He stopped and carefully poured a glass of water from the silver carafe on the table beside him. A small ripple of speculation spread through the room. When Livingston sensed that he had given the suspense enough time to build, he went on.

'Approximately two weeks ago, the law firm of Coleman & Prentiss, representing their client, Mrs Natalie Rogers Spear, presented us with an application to approve the sale of apartment 12B, previously occupied by the late Mr Bryan Rogers and now the possession of his daughter, Mrs Spear. Mrs Spear, heir to the estate, does not wish to occupy the premises and, accordingly, put it on the market. I hasten to add that although the apartment was listed through regular channels with the building agents, Ridgely & Ryan, this particular applicant, Mr Lester Weinberg, did not apply through the agents but, through friendship with one of our tenants, proceeded directly to Coleman & Prentiss, who accepted the offer with their client's approval.

'Your board met and reviewed the application which was financially in order. However, as is our custom, we then invited Mr and Mrs Weinberg to meet with us at an informal interview in order that we might form our opinions about their eligibility. Regrettably, after this interview five of the seven board members did not feel that the applicants would find this building suitable to their tastes, nor did we believe that you, as owners, would find them congenial neighbors. Accordingly, we so informed the owner and her attorneys and simultaneously sent word to the applicants that we could not approve the sale.

'Unfortunate as the results of this have been, it is now patently clear that our assessment of the character of these applicants was completely correct. Instead of accepting our decision in a mannerly fashion, the applicants have chosen to bring legal action against your corporation and individually against each of its board members, with the exception of the two who, through some breach of confidence, the applicants seem to have discovered voted in their favor.'

In the second row, an elderly lady with purple-white hair timidly raised her hand.

'Yes, Mrs Leslie?'

'How can they do that?' she asked. 'I always thought we had a right to say who could live in the building, just as you told us. What reason do they have for suing the corporation and the board?'

Jim nudged Casey. Here it comes, the nudge said. Let's see how Clarence Darrow is going to side-step his way around this one.

'A very intelligent question, Mrs Leslie,' André said. 'And, of course, the crucial one. The one on which the case completely rests. First, let me tell you that the applicants are undoubtedly good-hearted people. None of us has ever questioned their character or integrity. The gentleman is a successful, self-made businessman. However, through no fault of his own, he is somewhat lacking in polish and finesse. The same can be said of his wife. A most pleasant, even ingenuous woman, but one whose appearance and interests contrast strongly with what we think of as appropriateness and good taste.'

Paul Gordon spoke up. 'Those may be unfortunate characteristcs, but are they sufficient cause for rejection? Because a man is not formally educated or a woman has different fashion preferences, does that make them ineligible to own a co-operative?'

Livingston stayed cool. 'Not by any means, Mr Gordon. They are eligible owners in many buildings. Indeed, that is the very heart of the matter. We sincerely believe that they would be happy in any one of a number of co-ops, but not within the environs of 617 Park Avenue.'

Paul persistently pretended innocence. 'But I still don't understand. What is the basis of this law suit? What's the charge?'

'The charge,' André said slowly and dramatically, 'is that anti-Semitism played a role in the failure of the applicants, Mr and Mrs Lester Weinberg, to buy apartment 12B for the purchase price of one hundred and twenty-five thousand dollars.'

This time there was an audible gasp.

'Yes,' André said sorrowfully, 'we are charged with racial discrimination. An ugly phrase. And I need not tell *you*, Mr Gordon, one which is blatantly and unequivocally false. After his rejection, Mr Weinberg filed a complaint with the city's Commission on Human Rights, and they, in turn, brought suit against us. On behalf of the building, I have pointed out to the State Supreme Court and the presiding judge, Justice Alan Winston, that though the right to sell an apartment lies exclusively with the owner – in this instance the daughter of the deceased owner – the directors of the corporation have the right to reject the sale if the prospective tenant is not compatible. And, as I have explained to you, we do not consider Mr and Mrs Weinberg compatible.'

A middle-aged man in the fourth row raised his hand. André acknowledged him.

'Where do we stand now?'

'Justice Winston has, regrettably, found what he considers evidence of discrimination and has barred the sale of 12B to anyone, pending a further hearing into charges that Mr Weinberg was rejected because he is of the Hebrew persuasion.'

Elinor Simpson looked dismayed. 'Gracious, that does work a hardship on dear Mrs Spear, doesn't it? Do I understand you correctly, Mr President, that she cannot sell the apartment to anyone until the case is settled?'

'That is correct,' André said.

'But then we're being dreadfully unfair to her, aren't we? I would suppose that such things could drag on for months, and meanwhile she is obligated to pay the maintenance on the apartment, isn't she?'

Livingston frowned. 'I suppose there is some financial hardship involved for Mrs Spear. Incidentally, neither she nor her attorneys is named in the suit. Nor are our agents, since they were merely innocent bystanders, taking no part in the transaction. However, I continue to feel that the slight monetary inconvenience for Mrs Spear is insignificant in light of the serious effect these people would have on the status of this building and the value of this real estate. A fact, Mrs Simpson, which you must realize affects your holdings as well. As for the length of time the sale could be blocked, Justice Winston has given the Commission two months to complete their investigation into Mr Weinberg's charges. You see, it is quite involved. The city Commission on Human Rights files the suit, but it is up to them to prove the charges. The judge simply bars the sale of the apartment while this investigation is being completed.'

'What happens if the ruling is for Mr Weinberg – or against him?' Harry Stone asked.

'Let me take those questions one at a time,' André said. 'If discrimination is proved, the apartment will be granted to Mr Weinberg and we will be compelled to approve the sale. There is also an outside chance that he would bring action against the building and its directors for considerable sums of money, claiming damages for pain and suffering. In which eventuality, of course, we would have to discuss how payment would be made should a judgment be awarded. I am sure you would not want your directors personally penalized since they are acting, without compensation, on your behalf.

'However, should the ruling go against Mr Weinberg – as I confidently predict it will – our objection is vindicated and stands. And, of course, Mrs Spear's apartment is then "unposted", as the expression goes, and she is free to once again put it on the market, subject, as always, to final approval of the applicant by the board. Incidentally,' André said, 'I think you will be interested to know that Justice Winston warned the Human Rights Commission that it could be liable for damages by the owner of 12B if unlawful discrimination is not established. She has lost money because of this legal tangle, as Mrs Simpson pointed out.'

'Will we have to go to court?' Antoinette Stone asked. 'All that dreadful publicity! It's very difficult for those of us who are in the public eye.'

'I think not, Mrs Stone,' Livingston said. 'There will be a closed hearing, possibly two or three of them. But as an attorney and the president of the corporation I believe I can represent us. And,' he added modestly, 'I do have friends quite high up in publishing. I hope we'll be able to keep the whole thing out of the papers. We'll simply submit briefs and produce evidence that this whole charge is ridiculous. Frankly, hysterical charges of this kind are enormously difficult to prove even in those rare cases where they may be true. And in this case we have concrete evidence that they are not true. This building does not discriminate. We have proof of it.'

'Could you tell us what that proof is?' The question came from a dour, bankerish-looking bald gentleman in the third row.

'Yes, I can, Mr Burchard,' André said. 'Proof that we do not discriminate lies in the fact that one of our owner families is of the Jewish faith – Mr and Mrs Gordon who occupy 6A.' He indicated the fourth row where Paul and Mary sat.

With the exception of the Cromwells, every head in the room turned to look at them. Ridiculously, Mary found herself blushing. Equally without reason, Paul found himself angry at being singled out like some freak in a side show. But of them all, Jim was the most incensed. He rose to his feet.

'Our president is very articulate and convincing,' he said, 'but don't let him lull you into a false sense of security. Since this is a meeting of information, it seems to me you should have all the facts. Not just part of them. Mr Livingston has very pointedly excluded any mention of my part in this situation. I'm sure he did so out of a wish to spare my wife and me any unnecessary embarrassment, just as he has gracefully refrained from acknowledging my resignation from the board of this building. I believe that Mr Livingston is a man of good manners, and, in his own way, a man of good will. But I cannot in conscience sit here and allow you to believe that the directors of this building, with the exception of myself, *knowingly* approved a Jew. At my instigation, indeed my insistence, Mr and Mrs Gordon lied about their background and their religion in order to buy their apartment. If they hadn't, they, too, would have been rejected. Just as Mr Weinberg – who also was recommended by me – was rejected. I won't bore you with the reasons why I prevailed upon Paul Gordon to lie his way into this house. They were partly moral and partly materialistic. But they proved one thing: the majority of your board of directors is anti-Semitic, and I must warn you that I am prepared to go before the Commission and testify to what I have seen and heard behind the closed doors of their meetings. Mr Livingston won't be able to use the Gordons as his proof of liberalism, his "resident Jews", because I am in a position to refute that kind of hypocrisy.'

The Baroness was on her feet now, quivering with fury. 'So you will accuse us of hypocrisy, Mr Cromwell,' she said. 'Now isn't that interesting when you have just publicly admitted to being party to the most complete and utter form of it! Please spare us this dramatic confession. You are the worst kind of undermining schemer. You accepted our invitation to become a director, you sat in our meetings and you used that position to foist upon 'us, for your own, benefit,' a person whom we would not have accepted had we known what he was. Yes, Mr Cromwell, you are quite right. Your friends, the Gordons, would have been judged incompatible just as your friends, the Weinbergs, were. You knew it and were clever enough to deceive us. How you must have laughed! Well, let me tell you this. At least the rest of us stand by our views. Perhaps we have very personal reasons for prejudice or bigotry or whatever you now so high-mindedly wish to call it. But at least, we are open about it. Not sly, as you and your destructive friends are. I, for one, am not afraid to say it. You are correct – I would not knowingly countenance Jews as neighbors.'

'Only as lovers, perhaps?' Jim answered angrily.

Casey grabbed his arm. He shook her off roughly, staring defiantly at the Baroness. Before Felicia could answer, Livingston intervened.

'Mr Cromwell, you are out of order!' he said. 'And with all deference, Baroness, your remarks also are unseemly in an open meeting of this kind. If you and Mr Cromwell have personal grievances, I suggest you discuss them privately. Now be seated, please. Both of you.'

Through a blur of rage, Jim looked around him. Most of the tenants looked bewildered by this violent and incomprehensible exchange. Louise Basil was pale as death. Rosemary Murphy nervously twisted her handkerchief, obviously terrified that Jim was going to blurt out what she thought he knew about the Basils and Felicia. Casey grabbed his hand tightly. Paul leaned across her to give Jim a small, encouraging pat on the back. Only Richard Basil seemed unperturbed, almost indifferent to the exchange.

André Livingston spoke calmly. 'Ladies and gentlemen, I believe you are now in command of the facts about the issue at hand – Mr Weinberg's complaint against the corporation and directors of 617 Park Avenue. I shall keep you informed of developments and you will, as I stated at the beginning of the meeting, receive minutes of tonight's proceedings. Thank you for coming. I look forward to seeing you at the regular annual meeting.'

The group began to filter slowly out of the apartment. André spoke quietly to Dr Basil. 'I think we should strike that last exchange from the record.'

Richard's expression did not change. 'An excellent idea, André,' he said. 'It had nothing to do with anything, did it?'

'Exactly,' André agreed. 'Nothing whatsoever.'

Chapter XII

When the Basils returned to their apartment after the special meeting, Louise mixed herself a stiff drink. Richard said nothing, but he made a silent prediction that she would get even drunker than usual. The slightest bit of stress or tension was enough of an excuse for a bender, and the events of this evening, in particular the insinuation made by Jim Cromwell, would be the 'justification' tonight. He tried to walk past her into his bedroom, but she stopped him.

'You must be pretty proud of yourself, Doctor,' she said. 'How does it feel to be publicly accused of infidelity?'

'I don't know what you're talking about.'

'The hell you don't. Who did you think Jim Cromwell meant when he talked about Felicia's Jewish lover – Moshe Dayan?'

'Don't be absurd,' Basil said. 'Just because you know about the situation doesn't mean that anybody else does. Cromwell was taking a shot in the dark. One of those stupid coincidences that just happened to hit home. There's no way he could know anything about my friendship with Felicia.' He stopped abruptly. 'Unless,' he said slowly, 'you told him.'

Louise laughed. 'Bingo! Right on the nose!' She poured herself another drink. Richard grabbed it out of her hand.

'What did you tell him?' he demanded. 'You'd better tell me the truth, Louise, or by God I'll ...'

'You'll what? Divorce me? Kill me? Have me committed? Hardly. Not because you wouldn't like to do any one of those things. But *you'd* suffer for them, one way or the other. And that wouldn't do, would it? Other people can suffer, but not the esteemed Richard Basil. Nor the beautiful Baroness Von Brennerhof. Oh, no, you'll see to that, as you always have.'

He spoke evenly, menacingly. 'I'll ask you once more, Louise. What did you tell Jim Cromwell?'

'Okay, I'll tell you. I told him and his wife about how you were a big-shot Nazi who helped your Jewish girl friend escape from Germany. And how I, the inexperienced little American girl, was seduced into marrying you so you could get to this country. I told them how my poor father lied and cheated to cover up your record. What a terrible thing I did to him. I told them I wouldn't divorce you because I'm Catholic, and what I've had to put up with all these years while you and that woman carried on your love affair. I told them the whole truth. So now they know what you are. And what she is.'

Richard was stunned. 'You told the Cromwells that? All those lies?'

Louise looked at him curiously. 'What lies?' she asked. 'Every word I told them was the truth. Are you trying to say I don't know the truth, Richard? Because if you are, you're wrong. I remember it all as though it were yesterday. Every bit of it.'

God help us, she is mad, Basil thought. She really believes that twisted version of our lives. All these years it's been her only consolation: To picture herself as the heroine of this story, rescuing me, sacrificing herself, jeopardizing a mythical American father. He felt a stab of pity for her. Love was long since dead. Dead since the day he'd met Felicia in Mexico. But loyalty and protectiveness remained. He realized it now. How curious, he thought objectively, that at the moment I discover what a terrible thing she's done I should know the first real tenderness I've felt for her in years. Gently, he took her hand.

'It's all right, Louise,' he said. 'Cromwell got carried away tonight, but he won't tell anyone about us. I'm sure of it. You won't be humiliated. I promise.'

'I don't want anybody to know you were a Nazi,' she said pathetically. 'I shouldn't have told. I've never told anybody before. Except Rosemary.'

Richard rubbed his hand across his forehead. 'Rosemary knows, too,' he said flatly. 'The same story?'

'Of course the same story.' Louise was indignant. 'She's my only friend. Why wouldn't I tell her?'

He didn't answer. He was trying to put the pieces together. Something was wrong somewhere. If Cromwell believed Louise, why would he have made that reference to a 'Jewish lover'? It didn't fit if he accepted the fact that Felicia was a Jewish refugee and Richard her Nazi paramour. Cromwell must know the real story. But where did he get it? And why?

Making sure that Louise heard him, Basil dialed Felicia and

pretended to be talking to his answering service. 'This is Doctor Basil? Any messages? He did? What time? I see. Anything else? Okay. Thanks.' Louise was finishing her second drink. 'I've got to go out,' Richard said. 'Emergency. Dr Wilson called from Lenox Hill Hospital. One of my patients has just been admitted. I won't be long.'

Louise didn't answer. She'd heard that story many times before. She poured herself another Vodka. When the front door closed, she smiled. She took a childish delight in knowing that Richard was puffing his way up four flights of stairs. He wasn't as young as he used to be. Maybe this will be the first affair in the world ended by shortness of breath, she thought. What a prosaic ending to a grand passion.

* * *

Louise had accurately guessed Richard's destination. Felicia was waiting for him.

'What's this all about?' she asked impatiently. 'Really, Richard, you know I have an early morning plane back to Palm Beach. It's terribly inconsiderate of you to appear at this hour.'

He marveled at her composure. She really is the most self-involved woman I've ever known, he thought. Who'd guess that just an hour before she'd been involved in a ferocious argument, openly admitting her anti-Semitism and seemingly not giving a damn?

'I had to talk to you,' Basil said. 'I've just had a disturbing conversation with Louise.' He gave her an account of it. 'There's something very strange about all this,' he concluded. 'Cromwell must know the real story and thinks he can use it somehow to help Weinberg win his case. He must have stumbled on the true facts. Probably began to dig into our backgrounds after Louise gave him an inkling. Either way – whether he believes that you are an anti-Semitic Jew or a former Nazi – it's going to make ugly publicity if he brings it to Weinberg's attention. We'll be exposed as liars and worse. All I can think of is to try and reason with him. It won't do him any good to show that the house has other Jewish tenants. If anything, it will only strengthen the corporation's case. He must realize that. But he's such a wild-eyed zealot that he might do it just to prove some kind of moral point. Anyway, it's clear that I must get to him. And since you're leaving in the morning, I wanted you to know about it. And give your permission, of course.'

214

Felicia looked amused. 'Poor Richard. You do get so emotional about things, don't you? It always amazes me, coming from one in your profession. But then I suppose it's true that even psychiatrists can't be objective about anything that touches them personally. That's why so many of them are divorced, isn't it? Pity you can't view your own problems as dispassionately as you see those of your patients. No doubt it has something to do with the unstable characteristics of your race, as well. Jews are so revoltingly uncontrolled about the most inconsequential things. You know, for long periods I can forget your background. And then you go off on one of these Wailing Wall tangents and I am reminded of what you are.'

He tried not to think about what she was saying. It was better to stick to the subject at hand.

'Don't you care at all that the whole world might soon mistakenly believe you're Jewish? Or that they'll find out how chummy with Hitler you once were? What would either piece of gossip do to your precious social position, Felicia?'

'My dear, you are a child. You can't think for one moment that I would allow anyone to believe your demented wife's maniacal story. If it gets that far – which I doubt – I will make a statement of my own. I will tell how, out of the kindness of my heart, I helped a poor little Jewish couple. How I befriended them because the husband wanted to make a new life, and stayed quiet to help the wife avoid any possible reprisals toward the Jewish relatives she had so callously abandoned.'

'And what of yourself?' Richard asked. 'How do you think your famous friends will take the news of your own Nazi affiliations?'

Felicia shook her head. 'How can you be so unworldly? My God, it's lucky for you that I decided to help you. Otherwise, you'd still be languishing in some obscure Mexican village waiting for a proper visa into the States! All right, I will complete the explanation which is so simple it should be obvious even to you. First of all, dear Richard, I will affirm that I fled from the Nazis. I defy anyone – even Cromwell – to prove otherwise. My title should make my anti-Hitler sentiments quite believable. The German nobility, as everyone knows, was never on the side of that little upstart, Adolf Hitler. And even those who might not be convinced will be uncaring. You forget that we are talking about another world, long dead. No one gives a damn any longer about the political affiliations of the forties.' She laughed. 'For all I know, it may give me a greater aura of mystery and glamour in some circles.' She yawned delicately. 'You really must leave now. I have to get up at the most ungodly hour.'

Richard was stunned. 'So you don't wish me to talk to Cromwell.'

'I not only don't wish you to talk to Mr Cromwell, I forbid you to.'

He felt no anger. Only pain mixed with disbelief at his own blindness all these years. He had been so certain that Felicia really loved him. That she had not married him out of concern for what would happen to his career if the world found out about Louise's madness and the affair that had caused it. Now he forced himself to recognize the truth. Felicia's hatred of Jews made no exceptions. Not one. She despises every one of us, Richard thought. Did she, even in her wildest moments of passion, ever forget that I was not a Christian?

'I'll leave in a minute,' he said quietly. 'But before I do, there are a few pieces of unfinished business. Things I have to know.'

'Such as?'

'In retrospect it sounds like the question of a schoolboy, but with your loathing of Jews why did you get involved with me in the beginning?'

'In the very beginning I didn't know about you,' Felicia said calmly. 'It never occurred to me that you were Jewish. Just as it's never occurred to anyone in this building. Of course, I soon found out. In fact, if you remember, you were eager to blurt out your story. All that dreary business about the practice you'd just established in Berlin. And that maudlin account of Louise's family being sent to the gas chambers and how she'd lost her sanity because of it. By that time, I'd discovered what an extraordinary bed companion you were. And it struck me as amusing, somehow, to have such a virile Jewish slave. I must compliment you, Richard. I'd have dismissed the whole thing long ago if you were not such a satisfying lover. But you've always served that purpose admirably. Without complications. And on demand.'

'And I've been damned fool enough to think that my being Jewish has never mattered to you.'

'It hasn't, particularly. Most of the time I didn't think about it.'

'And you never intended that we'd marry, even if we could.'

Felicia stared at him. 'Marry? Don't be ridiculous. I never intended to marry anyone again. And certainly not you. A lover is an enormously useful possession, but a husband can be nothing but a nuisance. Even an acceptable husband.'

216

'I was never even your lover in the true sense of the word,' Richard said. 'You used the right word before: Possession. You owned me.'

'As you like,' Felicia said. 'Perhaps that is the right word. I was brought up to believe that Jews are fit only to be servants to my kind of people. They are only meant to fulfill whatever needs a superior race requires. Otherwise, they are superfluous and dangerous. As Hitler very well knew. Come, come, Richard. You didn't really believe I could feel any other way, did you? Your training has taught you that people are the product of their childhood. Surely you didn't think I could ever really love a Jew?'

'Yes, I thought you could. I thought there was a spark of humanity in you that I'd touched. I thought your love was strong enough to overcome those early, conditioned beliefs. Just as mine was big enough to forgive your ingrained prejudices, on the insane assumption that they did not apply to me. I even thought you felt as I did – that we were sacrificing our own wish to marry in order to spare a poor, unfortunate, defenseless woman like Louise. Now I see that you enjoyed Louise's misery. You used me all these years to continue her punishment and mine. Your sadism found a convenient and continuing outlet. You were able to torture at least two Jews by maintaining this relationship of ours, weren't you? You knew the anguish it caused Louise, the way it increased, deepened her madness. And through making her suffer, you also made my life a daily hell. You really liked that, Felicia, didn't you? I forgave you your past because I loved you. But you've never forgiven me mine.'

'Yours is unforgivable,' Felicia said coldly. 'You were born with it.'

* * *

Before he left the apartment the next morning, Jim received a call from Richard Basil, asking if they possibly could have lunch that day. Surprised, Jim agreed, and they set the date for one o'clock at The Running Footman, a comfortable restaurant not too far from the doctor's office.

'We must have hit a nerve last night,' Jim told Casey. 'Our live-in skull-stretcher wants to have lunch with me today.'

'Dr Basil? What do you think he wants?'

'Well, the man's not stupid,' Jim said. 'He's probably figured

217

out from that dumb crack I made last night that I know a helluva lot about him and Her Ladyship.'

'You mean you think he'll ask you to keep quiet?'

'I doubt that he'll ask me to take an ad in the *Times*.'

'What are you going to do, Jim?'

He frowned. 'I'm not sure. I thought a lot about all of this last night. My first impulse was to do nothing, as you know. But now maybe the fact of a second Jewish family could work for Weinberg instead of against him. I originally thought that the revelation would help the corporation's case, show that they really were not discriminatory. But if it's presented in the proper light, it might be bad for them.'

'I don't follow you,' Casey said.

'Look at it this way. It's all well and good to have two Jewish tenants, but if the board accepted both of them *without* knowing they were Jewish, how would that look?'

'That's brilliant! Of course! The fact of their being here would be negated by the fact that the building didn't know they were accepting Jews! You're right. It could make the board look more suspect than ever. Hey, maybe you've finally hit on the answer!'

'I'm not all that positive,' Jim said. 'Anyway, I'll see what's on Basil's mind before I go plunging ahead. Lord knows I've done enough of that already. All I need is to get Lester's hopes up again and then fall flat on my face. That would really end any dim chance we still have of getting the Weinberg account.'

'I'm glad you think that there is still hope,' Casey said. 'I was afraid you'd resigned yourself to the fact that it was a lost cause.'

'What hope there is, is damned small. And speaking of resigning yourself, there's something I ought to discuss with you. If we don't get Weinberg's business, I'm going to offer Tony my resignation from the agency.'

'Jim! Why? You aren't single-handedly responsible for this. We talked about that. Good Lord, it was Tony who cooked up the whole apartment idea in the beginning. You didn't even buy it at first. You were more certain than anybody that it wouldn't work.'

'Technically you're right, I suppose. But on the organization chart, this is my area, and no matter who else goofs up, I'm elected to take the rap.'

'Tony would never accept your resignation.'

'Between you and me, I don't think so either, but my New

England conscience is working overtime. We'd really counted on this one, Casey, and things are going to be tight at the agency if we don't get it. The least I can do to ease the pain is offer Tony a chance to dispense with the salary of one account supervisor and the expenses that go with him. Think I'm being an improvident moralist?'

'Probably,' she said, 'but that's the way you are. Anyway, I'm not going to worry because I think the whole conversation's academic. Tony won't let you leave. He'll need you more than ever to bring in a replacement for the Weinberg business.'

'I do wish you were the head of Steward, Sutton & Atherton,' Jim said. 'I'd love to work for somebody who had that much confidence in me.'

'Sorry, chum. You'll just have to settle for a legally wedded ego-builder, female, size eight.'

'Nice settling,' Jim grinned. 'I'll take two. They're small.'

* * *

His lunch with Richard Basil turned out to be still another in a series of unexpected events. Basil was already seated when Jim arrived. Without preliminaries, the doctor plunged right into the subject uppermost in both their minds.

'What do you know about my wife and me and Baroness Von Brennerhof?' he asked.

Jim stalled. 'What makes you ask?'

'Look, Cromwell, let's stop playing games. Louise and I had quite a talk last night. Apparently she chose you as the object of her confidences. I gather she told you the same pack of lies she's been feeding Rosemary Murphy.'

'All right,' Jim said. 'Yes, she did tell Casey and me a long and involved story about the three of you. It happened accidentally, by the way. We were called in by Rosemary one night to help keep Louise from smashing up the Murphy apartment and doing bodily harm to herself and other people. Incidentally, one of those people was you. I don't think she'd have gone through with it, but she said she wanted to kill you. We managed to calm her down. And that's when she told us.'

'But you don't believe her story, do you?'

'I did at first,' Jim said. 'Now I question it.'

'That's what I thought,' Basil said. 'Based on your rather ungentlemanly remark to the Baroness about her "Jewish lover",

219

you must have reason to doubt Louise's veracity. And you're right to.'

Jim didn't answer. 'Mind if I order a drink?' he asked finally.

Richard smiled. 'Sorry. I'm not what you'd call the gracious host today.' He beckoned to the waiter. 'What'll you have?'

'Bloody Mary, please.'

'Same for me,' Basil said. He turned back to his guest. 'Now let's talk straight. You've managed to stir up a hell of a fuss in 617 in the few months you've been there. Why?'

'Maybe I just don't get my kicks out of living in a building full of bigots,' Jim said.

'Bullshit,' the doctor said bluntly. 'I don't peg you for that kind of fanatic, Cromwell. You knew the building before you moved in. Grew up there. Why this sudden zeal to prove equality for all men?'

Jim was annoyed. 'Who's on trial here, Basil? You didn't ask me to lunch to lecture me on my personal beliefs or expect me to defend them. Let's get back on the track. The one you started on the minute I sat down. You've said Louise told us a pack of lies. Okay. I accept that. You've also indicated that you think I know the truth. Right again. Where do we go from here?'

'That's what I want to ask you,' Richard said. 'But first, let me ask you another question. What have you heard to make you question the story Louise told you? How did you figure out that she was lying?'

'Sorry. Both those things come under the heading of privileged information. I'll just tell you this. I did hear a diametrically opposed story from a reliable source. And I do think it's closer to the truth than Louise's version. Maybe you'd like to confirm it.'

'How can I confirm it until you tell me what you've heard?'

'You might try telling me the truth,' Jim countered. 'If your account matches the second one, I'll tell you. On the other hand, you'll be taking a risk. For all you know, you might be giving me a third interpretation. Maybe even more damaging than what I've already heard.'

Jim found this cat-and-mouse game strangely stimulating. Basil had backed himself into a corner. The suave, unreadable psychiatrist was on the defensive. He was probing, unsuccessfully, to find out how much Jim knew. He was running scared. But whether for himself, for Louise or for Felicia, it was hard to say. Maybe it was for all three. Jim had never liked Richard. Never trusted that super-cool exterior. Like a number of other people in the house, he was sure that the doctor was a sadist.

220

Never mind his reputation as a philanderer. What Jim despised was what the divorce courts called 'mental cruelty'. Cromwell would have been less than human if he had not secretly enjoyed the sight of the unflappable Basil now lifting his drink to his lips with a hand that visibly shook. What a son of a bitch he must be, Jim thought, to have driven that poor woman to the state she's in.

Richard took a sip of his drink and sat it down unsteadily on the plate in front of him. 'All right,' he said, 'I'll tell you the whole thing exactly as it happened.' For the next twenty minutes he talked, uninterrupted. His story confirmed the information from Berlin, embellished by his relationship with Felicia. It concluded, bitterly, with his account of his latest conversation with the Baroness and the reluctant admission of what a fool she'd made of him all these years.

'Maybe this kind of thing would be hard for a man like you to understand,' Basil concluded. 'Not that plenty of American husbands don't cheat on their wives. I see dozens of those wives every week in my office. They're always the ones whose nervous systems are shot by this kind of ego-destruction. Seldom the men who cause it. But I doubt that you're that kind. I'd make an assessment that you're one of the lucky ones, Cromwell. One of a vanishing monogamous breed. Lucky in other ways, too, I suppose. You never had to bribe and lie and crawl your way out of a society that didn't want you, that didn't give a damn for your intelligence or your ability but just spat on you and painted "Jew" in big, black letters on the front of your house.

'Hell, I'm not using that to excuse my unfaithfulness to Louise. When she saw her mother and father and sister and brother carted off to the gas chambers, her mind snapped. I knew we had to get out of Germany. I also knew that my life was incomplete living with a woman who lapsed into moments of madness. I got us as far as Mexico. Felicia did the rest. She had influence and power and a body available to anyone who could do anything for her. An unbeatable combination. Even knowing what she was, she fascinated me. I thought I loved her. I know now that it was the most classic kind of love-hate relationship that fulfilled some need in us both. She used me as a stud. She punished all Jews through me. And I took out all my vengeance on Nazis everytime I "violated" that superior Aryan body.' He laughed grimly. 'Physician heal thyself,' he said. 'I'm a pretty disgusting specimen.'

Jim sat silent, trying to absorb the story he'd been told. He weighed it carefully. It had to be the truth. Only desperation would bring Richard Basil to the point of such naked confession. Desperation and the hope that the revelation would win the kind of sympathy that would keep Cromwell's mouth shut. He looked inquiringly at Basil.

'Why have I told you this? That's what you're wondering, isn't it?' Richard asked. 'Or maybe you're not wondering. Probably you think it's a pitch for you to keep quiet about all this. Not tell anybody the truth about your three "honest, upright neighbors". Or at least the two who blackballed your friend. I'm sure that's what you think.'

'What else could I think?'

'As a logical man, nothing else. But that's not why I've told you the story. I want you to tell Weinberg the truth. About me and Louise and Felicia.'

'I don't get it,' Jim said. 'You want to expose yourself as a liar after all these years of covering up? You know there may be bad publicity. It could knock hell out of your reputation. To say nothing of the tension it'll cause in the house. What are people going to think when they hear you've been pretending you weren't Jewish and compounding the felony by having an affair with a woman of the Baroness' admitted anti-Semitism? If it's revenge you're after, it's understandable, I guess, but you'll pay a bigger price than she will. And so will your wife.'

Basil finished the last of his drink. 'I'm sure my motivations are complex,' he agreed. 'Undoubtedly I do want to punish Felicia. But I want more for society to punish me. I like to think I put on a pretty good front, Jim. But so help me God, all these years I've lived with a terrible guilt. I realize now that some of it had to do with what I was doing to Louise, but that's not the biggest part. I didn't cause her madness. The Nazis did that. Perhaps I deepened it, but I swear to you that had she been a normal woman, I don't believe I would have looked elsewhere for companionship, and probably not even for other sexual experiences. No, my reason for telling you this is that I'm tired of hiding. I'm ashamed of my own cowardice. Of being weak and frightened and as emotionally enslaved as I was physically threatened in Germany. Deep down, I guess I've got some kind of conscience or religion or whatever you want to call it. Like my ancestors, I'm seeking my own Day of Atonement.'

Jim began to understand a little. 'And you think that by helping my Jewish friend get an apartment you can clear your conscience?'

'Of course not,' Basil said impatiently. 'If there's a God, He's the only one who can forgive me. Not you. Not Weinberg. Not even that poor mad woman I'm married to. But I'm like a child. I have to crawl before I can walk like a man. There has to be a first step. Maybe the way to begin is to try to make up for black-balling Weinberg, for going along with Felicia. At least, I can be on his side. And yours and Gordon's. I've told you what I am and why I've pretended to be something else. I don't want to pretend any longer. You've shown me what I've become. You brought it to a head by your well-meaning blundering. I want to be able to look in the mirror again without flinching at that Godamned false face I've worn all these years. I don't know if it will help Weinberg. But it will help me.'

The almost-embarrassing frankness made Jim feel uneasy. As overly dramatic as the doctor's words were, Jim knew they were sincere. And uncomfortably, he applied them to himself. I've been pretty much of a phony, too, he thought. If I were candid, I'd admit that I don't really want Lester in the building. I want him to have the *right* to live there. But all my super-liberal speeches are motivated by business pressure. Would I have gone through all this for a stranger who couldn't do anything for me? Tony and I have sat back, safe and secure in our nice Christian wrappings, and played Russian Roulette with a lot of lives. Lester's and Paul's. And now the Basils. For that matter, we've even tampered with the Baroness' innermost secrets which, for better or for worse, really belong to her.

'You want to meet Lester Weinberg and tell him this whole story? Is that the idea?' Jim asked.

'I think it's the best way to proceed. He can use the information any way he wants. Or his lawyers can.'

'Has it occurred to you that your admission might strengthen the building's case? They can now point to *two* Jewish owners, you know. Might be just the ammunition they need to get them off the hook.'

Basil had anticipated Jim's own reasoning. 'I thought of that,' he said. 'But if Weinberg makes it clear that in both instances the board didn't know they were accepting Jews, that could be pretty damaging, couldn't it? And if there's an avowed anti-Semite in residence, that won't hurt his case either. I can give an affidavit swearing to both those things. It would have more credibility than one coming from you. You see, yours is partly hearsay. Mine is right from the horse's mouth. Or,' he said ruefully, 'from the animal's other extremity, which seems more appropriate.'

223

'Okay, it's worth a try. I'll set up a date with Weinberg. Naturally, you don't have to go into as much detail as this. Just the fact that you're Jewish and the firsthand account of Felicia's sentiments should be enough. I'll also make a deposition reporting the things she's said in my presence. So will Paul Gordon, I'm sure.'

There was an awkward pause. 'Damned decent of you to do this,' Jim said. 'Even though I felt that I had the facts, I don't know whether I'd have had the guts to use them. For one thing, I didn't want to hurt Louise.'

Basil nodded. 'I can understand. But you must realize that she is beyond hurting. It won't matter to her.'

'What about Felicia? And yourself?'

Basil gave a little laugh. 'Felicia will come out smelling like roses. She always does. As for me, now that I've diagnosed my sickness, I don't think it's as serious as I deluded myself into believing it would be. Hell, most psychiatrists are *expected* to be Jews, aren't they? So my patients shouldn't care. And I imagine that most of my confreres will kick the scandal around a little over lunch and then forget it as quickly as people always forget items they read in the paper. You know, when something is so important to an individual, he thinks the whole world is talking about it. Truth is, most of the world doesn't give all that much of a damn. No, unless I'm sadly mistaken, I've built a good name in my field. Even my stupid pretenses hopefully will be forgiven by my peers.'

'And your neighbors? Your fellow board members?'

'Naturally I'll do what you did: Resign from the board. As for the rest, I'll remember something my father used to say. "When other people start paying your rent, then it's time to worry about what they think of you." Let them give me the cold shoulder. I couldn't care less, and Louise won't even notice. Her kind of mental disorder is not unusual, you know. There are times, most times, in fact, when she can function perfectly. You'd never suspect the paranoia. And then there are those gut-tearing periods when she lapses into her state of imagined persecution.' He paused. 'Listen who's talking,' he said. 'I was becoming that way myself. It's like that sick joke about the paranoid at the football game. Every time the players went into a huddle, he thought they were talking about *him*.'

Jim laughed. 'Shall we order another drink?'

Basil nodded. 'Why not? My God, I feel wonderful! If this

is what confession does for Catholics, maybe I'll convert. Seriously, though, I am grateful to you.'

Jim waved off the undeserved compliment. 'Maybe we'd better place our lunch order, too,' he said.

'Right. I've been talking so much I forgot the time. I have a patient at three o'clock. Poor guy. He has a terrible hang-up about being Jewish.'

*　　*　　*

When he answered Jim's phone call, Lester Weinberg's voice had all the warmth of a man unexpectedly trapped into talking to an insurance salesman.

'Something I can do for you, Cromwell?' he asked.

'Maybe the other way around,' Jim said.

'Spare me,' Lester said. 'You've done enough already. Thanks to you, I've got a hostile wife and a battery of lawyers breathing down my neck. What do you want to do for me next – make it possible for me to donate my heart to Dr Cooley?'

On the other end of the line, Jim couldn't resist smiling. Crusty old bastard, he thought. He's really terrific. In the middle of this mess he can still hang onto his sense of humor. In his place, I probably wouldn't even talk to me, much less make jokes.

'I think I've got hold of a witness who can be useful to you. He explained about Dr Basil. Lester listened attentively.

'You sure this guy isn't playing some game of his own?'

'Hell, it's always possible,' Jim said. 'But I can't imagine what it could be. Anyway, if you're willing, I'd like to make a date for you to talk with him. As you would say, it might not help, but it couldn't hurt.'

Weinberg laughed grudgingly, a little relaxed now. 'Get you, Cromwell! If you don't stop picking up those Seventh Avenue expressions they'll drum you out of the Episcopal Church.' His tone became serious again. 'I still don't get it,' he said. 'How could any Jew from Germany be in love with a Nazi broad like that? Christ, he must be nuttier than his patients!'

'I know it's hard to believe,' Jim admitted. 'But I guess psychiatrists are as vain as other men when they fall in love. Basil's like the ordinary guy in that respect. Or the ordinary woman. You know, when you think you love somebody you see that person as you wish he was, not necessarily as he really is. I suppose it's an ego thing with everybody. Kind of like saying, "If I love him, he must be perfect." I don't know much about this

225

kind of thing, but I can understand a man deluding himself that way. Especially one who'd been through as much as Basil had when he met Felicia. He needed a woman. And he found one who was not only helpful to him but physically appealing as well. Objectively, the whole setup is impossible to accept. But emotionally, I can see how he could fool himself into thinking she cared. When you think about it, he almost had to, or go insane himself.'

'Yeah,' Lester said doubtfully. 'Maybe so.'

Jim plunged on. 'Anyway, he's faced the truth now, tough as it is. And he'd like to make some kind of amends.'

'Well, okay,' Lester agreed. 'I'll get the lawyers and he can make a deposition. You might as well come along and give them your story, too. That is, if you still want to.'

'Of course I want to. I gave you my word.'

'How about ten o'clock tomorrow morning? Think the doc can make it?'

'I'm sure he will make it,' Jim said, 'even if he has to switch some appointments. What about Paul Gordon? Do you want him here, too? He's not only willing to make a statement, he's anxious to.'

'Sure,' Lester said. 'The more the merrier. We already have testimony from Mrs Spear and that legal eagle of hers. What's his name? Pinky?'

'Binky,' Jim said.

'Binky, Schminky, what do I know? Anyway, we have their affidavits swearing that they accepted the application. So they're off the hook as far as the discrimination thing is concerned. All they have to do is keep paying the maintenance until the court releases the apartment for sale. I don't have to tell you that they're pretty anxious to get this over with.'

'When is the hearing scheduled?' Jim asked.

'Not for six Godamn weeks. The judge gave the Human Rights Commission two months to complete an investigation into the changes. So Binky's client is stuck for another couple of months' rent.'

Jim waited. He hoped that Lester was going to say something about his selection of an advertising agency. He could, realistically, wait until after the decision about the apartment, and Lester's silence indicated that he probably would. Unless, Jim thought, he announces that he's given the account to someone else before then. In any event, this was no moment to bring up the touchy subject that had sparked the whole thing.

'I'll get Basil and Paul and see you in the morning. By the way, how's Gertrude?'

'How should she be? Tell you, Jim, I've never seen her like this. Mopes around and looks at me like I murdered her mother. You want to know how low she is? I told her yesterday, "Go ahead and buy that Russian broadtail fur thing you saw at Revillon last month." And you know what she said?'

'No. What?'

'She said no she wasn't going to buy it. And when I asked her why not, you know what else she said?'

'Tell me.'

'She said, "Why should I get such an elegant outfit? Who'd understand a fur like that *on the West side?*" Now I ask you, is that my Gertrude?' Lester sighed. 'Tell you, it's going to be rough if we don't win this case.' He hung up without saying good-by.

Rough is not the word for it, Jim thought as he dialed Richard Basil. Let's call it by its right name: ruinous.

Chapter XIII

To the casual observer, it would have appeared that nothing unusual had happened to disrupt the serene pattern of life in 617 Park Avenue during the six weeks the building waited for the Weinberg hearing. In truth, most of the tenants almost forgot about the flurry of excitement caused by Livingston's disclosure of the anti-Semitism suit. They had had only a brief look at 'those troublemakers', the Cromwells and the Gordons, at the special meeting, and most of the residents didn't even recognize them when they chanced to meet in the lobby or the elevator.

Unfortunately, this was not the case with the board members. When Casey ran into Antoinette Stone at the front door, that indignant exponent of the arts stared through her as though she was some intruder who had strayed into the building. When Jim met André Livingston in the elevator, the president coldly and deliberately turned his back on this 'traitor to his class'. Even Rosemary Murphy disappeared from the Cromwells' life, undoubtedly forbidden by her mother to associate with such a disruptive element. Euralia reported, in one of her rare bursts of confidence, that Mrs Basil didn't seem to go to the Murphys any more, a fact which Casey reported happily to Jim. He had, of course, told her the whole story of the Basils, and they were pleased with this latest piece of information.

'Looks like the doctor really is atoning for his sins,' Casey said. 'If Louise isn't lurching up to this floor, it must mean that she hasn't been all alone in her apartment, getting bombed. At least one good thing has come out of this.'

'I hope so,' Jim said. 'I'm sure you're right. On the other hand, don't forget that our bitchy Baroness is still in Palm Beach. Maybe Basil doesn't have any place to go anyhow.'

Casey looked annoyed. 'That's really a hell of a thing to say,

Jim. I don't believe you mean that. Whatever you are, you're not as cynical as all that.'

'No. Of course I'm not. I think Basil meant everything he told me at lunch. He didn't even seem to mind repeating it in front of Paul and Lester and the lawyers.'

Casey took a deep breath. 'I feel better. Maybe he will really try to help Louise now.'

'He will. Not himself, of course. But he told me on the way back from Weinberg's that she was starting treatment with another analyst.'

'Nice,' Casey said. 'And speaking of nice, we still have one friend in the building. Elinor Simpson popped in this afternoon.'

'Oh? What was on her mind?'

'She wanted to know whether the "insinuator" as she calls it was working properly on our floor. Seems the incinerator was pouring smoke all over the back hall on the sixth. But I think that was only an excuse. She really wanted to talk about the Weinberg thing. I don't believe she understands it even yet.'

'It would be hard for her to understand,' Jim said. 'There's not an ounce of malice in that one. She probably can't comprehend things like discrimination. It just wouldn't occur to her to hate anybody for *any* reason. And certainly not for their race, color or creed. What did she say?'

'Not too much, actually. I tried to explain it to her in slightly less pompous language than Livingston used, but she just kept shaking her head and saying that such things weren't possible in 617. Oh, yes, she did come up with something wonderful at one point. She'd just finished saying that it was all like a bad dream. Then she smiled at me and said, "I must correct myself, Casey. Dear Edgar always told me that there's no such thing as a *bad* dream, because if it *seems* bad while you're having it, you're so happy to wake up and find it isn't true. And if it's a good dream, you enjoy it while it's going on." How's that for an outlook on life?'

'Enviable,' Jim said. 'I wish I could feel the same way about this Weinberg nightmare. I can't wait for the whole thing to be over.'

'Elinor would say you're wishing your life away.'

'Probably. But I'd trade six weeks for a conclusion. At this point, *any* conclusion. Good or bad. Just to have it off my mind.'

'Do you think Lester can win the case?'

'I'm not a lawyer, but it looks to me like he's got everything going for him. Anyway, we'll know in forty-eight hours. That's when the Commissioners hand down their decision. Think you can keep your fingers crossed that long?'

'On one condition,' Casey said.

'I can't afford a Revillon Russian broadtail.'

'No, idiot, not that kind of condition. You just have to promise me that from here on in you and those dopes at the agency will stop playing this kind of game to get a new account. Oh, I know it goes on all the time, buying your way into the heart of the prospective client. But it just isn't your style, not yours or Paul's or even Tony's. In the future, leave the skulduggery to agencies who are long on schemes and short on talent. Okay?'

Jim was amused. 'Meddler. Since when have you started telling me how to run my business?'

'Since you damn near caused a revolution on Park Avenue. And jeopardized a friendship to boot.'

'What friendship have I jeopardized? You were never friends with the Livingstons or the Stones or even the Murphys. And God knows you wouldn't have Felicia for an *enemy*.'

'I'm not talking about them. I'm talking about the Gordons. Do you realize we almost never see them any more?'

'I see Paul practically every day at the office. I don't notice any particular change in him.'

'Well, there's a change in Mary. She's not angry. I don't mean that. It's just like, well, she's withdrawn, kind of. When we talk on the phone she always has some excuse why she can't go shopping or have lunch, or why they can't come for dinner. And when I do see her, we skirt around the apartment thing. It's a sore subject.'

Jim frowned. 'I think you're imagining the whole thing. Good Lord, Casey, why do you keep harping on the fact that Mary is resentful or upset or whatever you think she is?'

'Honey, I don't know. But she's always been more sensitive than Paul. He delights in flinging this whole thing in the faces of the WASPS. But I know that Mary's touchy about the implications of their living here, now that it's all come out. I'm afraid that now she really equates us with the rest of the bigoted, so-called Christians.'

'Oh, come on,' Jim said impatiently. 'That's schoolgirl stuff. Mary's too sensible for that. You keep forgetting that Paul was more reluctant in the beginning. It was Mary who wanted the the apartment so much. Don't try to tell me that she's come all over hurt feelings because everybody in 617 knows she's Jewish.

And don't ask me to believe that she thinks we're part of the WASP conspiracy. How could she?'

'When you put it that way, I know it doesn't make sense. But I'm not imagining it, Jim. Something has happened to Mary. And to the way she feels about us. Don't ask me how I know it. I just know it.'

'Women,' Jim said. 'I'll never understand them.'

Casey nodded. 'I'll buy that,' she said.

* * *

Casey was right in her assessment of Mary Gordon's feeling, but Mary was at a loss to explain them, even to herself. A woman of more than average intelligence, she had always been able to do what she thought of as 'instant analysis'. She had that rare ability to figuratively 'step outside her own skin' and look at her problems as though they belonged to somebody else. Well educated and well read, she had more knowledge than the average layman of her own motivations. And though she had never been 'on the couch', she had read enough and talked with enough people in analysis to understand most of her resentments, guilts and subconscious reactions. For the first time in her memory, this talent for dispassionate self-examination had failed her. She was unreasonably, illogically angry. She felt used. By her friends, her husband's business associates, even by her husband himself. Strangely, she did not overtly resent the bigoted attitude of most of the people in 617. She understood it. She supposed it was because she expected nothing better of them. Her anger was directed at the Cromwells and Tony and Paul who had placed her in this unexpectedly defensive position. They had, as she thought of it, made her a guinea pig for their experiment in race relations. Every time she left or entered the building she felt the curious eyes of the other tenants on her, imagined that the staff was whispering behind her back. 'So I'm a Jew!' she wanted to scream at them. 'What do *you* think I am – a leper?'

Yet even while the anger boiled within her, she knew it was unjustified. She had made a free choice. She had nothing to be ashamed of, nothing about which to reproach the people she loved. When she avoided Casey she was ashamed. And when she saw her, she saw not a warm friend but a stranger who, by accident of birth, would forever be spared the humiliation of 'being different'. Common sense told her that Casey felt no less loving about the Gordons than she ever had; that none of the

231

theatrics and revelations of the past weeks mattered in the least to *her*. It was Mary who was defensive, bristling at an insult never even thought of, much less uttered. Finally, one bright afternoon, she realized that it was Mary who was angry at Mary. Not at anybody else. Alone in the apartment, she laughed aloud with relief. '*Schlemiel*,' she scolded herself, 'what's the matter with you? Going around feeling sorry for yourself, that's what you've been doing. Trying to make yourself believe that other people have done you wrong. What's the matter with you, Mary Gordon? Are you practicing to be the stereotype of the Jewish mother, wringing your hands and moaning about the sacrifices you've made? Some sacrifices! Why you dumb dame, you're furious at your own stupid, thin-skinned behavior! A bunch of Park Avenue windbags turn up their noses at you, and instead of getting mad at *them*, you try to pin the blame on the people who had enough guts to expose them! Whom do you really dislike? Yourself, you ding-bat!'

It was so absurd, so childishly simple, really, that she couldn't wait to tell Casey. She dialled the Cromwells and her friend answered.

'Hi,' Mary said. 'Euralia out?'

'Nope. Still can't break myself of the habit of picking up when the phone rings. Let's face it. I'm hopeless. How are you, Mary?'

'Less hopeless than I was a few minutes ago. You busy?'

'Not a bit.'

'How about coming down? We haven't really talked in such a long time.'

'I know,' Casey said slowly. 'Funny, I was saying that to Jim only last night. I miss you a lot.'

'Me, too. I'll put the coffee on. We can pretend we're two suburban housewives in a TV commercial.'

Their reunion was warm and lighthearted. Over coffee they gossiped about clothes and discussed Abby's new crush ('He's eight years old going on twenty-five and looks like a mini Paul Newman.'). It was Mary who finally approached the subject uppermost in both their minds.

'Paul told me about Richard Basil,' she said quietly. 'Funny. When I first heard about it, I thought I despised him. Now I feel kind of sorry for him. It must have been hell, all these years, hiding and hoping people wouldn't find out about him. Knowing he was betraying himself and everything he'd been brought up to believe in. Poor guy. He was living in one-dimensional life, wasn't he? He seemed like a plastic man because he'd acted

232

like one for so long. My God, Casey, what idiots people are! So afraid we won't be "accepted". So terrified that a bunch of people who don't matter "won't have respect for us". Always worried about what "they" will say – whoever "they" are.'

'I know. It's so easy to lose perspective. About all kinds of things. We all do sometimes.'

Mary looked pensive. 'Do we? *All* of us? What do you have to lose perspective about?'

'Lots of dumb things,' Casey said. 'You should know that. You've been part of some of them. Remember how scared I was of Euralia? That's a pretty good case in point. I got all steamed up about even interviewing her. Made a big deal of it, remember? And when you looked at it realistically, it was only a job. Neither of us would have been destroyed if we'd found we didn't get along. But I agonized over it like it was a declaration of war! And in all the agonizing, I was the only one who was really suffering, because the turmoil was going on only inside *me*. I've done that kind of silly thing a hundred times, over really trivial stuff. And I hate *myself* for it, even though I try to blame everybody else. With Euralia, I was blaming her and Jim and even Jim's poor dead grandmother for hiring her in the first place! Honest to God, sometimes I really think I need my head examined.'

Mary smiled. 'Listen, Casey, I'm boringly heterosexual, but I really love you. Even though now and then you're spooky.'

'Spooky how?'

'We've always been very ESP, you and I. What you said a minute ago about making mountains out of molehills really was right on target. I've been having a very big case of the sorry-for-myselfs these past few weeks. I thought I was mad at all of you for putting the Gordons on the hot seat in this damned Weinberg fight. My giant brain finally figured out that the only one who was really acting like a kid with the sulks was little old lovable me,'

'That's the best news of the season,' Casey said. 'You can't imagine how I've worried about it. I knew something was wrong, but I didn't know what.'

'I'm still not sure I can explain it. You and I once talked about what it was like to be Jewish. Remember? I told you that Paul and I'd never had a problem because we didn't push in where we were pretty sure we weren't welcome. I guess that's what happened. For the first time in my life, I pushed in where I knew I didn't belong. And I'm angry with myself for doing it. When

233

everything began to hit the fan around here, I got sore. I even began to think that you and Jim were tarred with the same anti-Semitic brush. How's that for a persecution complex? Think Dr Basil has any available dates on his calendar? Maybe I'm ready for him!'

'No way,' Casey assured her. 'You figured it out for yourself.'

'I hope so. Think of the money I've saved.'

'What about now, Mary? Do you still think you did the wrong thing?'

Mary considered that for a moment. 'I'm not sure. Yes, I guess I do think I did the wrong thing. Or we did. Paul and I. It would have been worthwhile if we'd been doing it for the right reasons. If we'd really believed in our hearts, that we were helping to fight prejudice. But you know that wasn't the basic motive, Casey. The real motivation was purely selfish, no matter how much we've tried to kid ourselves that it wasn't. I wanted a big, swell, Park Avenue apartment. And Paul wanted to help get Weinberg's business into the agency. It doesn't matter that we lied to the board. What does matter is that we lied to ourselves.'

'But your coming here did do some good,' Casey said. 'It did expose the discrimination in the building. And it probably saved the Basil's marriage. Maybe it will even save Louise's sanity.'

'I'll buy that last benefit,' Mary agreed. 'As for discrimination in the building, frankly I don't think it's meant a damn. All it will do will be to make them extra careful about screening the next dubious applicants. You wait and see. If you thought it was impossible for Jews to get in here before, just wait till the next time. The poor devils who try in the future will never even get their hands on an application.'

Casey frowned. 'I hope you're wrong.'

'I hope so, too. But I wish I were as sure of going to heaven.'

'What about the Weinberg account?' Casey asked. 'Do you think that's a lost cause, too?'

'I wouldn't predict what will happen to that piece of business. I can't get inside Lester's head. Or Gertrude's, for that matter. But I'll bet you a big lunch at Côte Basque that they'll lose the law suit.'

Casey looked surprised. 'You really think they will? Why? Jim says they've got everything going for them. Basil's testimony and his and Paul's. It would seem to me that it's an open and shut case of anti-Semitism.'

'There ain't no such animal. Just because you can prove that one person in a building publicly announced his dislike of Jews doesn't mean that the whole board of the building discriminated. Hell, Casey, I don't believe in Peter Pan or Perry Mason. And I think it would take a combination of magic and TV courtroom drama for Weinberg to make his charges stick. Livingston's no fool. You'd better believe that he'll have a brief-case full of ammunition at that hearing tomorrow. Want to bet?'

'I'll do even better,' Casey said. 'Win or lose, I'll buy the lunch. Day after tomorrow. I still have good cause for celebration.'

'What's that?'

'The rediscovery of our friendship. Deal?'

'Deal,' Mary said. 'And since you're such a big spender, I'll order everything out-of-season, under-glass and à la carte.'

Casey smiled. 'Be my guest,' she said.

* * *

The day of the hearing, Tony, Paul and Jim lunched together in the King Cole Bar of the St Regis Hotel. They sat on one of the circular banquettes, staring morosely at the oversized, over-publicized Mayfield Parrish painting of the legendary sovereign for whom the room had been named.

'I hate that tacky painting,' Paul said.

'What did you expect in the King Cole Bar?' Jim snapped. 'A montage of Marilyn Monroe by Andy Warhol?'

Tony laughed. 'Who needs *photographs* of beautiful chicks when Women's Lib has made it possible for us to look at the real thing?' He indicated a table of four famous models lunching nearby. 'You know, those lady Freedom Fighters just might have something after all. At least they've broken through the "men only" barrier in restaurants. I like looking at pretty girls. Good for the digestion.'

'Not everybody agrees with you,' Jim said. 'A helluva lot of guys really resent women barging into what used to be strictly a stag lunch spot.'

'That's *their* problem,' Tony said easily. 'Thank God it isn't mine.'

They lapsed once more into an uncomfortable silence.

'For Christ's sake,' Tony said finally, 'what's with you two? I feel like I'm having lunch with a couple of fugitives from Forest Lawn.'

Jim and Paul exchanged glances. Tony knew that the hearing

235

was probably ending just about now. How could he act as though the outcome didn't trouble him? Maybe he's getting so far removed from the day-to-day action that he doesn't realize the seriousness of this, Jim thought. Immediately he dismissed the idea. Tony was just as aware, just as concerned as the other two. More so, probably. It was his agency. The fact was that he was infinitely more professional and much more experienced than his two employees. He had lived through worse crises, Jim supposed. He envied Tony that cool objectivity. Maybe some day he'd grow up enough to be that relaxed. Or at least appear to be.

Paul's reaction to Tony's remark was somewhat different. Oh sure, he thought, it's easy enough for you to be unconcerned about the court case, Anthony Taylor Stewart III, Almighty Unassailable WASP. You're not on trial for being a Jew. In a second he was ashamed of his thoughts. Good Lord, I'm getting as uptight about this whole persecution bit as Mary has been. She'd told him about her talk with Casey. Confessed what an idiot she'd been. He'd been very understanding, able to admit that he, too, had had some of the same unreasonable resentments in the past few months. Now, he realized, he was doing it again: interpreting Tony's determined calm as a sign that he didn't care about Jews in general and Paul in particular. Maybe My People would have less trouble if we didn't run around with such a big chip on our shoulders, he thought. It does seem as though sometimes we holler before we're hurt. He made a determined effort to relax. This whole thing was getting to all of them. If it went on much longer they'd be fighting among themselves.

'I guess we can't get our minds off the Weinberg hearing,' Paul said. 'Makes us pretty rotten company.'

'Now that's the first intelligent thing you've said in twenty minutes,' Tony answered. 'You two are the rottenest company I've had lunch with since my lawyer told me how much my alimony would be.'

'We're going to be in lousy shape if Lester loses and takes his account someplace else,' Jim said.

'If,' Tony repeated. 'All I hear these days is "if". If Weinberg doesn't get the co-op. If Weinberg's account goes somewhere else. If he does take it somewhere else and we can't replace it. Well, let me add a raunchy "if" of my own: If my aunt had balls she'd be my uncle.'

The other two laughed. 'Okay,' Paul said, 'you can kid about it, but what happens if all those nightmares come true?'

Tony looked serious. 'We won't die from it. We'll take our medicine. Tighten the well-known belts. Hustle for some new accounts. Try to act as though we're not a bunch of kids playing advertising. Maybe we'll even get back to work. Any other questions?'

'Yeah,' Paul said. 'What's for lunch?'

* * *

When he returned to the office, Jim had a message to call Weinberg. For the next twenty minutes he invented reasons not to do so. He made a slow trip to the men's room. Stopped off in the photostat department to see if they had made copies of the layouts for one of his other client's new campaign. He even called Casey.

'Heard anything in the house about the outcome of the hearing?'

'No. Where would I hear? Haven't you had word?'

'There's a message to call Lester,' Jim said. 'I just thought maybe you'd know something. So I'd be prepared before I talked to him,' he explained lamely.

Casey felt sorry for him. 'Poor old James,' she said. 'I'm glad I don't have to make that call. Wait a minute. Why are we both presuming it's bad news? Maybe he won. Two night ago you said he had everything going for him.'

'I certainly did,' Jim said gloomily. 'And I'm famous for my accurate predictions. I said it to Wilbur, I said it to Orville, "This thing will never get off the ground."'

'Call me back when you hear, will you?'

'Sure. Right after they get through administering the adrenalin.'

He hung up and called Becky Rothman. You're still stalling, he told himself. Otherwise, why wouldn't you use the direct wire?

'Hi, Becky, it's Jim Cromwell,' he said. 'The Boss there?'

'Right here. I'll put him on.' Jim couldn't tell from her voice whether the news was good or bad. When Lester came on the line, any doubts were quickly dispelled.

'We lost,' Lester said flatly. 'Be talking to you.'

'Lester, wait! What happened?'

'Read about it tomorrow in the *Times*. It'll really re-enforce your faith in democracy.' Without another word, he hung up.

Jim got through to Tony. 'Lester just called. He lost the case.'

237

'What went wrong?'

'I don't know,' Jim said. 'He just said I could read about it in the *Times*.'

'Nothing else?'

'The whole conversation took five seconds. He did say he'd be talking to me. Whatever that means.'

'That could be a good sign,' Tony reassured him. 'At least the door's still open.'

'Jesus, Tony, you are the eternal optimist! It could also mean that he's going to tell us to get lost.'

'It could. But why jump to that conclusion? Don't swallow the cyanide until we know all the details. Keep your head.'

'I'll try. But if you drive by Fifty-ninth and Park tonight, that quivering wreck at the newsstand for the early edition of the *Times* will be one of your management account supervisors — Jim Cromwell, pastmaster of the aborted maneuver.'

He made two more calls. The first was to Paul.

'Just talked to Lester,' Jim said. 'No go.'

There was a brief pause. Then Paul said, succinctly, 'Shit.'

'Amen, brother. He says it'll be in the *Times* tomorrow. I'll get the paper tonight. You and Mary want to come up late so we can read the gory details together?'

'Why not? Who said the Irish had a monopoly on wakes?'

He phoned Casey and gave her the bad news. 'I told the Gordons to come to our place around nine. I'll have the paper by then.'

'Jim, I'm sorry. Is there anything I can do? Should I call Gertrude?'

'Maybe later. I don't know. Tony says not to jump to conclusions until we know all the facts. Under the circumstances, I guess it's the only sensible advice. I hope I can take it.'

'I'll have Euralia fix all your favorite things for dinner.'

Jim smiled. Even in the worst moments, Casey was so unfailingly female. 'It's the least she can do,' he said. 'Everybody knows that a condemned man is entitled to whatever he wants for his last meal.'

'Oh, come on, love. After all, you're not being executed.'

'No? Sez who?'

* * *

After dinner, Jim picked up the paper at the corner newsstand and brought it back to the apartment. The Gordons had arrived in his absence. The atmosphere was charged with anxiety.

'When I was a kid,' Mary said, 'I used to dream about being a great actress. Now I'm grateful that I didn't make it.'

Jim, turning the pages in search of the story, didn't even look up in response to this apparent irrelevancy. Casey and Paul looked curious.

'Terrific,' Paul said. 'What does that have to do with anything, for God's sake?'

'It has a lot to do with it,' Mary said. 'I used to imagine what opening night would be like. The applause and the curtain calls and then going to Sardi's to wait for the reviews. Well, let me tell you, if this is what it's like to wait for the notices, I'm glad I never got to be an actress.'

'I think,' Paul said slowly, 'that I will strangle you.'

Casey laughed. 'I think I will do the same to Jim if he doesn't find that bloody article pretty quick.'

'Okay, okay,' Jim said. 'Here it is. Page twenty-nine. Oh boy. Three columns and a by line. They couldn't have buried it in the obituaries. Not with our luck, they couldn't. Want me to read it aloud?'

'We hadn't planned on your keeping it clutched to your breast,' Paul said.

'All right,' Jim said. 'Here goes. The headline says: "CO-OP AT 617 PARK WINS DISCRIMINATION CASE."'

'Whose by-line is on it?' Mary asked.

'Who the hell cares?' Paul snapped. 'I'm sure it isn't James Reston.'

'It's somebody I never heard of,' Jim said. 'Thomas Butler, whoever he is.'

Paul held his head in his hands. 'You are all driving me nuts,' he said. 'Now will everybody shut up, please? Read the damned article, will you, Jim?'

Jim began to read aloud. ' "The city Commission on Human Rights ruled yesterday that a prospective buyer had failed to prove that he was denied a Park Avenue co-operative apartment because the building engaged in anti-Semitism. Previously, the State Supreme Court had barred the sale of the $125,000 unit at 617 Park Avenue pending an investigation of the charges filed by Lester Weinberg, chairman and chief executive officer of the Weinberg Shoe Company.

' "Mr Weinberg who currently resides with his wife at 240 Central Park West had been desirous of purchasing a 12th floor apartment in the building located in one of the most fashionable

239

areas of Manhattan's East Side. The complaint, filed on Mr Weinberg's behalf, stated that the board of 617 Park Avenue denied him admission because he is a Jew. Defendants named in the case were the 617 Park Avenue Corporation and four of its directors, Mr André Dubois Livingston, Mrs Eileen Murphy, Mrs Antoinette Lawrence Stone and Baroness Felicia Von Brennerhof. Not named in the suit was the agent for the building, Ridgely & Ryan, as the transaction was conducted directly with the current owner, Mrs Natalie Rogers Spear and her attorneys, Coleman & Prentiss. Both Mrs Spear and her lawyers had accepted the Weinberg application and were absolved from any accusation of bias. Also eliminated from the complaint were the building's three other board members serving at the time Mr Weinberg made his application: Mr James Cromwell, who has since resigned, Mrs Edgar Simpson, who voted in favor of the applicant, and Dr Richard Basil, who also has resigned and whose testimony figured importantly in the evidence presented by the complainant." '

'Wow!' Mary said. 'They've named everybody except the super!'

'Antoinette will be furious,' Casey added. 'They didn't identify her as a famous film star.'

Paul motioned them to be quiet. 'Go on, Jim,' he said.

' "The case began last January when Mr Weinberg made a firm offer to buy the apartment. He said he had approached the estate of Bryan Rogers through its heir, Mrs Natalie Rogers Spear, and had negotiated through her attorneys.

' "However, according to Mr Weinberg, at the interview with the board, he and his wife were subjected to thinly veiled slurs concerning their religious affiliation. Later the corporation disapproved the sale of the apartment without adequate explanation, Mr Weinberg alleged.

' "Mr Weinberg charged in an affidavit that a tenant of the apartment previously had told him that he would have difficulty obtaining the apartment in question because he was Jewish. In an earlier hearing before State Supreme Court Justice Alan Winston, the defendants denied that they had discriminated against Mr Weinberg. The defendants said at that time that one Jewish couple, Mr and Mrs Paul Gordon, already were owners of an apartment in the building and had been accepted almost at the same time that Mr Weinberg had been rejected.

' "In a surprise move, Mr Weinberg produced testimony to show that there currently were two Jewish owners in the building. In addition to Mr and Mrs Gordon, it was pointed out that Dr and Mrs Richard Basil, long-time occupants of 617 Park Avenue also were Jewish. Both Mr Gordon and Dr Basil supported, via sworn affidavits, Mr Weinberg's contention that both had managed to buy their apartments only by concealing the fact that they were Jewish. It was pointed out that because Mr Weinberg did not attempt to disguise his religion, his application was rejected and that an attitude of discrimination therefore existed within the building.

' "Mr André Livingston, while admitting that the building had not been aware that either the Gordons or the Basils were Jewish, maintained that it was pure speculation that they would not have been accepted had this fact been known at the time of their application. Such allegations, he stated, could not possibly be presented as fact. Mr Livingston, a well-known attorney, as well as president of the corporation, acted on behalf of the corporation and the directors named in the suit. He called the new evidence 'pure conjecture' and declared that it could not be substantiated. He denied that the building ever had engaged in racial or religious bias of any kind and pointed to the presence of an Irish Catholic board member, Mrs Eileene Murphy, as further proof of the building's liberal attitude towards so-called minority groups.

' "Alleged anti-Semitic statements made by another board member also were ruled out of the hearing on the grounds that Mr Weinberg was presenting hearsay evidence which was inadmissible. It was requested that the press not disclose the name of the member reported to have made the statements, although it was stipulated that the member did so in the presence of many witnesses, three of whom swore to such statements in the testimony given to Mr Weinberg." '

'I don't believe it!' Casey interrupted. 'My God, Felicia can't be sleeping with the whole press corps!'

'Maybe she's switched over to the judicial system,' Paul said grimly. 'Go on, Jim. Is there much more?'

'Not too much, except for the final wrap-up. "After the hearing, Commissioners Antonio Mazerola and Elizabeth Whitfield said in their joint opinion: 'The Commission is aware that discrimination against Jews does exist in the purchase and sale of co-operative apartments in New York City. Indeed, the facts in this case as brought out in the hearings, may justify a suspicion of unlawful discrimination. However, having carefully reviewed the evidence and having studied the briefs submitted by counsel, we find that the complainant has failed to prove his case.'

' "A spokesman for the Human Rights Commission said that Mr Weinberg could appeal the Commission's finding. The spokesman added that he did not know whether Mr Weinberg intended to appeal. Mr Weinberg could not be reached for comment." '

The room was quiet for a few moments after Jim finished reading. Finally, Paul spoke. 'What a travesty,' he said. 'Do you think Lester will appeal, Jim?'

'Not a chance. He's had it up to *there*. If you'd heard him on the phone today, you'd know how bitter he was. Can't say I blame him.'

'What do you think he'll do about the account?' Casey asked. Jim just shook his head. 'Take it someplace else.'

'I agree,' Paul said. 'But you know, I think Weinberg's a businessman above all. I'll bet if it were just up to him he'd name us his agency in spite of this. He realizes we meant well even if we loused it up. And he knows our campaign is a knock-out. But I think Gertrude will be the one who murders us. My money says that right this minute she's weeping her heart out on Gwen Crawford's flat little chest. Crawford-Thompson won't waste a minute pointing out to Gertrude that we were the ones who started all her unhappiness. By the time they get through with her, she'll lay the law down to Lester. "It's SS&A or me," she'll say. "Take your choice, Lester." '

'Do you really think she'll be so vindictive?' Casey asked.

Paul nodded. 'You bet I do. Hell hath no fury like a woman done out of an apartment. And, honey, this building really did a job on Gertrude. Who can she take it out on? Livingston? The Baroness? What can she do, switch to another channel when Antoinette's old pictures come on the "Late show"? No ma'am. Somebody's got to suffer for Gertrude's rejection. And we're first in line.'

'I think Paul's right,' Jim said. 'Lester is big enough to separate his personal problems from his business, but Gertrude doesn't have that kind of objectivity.'

'Nor that kind of brain power,' Mary added.

'Exactly,' Jim went on. 'Paul's diagnosis is probably accurate. She'll have to strike back at somebody, and in her tiny mind we've got to come on as the culprit. Lester won't be able to hold out against Gertrude's kind of pressure, even if he knows he should.'

'Well,' Casey said helplessly, 'at least it's over.'

'Yep,' Jim said, 'it's over. All but the shouting. And I'll get an earful of that when Lester gives me the gospel as written by Saint Gertrude.'

Casey went to the bar. 'I move we all have a drink.'

Paul joined her. He raised his glass. 'Here's to democracy, justice and freedom of opportunity in a land where all men are equal.'

'To everything except the anger of their wives,' Jim added. 'Poor Lester.'

Chapter XIV

Among the other board members, the reaction to the Weinberg verdict was predictable.

André Livingston, having dutifully given his fellow directors the full details of the case and their victory, modestly accepted their congratulations and went serenely to bed. He was snoring gently before the early edition of the *Times* hit the stands.

Elinor Simpson's first thought was, once again, to call Jim and say how sorry she was. Then she decided against it. What's done is done, she thought. She fretted that perhaps she hadn't been helpful enough. If Edgar had been around, he'd have thought of something really constructive to do. But Edgar wasn't around.

The Stones indulged in a little self-satisfied celebrating. At least, Antoinette did. Relaying Livingston's information to Harry, Antoinette could not resist expressing her relief. 'They can say what they will about this city,' she pronounced, 'but it still has its areas of integrity.'

'Integrity or ignorance?' Harry asked. 'Your precious board members think they're so smart, Antoinette, but they're stupid. They refuse to see the handwriting on the wall. Weinberg may have lost his case, but there'll be other Weinbergs in the future, you can count on that. And they may not be as decent and well-meaning as these people. One thing's sure, though. The next Jewish family that gets turned down here will have an even stronger case if they choose to claim prejudice.'

'Nonsense. You're forgetting that that dreadful Human Rights Commission made the final decision. If they choose to rule against the very people they're supposed to be supporting, what better evidence is there that we're innocent of bias?'

Harry went back to reading *Time* magazine. 'Forget it,' he said. 'You got what you wanted. It's just like one of your old

244

pictures. Little Nell's been untied from the railroad tracks in the nick of time.'

'Sometimes I don't understand you, Harry.'

'That could be the best thing that ever happened to either of us,' he said.

In 14A, the Murphy ladies wasted little time talking about 'the unfortunate incident' as Eileene chose to call it. The verdict was exactly what she had expected. The only surprise had been André's disclosure about the Basils. To this part of the outcome, Eileene addressed herself. Or, rather, addressed Rosemary.

'Your friend Mrs Basil is a liar,' she said flatly, 'and my door is never open to liars. Kindly be good enough, Rosemary, to tell Mrs Basil that we do not wish to see her again. She has taken advantage of our Christian forbearance. We shall not be so imposed upon in the future.'

'That's a blessing,' Constance chimed in. 'Good riddance. Your penchant for adopting weaklings has always been a nuisance, Roe. When we were children, it was hungry cats and stray dogs. Now it's alcoholic imposters.'

Rosemary looked puzzled. 'I don't understand. Just because she's not Catholic, does that mean that we no longer should be friends with Louise?'

'Her faith has nothing to do with it,' Mrs Murphy said. 'She is a shameless liar. And I forbid your having anything more to do with her.'

'I'm not a child, Mother. Have I no right to choose whomever I think I can help?'

Eileene was annoyed. 'If you wish to do missionary work, Rosemary, then perhaps you should join an Order. Otherwise, in my house you will do as I say. And let's hear no more about it.'

Rosemary waited until her mother retired. Then she quietly slipped out of the apartment and, for the first time in more than twenty years, went down and rang the bell of 8B.

A surprised but cordial Richard Basil opened the door.

'Miss Murphy! How nice to see you. Do come in. Louise will be so pleased. I've just been explaining the outcome of the Weinberg case to her. You know the result, I suppose?'

Rosemary nodded. 'Mr Livingston called Mother.'

The doctor smiled. 'Needless to say, he didn't call me, but I went out for the early edition of the paper.'

They were still standing in the foyer. Rosemary hesitated. 'I didn't meant to disturb you,' she said. 'Perhaps it would be

245

better if I came back another time. But I had to know, Dr Basil. How is she?'

'Making remarkable progress. Oh, she's far from well. Recovery in cases like hers don't come overnight, but I'm amazed by the change in her, even in six weeks. She's in good hands now. A colleague of mine, Dr Swanson, has taken her case. She's already begun therapy, and we probably will hospitalize her for shock treatments in the next couple of weeks.'

Rosemary looked horrified. 'Shock treatments? Aren't they terribly dangerous?'

'No,' he assured her. 'In the proper hands and under the correct conditions, they can often produce near-miracles. Don't worry, 'he added kindly, 'they'll be done under anesthesia. She won't remember a thing about them. But come in and see for yourself how much better she is already.'

Timidly, Rosemary entered the living room. To her delight, Louise was completely sober and seemed utterly at ease. I wouldn't have believed it, her friend thought. She actually looks twenty years younger. The haunted, hysterical fright had disappeared from her eyes. She seemed relaxed and happy, and her delight at seeing Rosemary was touching.

'How wonderful of you to come!' Louise said. 'Oh, I'm so glad to see you, Rosemary. Would you like something? Coffee, perhaps? Or a cold drink? Do sit down, please. How is your mother?'

The gentle little Irish lady fidgeted uncomfortably. 'Mother is fine,' she said. 'How are you feeling, Louise?'

'Better than I have in a long time. I'm going to a lovely doctor, a friend of Richard's. Such a nice, understanding man. I'm sure he must lose patience with me, though. Sometimes I just lie there on the couch in his office and can't think of a thing to say.' She laughed lightly. 'You must find that hard to believe, Rosemary. I always had plenty to talk about when I came to see you, didn't I? But then, you're my best friend. It was always easier to talk to you than anybody else. We must start visiting soon again. Your dear mother must think I've deserted you.'

Richard sensed the panic in Rosemary. 'Louise, dear,' he said, 'I think we would enjoy a cup of coffee. Why don't you put on a fresh pot? I'll entertain Rosemary while you're gone.'

Like an obedient child, Louise rose. 'Of course. I'll just be a minute. You two can get acquainted.' She wagged her finger playfully at her friend. 'Now don't you go steal my husband while I'm out of the room,' she teased.

246

As soon as she was out of earshot, Richard looked compassionately at Rosemary. 'This is hard for you, isn't it, Miss Murphy? I know what you came here to say, even if Louise can't realize it. Your mother doesn't ever want you to see her again. That's it, isn't it?'

Rosemary nodded miserably. 'I hope you understand. My mother is really a very fine woman. Very devout and charitable. She doesn't mean to be unkind. She's just very old-fashioned. I tried to make her see things differently, but she's too old to change. I know I shouldn't pay any attention to her. I should do what I want. Goodness knows, I'm old enough. But I just can't.'

'Of course you can't,' Richard assured her. 'We wouldn't expect it. Right now, Louise doesn't realize how ill she's been. Still is, for that matter. But I think perhaps she owes her life to your kindness and compassion, Miss Murphy. You need never feel guilty about deserting her. You were always there when she needed you. Which is more,' he said bitterly, 'than I can say for myself.'

'But what if she needs me again? Mother says she can't come to the apartment any more.'

'Hopefully the times she needs you will be few and far between,' Richard said. 'And when they happen, I'll be around. As I always should have been. Louise is beginning to get things into perspective. She has a lot to figure out. We both have. But as she slowly realizes the nightmare she's been living, I think she will be able to forgive me. Perhaps in time I'll even be able to make peace with myself.'

'Can she live with the truth, Doctor?'

'Swanson and I think so. We believe it will be an easier pain to bear than the lies she's been telling herself and you all these years.'

The relief of it brought tears to Rosemary's eyes. Then as she thought of Felicia a frown crossed her face.

'Will you move out of the building?'

'As soon as Louise is up to it,' Richard said. 'We don't want too much upheaval all at one time. But it's not going to be very comfortable for us here, now that our fellow tenants know all about us.' A trace of amusement crossed his handsome face. 'As for the other question that you're much too polite to ask, Miss Murphy, I'll answer that one for you, too. No, I am never again going to go above the eighth floor.'

As Louise returned with the coffee tray, her husband and her best friend exchanged understanding, mutually admiring glances.

'Thank you, Dr Basil,' Rosemary said quietly.

'No. Thank *you*, Miss Murphy,' he said.

* * *

In Palm Beach, the Baroness allowed herself to dwell upon the implications of Livingston's phone call. Sketchy though it was, enough was said to let Felicia know that that fool Richard had shot off his mouth recklessly to Weinberg and the others, including, of course, André. She had listened carefully for any intonation of reproach in the president's voice. As far as she could tell, there was none. Even if he believed that she'd been a part of the Nazi regime, André's own distrust of Jews would supercede his dislike of her old political affiliations. Of this she felt sure. Men like Livingston had always been her easiest converts in the days when she was discreetly propagandizing the Nazi cause. Though they professed a horror for the atrocities being committed in Germany, they had an even greater fear of the rich Jewish bankers and the intrusive Jewish businessmen who posed a threat to their financial and economic dominance. No, Felicia thought, if André ran true to form he would behave as though Basil, Cromwell and Gordon were the villains of this piece. He would conveniently forget the involvement of the Baroness in *l'affaire* Weinberg.

Serenely, she began to fill the bathtub, adding an extra helping of perfume to the water. She'd been introduced to a new man the evening before. Tall, handsome and charming, he was younger than she, but he was obviously interested. Interested enough, in any case, to invite her to dine that evening. She had heard that his money came from generous settlements from three rich wives, all anxious to be rid of him at any price. As she soaked, she wondered idly why. There was a rumor that he was bi-sexual. Felicia laughed aloud. What a delicious challenge, she thought. Richard had long since become a bore. Besides, age was taking its toll. He was no longer nearly as satisfying as he'd once been. How marvelous to be a woman, she thought, stroking her smooth skin in self-admiration. One need never lose one's appeal.

* * *

On the same night, Lester Weinberg sent the doorman out for an early edition of the *Times*. Not that he didn't know what it would say. The hearing had been a farce. Livingston had blocked every move, making his objections in that low-pitched, well-bred Harvard voice. It galled Lester to think how some of those Park Avenue plaster saints must be gloating tonight. He didn't like to lose. But even though he could, as the spokesman for the Human Rights Commission had said, file an appeal, Lester had no intention of doing so. He'd done everything he could. A lot of it against his better judgment. He should have let the whole damned thing drop after that first interview. In his heart, he knew right then and there that he was licked. But there were some things a man just couldn't roll over and play dead for. By God, he had his pride. And he had a wife who would never have forgiven him if he'd given up without a fight. She might not even forgive him now. At least for a while.

She was sulking in her bedroom. Had been, ever since he gave her the bad news. She hadn't even come out for dinner. Lester had toyed with the thick steak and the baked potato overflowing with sour cream, just the way he liked it usually. He hated fussy food. It was one of the reasons he detested those damned dinner parties that Gertrude's fancy agency friends kept asking them to. They thought they were being so swell serving things like squab. The memory of it turned his stomach. Those scrawny birds, all nasty little bones and no meat. It was like eating a canary. Still, he would even have settled for that unappetizing fare with company, rather than for this lonely meal which gave him an unwanted opportunity to think.

Gertrude would get over her disappointment. It was only a matter of time. He'd call up a couple of real estate agents tomorrow and start them scouring the city for a co-op so big it would make 617 Park look like a mobile home. Though he wouldn't admit it, Lester was rather relieved. He didn't like being deprived of something he went after – whether it was an apartment or a woman – but he had never been all that impressed with 12B. It didn't suit him. Moving into that setup would have been as out of character as marrying Grace Kelly or having the Duchess of Windsor over for gin rummy. Even at a dollar a point.

He heard the phone ring and supposed it was Cromwell. Lester glanced at his watch. It was a little after nine. Jim probably had also gotten the morning paper. He was surprised when the Weinberg's Haitian maid didn't call him. Instead, in a few minutes Gertrude appeared in the doorway of the dining room. She was red-eyed from an afternoon of weeping. But she was also, to Lester's surprise, fighting mad.

'Godamn patronizing bitch!' Gertrude said. 'Who the hell does she think she is, calling me up to sympathize like we'd lost our last dime?'

'Who, honey? Who called?'

'Who do you think? Gwen Crawford, of course. Couldn't wait to get on the phone with that "I-told-you-so" voice of hers. You should have heard her, Lester. "Oh, my deah, I'm so sorry you had to go through such a sordid experience",' Gertrude mimicked. 'But you know what, Lester? She wasn't sorry. She was glad!'

'How do you figure that?'

Gertrude slid into a chair. 'I'm starved,' she said unexpectedly. 'Hey, Carmen!' The maid appeared from the kitchen. 'Fix me a couple of scrambled eggs, will you? No toast. Thanks.'

Lester was fascinated. 'What do you mean, she was glad? She's supposed to be one of your girl friends, isn't she?'

His wife gave him a cynical look. 'Supposed to be is about right. Look, Lester, you didn't think I was really falling for all that bull, did you? I might kid myself about some things, but even I'm not stupid enough to think that the Crawfords are going to run after the Weinbergs unless they want something.'

'I still don't get it,' Lester said. 'Okay, they wanted something. The Weinberg advertising account. But what does that have to do with Gwen being glad we didn't get the apartment?'

'Jesus, I don't know how you ever got where you are,' Gertrude said. 'For a slick operator, you sure are a babe-in-the-woods about some things. My idiot Uncle Hershel could figure this one out. If we'd gotten the apartment, it would have been thanks to Jim Cromwell and his crowd, right?'

Lester nodded.

'So if we don't get it, Gwen figures SS&A has made a boo-boo. She also figures that I'm going to be so mad I'll raise hell if you give your advertising business to that agency instead of her husband's. Cripes, Lester, it's as plain as the nose on your face. She figures what happened today really clinches the deal for Crawford-Thompson. She's got it doped out that Stewart's agency is dead. And who's the first one in line to pay a condolence call? Gwennie herself. What does she think I am, some kind of Nosy Parker? Do you suppose she really believes I'd try to meddle in your business?'

Lester gave a wry smile. 'You mean you wouldn't?'

'Are you kidding? Listen, I've been having a good time letting those four-flushers fall all over me with their invitations and their palsy-walsy stuff. I've learned a lot from them. Enough so I don't always behave like a grammar school drop-out. But try to influence you about something that's going to affect my meal ticket? Forget it. You run the store as good as you always have. And I'll spend all the money you can carry home.'

'So the agency decision is up to me,' Lester said.

Gertrude dived into her eggs. 'Who else?' she asked.

*　　*　　*

The atmosphere at Stewart, Sutton & Atherton was heavy with that particular kind of depression that hangs over an advertising agency when it seems apparent that a new account is not going to come in or an old one is about to defect. As Joe Kauffman had told Jim, there are no secrets in an organization of this kind. From the chairman to the youngest kid in the mailroom, everybody knew about the Weinberg pursuit, including the efforts of Cromwell and Gordon to get the account's sole owner an apartment in their building. And everybody knew that the attempt had been a failure. Those who read the *Daily News* in the subway had missed the press coverage. But they had quickly been brought up-to-date by those who read the *Times*. At the coffee wagon there was speculation about how the loss of this account would affect the agency personnel.

'Heads will roll,' Paul Gordon's secretary announced. The others listened respectfully. She was, after all, close to the source. 'Got to be,' she went on. 'Paul's been worried about it, I know. Without that billing, we're over-staffed. They'll have to cut back.'

A junior account executive, still so lowly that he had no secretary to get coffee for him, shook his head. 'It seems like a dumb gamble to me,' he said. 'Whatever made them think it would work?'

Joe Kauffman's secretary looked at him pityingly. She was past fifty and had worked for a dozen agencies before joining the head of International. 'You've got a lot to learn about this business,' she said. 'Compared to some of the maneuvers I've seen tried, this one is simplicity itself.'

'Yeah,' the young account man said. 'So simple it didn't work.'

'Anybody seen Cromwell this morning?' an art director asked.

Nobody had. A twenty-year-old girl copywriter tossed her long mane. 'If he's smart, he's probably home preparing his resumé. And I advise you cats to start doing the same. That thing in my typewriter right now is not the next ad for Aunt Bertha's Buckwheat Batter.'

'That's right,' Paul's secretary said compassionately. 'You were one of the people hired to work on the Weinberg thing, weren't you?'

'Sure was. Me and about twenty other eager beavers. Your boss went all out on this one, kiddo. He must be having the guilts this morning.'

Kauffman's secretary sprang to the defense. 'Why guilts? If you don't know already, you'd beter find out that basic insecurity is the name of this business, sweetie. Advertising is just one big crap game. When you've been around as long as I have, you'll discover that in a weird way that's what makes it so fascinating. It's like living in Los Angeles: Any minute the whole Godamn cardboard town may slide into the mis-named Pacific. It's exciting. Keeps you on your toes.'

'Sure. So does standing in line for your unemployment insurance.'

'Okay, kids, let's break it up.' The voice was that of Tony Stewart's secretary who'd joined the group around the wagon. 'Nobody knows anything yet. Let's don't start the funeral till we're sure there's a corpse.'

The account man leapt at a ray of hope. 'You mean we still might get the Weinberg business?'

'All I know at the moment is that Weinberg *didn't* get an apartment. If you want to parlay that into a national disaster, it's your privilege.'

The copywriter sniffed. 'Easy enough for you to be so loose,' she said. 'It isn't likely that the chairman will function without a secretary, no matter what happens.'

Tony's secretary smiled spitefully. 'Bright girl. I congratulate you. Too bad you didn't go to Katherine Gibbs Secretarial School instead of taking those writing courses at NYU, isn't it?'

Paper cups in hand, they dispersed to their various desks and drawing boards. Some people might find the uncertainty of advertising stimulating, the young account man thought, but any rational human being has got to be crazy to get into it in the first place. It's like juggling hand grenades on a tightrope over Niagara Falls. Especially if you have a pregnant wife and a father-in-law who doesn't understand why you're not making a good living in the dress business.

Jim could feel the undercurrent of anxiety the minute he got off the elevator. It's as though they smell bad news, he thought. They know. Even the ones who've seen this kind of thing happen before never quite get used to it. If it were only Weinberg, the agency might somehow weather it without too much bloodshed. But Jim knew that the ad columns would be full of SS&A's failure to get the account the minute Lester made his announcement. He could only pray that some of their current accounts didn't run for the hills immediately thereafter. He'd never felt lower. Or more helpless.

Even Tony didn't try to feign optimism when he called Jim later that morning. 'Any more news?' he asked.

Jim tried not to sound bitter. 'What did you have in mind?'

'Lester. He called yet?'

'Not a peep out of him, for which I don't know whether to be grateful or sorry.'

'I think you'd better call him, Jim. I've got to get out some kind of internal announcement. Word is that the natives are restless.'

'I know. You can cut the gloom with a knife. Okay, I'll get back to you as soon as I get through.'

Lester did not come to the phone when Jim called. Instead he sent word via Becky that he'd like to see Jim in his office at three o'clock. At least he's enough of a man to look me in the eye when he gives me the word, Jim thought. Either that or he doesn't want to miss a moment of his revenge.

Shortly before three, Jim presented himself at Becky Rothman's desk.

'The boss says wait a few minutes,' she told him. 'Take a load off. There's a copy of the *Times* on the table, if you haven't seen it.'

'Very funny,' Jim said. 'Still doing one-liners, huh, Becky?'

The secretary calmly continued typing until two short buzzes on the intercom made her look up and nod at Jim. 'You can go in now.'

Lester was looking critically at a blue-suede pump and a brown patent-leather walking shoe when Jim came into the office. The two sample-size shoes looked ridiculous sitting daintily on Lester's king-sized desk among the welter of papers, the pile of cigar butts and the tarnished silver paperweight shaped like a woman's foot. Weinberg appeared to be absorbed with his merchandise.

'How do you like 'em?' he asked. 'New designer. Some Italian fruit we just hired.'

'Very nice.'

'Nice? They're sensational! There's half a million bucks in those two numbers or I don't know a moccasin from a mule! What's the matter with you, Cromwell? Aren't you interested in your client's business?'

For a moment, Jim couldn't believe he'd heard correctly. He could feel his insides relaxing. One stomach knot gone. Now a second. And a third. His relief was visible. And still he couldn't speak.

'What the hell you going to do – cry all over me?' Weinberg said. 'You act like you never got an account before.'

'I haven't, I mean I didn't, that is I wasn't sure . . . '

Weinberg laughed. 'If you weren't so Goddamn funny, I'd be sore at you. What did you think? That I'm so stupid I'd let the best damned agency in town get away from me just because two of their big shots are jerky enough to live in the wrong building and crazy enough to try to get me in? That's downright insulting, Cromwell. What am I, some damned fool who'd satisfy a personal grudge at the expense of my business? You think I'd bite off my nose to spite my face?'

'No. Of course not. It's just that I was afraid that you'd have lost confidence in us. Or that, quite understandably, Gertrude would . . . '

'Gertrude would put the squeeze on me to take my dolls and dishes someplace else? You don't know that little lady. She's smart as they come. Can spot a phony a mile away. Gwen Crawford and that bunch never had her fooled for a minute. No sir, not Gert. Tell you something else, Jim. When it comes to real class, your wife's got it all over Gwen and those finishing-school broads. Mary Gordon too, for that matter. They never sucked up to us. In fact, I'll bet you five hundred dollars that neither one of those girls approved of the little sleight-of-hand that you and Paul and Tony were trying to pull. Right?'

Jim grinned sheepishly. 'I'm afraid you're right.'

'Next time you big heroes better listen to them when you're figuring out one of your super-strategies.'

'I don't think that will be necessary,' Jim said. 'I think we're through with strategies. We'll stick to advertising.'

Lester looked serious. 'Don't be too tough on yourself,' he

said. 'I'd like to believe that all that dog-and-pony-show with the apartment wasn't entirely to get the Weinberg's business. Ninety per cent, maybe, but not all. You're a pretty straight bunch. I think you and Stewart really would like to crack the anti-Semitism thing. And I'm sure Gordon would. After all, he's one of us.'

'Thanks for the vote of confidence,' Jim said. 'And you're about right, percentagewise.'

'Well, just don't start taking more do-gooder pills yet,' Lester advised. 'We're a helluva long way from seeing the end of discrimination. And it'll come slower with the big shots than it will with the little people. Don't think you've changed anything in that apartment. Some day maybe. Not soon. Not in my lifetime, anyway. And probably not in yours.'

'I'm not convinced,' Jim said. 'Anyway, I'm glad we tried.'

Lester laughed. 'Sure you are,' he said, 'now that you've got an eight-million-dollar account in the bag. How glad were you an hour ago?'

*　*　*

The announcement of SS&A's appointment as the agency of record for the Weinberg Shoe Company was the headline of Al Shriber's advertising column two days later.

A week later James Cromwell and Paul Gordon put apartments 14B and 6A on the market, correctly listing them through the offices of Ridgely & Ryan, building agents, leaving the processing of the applications entirely in the conservative hands of a well-indoctrinated Carl Paterman.

Two months after that, both apartments were sold. One went to a Mr and Mrs William Lowestoff Taylor. And the other was purchased by a Mr and Mrs Hugh Patrick Doyle.

Both were unanimously approved by the board of directors of 617 Park Avenue.

MORE HELEN VAN SLYKE
NOVELS
AVAILABLE FROM NEL

All these books are available at your local bookshop or newsagent, or can be ordered direct from the publisher. Just tick the titles you want and fill in the form below.

Prices and availability subject to change without notice.

Hodder & Stoughton Paperbacks, P.O. BOX 11, Falmouth, Cornwall

Please send cheque or postal order, and allow the following for postage and packing:

U.K. – 55p for one book, plus 22p for the second book, and 14p for each additional book ordered up to £1.75 maximum.

B.F.P.O. and EIRE – 55p for the first book, plus 22p for the second book, and 14p per copy for the next 7 books, 8p per book thereafter.

OTHER OVERSEAS CUSTOMERS – £1.00 for the first book, plus 25p per copy for each additional book.

Name...

Address...

....